Outstanding praise for Scott Nicholson and *The Manor*

"A stunning and emotionally intense addition to the haunted house sub-genre."

Cemetery Dance Magazine

"There's no doubt about it; Scott Nicholson has the most serious ambitions to write truly literate horror stories the genre has seen since the emergence of Peter Straub. If your interests go beyond mere entertainment to appreciation for sincere efforts to raise the literary standards of horror fiction, *The Manor* is a book you can't afford to pass up."

Dark Fluidiiy

"Writing like the love child of Stephen King and Sharyn McCrumb, Nicholson really does bring a strong sense of place to the table."

The Mountain Times

"Nicholson has come to craft characters the reader can come to care about."

Winston-Salem Journal

"You'll be entertained by *The Manor.*"

Dark Echo.com

"Fans of Bentley Little and Peter Straub will love this old fashioned ghost story."

Baryon Magazine

"An edgy and frightening ghost story."

The Midwest Book Review

D0684922

Outstanding praise for Scott Nicholson and *The Harvest*

"A very atmospheric, often creepy and definitely well-written horror novel."

Science Fiction and Fantasy Chronicle

"Nicholson has constructed a small wonder with *The Harvest,* a story with the outlines of a B-Movie narrative, but with complex, sympathetic characters and an emotionally satisfying plot. Nicholson continues to prove himself a writer to watch."

Locus

"*The Harvest* combines Southern charm with the other-world . . . enjoyable to read."

Greensboro News & Record

"Horror story devotees get a certain macabre joy from a good creepy read. Scott Nicholson knows the feeling and is adept at passing it on to his fans, first in *The Red Church* and now in *The Harvest*. If this is your genre, Nicholson's books are worth a look."

The Herald Sun (Durham, NC)

"Scott Nicholson's second book, *The Harvest,* is a well-crafted novel that seamlessly blends elements of science fiction and horror in the tradition of H.P. Lovecraft and Stephen King. *The Harvest,* a standout suspense novel worthy of your attention, is a satisfying and frightening read. Scott Nicholson has shown himself to be a refreshing voice in contemporary horror and is definitely someone to watch."

About.com

"Nicholson is an old-fashioned storyteller, through and through, and his books are an enjoyable diversion when the pressures of daily life get to be too much."

Creature-Corner.com

"Stephen King and Dean Koontz fans need to sit up and take notice of this talented author. Scott Nicholson has created a new terror that will keep you up late into the night!"

Huntress Reviews

"Scott Nicholson gives us a tale that grips its claws straight to the bone in this scary novel that could have come from the pen of H.P. Lovecraft."

Baryon Magazine

"Extremely well-written with a cast of superb characters."
Eternalnight.co.uk

Books by Scott Nicholson

THE RED CHURCH

THE HARVEST

THE MANOR

THE HOME

Published by Pinnacle Books

SCOTT NICHOLSON

THE HOME

PINNACLE BOOKS
Kensington Publishing Corp.
http://www.kensingtonbooks.com

PINNACLE BOOKS are published by

Kensington Publishing Corp.
850 Third Avenue
New York, NY 10022

All Kensington Titles, Imprints and Distributed Lines are
available at special quantity discounts for bulk purchases for
sales promotions, premiums, fund-raising, and educational
or institutional use. Special book excerpts or customized
printings can also be created to fit specific needs. For details,
write or phone the office of the Kensington special sales
manager: Kensington Publishing Corp., 850 Third Avenue,
New York, NY 10022, attn: Special Sales Department,
Phone: 1-800-221-2647.

Pinnacle and the P logo Reg. U.S. Pat. & TM Off.

First Pinnacle Printing: August 2005
10 9 8 7 6 5 4 3 2 1

Printed in the United States of America

For Kelly Goldberg, a dybbuk in Dixie

"Life is what happened to the dead."
—Robyn Hitchcock,
    "If Death Is Not the End"

ONE

This was going to be another of those loser places.

Freeman could tell that right from the get go. The home looked just like all the others he'd waltzed through over the last six years. Sure, this one was built of stone and most of the others were brick. This one was in the mountains, surrounded by big oak trees and enough peace and quiet to drive you squirrel-shit nutty. At least the fence here wasn't topped with barbed wire like the one in Durham, where the homeless and the crack brains were always climbing over. As if a group home was a happy Neverland or something.

All group homes were bad news. But even from the road, he could tell this place was different. It had a face that ate children and grinned. This building had an attitude of "Go ahead, punk."

Or was *he* the one with the attitude problem? Hadn't a parade of counselors and shrinks and do-gooders thrown aside all their mumbo-jumbo disassociative-this-and-that and pretty much nailed "hopeless case" across his forehead like some kind of welcome mat to his brain? All of them except good old Dad, who had gone deeper inside his head than anybody.

Freeman looked over at the driver, Marvin something-

or-other. Not a doctor, just an ordinary guy. Dark skin, cheap aftershave, sunglasses, gum wrappers in the ash tray. At least Marvin bothered to peek over the sunglasses to meet Freeman's eyes, treating him as if he were a human being instead of a problem with legs.

Or maybe Marvin worked for the Trust.

Freeman thought about triptrapping Marvin, seeing if he could read him. But Freeman was down, and the trip-trap wouldn't work when he was this depressed. Plus, people with the Trust were pretty good at keeping their thoughts to themselves. They had shields. Whether this was due to some sort of implant or whether they weren't allowed to think, Freeman had never been able to determine. It's not like the Trust left secret decoder books laying around or anything.

"What do you think, Freeman?" the driver asked, nodding toward the long building and sprawling grounds.

"It's not so bad." Freeman figured there was no point riling good old Marvin. Might as well give him the benefit of a doubt. Surely, *everybody* didn't belong to the Trust. After all, Marvin had scarcely talked during the four-hour drive up from Durham and had sprung for a couple of Supersizes at McDonald's. So what if Marvin had kept the radio tuned to some saccharine gospel, adjusting the buttons as each station's reception faded? At least Marvin hadn't preached, given him the buddy-buddy, or, worst of all, asked Freeman about his past.

"Wendover's one of the finest," Marvin said, reaching over and turning the radio down a little. As they'd started the climb into the mountains, the Jesus–music had taken a definite turn for the twangy, white people singing with barely suppressed yodels. Freeman wondered how Marvin felt about the whites stealing his people's spirituals, putting organ music behind the songs, branding it "Southern Gospel" and making a fortune.

Marvin didn't look like it bothered him. Marvin didn't look like anything bothered him. He definitely didn't act like Trust material. Most of those goons were too cold and uptight, as if they'd watched too many Gene Hackman movies featuring Secret Service agents. But it was the ones you weren't sure about, the ones who bled red and wore ugly suits, that were the most dangerous.

Freeman gazed out the window again at the grounds. The fence was stone up to about waist high, topped with black wrought-iron bars ten feet tall. At the back of the property, the trees grew alongside the fence. Be pretty easy to hoist himself over if he got itchy feet, even with those sharp points on top. Pull a *Shawshank Redemption*.

The home was set a hundred yards from the fence, two-story wings set out from a three-story main entrance. The building looked like some giant bird, grounded by its own mass, its bones broken. The windows had little awnings over them, giving the appearance of brooding eyes. Even with the stone facade, the building bore that institutional look, as if it were always dark on the inside and independent thoughts would be locked in the broom closet for punishment.

A half dozen small cottages were scattered among the wooded edges of the compound, and a sheet of silver marked a lake at the rear of the property. The lawns themselves were closely mown, the oaks and maples clutching the ground with great gnarled fingers. A stand of willows swooned near the lake, as sad as a row of widows.

"Looks old," Freeman said.

"About seventy years," Marvin said. "Old for a person, maybe, not for a building."

When you were twelve, seventy was old for anything. Even God. Freeman tried to think up a clever comeback, like an actor who thought his improvisation was always better than the script.

"It was built under the Works Project Administration," Marvin said. "Right after the Depression."

Looked like the Depression had never ended here, as if

the shadow of hard times clung to every nook and cranny of the home, which would make it a perfect fit for Freeman.

They turned off the highway and headed for the front gate. It was open, the hinged bars swung wide. In Durham, the gate was always locked. Whether that was to keep people in or keep them out, Freeman wasn't sure. And the counselors hadn't volunteered much information.

Here, maybe they trusted people.

Yeah, right. "Trust" was just another of those power words that the personality police liked to slam you with. Trust, self-esteem, possibility-thinking, empowerment. And that biggie, hope. Nothing but a blowhard waste of alphabet.

And the Trust was a negative word to Freeman anyway. Dad had worked for the Trust. Or, as Dad liked to say, the Trust was just the means to Freeman's end.

As they drove into the shaded entrance, Freeman read the words "Wendover Home" set in metal scrollwork over the gate. The style of the letters was old-fashioned, like the script in some of those leather-bound books he'd stolen from the Durham Academy's library.

"This place been group all that time?" Freeman asked.

Marvin had been humming along with the radio in his rich bass. Apparently he knew white people's music. "No. It's only been a children's home for about a decade. Stood empty a long time before that."

"Bet this is some pricy real estate." They'd passed a collection of big houses on the way in, planned subdivisions with names like "Elk Run" and "Carolina Oaks."

"A lot of rich people keep summer homes up here," Marvin said. "Plenty of golf courses and resorts around. A couple of ski slopes, too."

Freeman took his eyes from the building that was going to be his next temporary home. He studied the mountains that rose up above the valley floor. The fall colors of red and gold were splashed amid the blue-gray and green. Long slivers of granite showed in the slopes, the peaks raw and jagged. Freeman found himself comparing them to the tall buildings of the city. No contest. Buildings were way creepier, because buildings were full of people.

"Think they'll let us go skiing?" Freeman had never been. He wasn't even sure he wanted to go, but being out in the open, in a hushed world of glistening white snow, seemed like something to wish for.

"I wouldn't know. I'm just a driver for Social Services."

Social Services. The enemy, almost as bad as the Trust. Knew what was best for you, whether you liked it or not. Marvin was way too cool to be one of *them*. Freeman edged closer to the car door.

They pulled into the cul-de-sac in front of the double doors and Marvin stopped the car before a wide set of concrete stairs. "Here we go," Marvin said. "Wendover."

Freeman glanced up at the windows on the second floor. A pale blur of motion appeared at one of them. A face? Someone watching?

Paranoid already. Good.

Freeman twisted his mouth into a frown. Better start off on the right foot, walk in mean, talk tough, squint like a miniature Clint Eastwood with saddle sores. Ready to eat nails and shit bullets.

Freeman got out of the car and tried out a strut. He took a breath of air and thought something was wrong. Then he realized that he wasn't smelling garbage and smog and car exhaust. The air was clean, cool, ripe with the fresh scent of pine and running water. So this was that Appalachian Mountain air that everybody had talked about when they promised he was going to a better place.

Marvin opened the trunk and retrieved the gym bag that contained all of Freeman's earthly possessions. Freeman looked up at the window again, real casual, so cool that he was probably exhaling frost. The face, or whatever it was, shimmered and disappeared.

Freeman's mouth fell open, definitely uncool. Must

have been the sun. A reflection of a cloud. Faces didn't just disappear.

Freeman shouldered his gym bag and followed Marvin up the stairs. Marvin even *moved* cool, with an athletic grace. Freeman was tempted to imitate the driver's smooth stride, but it was hard to be smooth and jerky-tough at the same time, so he stuck with the limping strut.

Marvin held open one of the doors and slipped his sunglasses into his jacket pocket. "Welcome home."

Home. Freeman had heard that before. At least a dozen times in the last six years.

The smell of the place wafted from the hall like liquid, sucked the fresh air out of his lungs and replaced it with a heavy corruption, like the funk of wet, moldy newspapers.

"Wendover, here I come," he said cheerfully, in hopes of fooling good old Marvin.

He stepped inside the building and it was like stepping from day into night without passing dusk on the way, his eyes slowly adjusting to the gloom. The hallway ceiling stretched twenty feet above. The floor was tiled, spattered gray and brown, the kind that hid blood stains and vomit. A strip of worn red carpet lay along its middle like a weary tongue.

"Mister Mills," came a high, thin voice. A man's voice, but not a manly, jock-itch man's. Some do-gooder wimp. Freeman looked up from the pointy toes of the shiny leather shoes before him.

"You talking to me?" Freeman said. De Niro in *Taxi Driver,* not Eastwood, but Freeman figured a Clint squint wouldn't fly in the bad light. He tried the line again, changing the emphasis of the syllables. "You talking to *me*?"

"Welcome." The man extended his hand. He was balding and his eyes were distorted behind his thick eyeglasses. The brushy mustache made him look like he was wearing one of those Groucho Marx disguises. His eyelids were heavy and purplish. The buggy, milky eyes blinked and the man licked his lips. Freeman's first thought was *Lizard Man*.

Freeman took the hand. It was clammy and moist, like the building's interior.

"Francis Bondurant," Lizard Man said. "I'm the director of Wendover Home."

"Hey, call me 'Trooper.' I've got a history with that one," Freeman said.

Lizard Man pursed his lips, and Freeman expected a long tongue to flick out at any moment and snatch a mosquito from the air. "Why, er, yes, Mister Mills. How was the trip?"

"Nice ride," Freeman said, with just an edge of toughness. No need to disrespect Marvin just to rack up an easy score against this guy.

"He was well behaved. A total gentleman," Marvin said, and Lizard Man seemed to notice the driver for the first time, though he'd been standing a few feet behind Freeman. Maybe the Liz wasn't cool with "coloreds."

"Behaved himself, did he?" Now that Lizard Man had an adult to talk to, he became just like the rest, talked right over Freeman's head as if he wasn't there. "Well, we hope he gets off to a good start here. Wendover has a reputation for helping the difficult placements."

Difficult placements. The Liz made it sound like a game, stats to be padded like a batting average against a rookie pitcher. Maybe Wendover was the roach motel of group homes. Difficult placements check in, but they don't check out.

"Here's some of his papers." Marvin pulled an envelope from somewhere inside his jacket. "You should have received the rest in the mail."

Lizard Man studied the papers, made sure everything was signed in the right place, then nodded curtly. The whole transaction reminded Freeman of a prisoner exchange in a war movie.

"Very good, sir," Lizard Man said to Marvin. "Are you rushing right back, or would you like to stay and rest a bit?"

Marvin rolled his eyes over the shabby interior: The oil painting of a sailboat that had lost its gloss, the paneled wainscoting that buckled from the wall in places, the ceiling tiles that looked as if someone had dashed coffee on them. "Thanks for the offer. But I've got a Bible Study to lead back off the mountain. Wouldn't want one of my youngsters to misinterpret the parable of the fishes."

"Amen to that," Lizard Man said, and Freeman could tell right away the man had fallen into the automatic Jesus–response and didn't know the first damned thing about the parable of the fishes. "Well, thank you for delivering this young Daniel from the lion's den."

"He isn't delivered yet, Mr. Bondurant. You and your staff will have to take him the rest of the way to salvation."

"Quite so."

To Freeman, Marvin said, "So long, Freeman. Hope it works out."

"Thanks for the lift." Freeman almost reached out to shake Marvin's hand, but didn't want to mess it up by fumbling around halfway between a high-five and a soul shake. So he just nodded. He was supposed to be tough, anyway. He wasn't going to be softened up with a few kind words and a fast-food meal. He'd been hit harder by better.

"See you around," Marvin said to them both, then glided out the door. The shaft of sunlight that snuck in during his exit gave a hint of the wide green world beyond. Then the door swung closed, slamming with the finality of a coffin lid.

Freeman was home.

TWO

Francis Bondurant was already building a mental file on his latest charge. As Bondurant pretended to read the reports on his desk, he secretly studied Freeman Mills over the rims of his glasses. The boy lounged in the over-stuffed leather chair in front of Bondurant's desk, looking at the art on the walls, prints of Brueghel, Goya, and Raphael. The kind of epic religious art that inspired young minds, or at least invoked a little fear.

"So, you had some trouble down at Durham Academy," Bondurant said, pressing his lips together in appropriate disapproval.

Freeman didn't answer, just scuffed his feet on the carpet.

Sullen was the adjective that Bondurant slid into the mental file. He had two cabinets full of documentation, reports, GAF scores, criminal records, and Social Services data, but he preferred to build his own portfolio for each of Wendover's clients. Through this method, he could work the healing powers of the Lord on these wayward children. He had to carry the children in his heart before he could lift them to higher glory. Even though Dr. Kracowski had requested and arranged Freeman Mills's transfer, that didn't mean the boy's troubled soul should be entrusted entirely to science.

"Do you want to talk about it?" Bondurant said. "Sometimes a little distance helps us put things in perspective."

"It's all in those papers." The boy shrugged, his face soft and feminine around his hard eyes. "Whatever they say, I must have done it. You know *they're* never wrong about anything."

"You versus them? Is that how you see things, Mr. Mills?" Bondurant put down his pen and folded his hands together under his chin.

"No. That's how *they* see things."

Bondurant smiled. This one was going to be a pleasure. The devil had reached into this child, whispered foul things in his ear, turned his heart to stone. But Bondurant wielded the shining sword and punishing scepter in the form of the paddle in his bottom drawer. "The Cheek Turner" was two feet of solid hickory and had adjusted the attitudes of larger boys than Freeman.

Bondurant read the psychiatric reports that the driver had given him: Bipolar disorder, periodic antisocial behavior, manic episodes of moderate severity, grandiose and persecutory delusions. One doctor had noted a suspected cyclothymic disorder, tossing in an asterisk and question mark beside the words "schizoaffective."

Diagnostic voodoo. Those doctors, with their own God complexes, couldn't see this boy's most obvious disorder. Freeman Mills needed to get right with God, needed to mend his sinning ways, needed to let Jesus in to cure that troubled heart. Bondurant removed his glasses and pretended to clean them.

"Suicide attempt," he noted. No need to skirt that. Let the boy learn that nothing would be glossed over at Wendover.

Freeman shrugged and absent-mindedly rubbed the scars on his left wrist. "It seemed like a good idea at the time."

A broken home. So many broken homes these days. Mother murdered when Freeman was six, according to the case history. Father, an accomplished physicist and clinical psychologist, convicted of the crime and confined to a psychiatric hospital. That punishment was divine justice to Bondurant's mind, but it still left an innocent victim. Except Bondurant was quite sure that none of these children were innocent, or else they wouldn't be wards of the state.

"Does your father know you're here?"

The boy shrank into the chair and his eyes shifted as if waiting for a shadow to loom over him. Bondurant recognized the mixture of anger, pain, and fear. Many of Wendover's children wore that mask. Especially when you mentioned their fathers.

"Why do you have to drag *that* bastard into this?" Freeman said.

"I need to understand you if I'm going to help you."

"Did I *ask* for help? How come all you shrinks make it your mission to fix me?"

Persecution complex. That's what the "shrinks" would say. But Bondurant knew that persecution itself wasn't a problem. The Sweet Lord Jesus Christ was the poster child of persecution, and the Lord had certainly overcome.

"Two arrests for shoplifting," Bondurant read aloud. "Running away from group homes. Vandalism. Tipping over tombstones in a Presbyterian cemetery. What possessed you to do that?"

Freeman said nothing.

Bondurant leaned back in his leather chair. "We'll not have that sort of foolish behavior here. Is that understood?"

Freeman nodded, looking as if he were near tears. The boy closed his eyes in an attempt to regain control.

Ah, a lesson in humility. Bondurant bit back his smile. "There's one simple rule at Wendover, Mr. Mills. May I call you Freeman?"

The boy nodded again.

"That rule is: respect yourself and respect others."

"Sounds like two rules to me."

"That's not a very respectful response, is it?"

"No, sir." Freeman's voice was barely audible, swallowed by the thick paneled walls of the office.

The telephone rang, and Bondurant glared at it, annoyed at being interrupted in this important task. He answered on the third ring. Kracowski was on the other end. "Francis."

Not a question, not a greeting. Merely a fact. The length of line between them didn't make Bondurant feel any more at ease, because Kracowski's office was just down the hall. He found himself adjusting his tie.

"Yes, Dr. Kracowski." Bondurant clenched his fist around the receiver. He couldn't quite accept that the younger man insisted on being addressed as "Doctor," while Bondurant himself could be called by his first name. No matter that Kracowski had helped bail him out of that Enlo mess. After all, accidents happened.

"There's trouble." Kracowski made the statement with no inflection. Was it *good* trouble or *bad* trouble?

"Of what sort, sir?" Bondurant nearly swallowed his tongue on that last salutation.

"Pillow case."

"What's that?"

"Womb therapy. Dr. Swenson told me it went badly."

Some of Kracowski's unorthodox methods, if discovered, would have the Department of Social Services conducting a full-scale investigation of Wendover. Never mind that Kracowski, and therefore Wendover as a whole, produced results, with several children already successfully integrated back into the home and society. Healing had to be done in a proper way, by the book. Kracowski must have read the book backward, torn out a few pages, and scribbled in most of the margins. And all that new machinery in the basement . . .

Bondurant had to suffer in silence and ignorance. He looked at the cross on the wall, the symbol of He who knew suffering. Bondurant smiled at Freeman to maintain the illusion of calm superiority. "How badly?" he asked Kracowski.

"The child is unconscious."

"I see," he said aloud, though inwardly he was searching for the kind of perfect verbal blasphemy that only a sinner could summon.

"We have it under control. It was a necessary part of the treatment."

"I'm sure there will be no problem." The child would probably have no memory of the treatment. One good thing about Kracowski, he didn't produce potential witnesses against himself.

"We won't need to administer atropine this time," Kracowski said. "A natural recovery should suffice."

Freeman rose from his seat, paced back and forth a few times, then walked over to the bookcase and ran his fingers over the books. Bondurant cupped his hand over the mouthpiece and called, "Excuse me, Mr. Mills, but I don't think anyone gave you permission to stand."

Then, to Kracowski, "Hold on, sir."

Bondurant pushed an extension button that buzzed a phone in an adjacent office. "Miss Walters, send in Miss Rogers. We have a new member of the Wendover family who needs to be shown to his room."

A static-filled voice responded, "Yes, sir."

Freeman ignored Bondurant and fidgeted before the bookcase. Just before the office door opened, Freeman looked Bondurant fully in the eyes for the first time and said, "She'll be okay once she starts breathing again."

Bondurant frowned. This boy was a little too witty for his own good. Coming up with words out of thin air, sticking his chest out, squinting, a study in defiance. Maybe it was the mania, the "up" cycle of the boy's manic depression, that brought on the misbehavior. Or his delusions of grandeur. But that would be granting him excuses, and Bondurant believed that evil was innate and that forgiveness had to be earned. Through pain if necessary.

The door opened. Bondurant deliberately kept his eyes fixed on Freeman's back. To look at Starlene Rogers inspired jealousy. "Freeman, this is Miss Rogers," he said.

Freeman turned, smiling at the woman. "Hello, Miss Rogers. It's a wonderful day in the neighborhood."

"Hello, Freeman," she said. "Welcome to Wendover."

"Take him to the Blue Room," Bondurant said. "I'll have his bag sent over later."

Bondurant risked a glance at Starlene. She was tall and a little stocky, a country girl raised on garden produce, home-butchered livestock, and Sunday sermons. Even in a navy pants suit, her curves suggested a particularly enjoyable route to eternal damnation. But her wholesomeness was a threat, her innocence made others seem unclean. Bondurant couldn't dwell on his resentment fully, knowing Kracowski was waiting on the line.

"Come along," Starlene said, holding out a hand to Freeman. The boy looked at her, trying on a suspicious expression, but Bondurant could tell it was an act. Starlene always put the children at ease. She had a quiet, relaxed manner that added to her charm. Bondurant found the quality annoying, suspecting an ulterior motive for her pretending to be so pure of heart.

She left with Freeman, who clutched his belly as if he'd eaten too much candy, and as Bondurant waited for the door to swing closed, he gazed at the bookshelf.

"Francis?" came Kracowski's impatient voice from the phone.

"Go on, sir."

"Just keep everybody out of Thirteen until I give the clearance."

"Yes, sir." Bondurant was used to accepting the man's orders without a thought. He found his attention wandering back to the bookcase. One of the leather-bound volumes was out of place. Right near where he'd placed the little bronze globe given to him by the Governor's Childhood Initiative Commission.

The globe was gone.

The little brat had swiped it. No, there it was, a shelf below. Bondurant realized he'd missed what Kracowski had just said. "Excuse me, sir. You were saying something about Thirteen?"

"The patient we're treating."

Bondurant hoped the home didn't become the subject of a scandal. Kracowski had managed to keep things tidy and under the rug so far, but the man's experimental treatments had gotten stranger and stranger. "And how is she?" Bondurant asked.

Kracowski's words sent a chill through him that was colder than the dead, damp air of Wendover's basement:

"She'll be okay once she starts breathing again."

THREE

Wendover's Blue Room turned out to be a large open dorm in the south wing of the building. Freeman supposed the name came from the sky-blue walls, a color probably chosen by some soft-skulled social scientist who'd decided that the sky promoted passivity. The room was lined with metal cots, a stained strip of gray industrial carpet running down the corridor between the two rows. The rest of the floor was of the same drab tile that had soaked up light in the hallway. If the walls had been olive or khaki, the place could have been mistaken for a boot camp barracks.

"I've got a feeling I won't have a private room," Freeman said to Starlene. Most of the two dozen cots had wooden trunks tucked beneath, and stray socks and comic books lay scattered in the shadows.

"The others are in class right now." She led him to a cot near the rear wall. "This one's yours."

Freeman pushed down on the cot. No give. Oh well, he wasn't here to catch up on his beauty sleep. And dreams were out of the question. "What happened to the kid who was here before?"

"Excuse me?" Starlene still wore that patient, saintly smile. She smelled nice, too, like bubble gum.

"I'm superstitious, okay?" He waited for her to try to tell him that this was the twenty-first century, that he was too old for such things, that Wendover didn't allow foolishness. She was a counselor, after all.

"He found a permanent placement," she said. "Might be a lucky bed."

Permanent. Freeman had noticed the word was easy for people to say who had families, homes, futures. "I could use a little luck."

"It's a new start, Freeman. I don't know what happened before, but you can put it all behind you. That's why we're here. That's why *I'm* here."

Freeman sat on the cot, wondering where his gym bag was. Probably that lizard-breathed Bondurant was rifling through his possessions, hoping to find some dope or booze or girlie magazines. "How many others are here?"

"Wendover houses forty-seven at the moment, counting you. We're licensed for sixty, but with this new state emphasis on reuniting children with their families—"

"Out of the frying pan and into the fire. Makes the numbers look good on paper, but does anyone ever go into the family home later to see what's happening? I mean, I've heard stories."

"A social critic, huh?" Starlene knelt beside him, not letting him look away. She had strong, straight teeth. Almost perfect. "Do you have a family?"

"Yeah. A virgin mother and a father who farts brimstone."

"Why are you angry, Freeman?"

Freeman realized his fists were clenched. She was trying to drag something out of him. They loved it when they thought they were getting inside your head and scrambling the circuitry. Life was easier when you played along, so they could feel good about themselves for "helping."

"It's not anger, it's more of an indefinite pain," he said.

"Your heart probably aches."

Actually, the pain was lower down, in the part he was

sitting on. But he saw no reason to be mean to her. She couldn't have much of a life if she spent all day with screwed-up kids. He should be the one feeling sorry for *her*, for having people dump their personal crap on her head. All she could do was smile and take it and cash the checks. But he couldn't show any pity. He'd probably have her for group or solo therapy, so he'd need to keep her at a safe distance. His edge was wearing off, anyway. The up cycle always came on like a rocket but left like a fizzled firecracker.

"I think it's my feet," he said. "May as well take off my shoes and stay awhile."

He put his feet on the cot and removed his tennis shoes. His big toe stuck through a hole in one sock. For some reason, a stranger's seeing his naked toe embarrassed him. He tucked his foot under his leg to hide the threadbare sock.

A bell rang, the noise reverberating off the concrete walls. As the echo faded, other bells rang throughout the building in a relay.

"Class is over," Starlene said. "You'll get to meet your Wendover brothers and sisters soon."

"One big happy family, I'm sure."

"We're all part of God's family."

First Bondurant and now this woman, coming on strong with the God job. Wendover must have taken a rain check on separation of church and state. At least Starlene wasn't being a Nazi about it. Her gaze was steady, her eyes bright. They were deep blue, or maybe it was the reflection of the walls. Her eyes were the kind that he imagined Joan of Arc had, martyr's eyes, ones doomed to see too much.

Eyes like his Mom's, back before death had shut them forever.

But Starlene wasn't his mother. None of them were, not the counselor with the whiskey breath at Durham, the frantic Spanish house mother in Tryon Estate, or the

Charlotte foster mother who'd made Freeman paint clay
figurines to "pay his keep" even though she'd received a
regular stipend from the state for that purpose.

Voices came from down the hall, the shouts of excited
and bickering children.

"I'd better go," Starlene said. "Your House Supervisors
are Phillip and Randy. They're good people." Starlene
went back between the rows of cots, no longer intimidat-
ing now that she was leaving. The threat of continued
kindness faded with her.

Freeman cased the possible escape routes. His cot was
beneath the only window, a smudged pane of glass some
fifteen feet up. A steel door was set off in the corner, a se-
vere-looking lock attached to the handle. A red light
blinked on an adjacent panel above the lock, as if the lock
required some sort of electronic password.

Freeman looked at the door that Starlene had exited. It
had the same sort of electronic lock. With fire codes, they
couldn't just lock the kids in and swallow the key, could
they? He hurried across the room in his stockinged feet.

The door wasn't locked, it opened with a groan of
hinges. He made a mental note to swipe some oil in case
he needed to do any sneaking out. The hall was empty,
Starlene's shoes making a flat echo around the corner. He
was about to close the door when he saw a man coming
from the opposite direction.

Must be a janitor. Except even a janitor ought to dress
better than this guy. He wore what looked like an ill-fitting
white uniform, gray with stains. The dome of his head
shone in the grim light, a few greasy strands of hair stuck
to the bald spot. The eyes were blank and empty.

He looked like a drunk or a bum. Still, he was a
grown-up, and Freeman had learned that, in the homes,
the lowest rank of grown-up was still way above that of
the kids. Freeman waved to him, but the man continued
his silent approach.

"Say, sir, do you know where my bag is?" Freeman

asked, not putting any defiance into his voice. Sometimes strange janitors could be turned into allies. If they weren't perverts.

In Durham, Tony Biggerstaff had bribed the weekend supervisors so that they smuggled in all the R-rated videos the kids could stomach. Freeman never knew how Tony paid them off, whether with cash, drugs, his sister, or himself. He never asked and Tony never confessed. But without Tony's sacrifice, Freeman would have never come to appreciate the Holy Trinity: Eastwood, De Niro, and Pacino. Beat the hell out of Smurfs and Japanime, and taught you a few life lessons in the bargain.

The janitor drew closer, pale lips quivering. The man's hands trembled. There was something odd about his gait. His bare feet protruded beneath the ragged hem of his trousers, making no sound on the tiled floor.

What kind of a janitor goes barefoot?

"Do you work here?" Freeman looked up the hallway to see if Starlene was coming back.

The man didn't answer. He was close enough now that Freeman could see the pores on the waxy face. Dark half-moons lurked in the shadows beneath the staring eyes. A strand of drool hung from one wrinkled corner of his mouth. The legs moved on, the arms limp at the man's side. The smell of dusty old meat wafted over Freeman.

The man passed Freeman, close enough to reach out and touch, but Freeman didn't dare. You never knew which of these home employees would snap, which one was important, which one you might need to impress at some time or another. You never knew which of them held your future in his hands. True, this dried-up geezer didn't look like a counselor, but you also never knew which little game was actually one of their staged tests. And if this guy was with the Trust, he definitely had games behind his eyes.

Freeman waited to be asked why he wasn't in class with the others, but the man shambled past, staring ahead as if Freeman didn't exist. The feet were creased with a mapwork of turgid purple veins, the bones knotted and calcified, but they rose and fell steadily. The man walked as if he had a destination just beyond the wall and didn't realize that the wall stood in the way.

Freeman had another thought. Maybe this man wasn't an employee of the home. Maybe he was somebody who'd never left, never found a permanent placement. Maybe this was what happened to unwanted people when they grew old. For a moment, Freeman imagined himself in that soiled uniform, condemned to a lifetime of directionless trudging.

Freeman thought about triptrapping him, getting into the geezer's brain, but the manic buzz of an hour ago had faded to zilch. Plus, every read came at a price, in headaches and confusion and loss of identity. For one thing, he'd learned that *everybody* was screwed up, everybody's thoughts and emotions were strange and twisted. One voice in his head was plenty enough, and maybe even one was too many.

The old man disappeared around the corner. Freeman stepped back into the Blue Room and let the door slip closed with a whisper of air. He felt more alone than he had in years. It was almost as bad as the closet Dad used to lock him in, where the wires and weird lights and pain first caused him to triptrap. And caused him to do bad things, think bad thoughts.

He went to his cot and sat quietly, like a death camp inmate, until the other kids arrived.

FOUR

Bondurant stood outside the padded room known as Thirteen, though no number was posted by the door. The room seemed to him more like "Room 101" from the George Orwell novel *1984*. In the novel, Room 101 was where characters faced their ultimate fears. Here at Wendover, the room was where Dr. Kracowski practiced his alternative therapies. The end results were similar.

"Is she conscious yet?" he asked through the open door.

"She's fine." Kracowski straightened from leaning over the bed that held the patient. The doctor was six-four, thin and pale, eyes dark and intense. He put his hands in the pockets of his white lab coat as if he'd read an instruction manual on scientific posturing.

On the bed, a cotton blanket pulled up to her chin, was the girl. Bondurant noted with relief that her chest rose and fell evenly with her breathing. Her cheeks were flushed and her eyelids twitched, but other than that, she looked like any healthy thirteen year old. He wondered what she was dreaming.

"She responded to the therapy," Kracowski said. "She suffered a little trauma, but when she comes around, she'll be farther along the road to recovery."

Bondurant wasn't sure he wanted to know more about

the technique the doctor had used this time. Womb therapy, Kracowski had explained, where they smothered the subject in pillows and urged her to be reborn. It sounded as sacrilegious as all his other therapies. Bondurant might as well enter a metaphysical bookstore and throw a dart at the shelves. Reiki, qi gong, channeling, past-life regression, primal scream, and dozens of other healing modalities made their way into the alphabet soup of Kracowski's treatments. Some of those were marginally accepted, but to Bondurant's mind all were as flaky and godless as traditional psychotherapy. And Kracowski did it all in the name of that ultimate devil's tool, science.

Kracowski also had his own original techniques, crafted from pieces of obscure disciplines and arcane spiritual beliefs. Those were the ones that scared Bondurant the most, but Kracowski kept them hidden away in his mental medicine bag. All Bondurant knew was that the new treatments were linked to the machinery in the basement and the solemn-faced visitors who checked on Kracowski's progress. Silent investors, with silent motives.

"How many know about this?" Bondurant asked.

"Four. Swenson. You. Me." He pointed at the girl on the bed as if he'd almost forgotten her. "And her."

Swenson. The knot in Bondurant's stomach loosened slightly. Paula Swenson was carrying on an affair with Kracowski. She'd certainly not want to mess up her chances at marrying into the doctor's millions by blabbing about a little mishap. The woman's marital odds were as poor as those of the several others who'd shared Kracowski's bed and research methods over the past few years. But Swenson didn't know these things, so she would keep her lips tight, if no other part of her vulgar body.

Kracowski felt under the blanket for the girl's wrist and checked her pulse. "Fifty-five," he said. "She won't remember a thing."

"You didn't drug her, did you?" Bondurant felt the

edge in his voice, and knew his tone was bordering on insubordinance.

"You know I'm not a believer in drugs, Francis. For many of these children, that's part of their problem."

"I didn't think so. I'm just always afraid of things that will leave a . . . trace."

"The only trace I want to leave is the mark of healing." Kracowski's eyes grew cold as he looked at the girl. She may as well have been a rare moth pinned to a cork board.

Bondurant paused at the door and looked down the hall to make sure no one was coming. Few of the staff were allowed access to the counseling wing. But some were too inquisitive for their own good. Starlene Rogers, for one. Always asking why the kids were taken from group therapy for individual treatment.

"I'm just being careful, Doctor," Bondurant said. "That's what you hired me for."

Kracowski made a scissoring motion with two fingers. "And don't forget how easily the strings can be cut."

Bondurant looked up at the younger man, hoping his hatred was concealed. Kracowski was a philanthropist, but his philanthropy ended with the giving of money. He rarely spoke of the spiritual work of Wendover Home, that of setting children on the path to God.

Bondurant suspected that Kracowski was a Catholic, or, heaven forbid, a Jew. But without Kracowski's backing, Wendover Home would have folded years ago, and the children would be scattered among various institutions, their chances for salvation further dimmed. And the doctor's newfound supporters had made the accounting ledgers a good bit healthier.

The girl's eyelashes fluttered and she rolled her head back and forth. A small moan escaped her lips. She tried to sit up, and Kracowski nodded in approval. Her eyes snapped open. She looked scared and confused, like a trapped animal.

"It's okay, Cynthia," Kracowski said. "You're safe now. We won't let them hurt you."

Bondurant wondered who *they* were.

Cynthia stared at the bare, padded walls as if expecting them to close in on her. She shivered under the blanket, though the room was warm. Bondurant thought he heard footsteps, checked the hall, and saw it was empty.

"Where did they go?" the girl asked, her voice brittle.

"Away," said Kracowski. "Far away."

"Are they coming back?"

"No," said the doctor. "Not anytime soon."

Bondurant tried to remember more about the girl. Cynthia. Cynthia Sidebottom. Bondurant wasn't good with details, since that wasn't part of his mission. But this child was one of the most damned, truly troubled, an unrepentant sinner. Her case file said she suffered from depressive disorder, but her arrest for prostitution told Bondurant more about her than did the reams of psychiatric analyses. This child was clearly hellbound.

Cynthia sat up and rubbed her head as if wiping away some half-remembered dream. She leaned forward, dangling her legs over the edge of the bed. "Where's the dyke?"

"You mean Dr. Swenson?" Kracowski asked.

"Whatever, yeah."

"Dr. Swenson wants to help you. We all want to help you."

Cynthia stared at the walls again. For a moment, nobody spoke, and Bondurant heard the bell in the opposite wing. The children would be returning to their dorms for a little community time before supper.

"If you want to help me, give me a fifty-dollar job and let me catch a bus back to Charlotte." She licked her lips in an obscene gesture. Bondurant pretended to ignore her, knowing she was only trying to shock them.

Kracowski's fists clenched, then he smiled and put a

hand on her shoulder. "Cynthia, you're resisting. You know that's not appropriate."

"Neither is your father act," she said. "Why can't you just use big words like all the other doctors, talk around me a while, then let me go?"

Kracowski knelt before her, his frame folded up like a sleeping stork's. "Because I'm the doctor who wants to fix you."

"What if nothing's broke?"

Kracowski leaned his face closer to hers and whispered something that Bondurant couldn't hear. The girl grew pale and glanced wildly at the walls.

"Don't let them get me," she said. "Doc, you got to help me."

Kracowski's mouth creased into a smile, a sick thing that seemed to throw the rest of his face into shadow. "That's why I'm here, Cynthia. To help."

To Bondurant, the doctor said, "I think it's time Cynthia returned to her room. We'll monitor her condition over the next several hours, but I believe she's fine."

Bondurant waited nervously while Kracowski scribbled a few notes on a clipboard. Cynthia raised herself from the bed and Bondurant took her arm to help steady her. As the blanket fell away, Bondurant noted with satisfaction that the girl was fully dressed. Not that he suspected Kracowski would delve into such distasteful sins. But strange things happened in this room, some of which might eventually spread their blight onto Bondurant himself.

Kracowski said, "Remember, Cynthia, your treatments won't be effective if you speak to others about them. It's just between you and me and Dr. Swenson. Understand?"

The girl nodded, the color slowly returning to her cheeks. "Yeah. Like a secret. I'm good at keeping secrets."

"So I've discovered." Kracowski gave her shoulder a gentle squeeze. "You're coming along fine."

"I'll get born one of these days," the girl said, then gave

another furtive glance at the corners of the room. "If they let me."

Bondurant didn't understand the strange relationship that Kracowski had with the children. He wasn't sure what to make of the coded language used in the treatments, and he didn't want to know too much. But the doctor insisted that Bondurant bear witness, perhaps as a special punishment, though more likely to make sure that Bondurant was aware of the stakes.

If any state officials came snooping around, Bondurant's job was to show the benevolent face of Wendover. As for what happened in the shadows of the old building, that was a matter for God to pass judgment upon. Bondurant was certainly in no position to judge, not with a six-figure salary and a respected place in the community at stake.

He led Cynthia down the hallway toward the opposite wing. They passed Starlene near the intersected corridors of the main entrance.

"Hello, Cynthia," Starlene said, throwing a quizzical look at Bondurant.

"Hey," the girl said, sullen now, as if the treatment and near-death had left her too weak to make her usual biting remarks.

"Cynthia has been receiving tutoring today," Bondurant said. "She's going to be one of our shining students."

"By missing class?" Starlene said.

Bondurant evaded the woman's gaze. She couldn't read minds. She was a worker bee, one of the counselors, nothing to worry about. She hadn't worked at Wendover long enough to learn not to ask questions. And if she got too curious, it was a simple matter to dig into her background records and find some excuse to fire her. If worse came to worse, accusations and allegations about her could surface.

"Dr. Kracowski is an expert in several fields, Miss Rogers," Bondurant said. "Ph.D.'s in Physics, Education, and Psychology, with an emphasis in Child Development

and Behavioral Science. Not only that, he finished the pre-
med program at Johns Hopkins. I think he, of all people,
is qualified to make decisions in the best interest of the
child. Isn't that right, Cynthia?"

Cynthia nodded, staring down the dark hall that led to
the Green Room, the dormitory where the girls lived.

Starlene said to the girl, "You look ill, honey. Are you
feeling okay?"

Bondurant fumed. The counselor was practically ignoring him, displaying open disregard for his authority.

"I'm all right," Cynthia said. "They said they would
leave me alone."

Starlene cupped the girl's chin and looked into her
eyes. "If you ever have any problems at all, you just come
see me, okay?"

A small speaker mounted in the hall clicked on, and
after a few seconds of hiss, Miss Walters's voice said,
"Starlene Rogers, you're wanted in the Lake Cottage."

"Remember what I said." Starlene walked down the
short flight of steps to the rear door, her shoes echoing
off the lath walls. Bondurant couldn't resist watching in
anger. Despite her charitable manner, she wasn't properly
beholding to her superiors. Bondurant would have to talk
to Kracowski about her.

Bondurant's stomach clenched. Starlene was beyond
the reach of his rage, at least for the moment. But the girl
was available, and her short-term memory was scrambled, one of the aftereffects of Kracowski's treatments.

"Come," he said, pulling her by the arm toward his office. "We've got some paperwork to look over."

Bondurant's palms sweated in anticipation of gripping
"The Cheek Turner" and delivering one more child unto
salvation.

FIVE

"Shoo. Hey, Dipes, did you drop a load or something?"

Freeman looked at the boy who had spoken. The teenager had a broad, beefy face and a crew cut. His eyes were small and piggish, gleaming with that cruel cunning that Freeman had seen in dozens of faces in group homes across the state. The porcine gaze was fixed on a thin, pale boy who looked to be about ten.

"I didn't do nothing, Deke," the thin boy said, a reaction so quick and rehearsed that Freeman could tell he had been the target of Deke's bullying before.

"Sure, Dipes. Better go change yourself, or we'll have to get the *nurse* to do it." At the word "nurse," Deke had launched into a mocking, effeminate tone. "Don't want her to see your stinky, do you?"

Since the boys had come into the Blue Room, Freeman had said nothing. He'd been sitting on his cot, pretending that the other boys didn't matter. One of the guys gave him an appraising, new-kid look, and another started to wave, but Freeman turned his attention to the book he'd swiped from Bondurant's office. The book was boring, one of those inspirational and motivational hardbacks that told you how to prosper with the help of the Lord. But holding the book allowed him to watch the room out of the corners of his eyes while trying to size up the pecking order. Deke seemed to be the biggest pecker of them all.

Deke began dancing around the thin boy, making a motion as if he were wiping himself with toilet paper. A few of the others were watching, and Deke grew bolder in front of his audience. "Come on, Dipes. Don't be a poopie pants."

Laughter rippled across the room. The boy who had tried to wave to Freeman was biting his thumbnail, glancing nervously at the door. Freeman wondered where the house parents were. He'd been in enough group homes to know that the children were never supposed to be left unsupervised, though it happened way too often.

Dipes retreated from the teasing, passing Freeman's bunk. Deke pursued his quarry, giving Freeman a smirk that said, "Watch me have a little fun."

Freeman quickly turned his attention back to the words on the page, searching for vapid inspiration. He felt sorry for Dipes, but his best bet was to stay on the sidelines for now. Maybe Deke had enemies among the kids, but the odds were just as good that Deke ruled the roost with no opposition. And survivors didn't survive by turning into Defenders of the Weak.

A tall guy in an olive army jacket, who had enough of a hint of facial hair to be fifteen, followed Deke like a second lieutenant. Dipes reached the corner and cowered as the two older boys jabbed at him and sneered. "Dipey wipes, dipey wipes," said Deke, his taunts somehow made even more obscene by his singsong chanting.

A couple of the other boys gathered behind Deke, making noises in imitation of passing gas. Three kids sat quietly on their bunks. From their expressions of relief, Freeman figured they were glad that Dipes was the victim this time instead of themselves. Then Freeman made the mistake of meeting Dipes's eyes.

Help me, those small dark eyes implored.

Deke was unbuttoning his trousers and crouching as if

he were going to moon Dipes. The young boy's lips trembled as he gazed past his tormentors at Freeman. The room smelled of sweat and a caged-animal tension. Freeman gripped the book in his lap so tightly that the pages wrinkled. He would be a smart soldier and keep his head low. Play all sides against each other while sizing up the situation. Like Eastwood in *The Good, the Bad, and the Ugly*.

It wasn't fair that Dipes was small and weak. But whoever said life was supposed to be fair? If life was fair, places like this wouldn't exist. If life was fair, Freeman would have had a different father and Mom would still be alive. If life was fair, you wouldn't need second chances.

"*Psst*. Hey, new kid," whispered the guy from two bunks over. He was one of the three who wasn't participating in the taunting. The boy's eyes were the strangest color of green that Freeman had ever seen, like sick moss.

Most of the other boys had crowded around Deke, so Freeman couldn't see what sort of new insult Deke had dreamed up. From the sound of the laughter, it must have been a good one. Freeman decided he could risk replying without attracting attention.

"What?" he said to the boy out of the corner of his mouth, Eastwood-style, as if he were annoyed at being distracted from his book.

"You going to help him?"

The other two kids watched from their bunks, awaiting Freeman's response. Freeman closed the book. "Are *you*?"

At the end of the dorm, Dipes started crying, and Deke imitated the boy's sobs. The fuzz-faced teen in the army jacket joined in as well. A few others added their wet grunts to the chorus.

The boy who had spoken to Freeman lay back on his bunk and stared at the ceiling.

To hell with it. Freeman stood and dropped the heavy book to the floor. It fell flat against the tiles, the noise like a gunshot. The crowd around Dipes fell silent, waiting for Deke's reaction.

Oh, crap. Freeman could feel the eyes on him, sizing him up. Freeman had been on the other side many times, checking out a recent arrival, wondering how the new kid's presence would affect the group dynamics. He'd already blown his chance to blend into the background. The next best thing was to channel old Clint, *circa* the Sergio Leone spaghetti fests, and grow a rawhide exterior.

"Who's this dickweed?" Deke asked the room. Freeman wondered if Deke knew what the phrase "rhetorical question" meant.

Dipes, forgotten now, wore a grateful expression as he slunk to his cot. Freeman yawned, then slowly bent over and picked the book off the floor. "Sorry. Dropped my book."

Deke crossed the room in a hurry, the teen in the army jacket clinging to him like a shadow. The crowd that had gathered around Dipes was now behind Deke, encircling Freeman's bunk.

Freeman held the book out so that Deke could see it. Deke snatched it away, his brow furrowed and his nose twitching as he tried to read the title. Finally he gave up and tossed it down, then kicked it and sent it skating across the floor like a rectangular hockey puck.

"Sucky book," Deke said.

"I agree," Freeman said. "A literal travesty."

They stared at each other, silence replacing the taunts that had filled the room a minute earlier.

"Where you from?" Deke said.

"Durham."

"Juvie court sent you?"

Being a juvenile court referral carried a little extra cache among junior thugs, but Freeman had taken a different road into the system. Not that he minded lying to Deke, he just didn't want to be recruited into Deke's army. Unless it was necessary for survival.

"Nope, never been caught," Freeman said, as coolly as he could, though the perspiration gathered under his armpits and his heart pounded like a monkey's drum.

Somebody kicked the book back to Deke, who picked it up. "What's your name?"

"Theodore Roosevelt."

The teen in the army jacket snickered. Deke's expression didn't change. "What kind of pussy name is that?"

"It's long for Teddy," said Army Jacket.

"Teddy bear," Deke said, his plump lips parting in a smile. "A pussy name for a pussy boy who reads pussy books."

"No, doofus, that was a president," said one of the crowd.

Deke rubbed his crew cut, doubtful. "So, Teddy, you mighta noticed, this fucking place ain't Durham."

"You can say that again," Freeman said.

"This fucking place ain't Durham," said Army Jacket. A few of the boys laughed. Deke elbowed Army Jacket in the ribs, punishment for hogging his spotlight. Silence fell over the room.

Deke held up the book. "How come you're reading this stupid book and you ain't even been to classes yet?"

"Stole it. From Bondurant's office."

"Bullshit."

Freeman shrugged, as if he could care less whether Deke believed him or not. He hoped his indifference would be taken for toughness and not arrogance. Deke was heavy-set and outweighed Freeman by forty pounds. Freeman might have the edge in speed, but he didn't want a battle on his first day.

"Why don't you read some of it?" Freeman said. "See if it's Bondurant's kind of stuff."

Deke opened the book, his brow wriggling as he struggled with the words. Freeman sneaked a glance at the boy with the strange green eyes. The boy flashed him a secretive wink. Dipes sat on a bunk in the front of the room, near the door, watching like the others.

Army Jacket shoved Deke's arm, making the boy drop the book.

"What'd you do that for, butterbrains?" Deke said, though Freeman noted a tone of relief in the bully's voice.

"You read that stuff, you'll turn into a pussy, too," Army Jacket said.

After a moment, Deke said, "Damn right," and kicked the book across the floor again. It bounced off the leg of one of the bunks and slid near a redheaded boy's foot. The redhead gave the book a kick and it spun to Army Jacket. The teen stomped on it and then scooted it to another of the boys. The crowd spread out a little and the boys kicked the book back and forth, the particularly damaging blows drawing shouts of praise.

Freeman sat back on his bunk and crossed his legs pow-wow-style. He'd have to deal with Deke eventually, but at least he'd created a diversion for the moment. This way he'd have an opportunity to learn the ins and outs of Wendover before the inevitable face-off. It's not like he had anything else to occupy his time, besides fending off inquisitive counselors, watching out for the Trust, and trying to keep his thoughts to himself.

And keeping other people's thoughts away.

Bondurant's words of inspiration were still taking a licking when the house parents finally showed up.

SIX

Starlene sat on one of the flat gray rocks that jutted from the ground beside the lake. The water, which smelled of moss and fish, distorted the reflection of the tall trees. A leaf fell to its September death, sending low ripples out from where it floated along the silver-blue water. Starlene thought falling leaves were like angels, except she hadn't worked out the part about how leaves rose up to heaven again after they had fallen. An angel shouldn't just drown and sink and then lie rotting on the mud at the bottom.

The kids had a short break between classes and dinner. They were allowed out on the grounds in the company of their house supervisors, and soon would be scattered across the lawn, laughing, chasing each other, almost forgetting their world had walls. For the moment, though, she had the grounds to herself.

Starlene looked at the rear of Wendover Home, at the cold stones that were always in shadow. Behind those windows were tiny hearts, grown as cold and hard as the stones that walled them in. Society's children. The troubled, lost, and unwanted. Starlene hugged her knees to her chest. God didn't send you anything that you couldn't handle, though, so she must be here for a reason.

At least the staff seemed to care about the kids. She'd

heard horror stories of the glory days when orphanages were little more than juvenile work farms. Though she'd only been at Wendover for three months, fresh off a Social Sciences degree at Appalachian State University, she got along well with the other counselors and house parents, especially Randy. Francis Bondurant was still a mystery, with something slippery behind his smile, but his reputation was solid with people who mattered. Dr. Kracowski was likewise elusive, keeping odd hours and holding private sessions at times when the young clients were supposed to be in class. Without Bondurant and Kracowski, though, she couldn't imagine such a difficult enterprise as Wendover ever lasting as long as it had. Better to offer prayers for them than to be suspicious.

Starlene took a granola bar from her pocket and peeled back the wrapper. She said a quick blessing and took a bite. She was about to take another, to convince herself that dry sweetened oats were tasty and not meant solely for horses, when she saw the figure on the far side of the lake. The figure stood at the water's edge, two hundred feet away, almost obscured by the branches of a weeping willow.

Must be one of the landscaping crew. She waved. The person didn't respond. On closer examination, the person appeared to be draped in some sort of gray-colored gown. Odd clothing for yard work. And didn't the landscapers get off work in the early afternoon?

Starlene squinted against the sunlight reflecting off the water. The wind had picked up a little and the golden willow branches swished around the shadowy figure. She waved again, the first unease fluttering around the granola in her stomach. What did the handbook say about reporting unauthorized persons?

The back end of the property bordered a couple of farms whose fields gave way to the steep mountain slopes that were coated in autumn's patchwork. A fence circled the Wendover lawn, but an adult could scale it without much difficulty. An adventurous local fisherman might have crept in for a try at the lake's bass, but casting a line would be awkward among those branches. She wasn't naive enough to think that clients never sneaked out of the home, but who would want to sneak *into* a place as imposing as Wendover?

She stood and shaded her eyes. The figure moved closer to the water's edge. She saw no fishing pole, and she was sure now it wasn't a groundskeeper. It was an old man, the sun glancing off his pale bald head. The breeze that skated over the lake ruffled the man's long gown. Starlene was reminded of a biblical movie, John the Baptist doing God's work in the water.

The man hesitated a moment, looking across the lake at the home. Starlene wished she had carried her walkie-talkie with her, but she had learned to treasure her rare moments of privacy. She thought of calling out to him or shouting for assistance, but something about the man's odd, hunched manner kept her silent. She crouched down on her rock.

Surely the man had seen her. But he showed no sign of being observed. Instead, he stepped forward into the lake. Another step, and he was in up to his knees. The water had to be forty degrees or so, but the man didn't hesitate. When he was waist-deep, an alarm went off in Starlene's head, the same alarm that warned her when a client was about to throw a fit or slip into a suicidal depression.

Starlene jumped from the rock and began hurrying around the lake. She broke into a full run just as the water reached the man's shoulders.

"Hey," she shouted. Her sprint brought her to a trail leading through a small copse of white pines. The sunlight dappled crazily off her face as she forced air into her lungs, drove her knees high, pounded her feet against the packed earth.

By the time she came out of the trees, the man had

disappeared. She shouted again, her breath rasping as she reached the willow.

Not even a ripple marked the surface where the man had gone under. Starlene knelt by the water's edge, peering into the murk. Surely some air would have escaped his lungs, bringing bubbles to the surface. The water along the bank should have been muddied by the man's footsteps, but the bed of sediment hung intact like a greenish skin.

Starlene gave one more glance at the home. The shadowed walls offered no help. What would Jesus do, if Jesus ever had to save a drowning man? A more immediate question, what would *she* do?

She peeled off her blazer and tossed it high on the bank. Shucking her sandals, she took a deep breath and arced into the water, praying that she and the man didn't meet headfirst.

The chill hit her like a fist, nearly causing her to gasp a mouthful of water. She opened her eyes to a disorienting universe of silver speckles.

Kicking her legs, she forced herself downward, fighting the natural buoyancy caused by the air in her lungs. Aided by the weight of her soaked clothing, she touched bottom and spun around.

Judging by the pressure against her ears, she was probably twelve feet deep. Here the water was darker and bluer, with loose particles of algae drifting around her stirred by her dive. Starlene pushed with her arms and turned in a circle.

No sign of the man.

She stroked with cupped hands, skimming the bottom. Above, the muted sunlight played against the surface, creating the illusion that the sky, too, was water.

Her lungs burned with held breath. No man, only mud. The cold water stung her eyes. Finally she made for the fresh air waiting above.

A shout greeted her as her head broke the surface. She shook hair from her face and treaded water, trying to orient herself. Another shout came, its direction disguised by the flat floor of lake. Then she saw them running toward the willow tree: Randy, followed by the huffing, gangly form of Bondurant.

"Are you okay?" Randy yelled.

Starlene nodded and took a gulp of air, then dove back under. This time she stayed shallow, peering through the gloomy water. The man was gone. If indeed he had ever been.

By the time she rose for her next breath, Randy had stripped his shirt and was at the water's edge. He waded into the water, eyes wide from the shock of cold. Starlene waved him back. After waiting to see that she was making steadily for shore, he climbed up the bank, then retrieved his shirt and her blazer.

Bondurant had caught up with them by the time Starlene was standing, dripping and shivering, on solid ground. Randy gave her his shirt to use as a towel. Her nipples had hardened from the cold and he looked away.

"What's going on?" Bondurant said, shifting his gaze from her chest to the spot in the water from which she had emerged.

"Some . . . man," she said, fighting to fill her lungs. "He was here under the tree, then he just . . . walked in."

"A man?" Bondurant said.

"Dressed in a gray gown. Like a hospital gown. I didn't recognize him, so I don't think he worked here. I yelled but he didn't even look up, just went under and disappeared."

"How long ago?" Randy asked.

"Couldn't have been more than four or five minutes."

"Even Houdini couldn't hold his breath that long." Randy went into the water up to his knees, then put his hand over his eyes to shield the sun. "I don't see any bubbles."

"We should call the police or the rescue squad."

Bondurant pushed his glasses up his nose. "A man, you say. Just disappeared into the water."

"Yeah."

"Miss Rogers, you expect us to believe a man would voluntarily walk into water that's not far above freezing?"

"Why else would I jump in myself?"

"The sun off the water could have played tricks," Randy said. "Happens a lot around here, seeing things. You know that from talking with the kids."

"I know what I saw."

She hunched under the warmth of the blazer as Randy waded back to shore. Bondurant raised one eyebrow at Randy, who shook his head.

"This is a very stressful job," Bondurant said to her. "Someone with your limited experience must go through a period of adjustment. The practical applications taught in the classroom are far different from what we have to do inside those walls." He paused, then added, "In the real world."

Starlene gazed across the calm expanse of water. She expected a gray-clad corpse to bob to the surface at any moment.

"We'll say nothing of this." Bondurant turned and headed back toward Wendover.

"I'm not crazy," she said.

Randy looked at the lake.

"I'm not crazy," she repeated.

"Let's go," Randy said, taking his shirt from her. "You better change before you freeze to death."

As they rounded the rocks on the far shore, Starlene looked back at the willow tree. Her legs and arms felt leaden, weighted by more than just her wet clothes. She hadn't imagined it. Had she?

Randy put a possessive arm around her. She let herself lean against him, all tan muscles and chest hair.

"I'm not making this up," she said.

"You heard Bondurant," Randy said. "Don't say anything."

"Oh, God. You don't believe me, either, do you?"

Randy didn't reply.

And she'd thought he understood her, that they shared the beginnings of a growing trust. "Randy?"

He faced her and put his hands on her shoulders. "One thing about Wendover is that you're not supposed to ask any questions. The sooner you learn that, the better off you'll be."

She looked into his ice-blue eyes. "What are you talking about?"

"That sounded like a question." He turned and walked up the path ahead of her.

She took one last look at the lake, shivered, then followed.

SEVEN

Dinner was barely recognizable as food. It was served on the same beige fiberglass trays that every other group home used. The beige always bled into the meat and gravy, muted the colors, and made it all taste bland. Could be worse, though. Could be Pepto-Bismol pink.

The dining room was small, but Freeman managed to find a corner table off by himself. Dipes came through the line with his tray and briefly caught Freeman's eye. Freeman looked away to dodge any lingering gratitude.

Just keep on moving. Nothing to see here, folks.

Freeman definitely wasn't in the mood to collect acquaintances. The thing with Deke and the book had been a convoluted act of self-preservation. He wasn't here to serve as Defender of the Weak, Protector of the Innocent. Leave that to the comic book heroes and Dirty Harry. His job was to survive long enough to figure a way to get the hell out, preferably in one piece.

One of Freeman's house parents sat at the table, a couple of chairs down. Randy. He had that weathered, beefy look, the kind of guy who was probably smooth with the ladies until they figured out his IQ was equal to the number on his old high school football jersey.

Freeman concentrated on his mashed potatoes.

Powdered. Why in the world did they have to be powdered? It's not like real potatoes were that expensive. Maybe the staff dietitian wanted to avoid the dark spots. You couldn't have specks in your potatoes when you were trying to build perfect people.

Randy leaned toward him. "So, Freeman, what do you think of Wendover so far?"

The dollop of potatoes was too small to hide behind. Randy showed teeth, the kind that could bite through his own leg if he ever needed to free himself from a steel trap. A kindness that could kill if necessary.

"It's fine, sir." Freeman stuck a generous forkful of mystery meat into his mouth as an excuse not to say more.

"You'll like it here. We have a lot of success stories."

And I'm sure you're about to tell me some of them.

But Freeman was wrong. Randy's fork went up and down as steadily as if he were pumping iron, packing away the beige food and building biceps at the same time. Freeman scouted the room.

Bondurant was nowhere to be seen. No surprise there. A warden could eat with neither the convicts nor the guards. Many of the counselors sat together at a long table. There were no empty seats there, and Freeman wondered if Randy had been forced to sit with him. Short straw gets the loser kid.

At the next table over, a group of girls hunched over their trays, giggling. All except the girl at the head of the table. Her skin was nearly as pale as her ash-blond hair. Black eyes, large and moist-looking, stared down at the plate before her. The food was untouched.

She suddenly looked up, directly at Freeman. An image flashed into his brain, a single word: *Trust.* He swallowed hard, sending the bland and thoroughly chewed meat toward his inner plumbing.

That was weird. It's not like I was trying to triptrap her or anything.

But she was already staring at her plate again. Freeman

took the opportunity to study her face. Even though she was a little sickly looking, with dark wedges under her eyes, she was pretty. Except, thinking of a girl as pretty seemed a little freaky. Prettiness made his heart light and his lungs stiff, as if he couldn't get any air into his body. Prettiness was pretty damned scary. Luckily, prettiness had always stayed a safe distance away. Bogart in *Casablanca,* wrong place, wrong time, that sort of thing.

He recognized the suffocating sadness in her eyes, though. He'd seen it often enough in the mirror. Maybe she hadn't yet learned how to shut it off, to bury it. But that was enough about her. He didn't want to be caught staring again. And he definitely did not want to fool himself into thinking he'd read her mind when he wasn't even trying.

Across the room, Deke was using his spoon as a catapult, flipping navy beans at some eight year olds. That was a tired trick. Maybe Deke had been here so long that he was behind the times, not up on cutting-edge goon techniques.

Starlene, the counselor who had taken him to the Blue Room when he arrived, entered the dining room. She had a towel around her neck, and her hair was wet. She was dressed in a red sweat suit, looking like a generous Christmas stocking. Freeman wondered if there was a gym here and if she'd been working out.

She collected a salad and a cup of coffee, then headed Freeman's way. So much for splendid isolation.

"You feeling better?" Randy asked her as she sat between him and Freeman.

"No."

Randy waved a fork at her salad. "I'm surprised you weren't in the mood for fish."

"I only eat the ones I catch. Except for the undersized ones like you, then I throw them back."

That's when Freeman figured it out. Ms. Sweat Suit and Mr. Muscles. The perfect jock couple, a match made in SoloFlex heaven. They probably had his-and-her headbands back at their condo love nest.

Freeman concentrated on his butterscotch pudding. It blended perfectly with the beige tray, and was the first pudding in the history of the world that could have doubled as wall spackle. He could imagine Deke stowing some away for later pranks on Dipes.

"I don't care what you and Dr. Bondurant think," Starlene said to Randy. "I know what I saw."

"We can talk about it later."

Grown-up talk. Freeman tried to will himself into invisibility. Starlene noticed his discomfort and said to him, "Sorry. I'm having a bad afternoon. Even grownups have them from time to time."

"Except grown-ups don't have to apologize." Freeman immediately regretted smart-mouthing her. But Clint Eastwood mode wasn't something you could climb into and out of at the drop of a hat. You had to stay in character. Unlike Kevin Costner in practically anything.

"I did apologize, Freeman."

He tried to triptrap her, just for the hell of it. All he got were ringing ears and the jolt of a live wire slicing through his head. He might as well have slammed his forehead against the dining room's cinder block walls. Some people were like that, natural shields, and even with the ones he *could* read, there was no way to control which stuff he got. Sometimes it was whatever the person had watched on TV the night before, or a favorite character from a movie. Sometimes it was a sick relative or money and how to get more money. Sometimes . . .

Sometimes it was the kind of stuff his dad used to think about.

"Is something wrong?" Starlene asked, and Freeman blinked himself back into the dining room.

"I just saw somebody I thought I knew." He poked at the pudding, then glanced at the pale, blond girl. She was

staring at him again. She was exotic, dangerous, Faye
Dunaway in *Chinatown.*

*Sure, something's wrong, Queen Starlene. Someday
when you have a few years, maybe I'll tell you. Until
then, ain't no shrink getting inside HERE. Because your
kind always has to find something, and you always have
to "fix" it, no matter if you break more stuff than you
glue back together. So you keep on YOUR side of the table
with Mr. Hunk-a-Hunka Burnin' Love there, and I'll sit
right here, and both of us will get along just fine.*

*Just stay out of my head and we'll be okay. That goes
for you, too, Miss Spooky Skeleton Girl who hasn't eaten
a bite.*

A bell rang, and Randy checked his watch. "Yard time,
soldiers," he barked loudly enough for the entire dining
room to hear.

Deke slipped in a quick lip-synch in imitation of Randy,
eliciting giggles from his goon squad. Chairs scraped and
flatware clattered as the kids assembled to dispose of their
trays. Freeman took a last stab at the pudding and slipped
a forkful into his mouth. It even tasted beige.

Starlene smiled at him, an alfalfa sprout caught between her teeth. Freeman felt guilty for trying to read her.
She was the only one here who had been nice to him so
far. Maybe he could use it later on, play that particular
character flaw to his own advantage. The best victims
were those blinded by their own sincerity.

Freeman ended up in line behind the skeletal blonde.
He wasn't sure if he'd slowed his pace to arrange the en-
counter or if it was coincidence. Her hair hung halfway to
her waist and looked so soft it was almost translucent
against her baggy black shirt. Freeman stared straight
ahead, hoping she wouldn't turn around and speak to him.

She scraped her plate into the garbage can. It was obvious she had stirred her food but had eaten nothing.

One of the counselors came over, a man in a vee-necked

sweater and carefully trimmed mustache. "How was your dinner, Vicky?"

"Fine, Allen," she said.

"Looks like you had a big appetite tonight." Not a hint of sarcasm.

"It was yummy."

He patted her on the shoulder. "We'll have you up to fighting weight in no time."

Allen left and Vicky brushed her hand across the spot he had touched, as if ridding herself of cobwebs. Freeman couldn't believe she had fooled the counselor so completely. Either she was smart, or Allen was stone dumb. Or maybe a little of both.

Freeman put his tray in the window slot. A conveyor belt carried the dirty dishes into the mysterious depths of the dishwasher's room. The churning of water and the hum of rubber belts reverberated inside the little space. Freeman stuck his head in to see if an actual human being did the work or if the system was automated like something out of *The Jetsons*.

Standing beside a large rack of glasses was the strange old guy Freeman had seen shuffling down the hall earlier. Maybe he was a janitor after all. No, not a janitor. Custodian. Everybody got a special name for their jobs these days so they could feel good about themselves.

The man didn't take any notice of Freeman. He probably saw dozens of kids come and go, change placements, rejoin their families, or have the juvenile justice system finally catch up with them. The man's blank eyes were undoubtedly a gift of evolution, a survival mechanism. The less you see, the less you know. The less you know, the better off you are.

Sounded like a pretty good philosophy. If the game was to be invisible, then the man in the dirty gown was a master.

Freeman tossed his fork into a pan of soapy water, then turned and found himself face-to-face with Vicky.

"By the way," she said. "You didn't accidentally read my mind. I read yours."

She walked away, joining the herd of kids gathering to go outside. Her next words slipped inside Freeman's skull without the benefit of sound: *You're not the only one who's special.*

EIGHT

Bondurant felt humbled here, the only place in Wendover that wasn't part of the domain he ruled. Two walls were lined with equipment: computers and monitors and racks of color-coded wires. Shelves of thick books covered a third wall, texts of everything from clinical cases to alternative religions to New Age healing modalities. A faint air of ungodliness cramped these quarters. Dr. Kracowski's office reeked of *seeking*.

Bondurant looked through the two-way mirror that bridged the office to Room Thirteen. Kracowski was attaching tiny electrode patches to a young, dark-skinned boy. The boy sat on the bed in gym shorts, socks, and nothing else except for the rubber circles stuck to his chest and his left temple. Bondurant pulled the boy's case file from his mental drawer.

Mario Diego Rios. Nine years old. Found at a bus station in Raleigh where he had gone without food for three days. His dad, a mechanic for the bus line, had locked him in an unlit storage closet. Little Mario still suffered nightmares, even after intensive talk therapy and Bondurant's prayer sessions. Since the abandonment, Mario couldn't stand to be in enclosed places.

Which was why the boy was trembling now, because

Thirteen was fairly cramped. Kracowski said something to Mario, which was picked up by a microphone in the ceiling. The displaced words came to Bondurant through the computer speakers.

"It's okay, son. I'm going to help you. But first you're going to have to do something for me. Can you do that? *Por favor*?"

The boy nodded, lips tight.

"You're going to have to think about something."

The boy looked at the door, then at the mirror.

"It's going to seem a little scary at first, but that's the only way I can help you."

The boy's brown face faded to light tan.

"You trust me, don't you, Mario?"

The computer recorded data from the patches that covered the boy's chest and head. The boy's heartbeat played out on a graph, along with a corresponding jagged line that had something to do with Kracowski's electrodes. An inset image showed a multi-colored map of the boy's cranial cavity on one corner of the screen. Bondurant concentrated on the graphics so he wouldn't have to see the boy's frightened face. Green, purple, and red fields marked a transverse image of the boy's brain.

"Think back for me," said Kracowski, his voice low and soothing. "Can you do that?"

Then, "Good."

The jagged line rose slightly as the boy's heart rate increased. The purple field on the brain scan shifted to red, measuring increased blood flow.

Through the microphone: "I want you to remember what it was like in the storage closet."

The line jumped, spiked, fell off rapidly, and jumped again. The red of the colored brain map pushed at the green.

"Dark," said Kracowski. "You feel the walls closing in, don't you?"

The line made a saw-tooth pattern, the peaks nearly touching the top of the computer screen. A tape machine whirred, recording the session. The computer printer spat out a paper version of the data being stored on the hard drive.

Kracowski's voice went even lower. "You're trapped, aren't you? You scream and nobody can hear you."

The boy's rapid panting was picked up by the microphone. Bondurant couldn't resist any longer. He looked away from the machines and through the mirror. Kracowski stood over the boy, fidgeting with the buttons on a small box that looked like a cross between a television remote and a control for a radio-operated toy. The boy's eyes were pressed so tightly together that they quivered.

"Now, Mario, what you're feeling is the negative energy inflicted by the experience," the doctor said, as if the boy could understand those big words. "The fear has disrupted your energy fields and blocked the normal flow of your emotions."

The doctor poised a finger over his control box. "I can help you. Now, it's going to hurt for just a moment, but I want you to keep thinking about that small, dark space."

Kracowski pressed a button and the boy shook uncontrollably for a couple of seconds. Bondurant glanced with concern at the computer monitor and saw that the bottom line had flattened. The boy's heart had stopped.

Bondurant clasped his hands together and asked Jesus to have mercy, on both the boy and on Wendover's good standing.

In Thirteen, the boy had fallen back on the bed. Kracowski adjusted the controls on his handheld box, then thumbed a lever. Both lines on the computerized chart took a wild leap, then ran together in synch. The gap between the lines had narrowed, the top one no longer jagged and inconsistent. The red on the brain map softened and faded to a placid purple.

Kracowski bent over Mario and lifted one of the boy's eyelids. The doctor smiled, turned to the mirror, and nodded, then began removing the electrode patches. Kracowski turned off the lights and left the room.

A few moments later the office door opened. Bondurant pretended to study the odd items on Dr. Kracowski's desk. A human brain, crenulated and obscene-looking, floated in a jar of formaldehyde. The label on the jar read, "Do Not Open Until Judgment Day." Bondurant shuddered at the sacrilege.

"Satisfied?" Kracowski brushed past Bondurant and dragged the sheaf of printed data toward his desk.

"As long as he's not dead."

"He's not only not dead, he's better than ever. How long have your therapists been working with the boy?"

"Six months."

"Six months of suggestion and mind games and feigned kindness. And the boy's claustrophobia didn't improve."

"Of course not."

"Post-traumatic stress disorder, adjustment disorder, possible Axis IV diagnosis of situational heart arrhythmia due to anxiety. Far too much negative energy, wouldn't you say?"

Kracowski sat behind the desk. Bondurant stood like a servant awaiting orders. "The boy's afraid of the dark. The Lord is the light," Bondurant said.

"You found one answer, and it works for you, no matter the question." Kracowski nodded at the bookshelf. "But there are ten thousand paths to knowledge or God or truth. According to quantum theory, we don't even exist as separate entities because our atoms have no substance when you get close to the center. According to the Taoist philosophy, the closer you get to the center, the farther you are from where you were going. According to Dr. Richard Kracowski, the center and the outer limits are exactly the same."

Bondurant looked at the dark window into Thirteen. "What happens when he wakes up and starts screaming?"

Kracowski tented his hands, the fingers like painted bones. "He won't scream."

"Every night since his arrival, he has insisted on a night light."

"That's one of your mistakes. You're treating the symptoms, not the underlying cause."

"Sure. We also fed him, taught him, gave him individual counseling and group therapy. We allowed him to grieve."

"You *allowed* him to grieve for a father who cared so little that he would lock away his own flesh and blood. You should have taught the boy to hate that bastard."

"That's not the compassionate care that Wendover represents."

"I'm not talking about the mission statements and slogans that you pitch at your child psychology conferences. I'm talking about perfect harmony and alignment."

Kracowski tapped the computer screen. The brain map was now a deep cobalt blue. "That, Mister Bondurant, is the color of healing. Cobalt blue is the color of God."

Bondurant watched the computer monitor as it paced out the boy's steady heartbeat. "So you heal them by killing them for a few seconds."

"Synaptic Synergy Therapy works. Low voltage at the proper emotional meridians, applied just long enough to disrupt the blockage. Multi-wavelength electromagnetic fields to influence the brain's neurotransmitters and blood flow. Radiopharmaceuticals to chart the brain chemistry. And add the power of positive thinking."

Bondurant turned. "No matter that it disrupts the heart's functioning?"

Kracowski smiled, his cheeks creased into shadowed pits. "A man of faith should know that the heart and mind are connected."

"The girl. Did you give her an SST treatment as well as the rebirthing therapy?"

"You *did* want to cure her promiscuity, didn't you?

Isn't that one of the things Moses forbade on his dear stone tablets?"

"God told Moses nothing about treating claustrophobia," Bondurant said.

"Did you ever consider," Kracowski said, leaning forward, "that God might have told *me* instead?"

Bondurant swallowed. Kracowski was taunting him, knowing who controlled Wendover's purse strings. And the silent investors had kicked in a ten percent salary bonus for Bondurant. With great power came great responsibility and a ton more bullshit to swallow. Bondurant was about to speak when the computer began beeping and the printer scrolled more paper toward the floor.

"The boy," Kracowski said. "He's waking up."

"For heaven's sake, turn on the lights over there."

"Oh ye of little faith."

"You haven't heard his screams. You're never around at night."

"I might be around more often than you think." Kracowski approached the mirror. "And cameras never lie."

Inside Thirteen, the boy's outline was faintly visible in the darkness. His eyes snapped open and his gasp was audible over the microphone. The heart rate graph rose in intensity. Bondurant clenched his fingers.

Darkness. He'll think he's back in the closet. Now he'll scream.

The boy sat up. On the monitor, the twin lines rose and fell in parallel motion. The brain image glowed in bands of red and indigo.

"See the upper reading?" Kracowski said. "That's his energy field as measured across the meridian points I devised. Did you notice how erratic the reading was before my treatment?"

"You mean before you gave him electroshock?"

"Mr. Bondurant, that's a crude comparison. I'm not a psychosurgeon. I don't try to cure by destroying the brain.

I don't give frontal lobotomies, or whatever term they use these days for systematic depersonalization. I merely drive away the traumatic residue that blocks the normal functioning of the brain's neurotransmitters."

Gobbledygook, Bondurant thought. Kracowski's technobabble was as bad as the counselors' psychobabble.

Mario looked around, unhurried, curious. It had taken three grown men to restrain the boy during his first night here, when the lights were turned off in the Blue Room and the boy fled for the exit, clawed at the walls, rammed his skull against the steel door. Now the boy sat in the dark as if meditating with open eyes.

"He's not screaming," Bondurant said.

"He doesn't seem to be uncomfortable in the confined space," Kracowski said.

The monitor showed the top line on the chart had leveled out while the bottom line rose and fell steadily. Kracowski waved a hand to indicate the pattern. "Calm as a nursing infant."

"I must admit, the treatment is impressive. How long do the effects last?"

"My initial research shows that it may be temporary. But even if the neurotransmitters must be, shall we say, 'realigned' every month, that's a much better success rate than any of your shrinks can claim."

Mario looked at the mirror, and for a moment, Bondurant was struck with the impression that the boy could see him. "What about potential cardiac damage?"

"No chance. It's as if a light switch was flipped off and then back on."

"Let's hope so. One incident, and the state licensing board and the Social Services investigators will sweep through this place like storm troopers. I don't think they would find your techniques in the chapter on standard practices."

"Your job is to keep them away. At least until I've

finished my *work*. Then they, like the rest of the world, will finally see the light."

Bondurant shuddered at the way Kracowski had emphasized the word work. He'd said it with an almost religious fervor. Kracowski might have made a good pastor. But the man found his pleasure in healing a troubled brain instead of leading a troubled heart to the Lord.

Inside the darkened room, Mario called out. "Hello? Are we finished yet? I'm hungry."

Kracowski pressed a button and the lights blazed in Thirteen. "I didn't say I could cure his eating disorder. Let's save that for next time."

Randy and Dr. Swenson entered from the hall and removed Mario's restraints. Dr. Swenson asked, "Mario, are you ready to play a game of cards?"

"Cards?" he said. "*¿Qué Clase?*"

Kracowski smiled.

Bondurant was afraid to ask if an SST treatment caused any other negative side effects besides temporary death.

NINE

Figured it wouldn't last.

Yard Time had been nice, and Freeman was able to score a good spot on the rocks, bathing in the sun with his eyes closed. He was surprised the kids were allowed near the lake since it might prove tempting to the potential suicide cases among them. Many of the kids had broken into groups near the main building. The shouts and rubbery thuds of a soccer match rose from the lawn.

Freeman opened one eye against the orange blaze of sundown. The mountains huddled like great beasts around the group home. Farms and pastures stretched beyond the fence to the base of the rocky slopes, giving Freeman a sense of unease, as if with two leaps the mountains would be on him, with no trees in the way to slow them down. He hoped he wasn't developing a case of agoraphobia to go along with his other problems.

Deke and his goon squad were hanging out in a worn spot amid the shrubbery, by the fence at the rear of the property. A gray thread of smoke spun from the shadows, either tobacco or marijuana. Deke probably had a steady supply of contraband, yet another way to maintain his throne and win tribute and loyalty from his dimwitted subjects.

"A penny for your thoughts," came a voice below him. A girl's.

Vicky.

Freeman's breath caught in his lungs, as if he had inhaled one of the high clouds. His pulse jumped in his wrists and his scar itched. He snapped his eye shut and wondered if he should pretend to be asleep.

"How about a dime?" she said.

Freeman blinked and sat up, feigning drowsiness. She'd claimed to have ESP, and unless she had learned to lie telepathically, he couldn't ignore her forever. And he wasn't sure he wanted to. "Hi."

"You're new."

Brilliant powers of observation.

But before he could twist his mouth into a frown, their eyes met and again Freeman felt his chest expand and his heart float. Or maybe his medicine was screwing with him. "Just got in today."

"First placement?"

"Nah. I'm chronic."

She rolled her spooky, dark eyes. "Nobody's *born* this way."

Oh hell. She's not trying to ask me about HIM, is she? Not Dad? Quick, change the subject, change the subject, change the subject.

He thought of some of the silly come-on lines he'd seen in those after-school specials that group homes loved to pipe in. What are you doing after the game? What's your cat's name? How was your summer vacation? None of them seemed to fit. Freeman had yet to see a heartwarming treat for the whole television viewing family that featured a bunch of caged mental fuck-ups.

"Maybe we get born with some of it," he finally said.

"Yeah. Believe it or not, I hear I was a chubby baby." She played with a dead leaf, running her finger over its veins, then over the veins on the back of her hand. Freeman had never so plainly seen the inner mechanics of a hand. Her knuckles were knots, her nails too large for the scant flesh of her fingertips.

Let's not talk about our problems. That's Rule Number One for faking sanity and normality. And the faster you can fool them into thinking you're normal, the faster you can get the hell out of Dodge. Because there's got to be a place out there where people aren't trying to crack open your skull twenty-five hours a day and probe it with their microscopes and questions. Second chances, no matter what Mom used to say.

Mindless chatter was way easier than talking about the real stuff, so he tried the obvious. "How long you been at Wendover?"

"Six months. Or two hundred years, depending on whether you're talking the calendar or how long it really feels like."

"I've been to worse. Just came up from Durham Academy. Two weeks before my transfer, a seven year old got gutted with a plastic knife."

"Harsh. We don't have that kind of thing here. But we have other stuff to worry about."

Freeman wasn't sure what would play better, De Niro in *The Last Tycoon* or Eastwood in *The Bridges of Madison County*. And he still wasn't sure if he wanted to get to know her. He'd already sworn off being Defender of the Weak, and Vicky looked pretty damned weak. "There's always something to worry about, if you look hard enough."

"That's what Starlene says," Vicky said. "About worrying. Says God doesn't send you anything you can't handle. It's easy for her, though. She's on a Jesus kick that makes Franklin Graham look like a hopeless heathen by comparison. And she has way better hair."

Freeman rolled up on one elbow. Vicky sat cross-legged on one of the gray-blue boulders. She looked across the lake, her face blank, as if she'd already forgotten her last statement and could care less about his response.

"I like Starlene okay," Freeman said. "She doesn't seem as weird as the others."

"Oh, she's nice, I guess. I just don't like people trying to solve my problems for me."

"Me, either."

"You don't look like you have any problems. Despite your little act."

Freeman didn't know whether or not to take that as a compliment. "I'll tell you who creeps me out—Bondurant."

"Good old Bondo-brain."

"He looks like a lizard."

Vicky's eyebrows lifted and a smile played at the corners of her bloodless lips. "Definite reptile material."

Freeman flicked his tongue out, a cross between Bondurant's nervous mannerism and a frog going for a dragonfly. Vicky laughed, and the laughter was like music, a melody in counterpoint to the wind in the trees and the shouts from the games. Freeman felt something was wrong, that he was falling from a great height. Then he realized what it was: he'd come terribly, god-awfully close to being relaxed and carefree for a moment.

When you let down your guard, that's when they get you. Pacino in Dog Day Afternoon.

A voice came from beneath the boulder. "What's so funny, bookworm?"

It was Deke. While Freeman had been distracted, lost on floaty, happy crap, the goon squad had circled around the lake and gathered below him and Vicky. Deke gave a yellow grin, teeth stained by whatever he had been smoking.

Freeman looked back at the group of counselors. They were seated together at a picnic table beneath an oak, lost in their own concerns, salaries and off days and certification levels. Randy was making a swimming motion with his arms. Starlene slapped him gently on the shoulder. Allen nodded at the couple as if he understood.

No help there.

Vicky eased a little closer to Freeman as Deke climbed

the boulder. "Getting you a little sugar, bookworm?" the fat boy said. "Smoochie smoochie with the Vomit Queen?"

Freeman saw two escape routes: dive into the lake, which was probably ice-cold even if he didn't break his neck trying the ten feet to the water, or roll off the back of the boulder and make a run for it. Even if he made it, what would happen to Vicky? His muscles tensed as he realized that once again he'd been drafted as a god-damned miserable Defender of the Weak.

Army Jacket and another of the goons were behind Freeman now. He'd hesitated too long. That meant he'd have to rely on his wits again. Outsmarting Deke, though it was hardly a challenge, was getting old pretty quickly.

"How did you like the book?" Freeman said. Vicky was practically touching him now.

Deke stood above the two of them, hands on his hips. "You didn't snag that from Bondo's office. You're a lying dork."

"You're entitled to your opinion, based on information and belief. And it's healthy for your self-image to freely express yourself."

"What the frig? Why are you talking like a counselor all of a sudden?"

"I want to help you, Reginald."

"My name's not Reginald."

Freeman rose to a kneeling position. He could feel Vicky's eyes on him. "And how long have you been experiencing this latent hostility?"

Deke nudged Freeman with his foot. "I ain't got no latent nothing."

"It's okay, Reginald. Own your feelings. Let it out."

Deke's cheeks turned pink. He clenched his fists, knowing his audience would expect a harsh response. "I'm going to pound you back to wherever you came from, dipshit."

Freeman talked fast, before the fist descended. "You

wouldn't resort to violence in front of a lady, would you? What does that reveal about your upbringing? What would your mother say?"

"Keep that bitch out of this, or I'll—"

"Ah. So you're using Vicky as a surrogate for your mother, and you hope you can win her affection by proving your mettle in battle." A tendril of sweat snaked down Freeman's neck. He hoped none of the goons noticed. He kept his face as blank as he could, as blank as that weird janitor guy's. What would Clint do? When he didn't have a gun, that was?

"You think I care about this hunk of bones?" Deke unclenched one fist and waved the fingers at Vicky. "I don't like girls who puke after every meal."

"If a girl was with you, she'd need to puke anyway," Vicky said. Freeman risked taking his eyes off Deke for a second to glance at Vicky. Her eyes flashed anger. To Freeman, she said, "Thanks for dragging me into this, Steve."

"My name's not Steve," Freeman said.

"Hey, wait a second," Army Jacket said. "I thought his name was 'Theodore' or something faggy like that."

"Shut the hell up," Deke said. "Let me do the talking around here."

"That's right, Reginald," Freeman said. "Learn to open up. Your feelings matter. Share with us. Now gift us with that winning smile, and burn us with optimism's flames."

Deke looked uncertainly toward the counselors grouped far away at the picnic table. "They spoon-fed you a heap of this crap, ain't they?"

"Think positive."

"You're weird, man."

"*I'm* weird? You're standing on a rock surrounded by a half-dozen kids you need to impress, you're trying to intimidate a guy you've never met before today and a girl who's a third your weight, you're probably fifteen and still in a juvie placement at an age when most of your buddies on the outside are working toward hard time, you have serious control issues, and probably an Oedipus complex waiting in the wings. And you say *I'm* the weird one." Freeman let out a fake sigh of exasperation. "Reginald, old chap, I've got a lot of work to do on you."

"I'm not fucking Reginald. My name's Deke."

Freeman held up his palms in resignation, shrugging at the goons. "Let's take the road to healing one step at a time."

"The only stepping I'm going to do is all over your face."

"Sadistic tendencies," he said to Vicky, as if consulting her for a medical opinion.

"And I concur on the Oedipus complex," she said.

"Hey, if I wanted to eda . . . to eda . . . if I wanted to do it to you, barf-brains, I'd have you begging for it in no time," Deke said to her.

"Erectile dysfunction," she said. "Premature ejaculate. Incipient impotency."

Some of the goons were grinning now, scratching their baby stubble. Army Jacket said, "I think she's talking about your wing-wang."

"Most certainly," she said. "I'm sure it's a specimen to rival Michelangelo's David in sheer phallic voluminosity."

"Like you'd ever get to find out," Deke said. His face was redder now, the color of the sun on the lake. He was breathing hard.

"I'm curious," Vicky said.

Freeman wondered how far she was willing to go. It was one thing to run intellectual circles around Deke, but if you started hitting below the belt, he might turn dangerous.

"Show her, man," said Army Jacket.

"Unzip," said another of the goons. A couple of others took up the chant.

Deke looked over at the counselors again, this time in

desperation. Suddenly the bell rang, and the shouts from the playground turned into disappointed groans and then silence.

Deke tugged at his waistband. "You got lucky, baby," he said to Vicky.

She rolled her eyes and said nothing.

"Let's get out of here before she pukes or something," Deke said. The goons followed their leader off the rocks and toward the main building. A couple of the goons glanced back at Vicky with looks of veiled appraisal.

"Well-played," Freeman said.

"You could have been more clever."

"I ran out of big words."

"Maybe I'll loan you a few, next time. My name's Vicky."

"I know. Did I mention I'm perceptive?"

"Perceptive enough to know how I figured out your name?"

"Let me guess. You read my mind."

Vicky stood and touched him on the forehead. "Nah. That's one place I don't think I want to go again."

She skipped down the slope of the boulder and headed across the grounds. Freeman was going to have to change his opinion of her: as slight and skinny as she was, she definitely wasn't one of the Weak.

TEN

Nah, can't be him.

Starlene was on the ground floor, headed for the offices in the central entrance, her arms full of reports. Bondurant had given her copies of Freeman's case history, and since the new boy would be in Group with her, she planned to stay one step ahead of him. She had been mulling something Bondurant had said, about the boy "knowing too much," when she'd seen the strange man in the gown again.

The man's shoulders slumped, his posture one of weary defeat. He gave a slow turn of his head and Starlene looked into the saddest, most empty eyes she had ever seen. The man nodded at her, then shuffled around the corner toward the west wing.

"Hey, wait!" Starlene hurried after him, her heels loud on the tiled floor. She'd lost him before, but now he had nowhere to disappear. She would drag the man down to Bondurant's office and then make Randy see she hadn't imagined the incident at the lake.

They were entering the section where Dr. Kracowski conducted his therapy sessions. Kracowski insisted on silence. Or, rather, Bondurant had, on the doctor's orders. Starlene had never met the doctor herself, and he seemed as elusive and mythical as the old man she was chasing. She reached the corner and turned, anxious and breathless. The hall before her was empty.

No. Not again. He was REAL.

Something glistened on the dreary tiles. Starlene knelt and wiped with her finger. Water. Behind her stretched a trail of bare, wet footprints.

"Hey," she called again, uncertain.

A door opened. A tall, dark-haired man came out, his clipboard loose in his fingers. He wore a white lab coat, the pockets frayed. His cheeks were blue with stubble. He looked as if he'd been napping in his office. "Lose something?" he asked.

"Did somebody just come by?"

"Somebody?"

"A man. Dressed in a gown, hunched over, no shoes."

The tall man smiled. "My dear, are you new here?"

Dear? He was talking like somebody from a 1950s sitcom. "I've been working here for eleven weeks."

"That explains it."

"What explains what?"

"Look-Out Larry. Our resident specter."

"Specter? You mean—?"

"Do you always ask so many questions?"

"Only when I think I've lost my mind."

"We don't lose minds around here, we find them. Look-Out Larry is a ghost, I assume. I've never seen him myself, since I don't believe in ghosts."

"This water is real," Starlene said, though most of the footprints had now evaporated.

"I see no water," the man said.

"Oh, you don't believe in water, either?"

The man smiled. "If I could make something disappear just by no longer believing in it, then I'm afraid God would have died ages ago. Excuse my manners. I'm Dr. Richard Kracowski."

He said his name with the air of one who knew his reputation had preceded him.

"Hello, Doctor. Glad to finally meet you. I'm Starlene Rogers, counselor."

"Ah, yes, Bondurant warned me about you."

"'Warned?' Sheesh. Tell me about Look-Out Larry, because that makes twice I've seen him today, and I've never had any reason to doubt my eyes before. And I don't believe in ghosts, either. But I do believe in God."

"Oh, so you've seen God?" Kracowski looked toward the ceiling. "Actually, I have this theory that Look-Out Larry *is* God."

"Sir, I'd love to debate religion with you sometime, but right now I'd rather figure out if I'm going crazy or not."

"Miss Rogers, the word 'crazy' is not in the lexicon anymore. Hallucinations are one of the hallmarks of schizophrenia, or, in certain diagnoses with which I don't agree, delusional disorders."

The footprints had evaporated completely now, and Starlene was no longer sure they had even been there. "So I'm schizophrenic because I thought I saw somebody who doesn't exist?"

"Either that or you're a religious visionary."

"But you said yourself that others have seen him. He even has a name."

The doctor leaned forward, conspiratorially. "Hate to tell you, but all the other people who claimed to have seen Look-Out Larry were *patients*."

Starlene looked both ways down the hall. "So more than one person has the same hallucination? I would think a man of science would take that as corroborating evidence."

Kracowski held up the clipboard, showing her the charts and graphs fastened to it. "Evidence is something that can be measured, quantified, proven. Surely you studied research methods in college, even if you ended up being a counselor."

Starlene didn't like the sarcastic bite that the doctor

put on that last word. It was bad enough to get strange stares from the members of her church and neighborhood, but to have to endure this from someone in the same profession—

"Maybe it was a trick of the light," she said. "These halls are dark. I mean, if it was a ghost, and I don't believe in ghosts, then I wouldn't have seen him. Right?"

"You're sounding cured already."

"Do me a favor?"

The doctor smiled again, his eyes half-closed. "For you, anything."

"Don't mention this to Mr. Bondurant? I wouldn't want him to think his hiring me was a mistake."

"Oh, I'm sure Bondurant knew exactly what he was doing. For the good of the children, right?"

Had Kracowski said that last sentence in mockery of Bondurant and the director's tight-lipped manner of speech? "I want him to trust me," she said.

"As far as I'm concerned, what happened here is a secret, between you, me, and our old pal Larry."

Starlene wanted to stuff Kracowski's clipboard into his smile. She cast a quick prayer of forgiveness, both for Kracowski's arrogance and her own surrender to anger. This was her first job, the counselor's equivalent of a combat zone, and she would be a good soldier. God had sent her here for a reason, and she didn't need to understand His purpose until He needed her to know.

"Excuse me, I've got a group session to lead." She headed down the hall to the stairwell, feeling Kracowski's eyes on her.

"A pleasure to meet you," Kracowski called when she was about to turn the corner. Starlene kept walking.

In college, Starlene had studied the phenomenon where medical students often noticed symptoms in themselves of ailments they were studying—med school hypochondria. The same was true of psychology students, though the symptoms were more nebulous. Maybe working with troubled children had snapped something loose in her own head. Were hallucinations contagious?

Sure. And mass hysteria in Salem had led to witch hangings. The human race had come a long way, and the field of psychology had come even further. Carving out pieces of people's brains in order to rid them of emotions was rarely done anymore, and even required the patient's permission. Electroshock wasn't automatic for every person who sought treatment for depression. Insanity was no longer touted as a spectator sport, as had happened at St. Mary of Bethlehem Hospital in seventeenth-century London, commonly known as Bedlam to the tourists who gave twopence for the show.

No, she hadn't seen a ghost. Because only crazy people saw ghosts, and as Dr. Kracowski had said, nobody's crazy anymore. Especially her.

And to see a ghost twice would mean she was two times crazy. She buried the idea of ghosts as she pushed open the door to Room Seven. She had children to help. She couldn't be worried about helping herself.

The room was sparse, with a desk in the corner and a dusty chalkboard on one wall. Posters proclaimed such timeless tidbits as "Hugs Not Drugs" and "A Smile Cures Everything." Out the window, the sun worked its way behind the distant, black ridge tops. The seven children sat in a ring of chairs. Two slouched sullenly: Deke the pudgy teen whom Starlene knew to be a bully, and Raymond in his ever-present drab olive jacket.

The others watched Starlene take her seat at the head of the circle: Vicky, pale and wide-eyed, whose dress hung about her as if draped from a clothes hanger; the new boy, Freeman; Mario, in too-short trousers, who rarely spoke; Isaac, who nurtured a serious persecution complex; and Cynthia, who called herself "Sin." Cynthia seemed to have recovered from her recent treatment, but a suspicious defiance sparked her eyes.

Ready for a good jousting match, Starlene?

Starlene loved Group. The setting was perfect for teaching socialization skills while also gaining the children's trust. In group therapy, she could be a "facilitator," though she hated that word for it. A facilitator was someone who was structured and inflexible, who "empowered" others while not taking much personal risk. She thought of her job as more like "witnessing," showing others the blessings she'd discovered and which all could share in.

"Hey, guys," she said, looking into each face in turn.

"You're late," Deke said.

"And I apologize. Adults have to apologize sometimes, too, don't they, Freeman?"

Freeman winced, twitched one corner of his mouth, and said nothing.

"You going to make us talk about something, or do we just got to sit here for an hour?" Deke said.

"I think it's better when we get things out in the open," Starlene said.

"Because sharing is caring," Freeman said.

She ignored his sarcasm. Many placements came to Wendover with a wall around their hearts. You couldn't hammer through the wall; battering at it only made the wall stronger. Love was better. Love seeped through the cracks and melted the wall away, eroded its base until the stones crumbled. "We do care, Freeman."

Deke glowered at Freeman, then at Starlene. He looked around the circle, at the children sitting in their straight-backed chairs, making sure he had an audience. "Not all of us care, Freaky Freeman."

Starlene was about to quiet Deke, then decided the group dynamic might be more interesting if she let the children lead the discussion themselves. If only Deke's natural leadership skills didn't turn nasty so easily. Six years in therapy, according to the case file, and Deke was no closer to adjusting to society than he'd ever been. Still, the Lord and her professional obligation required her to have hope for him.

But patience was a demanding virtue. That was one of the warnings that her psych teachers had burned home, that occasionally you'd feel like slapping little Johnny across the face. No matter that he had been abused and suffered a neurochemical imbalance and was diagnosed with an adjustment disorder, you sometimes had to wonder if a particular kind of vermin was, and always would be, a rat.

"Why do you think Freeman is 'freaky'?" Starlene asked Deke.

"He's weird. He likes books and stuff. He sits by himself. He don't talk much, and when he does say something, it's big words nobody understands."

"And how would you respond to that, Freeman?"

Freeman shrugged and slouched more deeply into his chair. "Do unto others."

"Ah, something from the Bible. That's a good rule to live by."

"Actually," Freeman said, straightening, "that's a basic tenet of many religions: Scientology, Buddhism, Islam."

"See what I mean?" Deke said. "Weird."

"He's a thief, too," Raymond said.

"Let he who is without sin," Freeman said.

"Hey," Cynthia said. "What about 'she'? Girls can sin as good as you can."

Raymond let loose with a wolf whistle. "And you ought to know, sweet cheeks."

"Like you'd ever be so lucky," she responded.

Starlene cut in before the verbal barrage turned crude. "Why do you accuse Freeman of being a thief?" she asked Raymond.

Raymond and Deke exchanged looks. Vicky, who had been silent thus far, watching the conversation as if it were the ball at a tennis match, finally spoke.

"Because they feel threatened," she said. "They're

insecure and overcompensate by trying to dominate the other boys. Any time a new guy comes here, Deke and Raymond and their gang have to knock him down in order to build themselves up."

"I ain't insecure," Deke said.

"Dysfunctional. Both psychologically and physically. Remember on the rocks?"

"At least I don't throw up every time I turn around," Deke said.

Vicky turned even paler, if such a thing were possible, though two red roses of anger blossomed on her cheeks.

"Guys," Starlene said. "Remember that we're all here for each other. We're all in this together."

"Bull hockey," Deke said. "Don't give me that 'brothers and sisters' crap. We get enough of that in chapel."

"Remember that part in the Bible about not coveting thy neighbor's ass?" Freeman said.

"That's not in there," Deke said, then turned to Starlene. "See how *weird* he is?"

"It's there," Freeman said. "The unexpurgated version of the Ten Commandments. The long form that usually gets trimmed down when they get posted in the courthouse or the classroom. Lots of other good stuff, too, about slaves and how God is a jealous God. The Big Guy said so himself."

"You seem to know a lot about the Bible, Freeman," Starlene said.

"He probably swiped a copy," Raymond said.

"Yeah, Weasel-brains," Deke said to Raymond. "I got one personally autographed by Jesus. Want to buy it?"

Raymond glowered, fists clenched. Deke held up his palms and smirked. Starlene left her chair and stood between the two boys. "Jesus said to turn the other cheek."

"His other ass cheek?" Freeman said. The kids erupted in laughter, even Deke, and finally Raymond.

Starlene sighed. Dirty jokes and sacrilege. Things

were going to be very interesting with Freeman around. Not to mention having a ghost in the Home. The good thing about doubting your sanity was you didn't have to worry about dying of boredom.

responding to his every command. It would burn down the sensitive media spotlight on the home. The good news about all those staff salaries you saved didn't have the kind of weight that...

ELEVEN

Bondurant didn't believe in ghosts. No sane man did, no holy man did. But the incident with Starlene at the lake was the third of its kind in recent weeks. Each of the three people had claimed to see a man in a dirty gray gown.

The first report had been from a kitchen worker, a wrinkled Scots-Irish whose family used to own the farmland where Wendover had been built in the 1930s. The man said the ghost was dressed just like the patients who had shambled down these halls when it was a state mental hospital during the Second World War. He'd been a boy back then, and as Bondurant had interviewed him, a childlike fear had crept into the old man's eyes. Bondurant had written him off as a superstitious hillbilly.

The second report was from a counselor, Nanny Hartwig, who had worked at Wendover for eight years. Nanny was a reliable sort, thick-bodied and dull and as patient as a cow. She'd never been rattled by the children, even when they threw food or cursed or spat. Nanny could slip a child into a restraint hold as smoothly as if it were a choreographed professional wrestling move.

But Nanny had shown up one morning to begin her three-day shift as a house parent, then disappeared. The other counselors noticed her missing and found her several hours later, huddled in a closet, gripping a mop handle so tightly that her knuckles were white. Nanny muttered incoherently about the man in the gown who had walked right through her. Bondurant had given her two weeks' vacation and hinted that she might consider therapy. In a church, not a clinic.

But this last sighting, with Starlene today, was the worst. Bondurant believed that the third time was a charm. The third time meant that the sightings couldn't be written off as imagination or drunkenness, because Starlene was of good Christian stock. Bondurant could lie to the Board of Directors, give positive spin to the grant foundations and private supporters, even snow the Department of Social Services if it came down to it, but quieting rumors among the staff was like trying to keep water from flowing downhill.

He'd considered approaching Kracowski about the sightings. Kracowski had an easy answer for everything. Usually the doctor could open one of his journals or spew some charts from his computer and Bondurant would be left standing dumbfounded, overwhelmed by terminology and formulas. Bondurant was always comforted by the doctor's confident manner. The very lack of humility that made Kracowski irksome also made his explanations believable.

Bondurant leaned back in his chair. The office was quiet except for the faint ticking as the clock hands moved toward nine. Darkness painted the windows and a few dots of stars hung above the black mountains beyond. The children would be settling down for evening prayers, boys in the Blue Room, girls in the Green Room. Except for the house parents on duty and the night-time cleaning lady, the staff was gone, either in the on-site cottages or far beyond the hard walls of Wendover to Deer Valley.

Bondurant opened the bottom drawer of his desk. His Bible lay next to the wooden paddle and a purple velvet bag. He lifted the bag. Crown Royal. The first sip bit his tongue and throat, the second burned, the third warmed him so much that he shivered. Someone knocked on the door.

Bondurant traded the bottle for the Good Book, slid the drawer closed, and parted the Bible to a random chapter. The Book of Job. That was one of his favorites, with suffering and a defiant and unrepentant Satan, and someday he was going to get around to understanding it. That and the damned parable of fishes.

"Come in," he said.

Nothing. He pressed the button on his speakerphone. The receptionist's office was left unlocked at the end of the day in case the staff needed to get to the patient files.

"Hello?" he said, listening as his amplified voice echoed around the outer office.

Still nothing.

Bondurant rose, annoyed that he should have to answer his own door. He swung the door wide. No one there. He crossed the receptionist's office and looked down the hall. There, in the dim angles leading to the cafeteria, a shadow moved among the darkness. One of the boys must have sneaked out of the Blue Room, probably on his way to swipe a treat from the kitchen.

"Hello there," Bondurant said, keeping his voice level. Even if you were angry, you had to feign calm. Otherwise, you ended up yanking the little sinners by their ears until they cried, or bending the girls over your desk and paddling them and paddling them—

Bondurant swallowed. The person had stopped, blending into the shadows. The hall was quiet, the air still and weighty. Bondurant's lungs felt as if they were filled with glass.

"Aren't you supposed to be getting ready for Light's Out?" Bondurant said, stepping forward.

The figure crouched in the murk. Bondurant cursed the lack of lighting in the hall. The budget never seemed to cover all the facility needs, though administrative costs rose steadily, along with Bondurant's salary.

As he drew nearer, Bondurant realized that the figure was too large to be that of a client. What was a staff member doing creeping around the halls at night? The house parents were supposed to stay with the children, to act simultaneously as guardians and jailkeeps. The cleaning lady would be cleaning the toilets in the shower rooms in the boys' wing, the same schedule she'd used for as long as Bondurant had served as director. Maybe it was one of Kracowski's new supporters, one of the cold and shifty types who acted as if they needed no permission or approval.

"Excuse me, did you know it's after nine?" Bondurant saw that the person was plump and squat, drab in the half-light. Nanny? Had she gotten headstrong and come back to prove she had in fact seen something that couldn't exist?

"Everything's going to be okay." Bondurant wished he'd studied psychology now, because he sounded to himself like a TV cop trying to lure a suicide away from a ledge. He held out his hand and closed the twenty feet of distance between them. What if she broke down and did something crazy, like bite him?

"You can tell me all about it," he said.

Fifteen feet, he wasn't sure the person was Nanny after all. Ten feet away, and he was still uncertain, though he could tell it was a woman.

She huddled face-first in the corner, shoulders shaking with sobs. But no sound came from the woman. She was aged, her hair matted and gray, her legs bare beneath the hem of her gown. The gown was fastened by three strings clumsily knotted against her spine. The skin exposed in the gap was mottled. The woman was on her knees, her broad, callused feet tucked behind her.

Bondurant hesitated. Perhaps he should get one of the house parents, or call the local police. But the police had long complained about Wendover's runaways and the extra security calls. This was different, though; kids ran away all the time, but how many grown-ups ever ran *to* Wendover? Before Bondurant could make up his mind, the woman turned.

Bondurant would have screamed if not for the numbing effects of the liquor. The woman's face was twisted, one corner of her lip caught in a rictus, the other curved into a crippled smile. Her eyelids drooped, and her tongue moved in her mouth like a bloated worm. What Bondurant had taken for sobs now seemed more like convulsions, because the old woman's head trembled atop her shoulders as if attached by a metal spring.

Worst of all was the long scar across the woman's forehead, an angry weal of flesh running between the furrows of her skin. The scar was like a grin, hideous atop the skewed mouth and slivers of eyes. The woman held out her shaking arms. The tongue protruded like a thing separate from the face, as if it were nesting inside and had just awakened from a long hibernation. The lips came together unevenly, yawned apart, spasmed closed again.

Oh, God, she's trying to TALK.

Bondurant took an involuntary step backward, forcing another breath into his chest. Sour bile rose in his throat, a quick rush of heartburn. He would have broken into a run if his legs hadn't turned to concrete. The woman scooted forward on her knees, a shiny sliver of drool dangling from her warped chin. Her soiled gown was draped about her like an oversize shawl. Her lips quivered again, the worm-tongue poked, but she made no sound.

Bondurant shouted for help, but he couldn't muster much wind and the cry died in the corners of the hallway. Bondurant gave up on mortal assistance and sent summons to a higher power.

He remembered the tale of the Good Samaritan, how the Samaritan had helped Jesus on the side of the highway. Or maybe it hadn't been Jesus, maybe it was somebody else, or Jesus might have been the one doing the helping. Bondurant was fuzzy on the details, but the long and short of it was that a Christian reached out his hand when someone was down.

Even if that someone was a twisted, shambling wreck that the Devil himself might have cast out from the lake of fire in disgust.

"It's okay now," Bondurant said, his voice barely above a whisper. "What's your name?"

Again the lips undulated, the sinuous tongue pressed between the teeth, but still no words came out. The woman raised one eyelid, and Bondurant looked into the black well of an eye that seemed to have no bottom.

"Let me help you up," he said. He closed his eyes and reached for her hands. A cold wind passed over him, shocking his eyes open.

The old woman stood before him now, arms raised.

The woman brought her hands to her face, curled them into claws and began raking at her eyes. In her frenzy, the gown came loose, one shoulder showing pale as a grub.

The woman's mouth gaped open, the tongue flailing inside, and her fingers pulled at the skin of her eyelids. Bondurant could only stare, telling himself it wasn't real, that Jesus and God would never allow something like this in the sacred halls of Wendover.

And, even through his fear, he was already scheming his cover-up, planning the story he would give to local authorities.

She broke in, I tried to stop her. No, I've never seen her before . . .

The woman's gown fell farther down her shoulders, and Bondurant could see more scars criss-crossing the flaccid breasts. Still the gnarled fingers groped, and the flesh gave way beneath her fingernails. The lips trembled as if trying to shape a scream, but only silence issued from that dark throat.

Bondurant had been trained to handle violent or aggressive clients. He knew a half-dozen different restraint techniques, from the basket hold to the double wrap. If he could only grab her, pin her arms behind her back, then—

Then he only had to wait either for her to get tired or for help to arrive.

He reached for her elbows and came away empty. She was moving away from him, retreating back into the shadows. Except she wasn't running away, he saw. She was *floating*, her obscenely-swollen toes inches above the floor.

The deformed mouth vomited its silent scream as she continued to rake at her eyes. Just before she disappeared into the wall, the forehead scar curved slightly, as if giving Bondurant a smile of farewell.

TWELVE

Freeman was dreaming of his dead grandparents' farm, a hundred and twelve acres of rolling woodlands, the green valleys pocked with cattle, a silver creek winding through the belly of the land. Freeman was in the garden near the barn, the smell of drying tobacco, manure, and hay dust hanging in the warm summer air. Broad leaves of zucchini plants and wires of runner beans surrounded him. He drove his shovel into the black earth, turning up nightcrawlers.

He turned the shovel and the worms spilled out, slimy and as thick as pencils. The shovel blade dipped again, and the ground fell away, becoming a huge black cavity. A monstrous worm reared up, glistening with mucus, its blind head probing the sky. The worm continued to swell, its girth like that of a rubbery tree.

Suddenly, the worm grew a hundred arms and the dark mouth opened: "Hey, Shit For Brains, what the fuck you doing jerking off in here when I need you?"

Now the worm wore Dad's head, and Freeman struggled against his blankets as the worm's millipedic arms reached for him, strangled him, slapped at him, smothered him, and, worst of all, hugged him—

"Psst. Hey, new guy. Freeman."

Freeman shoved away, cried out, the sunshine of his

dream gave way to six walls of shadow, and still the Dad-worm clutched at him.

"Whoa, man. Take it easy."

Freeman groaned and opened his eyes. In the muted night light of the Blue Room, he could make out the face of the mossy-eyed boy, Isaac, from Group. The boy was shaking him awake.

"You must have been in a bad nightmare," Isaac said in a loud whisper. He released Freeman and knelt by the cot.

Freeman blinked in the gloom, his heart pounding. Even in here, behind these dense stone walls, he couldn't escape that damned asshole. Dad was deeper inside his brain than a maggot in a corpse, whether he was asleep or awake. He wiped the sweat from his forehead. "Thanks."

"You were kicking up a storm. About broke my arm."

"I was getting away. I've had lots of practice."

"Who hasn't? You either get away or you're not around very long. You know how *they* are."

The Blue Room was fairly quiet. At the far end of the rows of bunks, a couple of boys were talking. It might have been eleven o'clock or three in the morning. "Where are the house parents?"

Isaac snorted. "Probably playing kissy-face with each other, for all I know. They make themselves pretty scarce after Lights Out."

Freeman lowered his voice. "And Deke?"

He pictured Deke pestering the smaller boys in the night, maybe even molesting them. The thought sickened him as much as the dream had.

"The fearless leader? Listen for a second."

Among the nocturnal stirrings and small talk, an abrasive, rhythmic sound rose and fell.

"That's his snoring," Isaac said. "He's big on sleep. At night, you can always count on being able to tell where he is. I'm Isaac, by the way."

"I know. Like in the Bible. You ever get sacrificed?"

"Not that I know of. You know how hard it is to put up with all this Christian baloney when you're a Jew?"

"I can imagine. But, if you're like me, you learn to fake it pretty quick. I've been in enough homes to know that the faith-based ones make for easier time, and have better food, too."

"Damn. Are *you* Jewish, too?"

"No, but I might as well be. Got nothing better going on."

"Jews don't trust their kids to be outside a Jewish family. When I got orphaned, my aunts and uncles tried to claim me. But the shrinks wouldn't let them, because, swear to God, I don't trust *Jews*, either. I mean, we're pretty peculiar sometimes."

The main door creaked open. "Hey, keep it down in there," came an adult voice. A flashlight beam sliced from nowhere and swept over the rows of bunks.

Isaac put his face near Freeman's and whispered, "Nazis."

"Ah, the fathers of modern psychiatry," Freeman said. "You know that's how the Germans got their taste for genocide, by wiping out nut cases in the 1930s. Then they started on the homosexuals."

"Hey, I thought the Jews were first."

"Nah. They were doing that stuff even before Hitler came along. All the while these doctors would twirl their mustaches and talk about what a great service they were doing by putting undesirables out of their misery."

"Some of the doctors were Jews, I bet," Isaac whispered.

"Well, Isaac, you present as a classic casebook example of 'paranoia.' "

"You talk like a shrink."

"No, I'm smarter than most of the shrinks I've gone up against," Freeman said. "My dad was one. Always shrink your shrink until they're smaller than you are. That's my philosophy."

"I'll bet you've got a lot of philosophies."

"Changes with the weather."

"So what are you?" Isaac asked. "Manic D? Plain D? Schizo? Socio?"

"Manic D with a cherry on top. At least that's what my case file says. What's got you?"

"Demons. Ugly little Jewish demons with hooks for fingers. Can't shake the bastards loose." Isaac shuddered as if one of the invisible demons had just landed on his back.

"You should see a doctor about that."

"Nah. They tell me that all I have to do is accept Jesus as my own personal savior and I'll be cured. I'd just as soon put up with the demons. A lot lower maintenance."

They were quiet for a moment. Deke's snoring cut through the still air, halted as he rolled over, then picked up again, the rhythm crippled now. One of the guys in a nearby bunk broke wind in his sleep, and Freeman stifled a giggle.

"On nights we have pinto beans, it gets really rough in here," Isaac said.

"There's more than one way to gas a Jew."

They shared a hushed snicker, then Isaac said, "That was a pretty clever trick, what you did with the book today. I've been here for two years, and that's the first time anybody's stood up to Deke."

"I didn't stand up to him so much as just confuse him a little."

"That's easy to do, I admit. But you could have got your face broken. Keep an eye on him. He'll be out to show the others you're not so hot."

"It burns me up that he picks on the little kids. What's the deal with Dipes?"

"It's not a good thing when you're old enough to change your own diapers. Somebody or something must have screwed him up bad. He won't talk about it."

"Join the club," Freeman said. "We're all people of difference, exceptional children. The troubled. The little bumblefucks that society likes to keep out of sight and out of mind."

The door to the Blue Room opened again, spilling a shaft of light from the hallway. A house parent entered the room, following his flashlight beam between the rows of cots. Isaac slid under the bed beside Freeman's, then flipped onto his own cot. Isaac was under the blankets by the time the light settled on him.

"Were you sleepwalking again, Isaac?" said the house parent, Phil.

Isaac sat up and rubbed at his eyes. "They've got pointy fingers," he murmured.

Freeman had to chew the hem of his blanket to keep from laughing out loud.

"Well, try to keep quiet," Phil said. He was thin, with styled hair and cologne that was so strong Freeman could smell it over the lingering odor of flatulence. The man's voice was girlish and whiny. "The other boys need their sleep."

"Sure thing, Phil," Isaac said, rolling his face into the pillow. He said something else which was lost in the bedding.

The light played across the room, resting for a moment on Freeman. He squeezed his eyes tight and concentrated on breathing evenly. The light moved on, and Freeman listened until the footsteps receded and the door closed.

"Nar—nar—narcolepsy," Isaac said out loud, imitating a snore.

"Fake sleep disorder," Freeman said. "Good one. If you hadn't already taken it, I might have added it to my repertoire."

"Yeah, I can pretend to fall asleep whenever some shrink is droning on about my learned helplessness. But if you're manic depressive, you got all the outs you need. Nothing like swinging both ways."

"And then there are the in-between days. Or even hours. I'm a rapid cycler. Up and down faster than a damned elevator."

"Shut the hell up," came a brusque voice from the end of the room.

Freeman flipped his middle finger into the semidarkness and settled into the covers. At least he'd made an ally. One thing he'd learned in group homes, you needed a few allies if you were going to pull through, as long as they didn't become baggage. Even a loner couldn't always make it alone, and sometimes a sidekick took a bullet for you. True in the movies, maybe true in the outside world. Maybe someday Freeman would find out.

But first there was a night to live through, and the dreams that sleep brought.

Dreams.

Which one would come next?

Dad as a giant whale, with Freeman in a tiny boat on a calm sea? In that one, a storm always blew up as Dad surfaced, the sky became a red hell of bloody lightning, the wind screamed like a thousand dying gulls, the waves rose up in monstrous hands of foam. And the whale opened its mouth, a mouth that swelled until it became a great black chasm and beyond that an everlasting night—

No, not that one. Freeman hoped he would never have that one again. He'd rather Dad be one of the Four Horsemen of the Apocalypse, with nothing under his black cloak but bones and disease. Dad with fluorescent yellow eyes glowing inside the hood. Dad with long claws clutching a gleaming scythe, come to harvest Freeman, who ran through the knee-high meadow until even the grass became his enemy, pulling at him, sucking him down—

No. Not that.

Think of something else.

He thought of Mom, but every time he thought of Mom, he saw only one thing: the bathtub with the red streaks on the shower curtain and—

NO SECOND CHANCES. THINK OF SOMETHING ELSE.

He mentally shuffled through all of the possible distractions. A mental film fest, Pacino and De Niro facing off in *Heat*. Do-it-yourself cartoons, the ones you make in your head, where the clowns are jolly and the painted smiles have no teeth behind them. Imaginary music, where the notes hang fat in the air and you can bob them around like balloons.

In his manic state, he could conduct entire symphonies, break down each piece in his mental orchestra, build to throbbing crescendos of air and color. Which was good, because when he was manic, he couldn't sleep. And when he slid down the brain tunnel into depression, he couldn't sleep, either.

Right now, in his in-between state, all he had to do was avoid the nightmares and he could shut his brain off for a while. His medication made his head itch, and the blanket was rough against his skin. They'd put him on some new stuff, Depakote, it was better than the lithium in some ways, but also brought a whole new group of side effects. Though none of the side effects were worse than the ones caused by Dad's experiments.

Like the triptrapping.

It was bad enough when Dad put him in the closet and made him read the cards, kept them hidden while Freeman guessed stars or triangles or wavy lines. Except Freeman didn't have to guess, he could *see* the cards as if he were looking through Dad's eyes.

And that scary first time when the words "Billy Goat Gruff" popped into his brain for no reason at all, with Dad sitting across from him in the garage that he'd turned into a workroom.

"Goat Gruff?" Freeman had said aloud. "Like in the story?"

"Sure. What we're doing, Freeman, is like when the goats triptrap over the troll's bridge. I'm on one end of the bridge and you're on the other, and you go trip-trap, trip-trap, trip-trap straight across and don't let the ugly old troll know what you're thinking. Because you know what will happen if he hears you?"

Freeman shook his head, and Dad jumped up, yanked Freeman by the hair, and pressed his mouth against Freeman's ear. His words spat like hot bullets. "*Because . . . he . . . will . . . GOBBLE . . . your . . . fucking BRAIN.*"

Then he let go of Freeman's hair, patted him on the head, and said, "This is our little secret, okay, Trooper? I've got some people breathing down my neck that would make the troll look like Little Red Riding Hood. You've got to work with me on this one. It's going to hurt a little, but I promise it will be okay in the end."

Dad had gotten more bizarre from then on, zapping him with electricity, telling Freeman the pain was for his own good because it made his mind more pure and open. Dad stuck him with needles and applied the tip of the blowtorch and locked him away in the closet for longer and longer periods of time, and he must have played games on Mom because she didn't do anything to stop the experiments.

In the closet, with Dad's weird machines humming, Freeman would triptrap into Dad's mind and scream and scream and scream because Dad's thoughts weren't nice at all. And Dad was trying to put thoughts back into Freeman's head, things he didn't understand and that made no sense. That was how he learned about the Trust and why Dad was so scared.

But then Mom was dead and all those strange people from the Trust showed up, took Dad's equipment away, and hauled Dad down to the police station. And Freeman went into protective custody and entered the foster system. And he didn't triptrap for years. Then the gift crept back, as if it had been a hideous monster hibernating in the base of his skull.

Some of the telepathic glimpses were fleeting, some were robust and overwhelming, some were pleasant, and some were pitch black. He'd practiced until he could control the ability a little, because he was afraid of the troll, though he never had figured out what Dad meant. Maybe it was fear, a big, black hungry thing inside. Though he tried to bury the gift, hoping neglect would make it disappear, he'd never been able to completely get rid of it.

He wasn't sure he wanted to give it up, either. Mind reading was kind of cool, even though it was freaky. And it definitely augmented his survival skills. He often knew which people to avoid and which people to mine for useful secrets.

But he was tired right now, and needed to shut down for a while. Thinking of triptrapping always made him remember Dad, and memory could murder. So tonight it was either music or the other thing that was foremost in his mind.

Vicky won out, and he thought of her until sleep pulled him under its dark sheets.

THIRTEEN

Bondurant rubbed his eyes. His hands trembled, fingers like blind snakes. The lights were low and he could pretend morning had finally arrived. The bottle of Crown Royal clinked against ceramic as he dashed some liquid amnesia into his mug.

The door to the outer office opened, and Bondurant froze in his chair, anticipating the knock on his door. This time, he wouldn't answer. And perhaps never again. If anyone, or any *thing*, ever wanted him again, they'd have to bust down the door. Or walk through it.

He heard the familiar bustling of Miss Walters, the beeps as she listened to the messages on the answering machine, the sliding of file cabinet drawers. Ordinary sounds marking the start of another day. The rich smell of coffee crawled through the crack under the door. Bondurant wiped his sleeve across his mouth and rose unsteadily from his chair.

He stumbled to the door and knocked. It was unusual behavior, knocking from the inside, but Bondurant appreciated the substantial weight of the oak beneath his knuckles. All real and solid things were to be cherished.

"Miss Walters?" He sounded to himself as if cotton balls were tucked in his cheeks.

The door opened a crack, and for a moment, Bondurant was afraid the vanishing woman from the night before was waiting, her forehead scar smiling.

But there stood Miss Walters, in the dreary cardigan she wore on Thursdays. She looked at him, sniffed, then nodded as if reluctant to notice too much. "Good morning, Mister Bondurant. You're here early."

"Umm . . . do I have any appointments?"

"Not until ten. You and Dr. Kracowski are penciled in for a meeting in Room Twelve. A couple of the board members are popping in for a visit."

Board members. Bondurant stiffened.

There were nine on Wendover's board, all of good, white, Protestant stock, seven of them males. The board met every three months, and the order of business consisted largely of self-congratulatory pats on the back followed by a lavish tax-deductible meal. But every once in a while, some of the directors felt the need to see clients firsthand so they could don expressions of appropriate pity when begging for grant money or private donations.

L. Stephen McKaye and Robert Brooks were two of the most outspoken directors and occasionally voted against the majority on policy decisions. They weren't easily fooled. Bondurant headed toward the coffeepot. He had a mission now, a role to play, business as usual. He would drive himself to a state of artificial alertness.

"You haven't seen anyone else?" he asked.

Miss Walters sat at her desk and rummaged through yesterday's mail. "Whom do you mean?"

"A woman. Maybe a housekeeper working on contract? Gray hair, hunched over, a scar on her face, older than you."

"Older than me?" Miss Walters fussed with a button on her sweater.

"I didn't mean that as an insult."

"I didn't see anybody."

Bondurant chewed on a swig of coffee. "She was dressed in a dirty gray gown."

"She'd fit right in around here." Her eyes moved across Bondurant's rumpled suit.

"Let me know if I have any other meetings. It's Thursday, isn't it?"

"All day long, last I looked. Except you know how us *old* people get a little bit confused."

Bondurant closed his eyes and steadied himself against her desk. He could fake it. All he had to do was concentrate on the pounding of his pulse through his temples and he could almost forget that he'd seen a woman disappear.

He'd faked worse, such as the incident reports that went to the state after a couple of Kracowski's "treatments." Officially, he had blamed one client's bout of unconsciousness on self-asphyxiation and the other's on an asthma attack. Both conclusions reached, of course, after a "lengthy internal investigation." If he could slip those reports by the Department of Social Services, then he could feign sobriety in front of two directors.

And he could also deceive himself into believing that ghosts didn't exist.

"You want me to refill that?" Miss Walters said.

He opened his eyes. "Sorry, just a headache, that's all."

Miss Walters knew better, but she was well practiced at faking it.

At least Thirteen had a window in the door. Not the kind of place you'd want to stow a claustrophobic, but you could turn around in it. Freeman had been in worse. Even the mirror on the wall didn't bother him. All group homes had these little "time-out rooms" with the two-way mirrors. If you had a bug in a jar, it wasn't much fun unless you could watch it crawl.

Randy had shown up in the middle of language arts

class right when Freeman was almost bored out of his
brain by Herman Melville. Randy said something to the
teacher and escorted Freeman down the narrow hall to
Thirteen, punched some numbers on the door's electronic
lock, then sat him on the cot. Randy had Freeman unbut-
ton his shirt, then applied electrodes to his chest and his
temples. Freeman hadn't worried, because people didn't
shock kids anymore. They were probably monitoring his
heartbeat to gauge his reaction to stress and fear.

He kept his cool even when Randy had him lie back on
the cot and fastened leather straps across his upper chest
and waist. When Dad had given him treatments, he'd
often inserted a hard piece of wood in his mouth so he
wouldn't bite his tongue. No mouthpiece, no shock. So
this was no problem. He stared at the mirror and relaxed
as Randy left the room.

Somebody was undoubtedly on the other side of the
mirror, making careful note of his reactions.

He let his knees twitch, then threw in some spasmodic
eyebrow movements. Let them think he had Tourette's
Syndrome. He'd met some Tourette's sufferers, and the
condition was a real bitch, but at least you could get away
with some random cussing and spitting.

The gimmick got old fast. The morning had dawned
overcast, and Freeman had felt the weight of the sky on
him even before rolling out of bed. Getting dressed was
an effort, even with Isaac making his goofy narcolepsy
face by squinting his eyes and blowing a raspberry snore.
Freeman was going from In-Between to the Gray Zone
and was probably on the elevator bottoming out at Pitch
Black Basement.

Blame the brain chemicals. The shrinks said his mood
swings were all the fault of serotonin, which didn't seem
to regulate itself inside his head. Love and chocolate,
they said, both gave you the same kind of high. He didn't
know about love, but he knew a chocolate bar was pretty
valuable inside a group home.

He'd never heard of either of those giving you the ability to read minds; unless you counted Mom, who seemed to know everything Dad said before he said it, and reminded Dad of it constantly. Maybe that's why Mom was dead and Freeman was sitting under a shrink's magnifying glass. While Dad was bouncing around in a rubber room somewhere.

But that line of thought was not going to do anything to help fight the depression that was coming on. No matter which textbook the psychiatrist showed you, there was no escaping the idea that depression was your own fault, that you should somehow be able to just "make yourself happy." That was a snake-eating-its-own-tail argument, because you then felt sorry for yourself because you couldn't fix what was wrong. Guilty by reason of self-awareness.

"Why blame yourself?" he said aloud. A small air vent in the ceiling undoubtedly held a microphone. These guys were pretty smart, up on all the mental espionage tactics. No doubt the Trust had a mole in here somewhere. Maybe they could open a drive-through therapy business. Pull your car up to the window, blather out a list of symptoms, and receive a paper slip as you paid your bill.

The slip could contain Chinese fortune-cookie platitudes, like "All the truth you need lies within," or "The journey of a thousand miles begins with a single step." You could even sell French fries on the side, or maybe an add-water baptism or instant communion—

"Who else is there to blame, Freeman?"

Freeman's eyes twitched again, though this time involuntarily. The amplified voice had no doubt come from the face behind the mirror. Freeman wished he were on an up, so he could triptrap the hidden person and nip the brain drain in the bud.

"I don't blame my *own* face," Freeman said.

"Excuse me?" came the male voice.

"I was just thinking that whoever's talking must be

watching me from behind the two-way mirror. Because I'm certainly not talking to myself."

"Disassociative personality disorder is not on your diagnostic axis."

The voice was metallic and clinical, and the transfer through electronics and speakers kept it from being trustworthy. Not that Freeman would have trusted it anyway.

"I've never been shrunk except face-to-face," he said.

"You've never been treated by me before, either. That's obvious, since you still have problems."

"You're quite sure of yourself, aren't you?"

"Success breeds confidence, Mr. Mills. That's one of the things you'll learn in our sessions together, while we're on the road to healing."

"Therapy is a two-way street." Freeman wasn't going to let this bug watcher off easy.

"Just beware the exit ramps."

"Not only are you too chickenshit to meet your clients face-up, your extended metaphors are pretty lame."

The room grew silent as the microphone switched off. Freeman made funny faces in the mirror while waiting. The Clint Eastwood squint worked well in the regular population, but you had to give the shrinks a little something extra. Maybe go over the top like Pacino in *Scarface* or Keifer Sutherland in practically anything.

Soon the voice came again. "Are you ready to talk about it?"

It.

Freeman hated that word, at least when said by somebody who always capitalized *It*. And It only meant one thing in Freeman's sessions: the long scar on his wrist. Now, with depression sinking in and the shrink trying this new tack, Freeman almost told all about It.

About Dad and the blowtorch, or Dad and the ground glass, or Dad and the electricity, or Dad the evil fucking troll who fried Freeman's brain until it worked like a cell phone and anybody could beep their stupid messages into it anytime they wanted.

Yeah, goddammit, I got somebody to blame. Now that you mention it.

But before he could speak, as his lungs froze and his stomach clenched like a fist around the beige breakfast waffles, the voice was replaced by Bondurant's.

"We're waiting, Freeman."

"No, I don't want to talk about it." Bad enough for one brain drainer to pick at your skull, but when you were double-teamed—

"Freeman, this is Robert Brooks. I'm a friend."

Yet another voice. Another "friend." This was turning into a joke. Shrunken by committee. Did these clowns honestly think they were going to catch Freeman off-guard, grill him as if they were TV cops, keep hitting him with new lines of questioning until his spirit broke?

"How can you be a friend if I've never met you before?" Freeman asked.

"We're here to help," said Brooks.

A brief argument flared in the background as Brooks forgot to switch off the microphone. Bondurant was telling somebody that Freeman was a kleptomaniac who should have his fingers held over the flames of hell.

The first voice that questioned him said, "Freeman, I'm Dr. Kracowski. We've arranged a little demonstration for a couple of our supporters. All you have to do is relax."

Relax. Freeman took a breath that tasted of mint ice.

"What I'm going to do will only hurt for a moment, and then you're going to feel better," said the faceless Kracowski. "Your depression will fade and you'll feel elated and energetic."

"How did you know I was depressed?"

"Because I'm trained to observe, Freeman. Because I listen. Because I care."

"What's this business about it only hurting for a moment?"

If there was any answer, he didn't hear, because—*zzzzifff*—his ears clanged and orange light streaked behind his eyes. The bones of his head tumbled like gravel in a clothes dryer. Hot wires jabbed into his spine and his intestines tangled into knots. A scream came from somewhere. Blood was sweet in his mouth.

Freeman stared at his reflection, scarcely able to recognize the boy in the mirror: the pain had written ugly years on his face, peeled back his lips, caused his head to tremble and his jaws to clench. Worse, he found himself unable to read his own mind. He fought for breath and waited for the wave of agony to crest.

For the briefest of moments, his reflection had that same stretched grin that Dad had worn just before ordering Freeman to visit his mother in the bathroom.

Like father, like son.

Pacino in *The Devil's Advocate*.

Eastwood in *High Plains Drifter*.

De Niro in *Cape Fear*.

It was the kind of grin that killed.

FOURTEEN

Richard Kracowski tapped a couple of keys, even though all the functions were programmed into the computer and ran automatically. Moving his fingers and studying the screen gave a bit of flair to the presentation. To a scientist, the cause and effect were plenty enough to satisfy; with these board members and McDonald in attendance, though, Kracowski felt the need to resort to some showy sleight of hand.

In Thirteen, the subject was recovering from the thunderburst that Kracowski's fields had just shot into his skull and soul. The boy's tremors faded, and a smile crawled among the slack features of his face. Kracowski had longed to see how this particular specimen would react to the treatment. Even for someone who had pushed the limits in both directions, Kracowski knew that this boy represented a paradigmatic leap in his research.

"What did you just do?" Robert Brooks said. Brooks was moist, his thick glasses misted by the humidity of his own skin. He covered the smell of sweat with a cologne so intense that Kracowski almost wished the man smoked cigarettes instead.

But Brooks was a key player, one of the money men, a fat industrialist who made a fortune in hosiery production.

Brooks's factories had once been located in the Piedmont, but he'd moved the operation to Mexico to take even greater advantage of the labor pool. He'd left hundreds of Americans jobless, taken a large tax write-off for the abandoned property, and had increased his personal wealth fourfold. Yet Brooks fancied himself a humanitarian because he chipped in twenty thousand dollars a year to Wendover.

Kracowski despised such men, and McKaye was of the same stripe: well dressed, milky, and of the belief that money bestowed virtuosity. The doctor had an immediate distrust of anyone who used a first initial in his name. That's why he avoided the politics of fundraising and left the handshaking to Bondurant. Kracowski put on the show, Bondurant sold the tickets.

And McDonald? The man stood quietly apart, a faint smile the only crack on the stolid face. Physically, he was as blunt as a toad and his head sat on his shoulders as if pressed into clay. His dark eyes seemed to soak light from the room, and the colors of the computerized charts reflected off McDonald's forehead.

Kracowski let Brooks's question linger for a few moments more, tapping the keyboard as the printer spat its data and the zip drive backed up the programming. The computer drives were encased in a ceramic-and-lead-lined box, and a counter electrostatic field had been created to protect the drives from the erasing capabilities of stray magnetism.

"I still have to hone a few details, but soon you'll be reading about it in the *Journal of Psychology*," Kracowski said.

"It's been very successful in early clinical trials," Bondurant cut in. "We'll all be proud to have it associated with the good name of Wendover Home. And, of course, associated with you gentlemen as well."

The boy on the other side of the mirror gazed at them, unseeing.

Brooks tugged at his tie, his jowls straining against the tightness of his collar. "That didn't look entirely healthy to me. What do you call this business again?"

Kracowski swallowed a sigh. "Synaptic Synergy Therapy. The principles are very simple. The brain operates on a series of electrical impulses and relays. You're no doubt aware of electroconvulsive therapy, which was popular in the middle of the last century."

"Shock treatment, you mean? Like in that Jack Nicholson movie, *One Flew over the Cuckoo's Nest*?"

"Hollywood and the mental health field are both built on illusion, Mr. Brooks. Electroshock still has supporters, and its effectiveness in treating some cases of depression is well documented. Some patients report short-term memory loss and depersonalization. Of course, the treatment can be taken to extremes, as happened in the 'Deep Sleep' controversy in Australia, where patients in drug-induced comas were given multiple and frequent shocks over the course of several weeks."

"That was legal?" McKaye asked.

"An acceptable risk. On the bright side, of the sixty percent who survived Deep Sleep, nearly a third escaped without permanent brain damage."

"That doesn't sound like smart money," McKaye said.

"The true test of any experiment is the outcome." Kracowski leaned back from the computer monitor and let the others see the numbers and various formulae scrolling across the screen. He knew it meant nothing to them, yet it conferred power to him. The witch doctors of the twenty-first century needed fast processing speeds and obscenely large hard drives.

"I'm feeling very much better," said the boy in Thirteen.

"Praise the Lord," Bondurant said.

"It's really a basic procedure," Kracowski said, before Bondurant could finish turning science into a miracle.

The doctor tapped some keys, brought up a three-dimensional model of the boy's brain, and zoomed the image until various folds and crenulations could be seen. "The brain contains a hundred billion neurons. Each neuron communicates with ten thousand others through connections called synapses, which relay a series of electrical events that in turn create chemical changes in the brain. The number of possible combinations of neurotransmitter connections is greater than the number of atoms in the universe."

Kracowski paused in his lecture. The men's eyes had glazed over, except for McDonald's, which gleamed with an unhealthy hunger. "Simply put," Kracowski said, "the brain is a universe unto itself."

Beyond the mirror, the subject was studying the ceiling. Freeman wouldn't be able to see the giant electromagnetic field generators that hung above the tiles, nor could he know that the bed he was sitting on was wired to deliver small voltage doses. A PET scanner was built into the base of the cot, highly advanced equipment hidden by a dull sheet metal grid. In the basement, superconducting magnets were sealed inside tanks of liquid nitrogen, which were themselves sealed inside tanks of liquid helium.

Kracowski had spent years designing his treatment rooms, each with slightly different specifications. Thirteen was the best of them, but Eighteen wasn't bad. Still, until McDonald and the Trust had moved in with some serious support and technology, as well as the exorbitantly expensive liquid forms of the gases, SST had been little more than a theory. Now it was the tool that would take quantum mechanics into the human mind. Quantum psychology.

"Didn't Dr. Kenneth Mills have a similar theory?" McDonald said. The others seemed to notice McDonald for the first time, with Bondurant wearing an expression of dislike. McDonald winked at Kracowski, knowing he'd lobbed him a softball over the heart of the plate.

"Mills had some primitive notions along these

lines," Kracowski said. "But his research was too incomprehensible and random."

"As far as you know," McDonald said. "Professional jealousy, perhaps?"

Kracowski spoke to Brooks and McKaye. "SST sends electric currents to the brain, while at the same time realigning the impaired electromagnetic fields, or EMF, that govern emotion," Kracowski told the group. "Recent research has shown that magnetism can increase blood flow. This treatment sends a carefully controlled set of wavelengths into the patient's brain, all operating at nonionizing radiation levels. You may have read about the alleged link between electromagnetic fields and alien visitation?"

McKaye started to protest, but Kracowski held up a hand. "No, I don't believe in aliens, Mr. McKaye. But true believers say that's why people can't remember being kidnapped and taken away, because of the intense EMF. And there are suggested links between EMF and cancer caused by exposure to cell phones or from living near high-voltage power lines. The research has been limited so far, and mostly designed to absolve the communications and utilities industries. There's so much we don't understand, but my work is showing the positive potential of appropriately harnessing the fields. If the brain is a universe, all I'm doing is putting the planetary orbits in order."

Bondurant nodded and said to McKaye, "From a religious perspective, he's restoring these children's faith in themselves, so that they might be worthy of the Lord. It's just another of His mysterious ways. Isn't that right, Doctor?"

"It's all harmony." Kracowski grimaced and looked at his computer. The boy's magnetic resonance scan was flickering, a disco lamp of green, red, and magenta.

Brooks pointed to the screen. "What in the devil is that?"

The boy's cerebral cortex was displaying an anomalous

reading. Kracowski checked the EEG. The graph twitched upward in a rapid-cycling peak, as if the circuits of the boy's brain had fused together and his synapses were overloading. The boy was having a seizure.

"That's impossible," Kracowski said.

In Thirteen, Freeman trembled, his teeth clenched, and his eyes rolled up inside his skull. His head flopped, knocking against the thin mattress so hard that Kracowski could hear it through the microphone.

"What's going on?" Brooks shouted.

"Better call an ambulance," McKaye said. McDonald said nothing, folded his arms, and watched the boy.

Kracowski met Bondurant's look of panic with a concerned but calm smile. "That won't be necessary, gentlemen. It's only part of the procedure. This boy's fields must be in particular disharmony to cause such distress."

"Is he breathing?" Brooks asked, straining to peer through the glass.

The boy twitched and writhed. Kracowski was relieved to note that the boy's tongue protruded between his lips, so at least he wasn't suffocating himself. The doctor clicked up another screen and checked the data. The treatment should be winding down now, a current in millivolts running through the boy's skin and bones. The electromagnetic pulses were running in a programmed and syncopated sequence, massaging the boy's emotional trouble spots.

"What's his diagnosis?" Kracowski asked Bondurant, even though he was familiar with the case file. He simply wanted Bondurant to run down the laundry list in order to make the resultant healing even more impressive.

"Rapid-cycle manic depression," Bondurant said. "Suicidal tendencies, kleptomania, antisocial behavior, cyclothymia, possible mild schizophrenia. Plus, he's an unrepentant little sinner."

"See, gentlemen? This boy is very troubled. The deeper the disease, the harsher the cure must be."

Brooks and McKaye stared at the epileptic boy. Brooks said under his breath, "If he dies—"

"I never let them die," Kracowski said, managing to convince even himself.

Soon Freeman Mills would be properly aligned, if he lived long enough. McDonald would have his weapon and Kracowski would have his glory. Kracowski would succeed where Dr. Kenneth Mills and all his predecessors had failed.

"Doctor," McDonald said. "I think these gentlemen have seen enough. Why don't you revive the boy?"

Bondurant's glasses had fogged from the heat of the laboratory.

"Let it finish," Kracowski said. He looked through the two-way mirror. Freeman thrashed beneath the restraints, his muscles twitching. There must have been some trick of reflection, because for the briefest of moments, Kracowski saw the boy standing at the glass, pressing his palms outward, his mouth open in a voiceless scream. Kracowski blinked and the illusion passed.

The boy was passive now, his jerks subsiding. Kracowski looked at the separate monitors, checked the EEG and the MRI scans. The boy's heart was working steadily, blood flow to the brain normal, pulse up a bit but stable. He was alive.

He was more than alive. He was cured.

And, if Kracowski had arrayed the wavelength sequences correctly, the boy would score unusually high on the ESP card test. But no need for Brooks, McKaye, or Bondurant to know about that particular side effect.

"Mr. Brooks, Mr. McKaye," Kracowski said to the pale men. "You have witnessed a miracle of science."

"Amen," whispered Bondurant.

"Did you see that?" McKaye said to Brooks.

"What?"

"The boy, standing at the mirror."

"He was on the cot."

"A trick of the light, Mr. McKaye," Kracowski said.

Brooks pointed to the EEG reading. "That's normal, then?"

"The boy experienced some spikes. Epilepsy is a kind of short in the electrical wiring of the brain. We don't know what causes it, but I can assure you, everything is functioning properly now. The treatment has his synapses working better than they ever have."

"Is that trouble likely to happen again?" Brooks wiped his face with a handkerchief.

"Never," said the doctor.

"You're very sure of yourself, aren't you, Kracowski?" McKaye said.

"I have to be. These young children are entrusting me with their brains."

Kracowski watched the computer absorb and store the data. The energy field was winding down. The lights in the lab grew brighter. The treatment was over.

Kracowski pushed the mic button. "How are you feeling, Freeman?"

The boy lifted his head. He motioned with his finger as if wanting them to move closer, though he could only see his own reflection.

"What?" Kracowski said.

"You sure he's okay?" Brooks said. "He looks like he's going to throw up."

"He's fine," Bondurant said.

"Doctor," Freeman said, staring at the mirror.

"You're cured, son," Kracowski said. "Healed."

"I'm very glad to hear that, sir."

"Your brain and soul are in harmony."

"You are a very good doctor."

"Is there any pain?"

"Pain?"

"While you were under, you had an episode."

"Is that what you call it when you die a little?"

Kracowski released the mic button.

"He's not supposed to know that, is he?" Bondurant said.

"He doesn't know anything. He's only a patient."

Freeman spoke, but his words didn't carry through the thick glass. Kracowski pushed the button.

"Neat little trick there, doctor. While I was dead, I saw a big ugly troll waiting under the bridge."

Kracowski flipped a switch, throwing Room Thirteen and Freeman into darkness. The green light of the computer screens and the colors of the magnetic resonance image of Freeman's brain intensified in the dimness.

"This exhibit is over, gentlemen," Kracowski said.

"I think we've seen more than we want to see," McKaye said. "We'd rather read about it in the journals."

Bondurant led Brooks and McKaye from the lab. Kracowski traced his finger over the multi-colored image of Freeman's brain.

"The mind is a universe," he said to the walls. "*My* universe."

"Don't get too full of yourself," McDonald said. "You think Freeman Mills ended up here by accident? You're not the only one who gets to play God."

FIFTEEN

Freeman sat under the trees by the lake. The air tasted gray. He felt like those Vietnamese POWs who played Russian roulette in *The Deer Hunter*. The ones who lost, whose numbers came up, whose brains splattered across the room. Not like De Niro, who could take it, or even Christopher Walken, who wasn't so tough but made it out alive anyway, at least for a while.

On the lawn near the main building, kids were playing games, running, shrieking. From this distance, he couldn't triptrap anybody. Up close, they had nearly overwhelmed him, swarming across the mental bridge like invading armies, their thoughts like bullets and their emotions like bamboo slivers.

If he stayed by himself, maybe he could sort things out. He remembered going into Thirteen, talking with some shrink through a two-way mirror, then some more shrinks, then everything going fuzzy. He had walked a strange land where shimmery people rose up from the dark floor and spilled out of the walls. People whose mouths opened in soundless screams. Scary people.

Then the lights were on in the room and he was staring at the ceiling, his muscles sore, and the shrink was talking to him through the microphone. Dr. Kracowski, the shrink said his name was. Actually, Freeman realized, the man hadn't *said* anything. Freeman had walked into his mind and picked out that little nugget of information.

Freeman mined other ores from the doctor's brain, obscure formulas and theorems, properties of electricity and wavelengths and other stuff that would have been dull in a classroom but became gold when discovered inside another person's head. And there were other bits, a woman named Paula Swenson, skin business that would have made him blush if he'd understood more of it. And something about Dr. Kenneth Mills. Dear old Dad.

But before Freeman could dig in and get a really serious read, Starlene Rogers had knocked on the door to Thirteen, Kracowski had run from the laboratory to get her away, and then Freeman was in *her* head: sunshine and roses and a mobile home in Laurel Valley, Bible verses and boys in pick-up trucks, a cat named T.S. Eliot, Randy the house parent who might have too much chest hair for her taste but was otherwise an okay guy, college psychology textbooks, peach lip gloss, Lucille the hairdresser who had a way with a curling iron, the coming Gospel Jubilee at Beaulahville Baptist, a strange old man in a gray robe.

The same old man Freeman had seen in the hall and again in the dish room. Except, inside Starlene's head, the man was wet and left footprints that stopped in the middle of the floor.

And then Kracowski was at the door, saying "Excuse me, Miss Rogers, this room is off limits to unauthorized staff," and someone released the straps and Freeman. sat up on the bed and then he was inside *Bondurant's* head, and Bondurant wasn't anywhere near the room. Bondurant's head was foggy, his thoughts not completing themselves before stumbling on to the next garbled batch. By that time, Starlene and the doctor were arguing and Freeman was wondering just how far and into how many minds at a time he could triptrap, and Paula and Randy showed up—

Something landed in his lap and pulled him back to the present, by the lakeside. He looked down and saw a shiny penny.

"For your thoughts," Vicky said.

"You couldn't afford them."

"Try me." She was pale in the sunlight, almost ethereal in her thinness. Her eyes were black storms in the calm of her face.

"Okay." Freeman looked across the water. Could he read the minds of fish?

"Of course you can't, silly. There's nothing there to read."

Freeman drew back as if she had drenched him with a bucket of the frigid lakewater.

"I mean, do you think they dream of worms or something? It's just 'swim, swim, swim.'" Vicky crossed her arms.

"You're not in here. Because I'm thinking that I want to see what you're thinking, but I can't."

"Because you think you're so freaking special. That you're the only one with problems, or with gifts."

"I wasn't thinking that."

"I wouldn't even have to read your mind to know that. It's written right across your face. 'Don't mess with big bad Freeman Mills, or there'll be hell to pay.' And this macho Clint Eastwood fixation is really pathetic."

"Why don't you dry up and blow away?" Freeman focused on the water until his tears made the surface appear to shimmer.

"Why don't you quit lying to yourself for a change?" Vicky turned and walked away, had reached the large rocks and was about to slip down the path between them when at last Freeman broke through her mental shield. At least a little.

"Keep moving, lard-ass," he shouted after her.

She froze, turned, and lowered her head.

"Your father called you 'lard-ass,' didn't he? When you were a little girl."

She knelt. Her shoulders trembled. Freeman wiped his own tears away, feeling guilty at the jab, yet pleased he'd been able to penetrate her shield. He thought if this were a movie, he would go to her now, hug her, show her he was strong and kind and understanding, like George Clooney in practically anything. Instead, he picked up the penny and held it to the sun.

"I'd almost forgotten that," Vicky said. "I think my first shrink got me to remember it, but the best things get buried deep. I guess you win."

One of the staff members passed by, Allen, the mousy guy, and waved at them from under the shade of the willow tree, letting them know they were safely under watch. No funny stuff. If Allen only knew.

"When did you quit eating?" Freeman asked. "Was it a gradual thing, or did you just wake up one morning and discover that oatmeal tasted like the sole of a tennis shoe?"

"I haven't quit eating. I still eat way too much."

"Yeah. You're, what, seventy pounds soaking wet?"

"Sixty-eight pounds and probably eleven-sixteenths of an ounce, if the two tablespoons of lunch have digested properly."

"A girl as tall as you ought to weigh at least ninety, maybe a hundred."

"If you believe the charts. But who cares about the charts? All I know is what I see in the mirror. A big fat buttery tub of lard."

"You're nothing but a sheet of skin stretched around a stack of bones."

"Bet you say that to all the girls."

"No, really. You're way too skinny."

"I'm a total lard-ass."

"Don't believe everything Daddy says. Daddies have been known to be wrong. Or psycho, in some cases."

Freeman stood, found a flat stone, and skimmed it across the water. It bounced six times before sinking. He walked over to Vicky and knelt beside her. He tried to concentrate, but he could smell her hair again.

"I'm sorry I was mean to you," he said. "I just get a little jumpy when it kicks in like this and I can read too many people at the same time—"

"Wendover causes it. Kracowski's little treatments. I used to read books with titles like *Mysteries of the Mind*, *Secrets of the Unknown*, parapsychology and ghosts, that kind of thing. I even practiced ESP every night, scrunching my face until I thought my eyeballs would pop. But I never got any good at it. Then I come here and, boom, I'm practically Miss Cleo overnight."

"Did Paula and Randy take you to the little room with the table and chairs?"

"And the deck of cards? Yeah."

"And Paula held up one at a time, showing the back of the card, and you had to guess what symbol was on it?"

"Yeah. A circle, a square, a plus sign, a five-pointed star, and a set of three wavy lines. Pretty corny. I mean, the Rhine Research Center was using that eighty years ago. Most parapsychologists use machines these days."

"Machines make it harder to cheat." Freeman flipped the penny and caught it, peeked, and held it flat inside his fist.

"Tails," Vicky said.

Freeman opened his palm. Tails.

"How many cards did you get right?" she asked.

"Twenty-two out of twenty-five."

"I got three."

"Three? You can do better than that by guessing."

"You think I want those nuts to know I can read minds? Are you crazy or something?"

"'Crazy' doesn't exist in the twenty-first century," Freeman said. "Only science and blame. This place is just a cover for whatever Kracowski is up to. Have you seen the Wendover fundraising brochures yet? 'Give from the

Heart to Society's Child.' We're the products of every-body's collective guilt."

"Then what are *you* acting so guilty about?"

Jesus Henry Christ, Freeman thought. *Don't let her get into that secret little spot in my head. The one where I've hidden you-know-what. The big troll.*

"I'm not guilty," Freeman said quickly, before his thoughts ran away to those shadowy cracks. "And I've done much better on the card reading. I used to get twenty-five out of twenty-five, back when I was six."

"Six? You could read minds when you were that young? Before Kracowski?"

"My Dad was into it."

"Whoa. When you said 'Dad,' I felt some bad vibes. What's up with that?"

"Nothing. You think too much for a girl."

"You haven't known many girls, have you?"

"Well, sort of."

"Don't bother lying to somebody who can see inside your skull, Freeman."

"Okay, okay. I've never kissed one, if that's what you want to know."

Vicky sighed with dramatic flair and shook her head. "I meant being empathetic with a girl. Caring about one. Having a friend."

"Don't need any damned friends." Beyond the lake, beneath the stone face of Wendover, the other children played. Freeman tried to learn the score of the soccer match in progress, but whatever juice had allowed him to jump his mind across the grass was now drained. Maybe he'd used it all up trying to sneak past Vicky's defenses.

"Sorry I called you a lard-ass," he said.

"That's okay. I'm sorry I jumped into your head with-out permission. Or, what do you call it, 'triptrap'?"

"My Dad's name for it. Did you have a treatment recently?"

"Yesterday. Those mirrors creep me out. And the humming, like a hive of metal bees in the walls."

"That's what causes it. The mind reading, I mean."

"Yeah," Vicky said. "I could read real good yesterday. Like in the lunchroom. I believe that if I had concentrated, I could have read every mind in the room. Or maybe not by concentrating, but its opposite. Shutting down, meditating, going blank."

"Letting the thoughts in." Freeman flipped the penny again, glanced at it. Heads. "Sometimes when you chase them, they get all mixed up with your own thoughts, and that's a good way to go crazy."

"Remember what I said about 'crazy.' "

"My power's going away already. I can feel it fading, sort of like a car radio going to static."

"It usually lasts a day or two for me. I've had four of Kracowksi's treatments. I don't know what he's up to, but I can feel the tingling."

Freeman rubbed his scalp at the memory of the seizure. "It's not too bad, though. Not like my Dad's experiments. But I'm not going to talk about *him*."

"Yeah, right. They say it only hurts for a little while. I've heard that all my life, and it hasn't stopped hurting yet."

"You ever heard of the Trust?"

"The Trust? No."

"Good."

"What's the Trust?"

"Never mind."

"I can't *never* mind. I have to *always* mind."

"Forget it."

"Listen, I know exactly what you're thinking," Vicky said. "I'm Jane Fonda and you're Robert De Niro in *Stanley & Iris,* and you expect me to take you on and teach you and open up a whole new world. Rescue you from yourself."

"No. I wasn't thinking that at all. That sounds like a dumb movie."

"I've seen worse, but not lately."

Freeman flipped the penny again, caught it, and held up his closed fist.

"Heads," Vicky said.

Freeman glanced at the coin, shielding it from her. Heads again. "No, tails," he said, putting the penny in his pocket.

The sun was sinking now, just touching the ridges in the west. Freeman looked across the lake, expecting one of the house parents to wave them inside. From here, they wouldn't be able to hear the bell that signaled dinner.

He saw somebody under the trees and thought at first it was Randy, the muscle jock. He tried for a quick trip-trap but the person was too far away, and the power really was on the blink. Then the figure came out into the muted light of sundown. It was the old man in the robe.

"You see him, too," Vicky said.

"The geezer in gray. I've seen him twice."

"What's he doing down there?

"Maybe he decided it was time for a bath."

Vicky stifled a laugh. "That's mean, Freeman. He might be the nicest person here, for all you know."

"I thought he worked at the home, like a janitor or something. Figured he must have been here so long they didn't give him a hard time about the way he dressed. Saved on uniform expenses."

The man moved closer to the water's edge, then paused and seemed to sniff the air. He looked toward Wendover on the rise of lawn above the lake, then at Vicky and Freeman. Freeman couldn't tell whether the man was smiling or grimacing as he approached the water, back stooped with the effort of descending the bank.

"The stupid old coot's going for a swim," Freeman said. He and Vicky stood so they could see better. "He'll freeze to death."

The old man put a foot into the water. Then he took

another step. He must have been standing on a rock, because he put another foot forward without sinking.

Four more of his shuffling steps, and still he kept on. He wasn't swimming, he wasn't bathing, he wasn't sinking. The old man was walking on water.

SIXTEEN

The kids were all accounted for, even Deke and his buddies. Starlene knew they liked to sneak off and smoke cigarettes in the laurels, but she didn't think cracking down on them would do any good, at least until she established rapport. She needed to earn their trust to be a good therapist. And at least it wasn't marijuana they were smoking. Probably.

Down by the lake, Vicky and Freeman were talking. That was a good sign for both of them, because Freeman had acted like a sassy loner and Vicky had been aloof ever since Starlene had taken the job at Wendover. The poor girl was a classic anorexic-bulimic, and maybe having a friend would help her self-esteem, which in turn might boost her appetite. She sighed. Sounded like a "Dr. Phil Get Real" platitude.

Starlene looked at her watch. Dinner was fifteen minutes away. House parents rotated shifts on a weekly basis, and her week off was coming up. After eating, she would make the long drive down to Laurel Valley, where her cat awaited in her cold mobile home. A good book and a prayer would get her to midnight, when sleep would probably come.

A restless sleep, as they all were these days. First it was

Randy who had intruded on her dreams, with his big arms and strong smile and his irritating overprotectiveness. Guys these days thought just because you kissed them meant you were obligated to roll back the sheets and let them wallow like hogs in the slop of your skin. Randy didn't understand the meaning of patience, especially that business about waiting for marriage. Chastity didn't seem to be a treasured virtue outside her Baptist church, and virginity was more a burden than a prized possession these days.

And Randy was so secretive, with his "Don't ask questions" attitude. She needed an ally on the inside. This job was tough enough without having to wing it alone. How could she have a lasting relationship with someone who believed in keeping things from her?

Now she had other worries to lose sleep over. This strange business with the disappearing man in the gown, for example. She hadn't hallucinated, no matter what Randy and Mr. Bondurant and Dr. Kracowski thought. She believed religious visions were confined to the Old Testament, not let loose in the modern waking world. Though, Lord knows, the truth often came cloaked in the weirdest of disguises.

And the boy, Freeman, who had left Room Thirteen dazed and trembling. He was another puzzle in this stone house of mysteries.

"The boy's doing fine now," came Dr. Kracowski's voice from behind her.

Kracowski stood under an oak tree with Dr. Swenson. Paula, the doctor liked to be called, especially by the men. She batted her eyelashes every time she introduced herself by her first name, and doubly enjoyed it after some man had peered at the nameplate on her breast a full five seconds too long. Starlene wasn't jealous, though she wondered what strategy the woman had employed to get through medical school.

Kracowski waited, looking at Starlene like a cat that

had swallowed cream. Pleased with his playmate or smug in his therapeutic genius?

"I don't know," Starlene said. "Freeman looked awful shaky when he left that treatment room."

"You don't trust me at all, do you?" Dr. Kracowski turned to Dr. Swenson. "She doesn't trust me."

"That's not really my place, sir," Starlene said. "My main responsibility is for the welfare of the kids."

"As is mine, Miss Rogers. We're all part of the Wendover team. Victory is measured by happy hearts and contented souls. One child at a time."

"What was that business with the electricity? I didn't think the home was authorized to administer electroconvulsive therapy. I'm pretty sure that neither Freeman nor his legal guardian authorized it."

"Wendover is Freeman's guardian now," Kracowski said.

"The treatment must have done his heart good," Dr. Swenson said, in her cheerleader voice. "He's well enough to be flirting with the Vomit Queen."

Starlene wanted to choke the woman for her use of the nickname, but Kracowski's grin stopped her cold.

"Now, Paula, just because the children can't hear us doesn't mean we can let down our guard," he said. "After all, if you name a puppy 'Butt-Ugly,' it will suffer from poor self-esteem and the resultant depression. Even though the puppy doesn't know the meaning of the words. It's all projection and perception, setting up expectations."

Starlene looked at her watch again. Three more minutes. She could put up with this insufferable pair that much longer, surely. This was nothing compared to the trials of Job or the rigors of a church bake sale.

"Tell me, Miss Rogers," Kracowski said, waving his hand to indicate the children playing and shouting on the grounds. "What do you see when you look at our young charges?"

"I see hearts in need of hope. And I think we ought to do more than just shock them senseless."

Swenson glowered. "Richard's treatments affect positive change at the subatomic level. He heals the whole person, from the inside out."

Kracowski laughed. "I don't need another advocate, dear. The results will speak for themselves once I collate my data and get my articles published."

"That's what it's all about with you, isn't it?" Starlene knew she was risking her job, but she'd had enough of Kracowski's subterfuge and pompousness. "As long as you get credit in the psychological community, you could care less about the kids."

"I care more than you can imagine, Miss Rogers. Those kids out there, the ones who receive Synaptic Synergy Therapy, they are *me*. Or, rather, the way I was when I was young. Lost, confused, unsure of my place in the world. I had so much anger inside."

"Did you plug yourself into a wall socket, or did you find somebody to talk to?"

"We're really not so different, Miss Rogers. I believe in optimism. That's a version of harmony, no matter if the harmony is induced by SST or through the attention of someone who pretends to care."

"I care," Starlene said. She watched Vicky and Freeman on the rocks by the lake. They seemed to be arguing about something. She hadn't seen Vicky so animated in weeks.

"I'm sure you do care," said Swenson. "You're brainwashed by the twin systems of religion and social sciences."

"Paula, don't rush to judgment," Kracowski said. "We all need faith."

"Faith," Starlene said. "I'll remember that tonight when I'm saying my prayers."

The sun was lower now, touching the cut of the

mountains, and shadows reached like fingers toward Wendover Home.

"I'll tell you what," Kracowski said. "Why don't you let me administer an SST treatment on you? If you're sound and healthy, it can do no harm. If you have any troubles, your emotional fields will be aligned to their proper state. And you'll see that I'm not some Victor Frankenstein running a chamber of horrors."

Starlene folded her arms. The evening was growing cold. Or maybe the chill originated from the challenge in Kracowski's voice.

"Sure," she said. "I'll be your guinea pig. You'd probably love to have a case involving an adult subject, anyway, to make your research more credible."

"Tomorrow morning, then?"

"I'm scheduled to rotate off duty tonight."

"I can have the schedule changed. Things will soon be very interesting around here. The state board is going to visit in a few days, and our directors are excited about what's happening here."

Down by the lake, Vicky and Freeman had stopped talking and were looking out across the water. Starlene followed their gazes, and that's when she saw the old man.

She was about to blurt out to Kracowski, to show him that the man with the wet footprints was *real*, that she wasn't prone to temporary insanity or hallucinations, but she saw the old man walking on water, four steps, five steps, and she was trying to deny the evidence of her own eyes when he disappeared.

Maybe she *did* need an SST treatment. Or maybe she just needed to have her brain fried to a crisp.

In recorded history, only one person had ever walked on water, and Jesus Christ was safely resurrected and borne aloft to Heaven. Unless Jesus had made his promised return right here in the Southern Appalachian Mountains, on the grounds of Wendover, then a different kind of spirit was on the loose.

SEVENTEEN

The conference room was quiet, the lights low. Francis Bondurant fidgeted with the glass in his hand. He longed for another drink, but he didn't dare let Dr. Kracowski learn of his vice. At least on duty and in public, he was a ginger ale man.

Across the polished table from him, Kracowski and Swenson sat side by side. This room was where the Board of Directors held its quarterly meetings, and was several doors down from where Bondurant had imagined seeing the old woman the previous night.

No, not imagined—she was REAL, she stared at me with that grinning forehead scar and—

Bondurant tossed down a couple of fingers of the ginger ale. He wiped his mouth with the sleeve of his suit, realized he was sweating, and loosened his tie. More oxygen to the brain never hurt, though surely his heart was thundering enough to send plenty of air to his skull.

"You're melting," Kracowski said. "What's going on?"

"It's like this, sir—"

Paula Swenson smiled at Bondurant's term of subjugation and moved closer to Kracowski. She had selected the alpha male and her eyes said she had nailed him until death or a hefty divorce settlement, whichever came first.

She cared not one bit for the children, for the Home, or for Wendover's good standing. She made her reputation on her back, not on her feet.

Bondurant clenched one fist beneath the table, imitating the grip of *The Cheek Turner,* picturing Swenson bent over his desk and squeaking, softly at first and then in real pain, as he brought the paddle down again and again and again—

"Now you're evaporating as well," Kracowski said.

Bondurant wiped the sweat from his eyebrows. "Too many things going on at once. Those two directors showing up on short notice, your experiments increasing in frequency, the staff changing over, and state inspectors coming by in a few days. This McDonald guy lurking around all the time. And these new supporters, I know they're a godsend, but it's hard to get a handle on them."

"Pressure is internal, not external," Kracowski said.

"That's a good one," Swenson said. "You'll have to write that down."

"I already have."

"It's just"—Bondurant paused to finish his glass—"the staff has become a little unsettled."

"Unsettled?"

"Well, it's about the . . . you know . . ."

"If I knew, your calling this meeting would have been unnecessary."

"Yes, sir."

"My time is quite valuable. Should you ever need a private consultant, you'll find that you couldn't afford me."

"Lucky for Wendover that you're willing to work for free," Swenson said, as if hardly happy about it.

"I'm not working, I'm playing. I'm playing the biggest game of all, isn't that right, Bondurant?"

"Game?" Bondurant's hands trembled.

"The God game. Healing little souls, that's what we do here, isn't it? Redeeming the sins of society. Fixing God's mistakes."

Bondurant wished he had a little something in his glass. He'd even risk some whiskey. The knot in his throat tightened. Nothing to do but say it plain. "It's about the ghosts."

Kracowski had been leaning back in his chair, casual, perhaps with a hand on Swenson's thigh under the table. Now he sat forward and stared as if trying to decide to what species Bondurant belonged. After a long pause, in which the room's air grew more dense, Kracowski smiled. "Ghosts."

Swenson giggled. "Spooky-boo. So that's what's been coming to me in the night? I thought it was *you*, Richard."

She squeezed the doctor's arm but he pushed her away. "Not now, Paula. The man's serious."

Bondurant wished that he, like the mad woman he'd seen, could disappear into the wall. Kracowski despised weakness, and belief in anything that couldn't be proven was a weakness. "We've had three staff members make reports. One even quit over it," Bondurant said.

"What did these reports consist of? The same old campfire story about the old man in the gown? I've heard that one myself. Ever since I was four. Do you know what an urban legend is, Bondurant?"

He nodded in response.

"Well, Wendover seems to have its very own urban legend, the one about the dreary little hunchback they call 'Look-Out Larry.' I'm quite sure the so-called 'ghost' predates the existence of Wendover Home, and local townsfolk will be more than happy to share the legends their grandparents whispered about this place. Every town has a ghost, and every old building has one."

"Wendover's only a dozen years old, but the building's been here for more than seventy years."

Swenson said, "Does that mean lots of people have died here?"

Kracowski laughed. "Nobody ever dies at Wendover. Do they, Bondurant?"

"Only for a little while," he said under his breath.

"What's that?"

"I said, 'Not like Enlo.'"

"Ah, the home where the little girl died from a restraint hold."

"*Alleged* restraint hold," Bondurant said. "That technique is approved by Social Services. The girl most likely had an undetected heart condition. But it should serve as a warning. Enlo was put on six months' probation."

"Too bad. You'd think a just God would let the girl's ghost return from the grave and dispense justice."

Swenson touched the doctor's shoulder. "You're funny, Richard. No wonder I like you."

Kracowski frowned at her. "Not in front of the staff. How many times do I have to tell you?"

Bondurant wondered if Kracowski really believed the staff didn't know about their little affair. But Kracowski wasn't common, he didn't deal in gossip, and, to him, casual conversation about personal matters was poison. He lacked humanity even though he professed to work in human services. Even though Wendover and its clients were sport to Kracowski, he took the game seriously.

"There's still the problem of the reports, whether you believe them or not," Bondurant said. "The staff members talk among themselves. Things get whispered."

"I'll take care of that." Kracowski's eyes grew even darker.

"Three people saw the man in the robe. I don't think all three are crazy."

"But maybe two of them?" Swenson said.

"By the descriptions, I think I know who the man might be."

"Ah," Kracowski said. "Here it comes. One of your long-lost prophets, no doubt. I hope it's Ezekiel, who saw the chariot of fire. Or Elijah and the burning bush. All the Old Testament's best lunatics were pyromaniacs."

Bondurant fingered the rim of the glass. He bowed his

head and prayed for strength. Confession was good for the soul, but the opening line was always a tough one. "You know that when the home was finished in the 1930s it became a state psychiatric hospital?"

Kracowski waved a hand. "Of course. Mary G. Mitchell Hospital. It was a training ground for some of North Carolina's finest doctors, and brought forth some solid clinical and theoretical research."

"Yes. But we all can agree that the treatments of the era weren't necessarily . . . humane."

"Science is built more on mistakes than on successes," Kracowski said. "And so, I might add, is religion."

"Maybe. But frontal lobotomy, coma therapy, forced sterilization, electroshock—"

"I don't perform electroshock."

"Certainly not."

"And then came the advent of the new class of drugs. The late 1940s and 1950s were a wondrous time for pills. It was more wonderful for the doctors than the patients. Instead of having to spend hours listening to troubled souls, you could scribble something on a notepad and send them off to the nearest pharmacy."

"Avoiding the real problem," Bondurant said.

"Neither of us approves of drugs," Kracowski said. "You, on religious grounds, and I oppose them because they distort the brain's harmonics."

"But then you get to fix them," Swenson said. "You can realign their energy fields."

"You're pretty smart for a doctor," Kracowski said to her, with an edge of sarcasm she didn't grasp. "But I'd rather the patient be healed in the first place and not have to submit to treatments. Harmony is the brain's natural state. We can blame civilization, socialization, and, yes, religion, for the pressures and stresses that have thrown the modern brain out of balance."

"I've read your theories, Doctor." Bondurant literally ached for that whiskey now. If only God would grant him eight ounces of ninety-proof bourbon. "But there are mysteries that science will never be able to solve. Like the ghost."

"You and your damned ghost. I still say it's nothing but wishful thinking mixed with the power of suggestion."

Bondurant's stomach tensed. This was going to be difficult. "I saw one myself."

The room grew so quiet that Bondurant could hear his heartbeat in his ears. Dr. Swenson stopped picking lint from her blouse.

Kracowski narrowed his eyes. "Your hunchback, I presume? Thanks to the power of suggestion?"

Bondurant shook his head, ashamed, scared. "No. This was a woman. Last night. I heard a noise in the hall and followed it. When I cornered her and asked her what she was doing, she turned and disappeared into the wall."

Bondurant wiped his eyes, hoping to erase the memory of her face. But that long scar grinned at him still.

"She had a scar across her forehead," Bondurant said, the words large in the hushed room. "A lobotomy scar. Done from the top, not up through her nose."

"And her clothes? I suppose she was dressed in hospital garments." Kracowski smiled and spoke as if he were narrating a B-grade horror movie. "Naturally, since she must have been the ghost of a patient who died here long ago. Evil lives in the walls, doesn't it, Bondurant? Evil, *evil, EVIL.*"

Swenson slapped at him. "Quit it, you're creeping me out."

Kracowski laughed. "I'm afraid our dear Francis has been working too many late nights."

To Bondurant, he said, "Reading the Bible in the wee hours? Or is it the whiskey that fulfills your spiritual needs these days?"

Kracowski had commented on his drinking, Bondurant's well-kept secret, of which neither the Lord nor Wendover's directors would approve. But he couldn't

answer in his defense because, through the small square
of glass set in the conference room door, the crazy old
woman was looking in, wearing her double grin. Kracowski, his back to the door, couldn't see. If indeed
there was anything to see.

"I don't want to hear any more foolishness about
ghosts," Kracowski said. "The breakthrough won't take
much longer, so keep your head until then. All that matters is that I continue my treatments. For the good of the
children."

"For the good of the children," Swenson said.

"For the good of the children," Bondurant echoed,
smiling weakly back at the woman at the window. But
she had already gone, into the wall or back through the
mists of time. Or maybe into the arms of the dead.

EIGHTEEN

Vicky slipped out of the shadows and crossed the hall. Sneaking out of the Green Room at night was too easy. She loved challenges, and Wendover hadn't provided many so far, at least when it came to security. Though the back doors were bolted and locked, some of the entrances had to be left accessible in the event of fire. No, they weren't entrances, because doors opened both ways. They were *exits*.

About once a week she sneaked outside, usually to lie in the grass and look at stars or count blue splotches on the moon. She had never been tempted to go over the wall and make a serious break for freedom; she could think of no destination that would allow her to escape her own grotesque body. She was so damned fat she should be easy to spot, like a Goodyear blimp in a circus tent.

The home had an overnight security guard, whose main duties were to quell fights among the boys or to make sure nobody was getting high on smuggled contraband. Watching out for runaways wasn't in the job description. He was probably watching TV in the rec room, eating greasy burritos and slamming Diet Coke, with a Snickers bar in his pocket for later, all sweet and gooey and peanutty, the kind that would make lumpy brown vomit and scratch your throat as it came back up. He had never caught her even though her footsteps were like an elephant stampede in the halls.

Vicky wondered what Freeman would think of her sneaking around. She reached out to read him, or "trip-trap" as he called it, but her mind was clouded. The effects of the last treatment had faded. She caught the dim hubbub of distant thoughts, but couldn't be sure where they came from, or if she was imagining them. Maybe it was all wishful thinking. Or the babble of angels. Or schizophrenia.

She went past Bondurant's offices. Light showed in the crack beneath the door. The old bastard was probably in there right now, fantasizing about paddling girls. Damned if she'd ever be bent over his desk. She'd feed him his glasses first, or die trying.

She heard voices inside the conference room and saw someone outside the door. She ducked back around the corner, then stooped low and waited. The old pipes in the walls thrummed as someone flushed a toilet on the second floor. Vicky leaned forward and peeked, but the hall was empty.

Bondurant, Dr. Kracowski, and the ditzy bimbo, Swenson, had been having a powwow. Vicky moved past the conference room, ducking under the window, her belly tight from being folded. From there, she had an easy jaunt to the front door. Though it was well lighted, the main entrance was the best place for an escape. The electronic key pad blinked red. They didn't expect anybody to dare sneak out that way, especially a four-hundred-pound water balloon with legs. She punched in the code, sixty-five star, then pushed open the door, and the sweet night air rushed over her.

Autumn had a taste, at least here in the Appalachian Mountains. Tonight it was dark orange, like pumpkin, invisible food that didn't make you stuffed to the eyeballs. The grass was moist with dew, and the lawn sparkled under the security lights. The mountains were unseen but they had a presence all the same, of a great weight looming on the horizon. She ran barefoot around the side of the building.

She was in the back of the home, passing by a row of shrubs, when she heard a noise in the shadows. A couple of times she had spooked a rabbit on her dark walks. But this sounded bigger than a rabbit. Lots bigger.

She turned as a chunk of shadow separated itself from the larger night. Just her luck. The guard, surprised while taking a leak in the laurels. Or knocking down a satisfying Snickers.

"Okay, you got me," she said. A shame, too. The night was glorious.

"Not yet, but soon enough." It wasn't the guard.

"Deke?"

"Yeah, Vomit Queen."

"What are you doing out here?"

"Fairy-hunting. Didn't find no fairies, though."

She looked around. The back entrance was locked for the night. The lake was too far, and though she might lose him in the pines, he would probably take her down as she ran across the open lawn. She could always yell and hope someone inside the building heard her. But all the windows to the rear were dark, and the walls were thick stone.

Deke came several steps closer and the moonlight caught his face. His eyes were pools of used motor oil. She didn't like the way he was smiling. She wondered if any of his buddies were crouched in the bushes, waiting for him to draw first blood before jumping the prey themselves. As fat as she was, there was plenty of meat to go around.

She edged away, trying not to look scared. Her nightgown was soaked around the hem. Deke stared at her as if he could see right through the flimsy cotton. *Creep, bastard, rotten scumbag.* Her hideous, bloated belly was nobody's business.

"Said I couldn't do it to you, huh?" Deke said. "That's

not what Slim Jim says. Want to meet Slim? He's been wanting so bad to say hello. And he ain't got no eda-whatever complex *this* time."

Deke tugged at his zipper as Vicky turned and fled blindly toward the back of the building. A row of old concrete steps ran beneath the back landing. She'd seen utility crews go down there during the summer, electricians and other guys with lots of tools in their belts. Last month, workers had unloaded a truck carrying something that looked like overgrown hot water heaters. She didn't know what was down there, but she didn't have a choice now.

Her bare feet slapped on the concrete. She hoped no junk or broken glass was laying around. It sounded like Deke was gaining ground. She didn't dare look behind her. Then she was beneath the landing, blind in a thick wedge of blackness.

"I thought you was supposed to be smart," Deke taunted from the steps. "A regular genius. All you done was make it easier for nobody to see us."

She held her hands in front of her, feeling in the darkness, and moved forward. The concrete vibrated faintly beneath her feet, and the hum of loud machines came from inside the basement. She brushed against some pipes, then the smooth metal of the service doors, and finally the door handle.

"Hey, honey, you ready for some Deke love?" Deke eased his way down the stairs, knowing she was cornered.

Vicky was glad she couldn't read his nasty mind right now. No way would these doors be unlocked . . .

But they were. One of the crews must have been working late and forgotten to lock up. Deke heard the rusty creak of the door swinging open. "You sneaking in there to throw up?"

She didn't answer, she was gliding into the darkness of the basement. She was at an advantage now, as long as

she was quiet. Assuming that the place wasn't a maze full
of dangerous junk, she could slip inside a few dozen feet,
wait for Deke to pass, then sneak outside behind him.
She ducked into a corner and closed her eyes, concentrating on her aural sense. She hoped her stomach didn't
start growling.

Deke tripped over something near the door. "Damn."
Then, in a menacing whisper: "Vomit Queen. Here,
Queenie, Queenie, Queenie. I got something for you.
Snap into a Slim Jim."

She marked his progress into the basement by his
clumsy clattering. The smell of alcohol hung in the stale,
moist air. The goon must have raided Bondurant's stash,
or else was stealing fruit from the cafeteria to make dormitory hooch. He was taking liberties with his already
limited supply of brain cells. Not that brain death would
be much of a leap for him.

"Vomit Queen," he yelled again, this time not disguis-
ing his anger. "Where's them big words *now*?"

Vicky opened her eyes. They had adjusted to the darkness, and she could make out a weird blue glow deeper in
the basement. Deke was at least twenty feet away now,
shuffling toward the glow. As long as her lard-assed
breathing didn't give her away, Deke would cruise right
past. Vicky was about to tiptoe for the exit when a noise
froze her.

It was a humming sound, low and throbbing, like she
imagined a fetus might hear in the womb. Mother's liquid heartbeat. The floor vibrated beneath her feet and the
glow became a lesser blue. Deke grunted something as
glass broke.

The hum grew stronger and fell into a familiar rhythm.
Vicky grew faint and leaned against the wall for support.
She recognized the sound. Not a sound, exactly. More like
a pulse. Like when Kracowski had given her the treatments.

The bluish glow throbbed in time with the rise and fall
of the hum. It reminded Vicky of playing near electrical

generating substations, the ones people claimed caused brain cancer. Only here in the basement of Wendover, the sound was not the dull whine of electric lines. This was something *alive*.

"Far fucking out," Deke said. "Hey, Vomit Queen, you see this?"

Deke had moved farther inside the basement. Vicky couldn't see his outline against the glow. She could escape now, but his voice sounded as if he had discovered buried treasure or else a body. Or maybe a refrigerator full of food, or some little kids to beat up. Vicky took one look at the dark doorway behind her, cursed her curiosity, and crept forward to see what had so amazed Deke.

As long as she kept between Deke and the door, she would be okay. And maybe she would learn something about the basement that would help her go AWOL during the night. A side door, a hidden set of stairs, information she could tuck away for future reference. Or maybe she'd discover some killer celebrity weight-loss secrets.

She followed Deke, and the glow became bright enough that she could see the shiny cables and lines running overhead. The basement broke into several corridors, and Deke headed toward the middle of the building. Vicky followed, figuring they must be beneath Room Thirteen and Dr. Kracowski's lab.

"Hey, you," Deke shouted. Vicky thought he was calling her at first, but then a shadow separated itself from the larger darkness. Vicky couldn't tell if it was a woman or a man. In fact, it seemed sexless, a shape that was only faintly suggestive of a human. It slipped down the main corridor, away from the light.

Deke followed it. "Come back here, Queenie."

Vicky knelt behind a row of tall cylindrical tanks. She pressed her hand against one. It was frigid to the touch. Above her, wires crisscrossed in a pattern that seemed an elaborate design, a technological spiderweb.

Deke's voice came from deep within the corridor,

followed by his muffled echo. "Hey, you can't hide from me, barf-brains."

Vicky crept to the mouth of the corridor. Though the glow from the open room carried only a few dozen feet down the corridor, Vicky could make out rows of metal doors lining each wall. Keeping low in case Deke happened to look back, she moved to the first door on her right.

The door had a little window set at head level. The window was glass with wire reinforcement. Behind the glass was a metal grid, as if to protect the glass from being broken from the inside. Like a meat locker where the cows were still alive and plenty pissed off.

She raised on her tiptoes and peered in. A pale face stared back at her through the window. Then she realized it was her own reflection, doubled by the two panes of glass. God, were her cheeks really that chubby? She exhaled slowly, then took a long breath of the stale basement air.

Silly fatso. Bad enough to be chased by a pervert and to sneak around in the dark, but you have to go and start seeing ghosts again.

"Come get some Deke love," Deke yelled from the darkness far down the corridor. If he were any louder, the counselors might hear him through the floor. Vicky didn't want to be caught because of Deke's stupidity. If the other kids found out she and Deke were together in the basement, they'd be making crude remarks until the end of time. She should get out, but first she wanted to see the room.

She pulled open the door. The room resembled a cell, small and square and windowless. Enough of the blue glow leaked in that she could make out the walls. They had an odd texture, though they were blotched with mold and stains. She went inside, listening for Deke, and put her hand on the nearest wall. It was soft.

Quilted with padded canvas.

A rubber room.

She backed out, ice water rushing through her veins.

Down the corridor were more of the rooms. How many people had been penned up down here, their shouts soaking into the walls, their prayers bouncing off the metal bars, their dreams swallowed by the cold stones that enclosed Wendover's foundation?

How many?

Deke screamed in the far darkness, and Vicky staggered toward the glowing generators and the metal cylinders, then past them to the door and outside. She swallowed a mouthful of the night air and had never been so grateful to see the stars. When her heart slowed enough for her to breathe, she crept up the stairs and traced her steps back to the Green Room, Deke's scream resounding in her ears.

NINETEEN

"You don't believe me," Freeman said, fidgeting in his chair, annoyed as always when some shrink wanted to do a vampire number on his soul.

Starlene Rogers sat across from him wearing a UNC Tar Heel sweatshirt and dark slacks, legs folded under her as if she had settled in for a long yoga session. "I believe you, unless you're lying."

She'd brought him to Four, one of the little rooms, the one-on-one places that were all the same once you cut to the chase: a place for you to squirm and lie and try to forget while some know-it-all hammered your feelings out of you.

But Freeman was Eastwood—tough, his skin was leather, his attitude was by-God bulletproof. Method acting at its finest. Who cared if Miss Starlene tried her little touchy-feely tricks? Freeman could wait it out. He'd shrunk a dozen shrinks, outlasted some real pros in the past, and he'd survived some real sons-of-bitches. Dad, for instance, the ultimate troll under the bridge.

The secret was in knowing how to tuck it away, tiptoe from thought to thought, to dream only in the safety of night. Or to just come right out and blow their little minds.

"I'm not lying," he said. "I can hear inside people's

heads. I know what they're thinking, at least sometimes. And I've learned that most people are pretty damned dumb. All they think about are TV shows and money and getting other people to do things for them."

"Freeman, you're aware of your manic and depressive cycle. Mania can cause people to believe they have superhuman powers."

"It's real. It's one of those things you just *know.*"

Starlene leaned forward, one of those trained gestures that meant she was pretending to care. Next she would probably touch his knee. "But there's no definitive scientific proof of extrasensory perception."

"Doesn't Kracowski let you in on his little card games? Maybe you ought to ask your friend Randy about it."

"What's Randy got to do with it?"

"He ever mention the Trust to you?"

"The Trust?"

"Never mind. You're better off not knowing."

"I can't help you unless you open up to me," she said. "That's the only trust I know about."

"See, I knew you were going to say that. You're just like all the others. You can't see that I'm different. I don't deserve to be locked away here with a bunch of losers."

"Do you think Vicky is a loser?"

Freeman watched the way Starlene's eyes fixed on her notes, like she was afraid to look at him. They were all afraid, when he was like this. They should be afraid. Because he would triptrap into their sad little minds and play games. He would see right through them, scramble their memories, make them pay, he would—

"Freeman. Please sit down."

Freeman blinked. He was near the door. He didn't even remember standing up. He walked back to his chair.

"Is Vicky a loser?" Starlene wrote something on her pad.

"She's okay."

"For a girl, you mean?"

"Now, don't *you* start in on that, too. I get enough of it from her."

"I saw you and her by the lake yesterday."

"We were just talking."

"Talking."

"Yeah." He debated launching into a patented Pacino rant, a cinematic soliloquy that enumerated the miserable, pathetic failings of God and the universe. "We were talking about reading each other's minds. And I know what you're going to say, you're wondering why we needed to speak if we could read minds."

"No, I wasn't going to say that."

"What were you going to say, then?"

Starlene tucked her pen and paper into the macramé purse beside her chair. She sat back, folded her arms, and closed her eyes. "Tell me."

Freeman's arms itched. He should have taken his medicine. It took the edge off when the ups came, when his thoughts were bright icy spears and the world was sharp and he could climb a mountain if they would only let him use his legs. But the medicine also chewed into his brain, flattened out all those fears. He needed his fears. They kept him alive. They kept the troll under the shadows of the bridge, where it couldn't grab him and eat him.

And he would survive. One day he would leave this place and be free. He would outsmart them all. Even God. But for now, he needed to blow this shrink's mind. That was a good start.

He closed his eyes. He tried to recall the feeling he'd had in Thirteen, when Kracowski's machines kicked in and shot his brain on a roller coaster ride. He even forced his legs to tremble a little. But Starlene was a stone wall. If she had any thoughts besides concern for Freeman's well-being, she had them buried deep.

"Tell me what I'm thinking, Freeman," she said, in that patient voice of hers.

Sweat arose along the back of his neck. He couldn't

fail, not after he'd bragged so much. Even if she had him blocked this time, he still had that stuff he'd picked up in Thirteen after his treatment.

"You have a cat named T.S. Eliot."

Starlene's eyebrows lifted. "How did you find that out?"

"Triptrapping, just like I told you." He was on again, riding the up, on a supersonic elevator to the top of the whole freaking world. No dumb shrink was going to put anything over on him. He just wished he knew who in the hell T.S. Eliot was. The name sounded familiar. A character actor, maybe?

Someone knocked on the door. Freeman moved to rise and answer, but Starlene held up her hand. "Who's there?" she asked him, whispering.

Freeman closed his eyes and triptrapped over the bridge, opened up the big sky inside, and the screams hit him like a hundred of Daddy's fists.

He gasped and fell to the floor, and still the screams ripped through him, tore his hair out by the roots, yanked his fingernails, shattered his rib cage, knocked his lungs from his chest, and ate his tongue.

They're underneath.

And then he was down with them, in the dark rooms where their shadows walked.

Something tugged at him, and Starlene's voice came as if from across a canyon. "Freeman? Are you okay?"

He was definitely not okay, because triptrapping had never been like this, it had always been one or maybe a few at a time, but now he was in a dozen, maybe a hundred, different heads. And these weren't ordinary heads.

God is a telephone and the Bible is written in shit on the walls; hats are part of a government conspiracy; how can you count to twelve if you can't say odd numbers; I am a tree I am a tree I am a tree and I leave.

You can only tell the doctors from the patients because the doctors get to go home at the end of the day.

If you kill yourself, pills taste better.

Pretty, pretty paper and a white, white room in which to write.

And more, lots more; words and thoughts and things that weren't thoughts but pieces of broken emotion stitched together, and through it all the wails grew louder, the voices combining now into a single scream and Freeman's head was going to explode and he rose away, trip-trapped backward, but it was like climbing the slick walls of a dark well, and the water below was the voice, the voice grew louder and the scream sluiced through him like liquid lightning and Starlene shook him and his bones rattled against the floor and he opened his eyes and oh sweet merciful God he was in the little room again, the floor was solid against his cheek, his tears tasted so sweet, this was reality, he didn't ever want to leave his own head again and someone knocked at the door—

"Freeman? What's wrong?" Starlene asked, kneeling over him and holding his shoulders.

He pushed his tongue against his teeth to make sure it was still there. "They're underneath."

She bent low, her breath on his face. "Your pulse is going wild."

"They said, 'Welcome to the party.'"

"Who said it?"

The knock came again. Beyond the door, Bondurant shouted, "What's going on in there? Miss Rogers, did you get clearance for this?"

Freeman pushed himself up. He didn't want to be on the floor, not with *them* underneath it.

As the echo of the last scream died away against the curves of his skull, a lone female voice stood out, calm and crystal clear, saying a single word: "Free."

TWENTY

"We need to go to the lake," Freeman said, and Vicky instantly understood this was a new code, a secret language between them.

She couldn't read him quite as well as she had tricked him into believing the day before, but she needed to cut through some of his crap, skip that middle ground, and get to the heart of it all. This situation was bad, and for the first time in her life, she didn't think she could survive it alone.

"Just don't try to hold my hand or anything," she said, as they turned down the worn path that led between the boulders.

"I'll leave that for Deke."

"Don't be a jerk. Did somebody pee in your corn flakes or something? You've been weird today, even for you."

Freeman slowed when they were out of sight of the counselors, then pulled Vicky into a rhododendron thicket. "I saw them," he said.

"Them?" Vicky felt the blood drain from her face.

"The people underneath."

"The same them."

"You've seen them?"

"Last night, I . . ." Would Freeman believe her? She didn't know if she could stand keeping it in anymore. He wasn't triptrapping through her head, either; at least she couldn't feel that strange tickle, so he wouldn't know for sure that she was telling the truth.

"Tell me," he said. "I won't laugh at you."

Sure. She'd never been laughed at. Vomit Queen was a term of endearment, after all. Daddy had never, ever criticized her. Mommy had never locked herself in her room with a bag of Oreos. And Vicky liked what she saw in the mirror. Sure.

Big deal if Freeman laughed. He was just another guy who thought just because he was finally growing his first pubic hair he was a real man, and it was common knowledge that all men were jerks. So even if Freeman were a jerk-in-training, she could bounce that laughter away like an overweight Wonder Woman blocking bullets with her golden bracelets.

"I saw a ghost," she said, before she had time to change her mind for the third time about trusting him.

"Did you . . . you know, read it, or whatever?"

"No. I saw one with my eyes. I sneaked out last night—"

"Outside? You mean you know a way *out* of there?" Freeman pointed behind the boulders in the direction of Wendover.

"Yeah, but that's not important right now. Anyway, Deke chased me into the basement—"

"You were out with *Deke*?"

Had jealousy flickered across his face? "If you keep interrupting, we'll never get anywhere. Deke chased me into the basement, then I hid in the dark. There's all kinds of weird equipment, electrical generators and tanks and stuff. I think it has something to do with Kracowski's experiments. There's a bunch of rooms down there, too, like hospital rooms or jail cells. Deke went down one of the halls, and I followed him."

"Behold the power of love."

"Stuff it. We saw somebody, and I thought it was the geeky night watchman down there with a girlie magazine and a candy bar. But the person was shiny, and elusive as heck. I couldn't get a good look, but Deke followed him or her into one of the rooms. He started whimpering—"

"Deke, afraid of the dark? Wait until his goons find out."

"He screamed, and I got scared and left. But now I know what I saw. A ghost."

"It wasn't the man on the lake?"

She could smell the water, though it was hidden by the rocks. She wondered if the old man was out there now, doing his miraculous two-step. "No, I think this was a woman. If dead people have sex."

"Gross."

"I meant, are dead people either male or female? It's not like they need to reproduce or anything."

"I guess they stay whatever they were. The old man looks like a man, doesn't he? At least, as much of him as we can see."

"I don't know what happened to Deke, but I haven't seen him today."

"He wasn't in the Blue Room this morning."

"Well, none of the counselors are freaked out about it. They'd be running around like headless chickens if somebody ran away."

"They *are* headless chickens. How do you think they became shrinks?"

Vicky laughed despite herself. Freeman was a weird one, all right. Maybe even weird enough to trust some more.

Freeman grabbed her arm, squeezed her fat flesh. "Shhh."

Someone was coming down the trail. No, *two* someones.

Vicky pressed back into the thicket, but the branches weren't dense enough to completely hide them. "Do we run for it?" she whispered.

"Why? We haven't done anything wrong."

Dr. Kracowski passed by, with Dr. Swenson right behind him. Vicky put her hand over Freeman's mouth. His manic belligerence might drive him to yell some insult. She wanted to see where they were going, because they walked like conspirators, alert and quiet. If you wanted to spy on sneaky people, you had to be sneaky yourself.

When the pair disappeared around the bend in the path, Vicky said, "Let's follow them."

"You're really into following people, aren't you?"

"So I'm a stalker. Don't you have any curiosity?"

"Enough to kill the cat, but I suspect he died from rat poison. Which is why you shouldn't snoop around too much."

"Hah. This from the guy who brags about triptrapping through other people's heads. You don't mind your own business, so why should I?"

"Okay, okay. Let's go."

They pushed their way out of the thicket, Vicky's arms scratched by the branches. They climbed over the boulders and slipped through a dark notch in the granite. The two doctors had stopped at the water's edge, in a stand of young maples. It was the only part of the lake shore not visible from Wendover.

Vicky and Freeman hid in the shadows of the boulders and waited. The doctors talked quietly for a moment. Vicky's face itched, and she fought an urge to sneeze. Freeman squeezed her hand. How could he stand to touch such grotesque flab?

A man came down the path from the opposite direction. He was dressed in cotton slacks and a white shirt with the top two buttons undone. He was broad chested, tan, short, and he wore sunglasses. The man was obviously trying too hard to disguise himself as a mountain tourist.

"Doctors," the man said in greeting.

"Hello, McDonald," Kracowski said, making no move to shake the man's hand. Swenson stood silent beside him.

"What happened last night? We captured the boy prowling around in the basement."

Freeman squeezed Vicky's hand more tightly. The visitor, apparently satisfied that no one was watching, removed his sunglasses. His eyes were cold as marbles.

"That was an unfortunate mishap," Kracowski said. "The security man has been properly scolded. Did the boy see anything?"

"Enough. We've got him in brainwashing right now."

"Please," said Kracowski. "I don't like that word."

"Right, Doc. What do you call it? 'Synaptic realignment'? Your technique may be new, but ours has a pretty decent track record."

"Not so decent that your bosses aren't interested in my work."

"We all work for the same boss. Don't forget who funded your equipment. You think liquid nitrogen and advanced superconductors are cheap? Not to mention the extra security measures we're going to have to take now?"

"You rented me, you didn't buy me." Kracowski knelt by the lake and stared across the water. "What do we do now?"

"Nothing," McDonald said. "You continue just as before. We're bringing in some of our own people. Bondurant can't handle this."

Kracowski said, "You promised no meddling."

"We have a large investment to protect and we expect results."

"I'll share everything when the time comes. This is an incredible breakthrough. I'm not sure your people understand the implications of my work."

"Turning out happy campers." The man laughed, Kracowski's jaw clenched. "This isn't the CIA and the KGB racing to see who can bend the most spoons with telepathy. This is bigger than governments. You work for the Trust, and don't you ever forget it."

"There might be more," Kracowski said. "There could be side effects that I didn't consider."

Swenson finally spoke. "Don't worry about the children. None of them have shown any long-term damage. Nothing that can be traced back to the treatments, anyway."

"I'm not talking about that." Kracowski stared off across the lake. "I'm talking about the old man in the gown."

Vicky swallowed a gasp, her heart pounded against her ribs. Freeman's face grew pale and he bit his lip. So Kracowski knew about the ghost. Their minds hadn't been playing tricks on them.

"You don't believe those stories, do you?" Swenson said. "Bondurant's a drunken fool."

"Starlene Rogers isn't. And others have talked as well."

"You'd better keep your staff in line, or we'll have to take over completely," McDonald said. "You're not the only person who's worked on ESP techniques."

"Don't threaten me," Kracowski replied.

"Don't worry," the man said. "Wouldn't want anybody messing in your little sandbox, would we? Just make sure the Mills boy doesn't notice his puppet strings."

Kracowski reddened and stepped toward the man. Vicky thought Kracowski was going to throw a punch, but Swenson tugged his shoulder and pulled him away.

"Forget it, Richard," she said.

"Fucking spook," Kracowski muttered.

"You shouldn't hate me," the man said. "I'm the best thing that ever happened to you. You have a laboratory with the most advanced equipment that secret slush funds can buy and you've got an endless supply of guinea pigs. You've died and gone to mad scientist heaven."

"Actually, whenever you show up, this place feels a lot more like its opposite."

McDonald laughed. "I never thought Dr. Richard Kracowski would come off as 'holier than thou.' Save your bullshit for the kids. I've got a job to do, and it's getting done, one way or another."

The man's chilling smile dropped and his eyebrows arched, and suddenly he looked as if he could chew bricks. "I know you're full of yourself, but you're just a little piece of a big picture. Daddy can cut off the sugar just like that."

The man snapped his fingers for emphasis, and this time Vicky was sure that Kracowski would jump him. But he only turned away and looked across the lake again. McDonald glanced around one last time, and Vicky pulled Freeman deeper into the bushes. The man exchanged glances with Swenson, then went down the path and disappeared, headed toward the back fence.

Swenson went to Kracowski and put her arms around him. "They're just a means to an end," Swenson said. "We know it's about the search for truth. We're using them more than they're using us."

"They don't understand the implications," Kracowski said. "This is bigger than governments and politics and little boys with big toys. It's about the wall between life and death; between this world and the world beyond. It's about breaking down the ultimate barriers of the mind."

"But we need more evidence."

"I don't want the Trust to know too much. I've been careful to keep different parts of the research in different places. It would take McDonald's best hackers years to track down everything."

"You don't trust anyone, do you, Richard?" She hugged him more tightly.

"Trust. The one quality that Synaptic Synergy Therapy can't impart."

"What do we do now?"

"More research. More work. More patients."

"Do you really think you're close to the answer?"

Kracowski nodded at the surface of the lake. "Ask *him*."

He headed back toward Wendover. After a moment, Swenson followed.

When they were gone, Vicky relaxed her stomach muscles. "What's going on?" she whispered.

Freeman shook his head. "Clint in *Absolute Power*. Double cover-ups."

Behind them, a twig snapped.

TWENTY-ONE

"You guys shouldn't be down here," Starlene said.

"It's okay, we've got our clothes on," Vicky said. Freeman swiped the air in front of Vicky as if feigning a slap.

Starlene wanted to ask them about Kracowski and Swenson, whom she'd passed on the trail, but she didn't think spying and gossiping, and probably mind reading, were proper Christian behaviors. Instead, she said, "You guys come looking for the old man?"

"You mean the one you don't believe in?" Freeman said.

"I didn't say that. And I didn't say your experience yesterday wasn't real."

"You just think I *thought* it happened, like a dream or something."

"We all make our own realities."

"Especially the people in the basement."

Starlene looked to Vicky for help. The girl lowered her eyes. She was allied with Freeman.

"There's no one in the basement, Freeman," Starlene said.

Vicky grew animated, her knotty elbows and hands moving as she spoke. "How do you know? You ever been down there?"

Starlene shook her head. "No, but the door's kept locked. Same with the stairwell entrances."

"You wouldn't believe all the stuff down there. Lots of high-tech equipment, tanks and tubes and generators and wiring. And some creepy old cells."

"What are you talking about?"

"Come on, I'll show you." She scrambled out of the rhododendron and led them up the trail. "I was there last night."

By the time they reached the open lawn, the bell sounded and the children gathered to go inside. Starlene waved to Randy. He'd be rotating off duty tonight. If Starlene wasn't so hardheaded, she would be off, too, and maybe they could have caught a movie together. Maybe Randy would kiss her without trying to ram his tongue all the way down her throat. Maybe he'd even talk with her about what was going on at Wendover.

But tonight, she needed to be here. Not only for the kids, but for herself as well. The old man wasn't just a figment of her imagination, others had seen him. Could this place be the site of a miracle? Did visions come to those in the modern day? Did God still send messages to the people He loved?

Starlene saw Bondurant watching them from his office window as they approached the building. He didn't wave.

"Time to go inside," Starlene said to Freeman and Vicky.

"First things first." Vicky ducked under the stair landing and went down the steps leading to the basement. Starlene watched from the top of the steps as Vicky pulled and pushed on the door, then banged her shoulder into it.

"Dang," Vicky said. "I swear it was open last night." She pointed to a large, gleaming lock and hasp. "That's new."

"Come on up," Starlene said.

"You don't believe her," Freeman said.

"Are you reading my mind, or is that just your opinion?"

"Just because you're a shrink doesn't mean you know

everything." Freeman brushed past her and went down to Vicky. They talked for a moment in hushed voices. Then they ascended the stairs together.

"I'm sorry," Vicky said. "I made the whole thing up."

"Yeah," Freeman said. "We didn't see an old man walking on water and I didn't get inside the heads of people who live in the basement. But it's okay for us to be wrong. After all, we're *troubled*, right? We're society's mistakes."

The second bell sounded, meaning they were late for lunch. "Look," Starlene said. "You guys don't have to hate me. It's hard for me to stay clinical and detached, but that's what I'm supposed to do."

"Trust," Freeman said, as if spitting. "Isn't that one of your special little words?"

Freeman and Vicky went up the landing and entered the building. Starlene started after them, then hesitated. She hurried down the stairs to the basement. The lock *did* look new, not a scratch or speck of rust on it. Sawdust, steel shavings, and crumbled masonry lay in small piles on the ground. The hardware had been recently installed.

"Is that to keep us out, or to keep *them* in?" Bondurant smiled down at her from the top of the stairs. Without waiting for an answer, he said, "You've seen them, haven't you?"

"Them?"

"The ones who live in the walls." Bondurant took a staggering step down. His face was bright red, his eyes wild. He slapped the stone foundation of the building. "The ones that God wouldn't let into heaven."

"I–I'd better get going. I have a group session after lunch."

Bondurant fumbled in his pocket and came two steps nearer. He brought out a key. "Don't you want to look?"

He lost his footing, and Starlene thought for a moment he was going to tumble down the steps. But he grabbed the handrail and regained what he could of his balance.

The smell of whiskey filled the cramped alcove beneath the landing. Wendover's director was as drunk as a lord.

"Mr. Bondurant, you look like you're under the weather. I think you ought to go lie down."

"I'm afraid I'll go to sleep if I do that." He was nearly all the way down the stairs now, and Starlene considered bolting past him. She'd never quite trusted him, even though he knew some Bible verses and professed faith in Jesus. But this man could crush her career with one negative reference. Though he looked out-of-his-mind insane— purple welts under his eyes, hair oily and mussed, hands trembling—he still carried a lot of influence with the state's behavioral health care system.

"And, please, call me Francis," he said, mushing his sibilants. He'd dropped his careful manner of speech. She moved aside as he tried unsuccessfully to slide his key in the lock. "Damned red tape."

He gave her a bloodshot look, and his gaze crawled down her body like a spilled basket of snakes. "It's bad enough to get regulated by the state. Now the federal government says 'Do this and that.' And all this talk about children's rights, like *we're* the bad guys."

He licked his lips, and Starlene saw why the children compared him to a reptile. "We do the best we can," she said.

"Goddamned right we do." On the fourth try, the key slid in the lock and the hasp popped free. "We're in service of the Lord, but all these layers of deception get in the way of the real work. You know what that work is?"

"Healing. Loving. Caring."

He banged his foot against the door and it swung open. "Hell, no. The real job is about looking good on paper. That's what brings in the money. That's why Kracowski is the best thing that ever happened to Wendover."

Bondurant shouted up the stairwell. "You hear that, Kracowski? You're the best goddamned thing that ever happened."

Starlene stood clear of Bondurant, who swayed and leaned against the door jamb. She couldn't resist looking past him into the dark basement.

Bondurant held out his hand and gave a wiggly grin. " 'Fraid of the dark?"

More afraid of YOU, she wanted to say, but this might be her only chance to see inside the basement. Vicky and Freeman had been trying to tell her something, but she'd been unable to cut through her own educated biases to listen. Maybe her faith was a bias, too. Now the door was open. It was up to her to walk through.

"She smiled at me," Bondurant said, spraying her with his liquor spittle.

"Who?"

"The woman. The woman in the wall."

Starlene barely heard him, because she saw a glow emanating from inside the basement. It was an eerie, diseased half-light. She felt herself being drawn forward, almost against her will. Behind her, Bondurant pressed close against her, his stench as repellent as his body heat.

"She's here," he whispered, and closed the door behind them. Starlene knew this was dangerous, that the drunken fool might do something embarrassing, but her fears were overwhelmed by what she saw before her.

The metal tanks themselves would have been cause for wonder, set in rows with coils and wires around each. The wiring that Vicky had tried to describe circumvented the ceiling, and several sizes of conduit ran overhead. An array of expensive-looking machinery lined the walls behind the tanks. The technology was a vivid contrast to the musty gray of the stone foundation, but that wasn't what caused Starlene's blood to freeze in her veins.

An old woman, Bondurant's "woman in the wall," stood in the glow of the generator components.

The woman had an ugly scar across her forehead, her facial wrinkles so deep that it looked to be the work of several hundred years of gravity. The woman's eyes were set back in her skull like the openings of small caves, holes that allowed no light to enter. From the tattered condition of the woman's robe, she looked severely neglected.

Starlene's first instinct was to help the woman. "What are you doing here?"

The woman's mouth opened, as slow as dust. Bondurant had pulled a flask from somewhere and was busy assaulting his central nervous system. "She lives here," he said, after removing the flask from his lips.

"Here?" Beyond the tanks set in the middle of the room, a series of dark corridors broke off from the main floor area. Starlene saw a few doors that promised even deeper shadows.

"When she's not in the walls, I mean," Bondurant said.

The woman's lips moved again, slowly, and Starlene thought the woman had spoken. Maybe sound wasn't what the woman emitted, because the top of Starlene's spinal column tingled and the words "A white, white room in which to write" flitted across her head and were gone. Except the voice had been a man's, not an old woman's.

Bondurant put his arm around Starlene, the gesture more boozy and paternalistic than sexual. "We got plenty down here. They're the best kind of patients you could think of. Don't have to feed them, they never complain, and no Social Services bastards breathing down your neck."

"You mean they *stay* down here?" The cobwebs, the stained concrete floor, and the wet smell of corruption made the basement seem more suited for a colony of rats.

"They don't stay here all the time. They used to, then they got in the walls. And now, sometimes, they get out." Bondurant waved his hand toward the ceiling, indicating the rooms above them.

They took it by hook and by crook.

The words were there, inside Starlene's head, like voice-over edited into a movie soundtrack. The woman's lips hadn't moved, but Starlene was sure the words had been the woman's.

I got half a mind to tell somebody about it, what they did. But I only got half a mind.

Maybe Freeman had been telling the truth. He'd exhibited some remarkable guess work during his session with her. But mind reading was a little too loopy, a little too unnatural, a little too much like something God would never allow. Yet so were old men who walked on water and disappeared. And shadowy secret agent types making deals with doctors. And expensive equipment hidden in an underfunded children's home.

"Who are you?" Starlene asked the woman.

The woman said nothing, just turned her stooped body and shuffled back towards the shadows. It was only after she'd reached the throat of the widest corridor that Starlene's legs obeyed her brain enough to follow.

"You don't want to go back there," Bondurant said.

"She needs help," Starlene said, angry. "How could you stand it, knowing she was living down here in this filth?"

Bondurant's drunken laughter bounced off the stone walls. "I don't think 'living' is the right word."

Starlene paused in mid-stride, and stood breathless in the center of the metal cylinders. Ahead of her, the woman had faded to nothing.

The woman's final words reverberated inside the bone cave of Starlene's skull: *Got half a mind. Off to find the other half.*

TWENTY-TWO

"Starlene went down there," Freeman said. The sound on the rec room TV was turned down, and a cat food commercial was playing. He looked out the window at the sun sinking behind the impossibly distant mountains. Eastwood in *Escape from Alcatraz*.

Vicky had "finished" her meal, and the counselors hadn't noticed that she'd only eaten one teaspoonful of food. Freeman had no appetite, so they left the cafeteria early. They were allowed to wait in the rec room near the offices while the rest of the kids ate. Randy had cast a suspicious eye at them, but then had to go break up a shouting match between Raymond and a second-string goon who was probably making a play for Deke's vacated throne.

"I guess Starlene can find out for herself," Vicky said. "You can't talk any sense into a grown-up's head. They already think they know everything."

"She's not so bad. Not like The Liz or Doctor Krackpot."

"Who do you think those people down there are?"

Freeman looked at the ugly swirl rug beneath his feet. He narrowed his focus, deliberately keeping his attention above floor level. He was pretty sure he wasn't keen enough to triptrap into the heads of the people underneath, but he didn't want to take the chance right now. "I'm not sure, but they're somehow *wrong*."

"Do you believe in ghosts?"

"No, but that doesn't mean that ghosts don't believe in *me*. I didn't believe in ESP, either, until it jumped up and bit me."

"Do you believe in anything else?"

"Sometimes."

Vicky sat back in the worn armchair and crossed her thin legs. "When it's dark and all the other girls are asleep, I talk to God."

"Now that's what I call ESP."

"No, really. And I feel like He's talking back to me."

"Starlene got to you, didn't she? Fed you the company line. Well, has your life gotten any better since you've developed a meaningful personal relationship with a thing you can't see?"

"Why do you always get so defensive over things that have nothing to do with you?"

"Why do you vomit every time you eat?"

Vicky pointed at the scar on Freeman's wrist. "You disappear your way, and I'll disappear mine."

Freeman moved away from the window to the entrance of the rec room. Through the glass cafeteria doors, he could see the counselors stooped over their food. All he had to do was walk away. No one would even notice he was missing, at least not until after-dinner group sessions.

He headed down the hall past the main office. The office lights were off and Bondurant was nowhere around. Vicky called Freeman, but he pretended not to hear. She wasn't the only one who knew how to escape. He'd been doing it for years, both inside and outside his head.

Freeman paused at the front entrance. A keypad beside the door blinked, a security system that required a code. The door's release bar would set off an alarm. Still, if he ran fast enough and reached the fence at the back of the property, he could cross over the farms and hide in the woods. From there, he'd have a decent shot at making it to . . .

Where?

He had nowhere to go.

Just like always. He put his back against the cool glass and slid to a sitting position. Vicky was waiting.

"I know the code," she said. "That's how I get out."

"What did you do, read the night watchman's mind?"

"No. Cynthia . . . did things for him in trade."

"Does Cynthia want to get out, too?"

"No, I think she just likes doing it. She told me what she did, and I didn't believe her until she gave me the code. I think she wanted to shock me."

"Did it work?"

"I've heard worse. Like your saying you could triptrap into my head and not being afraid of what you found. That's *way* worse."

Freeman looked up. Vicky's eyes blazed with intensity. Even if he could have triptrapped her at that moment, he wouldn't have dared. She punched three keys, a green light flashed, and she pushed the door open.

The evening Appalachian air swept over them, whisking away the mildewed odor of Wendover. Freeman rolled to his feet, grabbed Vicky's hand, and then they were off, running silently across the lawn. The grass was damp from an early dew, and Freeman's sneakers were soaked before they reached the boulders. One of the second floor windows lit up but they didn't stop.

"Is this the best way to go?" Freeman asked.

"There's a place on the far side of the lake where you can climb a pine tree and jump over the fence. You land in a laurel thicket. Get a few scratches, but no broken bones."

"Sounds like you've done it before."

"You're not the only one with secrets."

They slowed when they reached the cover of the boulders and Freeman let go of Vicky's hand. The moon was three-quarters full and glowed off the skin of the lake.

Among the scant patches of forest, reflected light spilled silver across the ground. They moved down the path, Freeman's ears straining for the slightest sound.

It wasn't sound but sight that stopped them.

They rounded the bend, and the old man in the gown stood on the path in front of them.

"You can't go this way," the man said, or maybe he hadn't said anything, only put the words in Freeman's head. His lips hadn't moved at all, just parted as if he wanted to draw a breath but couldn't.

"Did you hear that?" Vicky whispered.

Freeman nodded. "I didn't even triptrap."

The old man stood there, unmoving. Moonlight caught his flesh where the gown was ripped. His skin was milky, translucent, as if you could poke a finger in and it would keep on going.

"Who are you?" Freeman said, wondering if he even needed to speak in order for the man to understand.

"I live here," the man said or thought. He waved his hand across the lake. "I used to sleep here. But they woke me up."

"They?" Vicky said.

"I kept them."

Freeman looked behind Vicky. He couldn't decide if he was more afraid of the old man or of Bondurant and Kracowski and whatever was happening in Wendover. They could rush past the old man and make it to the fence. Even if the man had any muscle inside the ragged gown, he looked to be a hundred and twenty.

"I saw you in the home," Freeman said, waving in the darkness toward Wendover. "You say you live here?"

"Here, there, nowhere," the man spoke-thought. "It's all the same."

"Are you . . ." Vicky said. "Are you *dead*?"

"Not dead. Not anymore. The dead get to sleep. The dead are lucky."

Freeman pressed backwards against the rhododendron

branches. "You're one of the people underneath, aren't you? The people in the deadscape."

"You can't go this way."

"We don't want to go back to the home. It's too scary."

Vicky gave Freeman a look that said *So even a snake-eyed tough guy suffers a moment of weakness now and then*.

"You can't go this way," the man repeated in a voice like the lost wind over an empty grave.

"We're in a hurry," Freeman said. "Any minute, the counselors are going to notice we're gone."

"Please," Vicky said. "We haven't done anything to you."

The old man looked out over the lake, eyes as blank as water. "Drowning isn't so bad."

Freeman nudged Vicky away from the old man and stepped between them. "You're not going to hurt us. I won't let you."

The man's lips finally moved, lifted into a wrinkled smile that might have been hiding swallowed light. "I don't *need* to hurt you. They're doing a good enough job of it already. Wendover gets us all, sooner or later."

As they watched, the man's form softened and blurred, the edges blending with the moonlit night. His body broke into milky ropes, which then unthreaded themselves until at last only a pale mist hung in the air. The mist drifted from the path, down the grassy slope of the bank to the water's edge. There, it slowly dissolved, and Vicky and Freeman were left with nothing but the distant chirping crickets and the fireflies blinking against the thicket.

The old man's words came again from the sky, t......g like dead snow: *You can't go this way*.

Neither of them spoke for a moment. Freeman's heart was pounding so hard he could feel his pulse in his temples. A bullfrog croaked and splashed. From the darkness beyond the rhododendron came the hoot of an owl.

"Let's go," Freeman whispered.

"But he said—"

"Who cares what he said? He's gone and, besides, he's dead. What can he do to us?"

"I don't like this."

Freeman glanced at the night sky. The moon had risen higher. The ground was well-lighted now, and they could make good time if they kept moving. Every minute counted when you were serious about running away.

"Do you trust me?" he asked.

"Trust doesn't mean anything. You trusted Starlene Rogers, but you left her back there at Wendover, in that creepy basement. No telling what's happened to her."

"She's a grown-up. She's one of them. The enemy. You have to stomp people who get in your way, like De Niro in *Raging Bull*. She'd end up shrinking you to nothing if you gave her half a chance."

"I'm going to be nothing anyway."

"Someday we're all going to be nothing. But we have to keep trying, keep dodging, keep running as long as we can. I don't know about you, but I'm not going down without a fight."

Vicky pulled away from him and sat on a flat stone at the edge of the path. "And I thought you were brave. You really fooled me, didn't you?"

Freeman walked away from her, to the edge of the lake. He looked across the water where the mist had disappeared.

"You can stand up to a bully like Deke," she said. "But you can't stand to look inside yourself. You play tough but you're nothing. You're as scared as any of us. Clint Eastwood, my ass."

"No fair. You don't know anything about me."

"I went inside your head, remember? Triptrapping works both ways when you're dealing with somebody else who can do it."

"You didn't see anything. I've got all that stuff locked away. I'm over it. Nothing's bothering me anymore."

"Except your Dad. And what he did."

Freeman balled his hands into fists. He wasn't going to lose it. Not like Clint in *Dirty Harry*. Though it would feel so goddamned *good*.

The heat rushed through him and he fought the pain in his head. He wasn't going to cry in front of a stupid girl. Especially one who was nothing but skin and bones, who was so messed up she couldn't eat a solid spoonful of food. Who was *she* to tell him what was going on inside his own head? The best shrinks in the state system hadn't been able to touch him. He was fucking by-God bullet-proof.

"I know about the acetylene torch," she said quietly. The water lapped at the shore with a series of tired sighs.

"He didn't burn me on purpose."

"Not the first time. And I know what happened to your Mom. What you saw—"

Freeman wheeled and stormed over to her. He could break her in half, she was so scrawny and brittle. He could slap her and make her skull shatter like an eggshell. He could rearrange her face until she shut her big fat mouth.

"You don't know a goddamned thing about my Dad, or my Mom, or about *me*," he yelled, so loudly he could hear his own echo across the water. Anyone listening from Wendover could have heard him, but he didn't care.

"Admit you're scared, and I'll show you the way out."

Freeman had lied plenty of times in his life. Lying was a survival skill when you were in the system, when you were one of society's mistakes. And right now, he could lie and get his way. He could fool Vicky into thinking he was scared, because girls seemed to get the emotions of anger and fear mixed up. He could play her, manipulate her the way he'd done with every group home shrink and sociologist in the state.

But Freeman wasn't going to lie, not this time. "I'm not scared. I just want to see what it's like to live one night under the stars, to not have somebody tell me when to go to bed and when to wake up, or make me get in touch with my feelings. Or shock me like a freaking lab monkey until I do tricks and turn flips. Even if they catch us, I need one night where I belong to *me*."

"You know something, Freeman? You're a selfish bastard. You had people looking up to you, kids like Isaac and that boy Dipes."

"He's okay for a little brat."

"See what I mean? Even Cynthia said she thought you were cool. You give other people *hope*, Freeman. But all you're worried about is your own damned neck. All you want to do is run away."

"You're one to talk."

"I only run away for a little while. I don't know if I can handle the world outside these walls."

"All the more reason to take off." Freeman's anger had left him, his soul a deflated tire.

Vicky stood. "I wonder if the old guy in the lake is coming back."

"He said we couldn't go this way. But I think he's as bad as the rest, just trying to keep us boxed in. Even the dead people are against us."

Vicky laughed, a sound that was out of place in the still night. "You've got a hell of a chip on your shoulder, don't you?"

"You can stay here if you want. I've had enough."

Freeman turned and jogged down the trail. He tried to tell himself it was the mist off the lake that blurred his vision, but the truth stung like salt. Clint Eastwood never cried. Clint Eastwood never looked back, either.

He gained speed, hoping the cold air in his lungs would shock him into numbness. The path thinned and branches slapped at his face. Soon he was among the tall stands of oak and hickory that bordered the rear of the property. The foliage blocked the moonlight, so he crept forward in the silent dark, the fishy smell of the lake now mingling with the odor of rotting leaves.

He reached the fence as the moon broke through a gap in the branches overhead. The light caught the curled razor wire atop the fence. Insulators hung on poles, and several lines of bare wire ran along the top of the stone wall. The air tingled with ozone.

They had electrified the rear fence.

The dead man had tried to warn them. Somebody didn't want them to leave. A low growl came from the dark woods beyond the fence. It sounded to Freeman like what a troll might sound like, a monstrous creature whose claws could shred skin, whose teeth could grind bones, whose tongue could lick a skull clean.

Freeman hadn't felt this afraid since—

He held his scarred wrist to the moonlight. There was more than one means of escape. Except, if he died here, he might become one of those people underneath, the squirrel-shit nutty, the scared, the obsessed, the forgotten.

Eternal losers.

The ones even God couldn't heal, the ones who had never been defended or protected. Doomed to seek peace in a charnel house of the insane run by the insane. Freeman suspected this was one fight that would even have Clint holstering his six-shooters.

TWENTY-THREE

Bondurant pressed close behind Starlene. God sent along these tests once in a while, and God had so far given Bondurant plenty of latitude. God forgave the drinking, smiled down upon his punishing of the children, and looked the other way when Bondurant falsified state reports. God forgave, just like the Good Book promised. God loved the sinners perhaps even more than He did the saints.

Sometimes He let the sinners crawl up from hell just to be reminded of what they had lost. This basement was close enough to hell for Bondurant to feel the cold, spiteful breath of the dead things.

"What does it mean?" Starlene said, not understanding the scope of this new reality.

As if everything had to have a meaning. When you gave it all over to the Lord, everything fit the plan. A season for this and that, after all, whatever it was that the Book of Ecclesiastes said. For every season and all that happy bullshit.

But that was for later. Right now, he just needed to keep these ghost voices out of his head long enough to set Starlene on the straight and narrow.

"Don't mind her," Bondurant said.

"Who was that? *What* was that?" Starlene peered into

the darkness as if she could will the visions free of the walls into which they had evaporated.

"Nothing. Just one of Kracowski's tricks of the light."

"Kracowski? Is that what all this machinery is for? His treatments?"

"The Lord's work."

Sounds came from the dark corridor. This wasn't a ghost. This was something larger, something real, something not used to the dark. The ghosts were always silent. Even when they "spoke," you could still have heard a candle burning.

The glow cast by Kracowski's machines outlined Starlene's hair and gave her an aura. Bondurant reached a trembling hand to punish her. Those two brats, Freeman and Vicky, knew he was down here with Starlene. They'd probably tell Randy or one of the other counselors. He'd have to hurry and make her pay for her sins while he had the chance.

"Who's there?" Starlene called into the yawning black corridor.

He wished she'd shut up. Her mouth was good for only one thing, and that was apologizing to God for her wayward and wanton soul. Why did she waste her lips on asking questions?

Bondurant touched her hair, sought to clutch it, but she moved away. The bitch was ignoring him.

Me! Francis Bondurant, Director of Wendover, a member of the state's Board of Social Services, a man who crushes careers like yours with one rubber stamp. I'll give you a goddamned lesson in placement, all right. Let me get my paddle and I'll teach you to mind your own business.

Bondurant followed her into the circle of blue light. He staggered a little and fell against one of the tanks. It was cool to the touch. He drew away and went for her. She kept walking down the corridor.

Perfect. If he could corner her in one of the old cells, he

could lock her in, accomplish his mission and be absolved in time for his after-dinner meeting. The cells were nasty, and he'd leave her in there until she begged forgiveness in front of God. Kracowski's ghosts could watch if they wanted, as long as they didn't put their crazy words in his head again. He had enough crazy words in there already.

Words that the Good Lord might not approve of, but as long as Bondurant didn't utter them aloud, all would be forgiven. All would be forgiven anyway, because that's just what kind of guy Jesus was.

Starlene had entered the cell block now, and the stench of rot and mildew made Bondurant's stomach roil. He fought down the tangy whiskey bile and felt his way along the coarse stucco wall.

"Are you scared of the dark?" he said.

Dark don't walk, dark don't talk, dark don't do nothing but smarty smarty smarty.

At first Bondurant thought Starlene had spoken, because she'd paused near the door to the first cell. But that wasn't her voice. This was one of Kracowski's ghosts.

"Did you hear that?" Starlene whispered.

"God speaks in many tongues," Bondurant said.

She didn't know enough to ignore the voices. Bondurant had nearly wet himself the first time he'd seen that ragged, stooped old woman with the forehead scar. And when the ghosts started talking to him, putting words right in his head, he nearly signed himself up for a skull session with one of the counselors. Now he'd been exposed to enough of them that he could almost tune them out, as if they were an irritating rock music station on the heathen radio.

He could ignore them, but he couldn't shut them up. So he accepted them as they came. They were harmless. Like pets you didn't have to feed.

You can't keep me here. Don't you know who I am? I'm Eleanor Roosevelt, you fools. Can't you tell by my hat?

"Eleanor Roosevelt," Starlene said.

"Don't listen to them," Bondurant said. "They're trying to drive you mad."

"What's going on here? I don't believe any of this."

Unbeliever. She had stopped moving and that gave Bondurant his opening. Take advantage of weakness, that was the way of the world. The black rectangle of a doorway stood out against the dim blue light of the hallway. He would shove her in there.

Shuffle, shuffle.

That sound again. Almost swallowed by the black throat of the corridor. Something bigger than a ghost.

Maybe it was more than one. A dead parade, communion time for the criminally insane, in lockstep search for their scattered reason. Whispering in the walls like mutant rats. Marching in aimless uprising against the agitators of their sorry souls.

But they had no *right*.

They were the imprisoned, and he was the jailkeep.

Wendover was *his*, damn it. Bad enough when Kracowski moved in with his machines and his theories and his secret funding. Now these restless idiot spirits had invaded, crowding his domain and changing the rules. Playing with his head. Making him think their weird thoughts, lending their pain, forcing him to empathize.

A white, white room in which to write.

Not that one again. The same voice, the same sentence over and over. This one was male, cracked, the sentence always taking a different rhythm but the words and their order always the same. An eternal revision that always yielded the same outcome. Crazy as a fucking bugbed.

Crazy as a fucking bugbed.

Whoa. Wait a second. Did he *think* that, or had one of the ghosty things echoed it back into his head?

"Did you hear that?" he asked Starlene, and he was ashamed that his throat caught. No weakness allowed. He was the one who took advantage of weakness. Wendover was his.

"Crazy as a bad-word bugbed," Starlene said. "Yeah, I heard it."

Starlene moved away from the doorway, spoiling Bondurant's opportunity to seal her in a temporary tomb. He was too drunk, and in the darkness he'd lost track of her. He brushed his knuckles along the walls, scouring the flesh on the rough masonry. He sucked at his bloody wound.

Shuffle, shuffle.

Recreation hour in the ward of the damned.

"What's going on, Mr. Bondurant?"

What's going on was the whole world was turning upside down, and Starlene couldn't see it because she was blinded by purity. This was Ground Zero for Armageddon, the first testing ground of faith.

The blackness was a solid thing, pressing like a suit of wet clothes, forcing itself against his eyeballs and his eardrums and winding through his mouth and wiggling into his lungs and—

I've half a mind.

Her.

The one with the scar.

She was with them, somewhere in this darkness, making words go into his head even when he *DID NOT GODDAMN WANT THEM IN THERE.*

Bondurant had lost track of Starlene. He reached an intersection of corridors and listened for her footsteps. All he heard was the soft shuffling. He was having a hard time concentrating with all those voices in his head. The rows of cells were invisible mouths that whispered feverish, foul things.

White, white room—

—my wife is a hat—

—tin foil gods and metal scarecrows—

—artcrimesexpill—

—seven nine eleven thirteen—

He tried to steady his breathing so he could locate

Starlene in the dark, but he was panting too hard from anger and fright and confusion and things going in and out of the walls. The blank canvas before him became a softer gray, then a fuzzy suggestion of shape.

Then she appeared.

She glowed softly, naked, her face shadowed, the rest of her suffused in a yellow light. She was the Whore of Babylon and the mother of all creation. A promiscuous virgin with a hell of a stage show.

"It's a miracle," Starlene said from somewhere to his left.

In the light cast by the woman, Bondurant saw Starlene leaning against the wall in the doorway of a cell. He gave her only a glance; this nude, see-through woman demanded all his attention.

This woman's beauty made even the wholesome Starlene pale in comparison. Bondurant took a step toward the woman. Her mouth opened, and looking into her throat was like looking down the corridor, a long blackness stretching to a deeper dark. The woman was smiling, but her smile had far too many teeth in it.

A time to sow and a time to reap.

The words oscillated around the bone of his skull like a ringing alarm clock dropped down a well.

Crazy as a bugbed bugbed bugbed.

The woman held out her arms as if she wanted to embrace him, and despite his fear and awe, Bondurant felt a stirring in his groin.

Now Bondurant realized what was odd about the woman. His eyes had traveled all over her figure, he'd played with her curves in his mind, licked his lips as he imagined his hands on her, his palm stinging her softest flesh as he meted out the punishment every woman deserved. Last of all, he looked at her eyes.

Eyes that saw nothing, because the sockets were empty. The makeshift skin around them bore runnels carved by fingernails.

Her voice came like icy rain: *The better to see you with, my dear, precious, sweet Little Red Riding Hood.*

She opened her palms and revealed her loose eyes, red strings of flesh dangling from them.

Starlene screamed. Bondurant choked on a prayer, sprayed a geyser of vomit on his shoes, and stumbled backward in the dark.

The Miracle Woman smiled, too many teeth and not enough eyes.

TWENTY-FOUR

Kracowski glanced at the computer screen, then checked his meter. "A hundred-and-twelve milliGuass," he said.

Paula, standing behind his chair, rubbed his shoulders. "It's only numbers, honey."

Kracowski knew he might as well be talking to the wall as talking to Paula, but he'd talked to walls too often lately. "These anomalies are not what I expected. Synaptic Synergy Therapy is designed to heal my patients, not cause them to have subjective experiences."

"Well, the ESP data is strong enough to convince even the biggest skeptics. And everything's subjective, honey."

"Except the truth."

He cleared the meter, changed its coordinates so that it detected another area of the basement. "Look at these spikes. The electromagnetic fields created by my equipment should be consistent. These are all over the place."

"So? If it bothers you, just ignore it."

"I can't ignore it. These readings aren't consistent with my theory."

"Change your theory, then."

Kracowski pushed away from his desk. "I was so sure I was right."

"You *are* right, Richard. You just found more than you bargained for."

He went to the two-way mirror and looked into the darkened space of Room Thirteen. He had helped those children. He had aligned their minds into harmonious states. He had restored them, made them whole, healed what the religious-minded such as Bondurant called their "souls."

But souls didn't exist. The human body was a complex bag of chemicals, mostly water. The brain was nothing but a series of electromagnetic impulses. Thoughts and dreams were merely a random alignment of those impulses. Things like wishes and hopes and love and fear were specific patterns of neural activity, a battery of switches thrown on or off. Never mind that the number of possibilities were nearly limitless. "Nearly" was the key word. Everything had its limits.

Money.

It didn't buy happiness, and Kracowski knew this truth better than most.

Love.

That heralded and holy set of specific mental disorders, praised by poets throughout human history, chased by the weak who expected a miracle cure for their individual shortcomings, embraced by the masses as something worthy of sacrifice. If only they knew that Kracowski could create a series of electromagnetic wavelengths that aligned the synapses so that the subject experienced all those physical and emotional sensations: quickening of pulse, widening of pupils, flushing of skin, racing of blood to erogenous zones.

Fools fall in love, indeed. Research had already shown that those newly in love displayed the same synaptic patterns as those diagnosed with obsessive-compulsive disorder. A rose by any other name.

Faith.

Faith had its own built-in limit. Faith was the answer to

its own question, a circular logic that satisfied simpletons around the world. No matter whether they called it God or Buddha or Allah or Moon or Krishna. No matter whether you met it on your knees or from the heights of a Himalayan monastery or in any of the modern brainwashing facilities they called temples, churches, and synagogues. All religious faith was selfish because all believers ultimately sought to save themselves, not others.

Science.

Ah, that was the one that might not have limits. Or the one discipline that might impose them. Truth. Knowledge. Facts. Hard evidence and data. That was almost something worthy of worship.

Except when the facts suggested that the entire truth would never be understood. Which was happening right now.

Telepathy and clairvoyance were theoretically possible, if one believed that the brain's electrical impulses weren't confined to the flesh. He could accept a world of mind intersecting with the world of space and time. But the existence of a soul separate from the body smacked far too much of metaphysical idiocy.

He'd been given a starting point, the abstracts and data that McDonald's people had compiled over the previous decade, the backlog of Dr. Kenneth Mills' experiments. ESP was producible as an innate ability that could be induced with a balance of force fields and systemic shock. But these latest experiments had skewed toward the spiritual, the unprovable, the unbelievable. That bothered him. That scrambled the harmony of his own synapses. It misaligned his neural patterns and disturbed his sure vision of the universe. It pissed him off.

"What are you thinking about?" Paula said.

He tapped his forehead against the mirror a couple of times. "I'm thinking of you, dear. What else?"

"I love it when you talk that way."

Her perfume cloyed the air. If only she knew that the

THE HOME   183

natural pheromones in her perspiration were far more
sexually alluring to the human male than perfume's scent.
Still, she satisfied a need, and she was only temporary.
He could always air out his office after she left.

"Hey, what's this?" she said.

She pointed to one of the video screens that monitored
the equipment in the basement. The picture was greenish
and fuzzy. The Trust had coughed up a fortune for the remote electromagnetic resonance system, spending millions
on superconducting magnets and advanced circuitry, but
the infrared video system was low budget. All Kracowski
made out on the screen was a soft blur of movement.

"No one's supposed to have access to the basement,"
Kracowski said. "That equipment is delicate."

"I thought McDonald had some guards down there."

"They're under orders to stay away from the equipment." Even as he spoke, he remembered McDonald's
words as the equipment was being installed. *Orders
change*, McDonald had said, ex-Army bastard that he
was. Kracowski peered at the screen. One of the figures
separated from the green dimness and backed away.

"Bondurant."

"What's he doing down there?" Paula asked.

"He's the only one on staff with a key."

"Look. There's somebody else down there."

Kracowski cursed a god he didn't believe in. The magnetic pull of a regular MRI scanner was about 20,000
times the force of the earth's magnetic fields. It was
strong enough to rip a pacemaker right out of a patient's
chest, which was why MRI patients got a thorough
going-over before being slid into the tube.

The equipment in the basement generated a field a hundred times stronger than that, at least in certain localized
points. The magnetic field was strong enough to hum and
created static electricity and microshocks. If the anomalous fluctuations continued, they could create a serious
danger by pulling hardware from the walls. A loose piece

of metal might fly across the room and pierce one of the tanks of liquid helium. The helium wasn't explosive, but an accident could set Kracowski's work back by several months, not to mention drawing the interest of a lot of busybodies in the state Social Services Department and the county planning department.

Bondurant's playing around down there, probably half-drunk or worse, was a disaster waiting to happen. He was already disrupting the careful alignment of the fields. The man might have iron or steel items in his pockets that could destroy valuable equipment. If the liquid helium or liquid nitrogen tanks were pierced, the basement would go into an instantaneous, though brief, deep freeze.

Kracowski opened his desk drawer and got a key and his flashlight. There were three ways to access the basement from inside the building. One was from Bondurant's office, another via a locked door in the main hallway labeled *Custodial Staff Only*.

Kracowski went to his bookshelf and removed his copy of H.G. Wells's *A Short History of the World*. He reached into the space on the shelf and fumbled for the hidden button. What had seemed clever when McDonald's people were installing it now seemed like a spy movie trick, unnecessary and overdone. He pressed the button and an adjacent bookshelf swung forward, revealing the metal door and the third way downstairs.

"Hey, that's cool, Richard."

Leave it to Paula to be impressed by extravagance. He unlocked the door and switched on the flashlight, playing its beam down the dark stairwell. Cobwebs draped the doorway, and he brushed them aside as he headed into the gloom. The stench of must and mildew rose from the dank basement. He glanced back once and saw Paula waiting at the door, her silhouette stooped with tension and excitement.

Kracowski slipped down the stairs to the narrow hallway that branched off from the main basement corridor. He splashed his beam into one of the cramped cells. The cells were a hellish testament to the mental health field of the 1940s, when terror and pain were more common psychiatric tools than nurturing and synergizing. Frontal lobotomies, pharmaceuticals, insulin-induced comas, and electroshock were the glorious toys of those spearheading the charge into a brave new world of the mind. Too bad the psychiatrists hadn't recognized and dealt with their own delusions of grandeur.

Too bad they weren't as flawless as Kracowski.

He heard shuffling in the darkness of the main corridor. He switched off his light and listened. He recognized Starlene's voice immediately.

"Hello? Who's there?" she called from the darkness.

He should have figured Starlene would start snooping around. She'd already asked far too many questions about his experimental treatments. With her simple religious faith, she automatically assumed that all cures that weren't divine in origin were the result of unspeakable dark powers. That's why he wanted her to submit to the treatments herself, so she might understand what he was trying to accomplish.

And perhaps she could be "cured" of the need to submit to an invisible authority and beg forgiveness for imagined sins. If not cured, perhaps she'd be frightened enough to keep her mouth shut. If worse came to worse, her memory could be erased.

"Come out where I can see you," Starlene said. Her voice echoed down the corridor. Bondurant must have fled the basement, because Starlene's footsteps were the only sound besides the hum of the equipment.

Kracowski eased down the hallway and waited. The air was thick with the stirring of ancient dust and he fought back a sneeze. That's when he saw her.

At first he thought it was Starlene coming down the hall toward him. Then he realized the woman wore no clothes. She carried her own light with her. No, not with her, *within* her. She drifted toward him like dawn's smoke on a meadow, then, before he could discern what was wrong with her face, she was gone.

But not before putting words in Kracowski's head: *You can see the truth if you look through my eyes.*

Kracowski nearly dropped his flashlight. He looked around to see who had spoken, to see where the woman had gone. Translucent women didn't exist, and women who didn't exist couldn't appear out of nowhere. A mind could not live separately from the body. Kracowski flipped on the light again and swept the beam across the hall and into the nearby cells.

"Where did she go?" Starlene said, approaching from the shadows.

"Access to the basement is limited to authorized personnel only, Miss Rogers," Kracowski said.

"Was *she* authorized?"

"You should be concerned with your own violations, Miss Rogers. This early in your career, you'd better keep your record spotless."

"I can't pretend I didn't see her."

"Saw whom?"

"Don't pull that with me. Mr. Bondurant saw it, too." Starlene waved into the darkness behind her. "I believe he ran away."

"I'm not sure what sort of manifestation or illusion you thought you saw. My Synaptic Synergy Therapy and the resultant electromagnetic fields might have uncertain effects. I'm still studying how it changes neural patterns. It's possible that you may have been exposed to a high field fluctuation. That may lead to hallucinations."

"She called herself the 'Miracle Woman.' Except she didn't talk at all, just put words right in my head."

Miracle Woman. That was all Kracowski needed, more religious hysteria among the staff. At least that could be a good cover story if Starlene made some sort of report to the state board. He could say she was suffering from delusions. By the time Kracowski was through, he'd have them wondering whether Starlene should be *receiving* help instead of giving it.

He shined the light in her face so that she blinked. "Why are you down here?"

"Bondurant. He—" She seemed to change her mind about what she wanted to say. "I'm trying to figure out how your gizmos down here work. And how it's supposed to heal these kids."

"You believe in the power of talk, the power of suggestion. Nurturing, compassionate attention. But you're trying to pour love into cracked vessels. I not only patch the cracks, I reshape the vessel."

"Freeman said he 'heard' people down here. He claims to be able to read minds."

"A rare but reported delusion among those with bipolar disorder, at least during a manic episode. And he's a rapid cycler, isn't he?"

"I've observed him swinging from up to down in the course of minutes. But he's hearing voices, and I'm hearing voices, and I'm seeing people that I don't want to believe are real."

"I can assure you they are not real. Like I told you before, I've heard plenty of ghost stories about Wendover, and I've not seen a ghost yet."

"You didn't see the Miracle Woman?"

"You saw nothing." Kracowski took the beam from Starlene's face and played it down the hall. "If it's not there, it can't be quantified. If it can't be quantified, it doesn't exist. If it doesn't exist, then I'm not interested."

"If you're so brave, then why don't you give me the flashlight and you can stay down here in the dark?"

Kracowski tilted the light under his chin, knowing it made sinister shadows on his face. "Maybe the crazies are standing right in front of you."

"That doesn't sound like something a rational man of science would say."

"If I scare you away, maybe you'll leave my equipment alone."

"I wouldn't dream of interfering with your research. After all, you have the whole world to save, right? Lots of troubled, lowly humans to heal. The masses. Those who aren't perfect like you."

She headed for the main corridor, into the thick stretch of black, her shadow bobbing along the wall like oil in a sick ocean.

"You saw nothing," Kracowski said.

"Like I didn't see that man at the lake," she said without slowing. "And those wet footprints in the hall. I'm seeing a lot of things I'm not seeing lately."

"They don't exist until I say so."

Starlene paused at the edge of the corridor. "God is the one who makes those decisions."

Then she was gone, into the black and across the blue where the hum of the machines carried suggestions of things beyond science.

TWENTY-FIVE

Six hundred pounds of night sky pressed down, the mountains closed in, the trees were bad things that wanted to strangle him.

Just like that, standing by the fence with the whole world against him, Freeman jumped the elevator into the down cycle, no stops. He was smart enough to tell the difference these days, thanks to Dr. Krackpot's treatments. Sure, depression was only a bad mix of brain chemicals and crossed wires, but he couldn't stop thinking of it as God's idea of a good joke.

Only moments before, he'd known everything, he was smarter than God, he could triptrap into every skull in the world if he wanted. Now there was nothing but big dark.

The path by the lake was tar, his feet as heavy as stumps. The black blanket of depression over his head dulled his senses and choked off the oxygen to his head. Seeing the electrified fence had flipped the big switch in his brain. He was stuck at Wendover, hopeless, helpless, just another stooge in the loser factory.

Even worse. He was starting to shrink himself and trying to figure things out. The good old enemy within. The troll under the bridge.

"Freeman?"

Oh, no.

Not her.

Not now.

All he wanted was to be alone, to slink back to his mattress and burrow under the pillow in the fart-filled wonderland known as the Blue Room. To be alone with bleak thoughts. Him and his misery, a match made in heaven.

"Freeman, I'm sorry."

Sorry. That was a good one. The word that everybody went for after they'd screwed you over and messed you up. *Sorry* was one of his dad's favorite words, right after *shithead* and *motherfucker* and *sausage-brains* and all his other pet names.

Freeman moved past Vicky in the darkness, letting despair drag him back toward Wendover. The lake caught the silver moon and soft ripples whispered forgotten names, as if the water held the spirits of those long dead. Let the ghosts come and eat him up or pull him down with them for all he cared. Maybe he belonged with those crazy fucks.

"Freeman, talk to me. Don't be like this."

Like what? He wasn't being like anything. She didn't need to follow him. Why couldn't she find somebody else to worry about, somebody who gave half a damn?

He walked on, and the path may as well have been waste-deep mud. Depression. Tidy little name the shrinks had for it. They were so goddamned smart. Depression, like sinking into a hole.

"I can't triptrap you, Freeman. You're shielded. So you have to tell me. What's going on?"

Triptrap was for idiots. Who cared what anybody else thought? When you walked across the bridge into somebody else's head, all you saw was their fuck-ups and problems and pain and sorrow. He had a Pandora's box worth of troubles tucked away in his own head. Why go out of his way to find more?

Vicky grabbed his arm and tugged. He blinked out of his

stupor of self-pity and saw they were on the Wendover lawn, the few lighted windows of the building gazing like monster eyes. Off to the left, almost hidden beneath the trees, were the counselors' cottages. The buildings were dark and silent.

She tugged again. "Freeman. I'm scared. Talk to me."

Oh, God. Defender of the Weak, Protector of the Innocent. What a crock. Defending the weak had almost cost Clint his neck in *The Outlaw Josey Wales*.

Still, Vicky had been nice to him, or at least acted like it. Damn, he hated when they were as good at pretending as he was.

"Forget about it," he said. "We're all stuck here."

"Stuck? Just a few minutes ago, you were all excited about making a run for it."

"They outsmarted us. They always win. No matter what you do, they're one step ahead. Haven't you figured that out yet?"

"No, Freeman. There's always hope."

Freeman swallowed a laugh. It turned his stomach and he almost choked. Maybe he'd ask Vicky to give him some pointers on self-induced vomiting so he could get rid of all the lies they had fed him over the years.

"Let me explain," he said. "There's a bunch of crazy dead people in the basement, electric razor wire on the fences, and the key to the front gate is in the pocket of a man who zaps little kids for fun. And the Trust is behind it all. I thought the Trust was out of my life forever, once Dad was booked into a rubber room. But they're back and I have this bad feeling they brought me to Wendover for more of their fun and games. Now what part of that is supposed to make me break into a chorus of 'Tomorrow'?"

Vicky stopped him. "I thought you were special, but you're just like all the rest, aren't you? *Aren't* you?"

He had to look at her. He owed her that much, at least. He wished he hadn't, because those big dark eyes caught the moon just like the lake water had. That's all he needed, for her to squeeze out a few tears here in the middle of the night. If he lived a million years, which was a million more than enough, he'd never be able to figure out girls. Even when he could get right inside their heads, they still made no sense.

"Come on, let's go." Freeman took Vicky's arm. "All we're going to do is get in trouble. And that dead guy in the lake back there might decide he's lonely."

She jerked free. "You're so stuck on your own problems that you don't see everybody else has them too. And sometimes you're the *cause* of their problems."

Damn. She was crying.

Freeman was helpless. If he were on an up, he might have sneaked into her head and tried to relate to her. Even though he'd be doomed to failure. Girls never said what they really meant, and they never even *thought* what they really meant. When you tried to fix one thing, it turned out to be something completely different that was broken.

He reached out to pat her shoulder, something even Clint Eastwood could manage, but she turned her back. What to do now?

She took several slow steps away. He thrust his hands into his jeans pockets and looked at the stars. Insects fiddled among the trees and two bullfrogs swapped croaks across the banks of the lake. He wished he could dissolve into the night, do like the old man's ghost and melt away like a fog. But he couldn't, because he was made of God's stuff, flesh and bone and blood.

Damn.

He was the troll beneath the bridge, and she was the little goat Gruff.

He was gobbling her up.

Him and his evil mouth, his bad teeth, his stupid mean claws.

Freeman went for that word, the one he'd heard too many times and hardly ever used himself. "Sorry."

"You're only sorry for yourself."

"No, really. I didn't mean to hurt you."

She spun so fast that he almost fell over backwards. She came on like a two-fisted prizefighter, De Niro as Jake La Motta in *Raging Bull,* Clint as Dirty Harry, Pacino as Michael Corleone in the Godfather movies, her words stinging like uppercuts and jabs. "Didn't—mean—to—*hurt*—me! You're the goddamned *champion* of hurt, Freeman. I never met anybody like you. And I never wanted to, either."

Then she stormed off across the grass heading toward Wendover, small and lost against the dark structure. Freeman followed, his heart like a trapped bird against the cage of his ribs.

They were nearly to the building and Freeman was thinking of something to say, maybe ask what was the best way to sneak inside, when Vicky stopped.

Freeman thought she was going to give him more pieces of her mind, but she pointed to a window on the second floor, one of the few that wasn't dark. A shadow moved against the muted light, a head ducking back. Someone had been watching them.

"Who was it?" Freeman asked.

"Couldn't tell."

"Do ghosts have shadows?"

"Maybe ghosts *are* the shadows."

"Vicky, this place is major messed up."

"It was bad enough back when it was just us kids with all our problems. Even without the disappearing man and the people in the basement, and now you're babbling about some Trust that's behind all this. I don't think I can take anymore, Freeman."

They approached the back stairs, the night cool with crickets. The moon stretched the dark shadows of trees across the lake. Freeman took Vicky's arm and she didn't stop him; he let her lean against him as they headed up the steps. Freeman felt lighter now, as if some of the world's weight had fallen from his shoulders.

He stopped in his tracks. Realization, big time.

Depression didn't just slink away, even for a rapid cycler. Depression clawed its way to the surface from a spot deep in your guts. Yet Freeman felt something so rare that he had to pinch himself to make sure he wasn't sleepwalking into a good dream.

The feeling wasn't happiness, exactly. He'd known little enough of that in his life, but he could recognize it from a safe distance. And it wasn't joy. And it sure as heck wasn't the L—word. But being with Vicky was starting to feel like a habit. A good habit.

"Don't get weird on me, Freeman."

He smiled in the night. A smile. Yeah, that was weird, all right.

Her hand pressed against his. She was giving him something. He took it and closed his palm around it. A penny.

"Don't make me have to come in there," she said.

The trouble was, she was already *in*. She was attached to almost every thought he had lately, at least when he wasn't depressed. He could close his eyes and smell her soap, see the freckle two inches below her left eye, feel the fine bones of her fingers. She was in way too deep, and he didn't know how to get her out.

Could you vomit thoughts, clean out your skull and make it all nice and empty? Brain bulemia? Start from scratch, with no past and no Dad and no scars and no feelings? No ESP?

Would God, if the bastard was as real and caring as Starlene made Him out to be, let a boy have a new beginning, this time without playing against a stacked deck?

No.

That was what they called *hope*, and Freeman knew the word was nothing but a loaded gun in a shrink's arsenal. Hope didn't exist in the real world, where ghosts walked and little kids got shock treatment and barbed wire marked the edges of the universe.

"I'm not thinking anything," he said, squeezing the

penny and wishing he had the guts to say something strange, deep, and tough-soft, like maybe Pacino in *Scent of a Woman* or *Sea of Love*.

"Don't hold out on me. You know you can trust me."

"I'm thinking we ought to be getting back inside before someone notices we're gone. All we need is for Bondurant to be breathing down our necks. He'd probably sign us up for an extra session in Kracowski's secret little room."

"Or else give us a spanking," Vicky said.

"Spare me."

"Think we should try to get in through the basement?"

Freeman heard a sound from beneath the landing. "I don't think so," he whispered.

Someone spoke from the darkness below them. Freeman barely recognized the voice as Starlene's, it was so shaken.

Starlene spoke again, this time more clearly. "Hey, guys, what are you doing here? It's past Lights Out. You could get in big trouble."

Freeman almost wanted to laugh at that. Dead people coming out of the woodwork, and he was supposed to worry about having his dessert withheld.

"You shouldn't have gone down there," Vicky said.

Starlene came out of the dark hollow beneath the landing. "I just wanted to check out what you guys said."

Freeman and Vicky exchanged glances. A grown-up who acknowledged having doubts? What was the world coming to?

"What did you see?" Vicky asked.

"I'm not sure."

Freeman tried a triptrap on Starlene, but the air was too murky, his own thoughts too cloudy. He only gave himself a headache. If he knew what she'd seen, then maybe he could convince her that he wasn't crazy. Or maybe she had seen something that had her doubting her own sanity.

Nah. No counselor in the history of the human race

had ever been less than perfect. Shrinks were the baseline from which sanity was judged. Though Starlene had shown glimpses of being human, when you got right down to it, she was still a hard-headed know-it-all who gave Jesus Christ credit for all good things and blamed her few failures on other people.

"Nobody's sure about anything lately," Freeman said. "What about Kracowski's machines?"

"All I can say is they look expensive. And they put off a lot of strange vibes."

"Listen," Vicky said. "You two can stand out here all night if you want. I'm going inside."

"You might get in easier with this." Starlene pulled a keychain from her pocket. "Unless you already know how to break in."

Vicky gave an innocent look, widening her eyes and letting her mouth go slack. Nothing looked as guilty as feigned innocence.

"Vicky's a saint," Freeman said. "It would never cross her mind to do anything against the rules."

"As if you've crossed her mind lately?" Starlene asked.

"I thought you didn't believe in ESP."

"I'm starting to believe in a whole lot of new stuff." She looked at her watch. "Almost eleven. You guys think you can sneak into your dorms without getting caught?"

"You mean you're not going to report us?"

"No. I'm on your side, remember?"

Starlene led them to the back door and unlocked it. Then she reached inside and keyed the pad, deactivating the alarm.

"Whatever you do, stay away from the lake," Freeman said to Starlene.

"I know how to swim."

"I'm not talking about swimming. I'm talking about jumping into the water and looking for an invisible man."

"Hey, how did you . . . Oh."

"We aren't as dumb as we look," Vicky said.

They slipped down the hall, looking out for the night watch. Whoever had seen them from the upper window might be lying in wait for them. Bondurant was rumored to roam the halls in the middle of the night, paddle in hand. And that wasn't even considering the danger from crazy spooks who dangled from unseen strings and threw weird sentences into your skull.

Wendover itself seemed like a skull, a hard shell housing random and unexplained dreams. Freeman wondered if a building could be insane. If what Vicky said was true and this place had been a nuthouse back in the glory days of psychosurgery, then these walls had absorbed more than their share of screams. Freeman shuddered and wondered where screams went to die.

They slipped past the main offices. No light showed beneath the door, which either meant Bondurant was gone or else was sitting in the dark. Probably dreaming about the next kid he got to paddle. Freeman never wanted to triptrap into Bondurant's head again. He'd rather swap thoughts with a ghost than with something as vile as The Liz.

"Walk me to my door?" Vicky whispered. In the grim fluorescent light, her face was an unhealthy shade of greenish white.

"You scared?"

"No. I'm too dumb to be scared."

"Yeah. You're real dumb all right. So dumb that you play games with the security guards and you've got the counselors eating out of your hands."

"Sorry about that, back there," she said, sweeping her hair from her face, a gesture that made Freeman's heart pause. "When I got all emotional."

"Happens to the best of us."

"I'll try not to let it happen again."

"That would probably make life easier. Even if you have to fake it."

They were silent the rest of the way to the Green Room.

The door was ajar, and Freeman thought about all the girls in their bunks wearing nothing but their underwear. The dormitory was dark, and Freeman didn't know if one of the counselors was inside waiting for Vicky to enter. He figured he'd best not hang around, no matter what.

Before he left, Vicky grabbed him and put her mouth to his ear. "Thanks for the walk," she whispered. Then she kissed him on the cheek.

What would Clint do?

Stand there like a wooden statue, that's what. He almost wished he had a big chew of tobacco, so he could lean over and spit on the floor in lieu of a response. Or wince and twitch one corner of his mouth. Feel nothing, even if you have to fake it.

She was through the door and gone before he could think of something to say, and he was glad, because he would have resorted to Clint's classic line from *The Outlaw Josey Wales*: *Reckon so.*

TWENTY-SIX

Dr. Kracowski stared at the two-way mirror. "Impossible."

"Things are only impossible until they happen."

Kracowski watched McDonald's face in the reflection. They were in Thirteen, the room of miracles. That is, if Kracowski believed his own eyes instead of the empirical data. For the first time in his life, a shadow of doubt crossed the doctor's mind. "Is that why the Trust funded me?"

"We've been in the paranormal business for decades. Uri Geller was just a Cold War smoke screen. Think of the practical advantages of ESP, clairvoyance, remote viewing. You could sit in on any meeting, no matter how top secret."

"Congress would never fund such foolishness."

"Yeah, and they would never fund a space-based missile system, either. What's a few billion siphoned off here and there? When it comes to national security, most politicians know enough to keep their noses out. And when did I ever say I was working for one government?"

"Okay. You want me to believe in Illuminati conspiracies, and you want me to believe in the supernatural. That's a lot to ask of a non-believer."

"You're not the first one to make a breakthrough."

McDonald waved to the floor. "But your machines downstairs are doing something even our think tank people hadn't considered. Kenneth Mills never even had a clue, and in many ways, he was the pioneer in this field."

"You're fond of mentioning Mills, aren't you? Maybe he was brilliant, but his end results weren't. His wife's dead and his son suffers from a half-dozen behavioral disorders."

"Mills had a few personality flaws, sure. Like any genius. But his work with EMF opened the door to other people's heads. And you've taken things to the next level, Doctor. A level that, I'm afraid, is a little higher than we expected."

"And you're thinking I can't be trusted?"

"No. Like I told you, orders change."

"That explains the electric fence."

"We just think it would be best to keep everyone quarantined until we know more about what we're dealing with."

"Quarantined? You make it sound as if we're cultivating anthrax or manufacturing nerve gas."

"It's strictly 'need to know' at this point. If a few of the staff members went around town telling ghost stories, somebody might start snooping. And snooping leads to more snooping. Before you know it, along comes an idiot reporter looking for a Pulitzer and a book deal."

"Ah, that clichéd little cloak and dagger bit. Who do you *really* work for, CIA or FBI or National Security Council?"

McDonald gave a toadish creak of laughter. "We're the guys who keep an eye on *them.*"

"I think, McDonald, or whatever your name is, that's the first lie you've told me." Kracowski sat on the little cot where he had cured so many troubled children. He looked at the ceiling and wondered what it would be like to undergo an SST treatment himself. He didn't think he would notice any difference, because his neural patterns were perfectly aligned. There was nothing to cure. But would he be able to read minds? Or see ghosts?

He shook his head at the memory of the incident in the basement, those cold words slithering into his head.

"So all you have to do is keep with the program," McDonald said. "We're bringing in some of our people to verify your results. Independent observers, that sort of thing."

"What you're trying to say is you're going to keep the lid on this forever."

"Maybe not forever. The United States government didn't keep the atom bomb secret once they started wiping out cities."

"I still don't see how you expect these"—Kracowski spat the next word—"*ghosts* to be manipulated. If they even exist."

"I think you can take 'if' out of the equation." McDonald pointed to the two-way mirror.

Kracowski turned, and an image flickered in the glass as if trapped between the double panes. The image took a silver and white form, built itself a face. It was the woman, the one Kracowski had seen in the basement. This time, he had a corroborating witness to his illusion.

As they watched in silence, the woman ran her milk-vapor hands along the glass as if searching for a weakness, some small crack through which she could slip.

Kracowski realized he hadn't taken a breath in half a minute. McDonald was just as still. The woman's eye sockets, empty as abandoned mines, stared out as if not understanding this strange and solid world she had encountered. Her amorphous flesh pressed against the glass, and Kracowski found himself taking mental notes to record later in his journal. He was halfway through the first sentence when the image dissipated like smoke.

The room had grown so quiet Kracowski could hear the dull vibration of the machines in the basement. Even in a state of rest, the massive magnets had a gravitational pull. And perhaps some other kind of pull as well.

"Electromagnetic energy," Kracowski said.

"Looked like a *ghost* to me."

"No. Perhaps that's the force that draws them into our plane. This little intersection of dimensions we call 'reality.'"

"Reality. I'll believe it when I see it."

Kracowski waved his hand. McDonald was now insignificant, a spectator to Kracowski's brainwork. "From what little I've read about paranormal investigators, they use anomalies in electromagnetic readings as 'evidence' of otherworldly activity. Presumably, the ghosts disrupt the force fields when they appear. But what if it's the other way around? What if the electromagnetic fields *attract* them to our set of dimensions?"

"Just a few minutes ago, you were strictly by the numbers. Now you have a theory for cooking up ghosts."

"I'm a scientist, McDonald. A scientist's main job is proving why certain theories will never work. Discoveries are almost always made by mistake. Not many scientists are lucky enough to make a true discovery in their careers."

"And you're not making this one. Remember who you're working for." McDonald looked at the small camera lens in the corner of the ceiling.

Kracowski went to the door and tried the handle. Locked. He turned, his cheeks hot.

McDonald dug in his pocket and held up a shiny object. "I carry the keys from now on."

Kracowski nodded toward the glass where the image had appeared. "I don't think *they* need keys. And I'm not sure barbed wire is going to hold them, either."

"We'll see. Until then, you keep cooking them up, and I'll worry about what to do with them."

As McDonald unlocked the door and tapped out the code on the newly installed electronic lock, Kracowski stared at the mirror and wondered how he could best get inside McDonald's head.

TWENTY-SEVEN

Freeman thought he'd slipped to his cot unnoticed. But seconds after his head hit the pillow, a low whistle came from his left. Isaac's silhouette was all Freeman could see of his friend. No, not a friend.

Freeman would have no friends here. Not Isaac, not Dipes, not Starlene, not anybody. Not even Vicky, no matter how much she made his heart float. He was permanently retired from the job of Defender of the Weak, Protector of the Innocent. Isaac was just another stooge, another loser kid, competition for food and oxygen here in God's favorite little game, Survival of the Fittest.

"Psst." Isaac was sitting up now. He wore striped pajamas that looked like those worn by concentration camp inmates.

Freeman pulled the blanket over his head, the institutional rayon scratching his cheek. He smelled his own feet. Tomorrow he'd have to shower, get naked in front of Deke and his Goon Squad. No, wait. Freeman yanked the blanket away and peered down the row of cots. Deke was still gone. He had never returned from the basement.

Isaac hissed again.

Freeman lay on his back and stared up. The faint blue safety light by the door made the ceiling look like a starless night with a moon somewhere over the horizon. Or maybe it was the surface of the ocean and they were drowned. It really didn't matter if they were all dead yet or not. Either way there was no escape.

Isaac was by his ear now, pesky as a mosquito. He whispered, "What happened?"

"What do you mean, what happened?"

"You got rid of Deke somehow, didn't you?"

"I don't know."

"He wasn't at dinner, he missed Group, and even Army Jacket's looking a little lost. I'll bet you and Vicky—"

"Never put her and me in the same sentence."

"Or maybe it was Starlene. Or Kracowski? Did the mad doctor shock the monkey into a pile of ashes?"

"Are you on Ritalin or something?" Freeman asked.

"No, why?"

"You're talking way too fast."

"Bondurant made some of us go into his office. I've been there before. Never got a paddling, though. I hear that's one of his deals."

"What did he do to you?"

"Just asked if we'd been in the basement."

Freeman pulled the blankets tighter and tried not to think about the things under the bed and floor. "They got us trapped."

"What are you talking about?"

"Wires. On all the fences. Can't climb over without getting a shock that makes Kracowski's treatments seem like a tickle."

"Why?"

"Something to do with the Krackpot's equipment, I think. And there's a mysterious agency called the Trust that dabbles in this sort of weirdness. We're the guinea pigs. But I don't know what the experiment is."

"No way. That would never happen in the land of the free. And I thought *I* was paranoid."

"Isaac. You're a Jew. What the hell do you know about freedom?"

Isaac knocked on his own skull. "I'm free up *here*. If you have that, then you win."

Did Freeman have that sort of freedom? All he had was a screwed-up dad and screwed-up memories and rapid-cycle manic depression and a gift for triptrapping and, worst of all, he was falling into some sort of stupid attraction for a girl.

Attraction? Am I falling in love, or are my neurotransmitters fucked?

Now he was positive he was on the down cycle.

"Bondurant was drunk, as usual," Isaac said. "He asked me if I'd seen the Miracle Woman."

"Miracle Woman?"

"His eyes got all funny when he said her name. He looked at the walls like he expected to see cockroaches."

"Isaac, do you believe in God?"

Isaac said nothing. Somebody coughed in the far end of the dorm. The stench of dirty laundry and bad breath hung thick in the room. The kid to Freeman's right was snoring.

A voice came from the foot of Freeman's cot. "He don't believe in anything."

It was Dipes. Dipes, who never uttered a word.

"Yes, I do," Isaac said.

"Hush, because here comes the counselor," Dipes said.

Isaac scrambled back onto his cot, Dipes ducked, and Freeman closed his eyes. Ten seconds later, the door to the Blue Room opened. A flashlight beam bounced around the room, froze on Freeman's head for a moment, then the door slammed.

"How did you know he was coming?" Freeman said to Dipes.

The thin boy shrugged in the dim light. "Just knew. I've been knowing things lately. Knowing what's going to happen before it happens. Like I saw Deke disappear in the basement, then one of those creepy guards took him to a secret room. And I ain't seen Deke since. Can't say I miss him none, though."

"Freaky," said Isaac.

"Wait a second," Freeman said. "How many of Kracowski's treatments have you had?"

"Five," Dipes answered. "He said I was one of his favorites. Said I had so many problems I'd make a good case study."

"Aren't you better yet?"

Dipes said, "Look, someday when you got a few hours I could tell you the whole deal. But I don't think we have a whole lot of hours left."

"How come?" Isaac said.

"Because it's going to open up."

"What's going to open up?" Freeman was impatient, and had to remind himself that he was talking to a nine year old who still wore diapers. And who now claimed to have powers of precognition, the ability to see the future.

"The door," Dipes said. "The door to the deadscape."

Isaac said, "What's the deadscape, anyways? People keep talking about it, but what does it look like?"

Freeman had seen the deadscape as plain as day. To him, that world was as real as this one. Not everybody could triptrap, though. At least, not yet. But, if Kracowski's experiments were giving people psychic powers, then who knew where it would end? What would happen if everybody in the world could read each other's minds? How would Freemen feel when his power was no longer so special?

He asked Isaac, "Haven't you had a treatment yet?"

"No. Maybe I'm not screwed up enough to need curing."

"Give them enough time and they'll find something," Freeman said.

"Well, they're careful with me because my grandparents want me out of here, but no way am I going to get conditioned by some creepy old Jews. They believe Christians are out to wipe them off the face of the planet."

"They probably are," Freeman said.

"Plus they'd make me get good grades."

"Better the devil you know, huh?"

Dipes tapped on the rail of Freeman's bed.

A couple of guys were talking across the aisle. One of them snickered.

"Tell us what happens," Freeman said to Dipes. "What you see."

"I don't know what the deadscape is, all I know is there's a white door in the floor. And the door swings open, and it's real bright, and all these people pour out and their eyes are crazy and they want to get us—"

"Calm down," Freeman said.

"They're people, but they don't have no bodies. They scream, but their lips don't move. And we start dying. And I'm scared."

Freeman fought off an urge to hug Dipes and comfort the little guy. The only way to survive this thing was to worry only about himself, *numero uno*; the budget Clint Eastwood a.k.a. the Kid, starring as The Man With No Name in his most insensitive role ever. Because the future was looking pretty bleak, even from the spiderhole view of a manic depressive.

Whatever he'd seen in the deadscape was more than just a triptrap illusion, and couldn't be explained away by screwed-up brain chemistry and misaligned neurons. Whatever walked down there was real. He believed without a doubt Dipes could see the future. At Wendover, everything was now believable, even the impossible.

Especially the impossible.

Isaac pulled his sheet over his head and made "whoooh" noises in imitation of a ghost. He lifted the sheet and stared at Freeman and Dipes, his face made eerie by the blue lighting. "Okay, let me get this straight. You're trying to tell me a bunch of restless spirits are living in the basement—

I mean, are *dying* in the basement. And they're going to crawl out of the floor and do bad stuff to us. Okay, I'll buy that, since we all know that ghosts do bad stuff because they're jealous of us breathers and—"

"Isaac, you talk way too much." Freeman wished they would go to sleep so he could be alone with his thoughts of Vicky. He'd had enough doom and gloom for one day.

To Dipes, he said, "When does this door of yours open?"

"I can see the future, but I ain't learned to tell time yet."

"Guys," said Isaac. "Ghosts aren't real. And nobody knows the future but God."

"What are you fuckwits talking about?" It was Army Jacket, who had crept out from the shadows.

Freeman felt brave in his despair, so he said, "Where's your buddy?"

"What buddy?"

"Deke."

Army Jacket's eyes were black as beetles. "He ran away. He could blow this joint any time he wanted to."

"Sure. And he didn't invite you to run away with him. A goon like him *needs* a brainless sidekick. It's hard to picture Deke out there in the real world, getting by on his wits."

"Don't be a smartass."

"Somebody around here better be smart. Because we're in trouble."

"What the hell is this 'ghost' stuff?"

"Ghosts are what got Deke. Down in the basement."

"Bullshit. That's baby crap."

Dipes stuttered in the presence of his tormentor, but managed to say, "Wuh—we had those treatments. Now we can see through the walls."

Army Jacket snickered. "I had the treatment, too, and I'm not crazy yet. Unless they're giving you some pills or something. If they are, I want some."

"Ghosts aren't real," Isaac said.

"Oh, yeah?" Freeman said, pointing to the wall on the far side of the dorm. "Try telling *her* that."

Against the painted cinder blocks, flickering like the image cast by an old film projector, the woman without eyes smiled her dead smile.

TWENTY-EIGHT

Bondurant stepped back from the window. Dawn was still an hour away, and he knew he'd be unable to sleep until the sun rose. No matter how much he drank.

Since fleeing the basement, he'd wandered the halls of Wendover, flashlight in hand, trying to forget what he'd seen. Or what he thought he'd seen. The memories were blurred now, softened by Kentucky bourbon and that trick of the night that allowed you to delude yourself.

Now he was checking out the dark rooms on the second floor where classes and group sessions were held. All the rooms were empty.

No, not empty. The stink of something strange clung to the shadows, and a couple of times he'd seen movement from the corners of his eyes. But when he turned his head, the fluttering shapes evaporated.

Bondurant sat in one of a circle of chairs and flipped off the flashlight to save batteries. He closed his eyes and felt for the chair beside him. Kids sat here and tried to solve their problems, trapped in this evil church of psychology, with an overly educated counselor serving as minister. If Bondurant had his way, the little sinners would bend in prayer instead, talking to God instead of each other.

Bondurant felt for the flask in his coat pocket, pulled it out and twisted the lid free. He held the flask in the air.

"The Lord is my shepherd, I shall not want," he said. The words bounced off the cinder block walls.

He put the flask to his lips, tasting the sting of liquor around the rim. He drank, but only a few drops remained. He pushed his tongue against his teeth and took a deep breath. Wendover's air was full of dust and dead things.

The bourbon was gone. He was alone.

"I don't have a problem," he said to the dark room.

That's what they always say. He'd read enough case files to know that even young children could become alcoholics. But Bondurant wasn't an alcoholic. Alcoholics had problems with drinking, and he had no problems. He occasionally sinned, but his sins were forgiven because someone had died for them. Someone else's blood had washed those sins away.

The solution was so simple that he could never understand why the psychological establishment didn't embrace it with joy.

His head swam too much to wrap completely around the angry thought and he slumped in his chair. This was his church, he realized. Not a church in the way the Baptists built them, strong and expensive, like military bunkers. This was a mental church, standing under a steeple of his own solitude and power.

Out there, in the real world, he was nothing but a suit and a handshake. Even at his expensive home in Deer Run Estates, he was just a shadow passing between the furniture, no more substantial than the photograph of his ex-wife that rested on the mantel. Here at Wendover, he was important. He had value. He was admired and appreciated, even loved.

Loved by the weak, and by those he tried to lead to salvation. Those who sat in this circle of chairs.

His group.

Lost in the blackness.

"What would Jesus do?" he asked the silence. No one answered. Some group this was. You come in expecting to be understood but all you got were stupid stares.

He spoke louder now, a preacher at the lectern. "Jesus would say, 'Take another drink,' that's what Jesus would say."

"Sounds good to me," came a voice from the darkness.

Bondurant shuddered himself alert, thinking he'd drifted into unconsciousness. "Who said that?"

"Me," said the voice.

Bondurant's hand trembled around the flashlight. He put his thumb on the switch, but was afraid to see the thing that had spoken. It was a female voice, calm and doomed and coming from a chair across the circle. He wondered if it was the woman with the smiling scar, the one who had disappeared into the wall. She had never spoken, though, except with her eyes. This one had a voice.

It couldn't be one of the staff. He would have heard the door open, and the halls were all lit by faint security fixtures. No one had entered. Except through the walls, or maybe down from the sky. Or up from the floor. From the deadscape.

"You're not supposed to be in here," Bondurant said.

"I belong here."

"Who are you?"

"Me."

Bondurant's pulse pounded against his skull. He was drunk and dreaming, that was all. He wasn't sitting here talking to nobody. "I'm Francis," he said.

Three voices came in unison from the darkness. "Hello, Francis."

He groped for the flask again, then remembered it was empty.

"Do you have a problem, Francis?" came one of the voices, this one from his left, a female voice scratchy from cigarettes.

He looked at the window, a square of lesser gray

against the black. He prayed for sunrise. The Lord would deliver. That was one of His favorite tricks, tempting the faithful with despair and fear. But Bondurant's faith was strong.

"I don't have a problem," he said, surprised that his voice was steady.

"Sure," came a man's voice two chairs from Bondurant's right. "None of us got problems. Only solutions, right?"

"Amen," said the woman across the circle.

"Wait a minute," Bondurant said. "You guys are talking about my drinking, right?"

"Ah, so you admit it. That's the very first step."

"Step," he said. "I'm not going anywhere."

"We understand, Francis," said the scratchy woman. "We've been there. We know what it's like."

Bondurant wanted to stand and stagger for the door, but his legs were limp. He wiped the sweat from his palms onto his slacks. His necktie was choking him, and he struggled for breath. The room with its invisible walls and invisible people seemed to grow smaller.

"Leave me alone," he shouted.

"We can't," said the man. "We love you too much."

"I have the love of the Lord," he said. "I don't need yours."

"Ah, so you accept a higher power. That's another step toward healing."

Bondurant found the strength to rise, though his legs quivered like saplings in a thunderstorm. "*I don't need to be HEALED.*"

Silence.

Bondurant clenched his fist around the flashlight, ready to lash out.

The woman across the circle whispered, "So much anger. So much pain. Francis, you don't have to fight it anymore. Just surrender."

He sat again, slumped, defeated, scared.

The man spoke from darkness. "We know it's hard. You're under a lot of pressure. All these brats to take care of, who wouldn't need a drink?"

Bondurant put his head in his hands and nodded.

"Social Services breathing down your neck all the time, fund-raisers, a board of directors to please, everybody expecting you to keep on smiling no matter how much shit they feed you," said the scratchy woman, only she was no longer to his left, she was standing behind him.

A new voice came, a child's voice, small and lost. "It's okay, Mr. Bondurant. We forgive you."

"Forgive," he said. Only the Lord's forgiveness mattered. Sins weren't measured on earthly scales, only by He who judged. No mere child had the right to feel sorry for Bondurant.

"For the spankings," said the child.

Bondurant felt as if a sock were stuffed in his throat. He only spanked in those instances when he knew he wouldn't be reported. Like all successful predators, he chose his victims carefully. And now some stupid little snot-nose was telling him it was *okay* to bend the sinning little shits over his desk.

Well, he knew it was okay, because the Lord had assigned him the mission. Who cared what the Department of Social Services thought when he had higher authorities to please? The rod and staff comforted. He turned their other cheek until they howled for mercy.

Because, beyond everything else, Bondurant was merciful. He'd learned that from the Lord, and from the Scriptures. Mercy tempered all acts, though sometimes you had to be righteous and vengeful.

"You need to open up," the scratchy woman said.

"Open up?" Bondurant didn't know what frightened him more, sitting in a room with people who didn't exist or being put on the spot.

"Don't be afraid," whispered the child, and now his

voice was very close, so close that Bondurant should have felt the exhalation on his face.

Bondurant recognized the voice. Sammy Lane, the boy who had died in that botched restraint hold two years ago at Enlo. That was the home's most shameful moment, bringing the Social Services storm troopers into Bondurant's life. Sammy became the poster child for reform, his grinning photo splashed across the newspapers for weeks until another controversy pushed the death to page five. Then he was gone, nothing but a black mark on the system's record.

Until now.

Sammy was back, offering Bondurant forgiveness.

"I didn't have anything to do with it," Bondurant said. "I wasn't even there when you died—I mean, when it happened."

"They said you gave the order," Sammy said. "And I wasn't being mean or anything, this girl pulled my hair so I kicked her, and the counselor twisted my arm behind me and took me to the time-out room, and of course I hated it because nobody likes to be locked in the dark, so I shoved the counselor and he wrapped his arms around me and told me to calm down and I couldn't breathe but he wouldn't let go and I didn't have enough breath to tell him to stop and the next thing I knew I was dead." Little Sammy paused. "But it's okay now."

Bondurant wept, the salt stinging his bloodshot eyes. He was innocent. The investigation had cleared him. Even the counselor had gotten off, taking a plea agreement that barred him from ever working in child services again. Everyone was satisfied with blaming it on the system instead of individuals. Enlo's financial support had suffered a little, but Bondurant waxed his smile and faced the storm and then the storm blew over. And Bondurant took the director's chair at Wendover. Everyone had forgotten.

Except Sammy.

"We all have problems," said the scratchy woman.

The man said, "My shrink asked me all these questions, but she was a woman so I couldn't answer. Reminded me too much of my mom. Later, I wrote the
answers on little pieces of paper and slipped them in the
back of the television in the rec room."

"That's crazy," said Bondurant, glad he didn't have to
respond to Sammy.

"They said *I* was crazy but I was only in love," the
scratchy woman said. "Love is nothing but internal
bleeding."

"It's not my fault," said the man from the darkness.

"I didn't love you, I loved the doctor. They took away
my cigarettes so I chewed tin foil. I pulled the staples out
of magazines and swallowed them. Then I found some
loose nails in the paneling and ate them. By the time they
opened me up, it was too late."

"I don't want to be opened up," Bondurant said.

The woman who was standing too close behind him
said, "Let out what's inside."

A cold touch like the end of a frostbitten finger trailed
down the back of his neck. "I'm scared," Bondurant said.

"We're all scared."

"We're all scared," whispered Sammy, in his tiny voice.

The gray around the window had grown lighter. Bondurant closed his eyes. The sun was climbing over the
mountains outside, and soon he would be able to see the
things that were talking to him in this empty room.

"Well," came a new voice, a strong and confident man's.
"That's enough for one session. We don't want to solve
all our problems, or I'll be out of a job."

Bondurant forced his eyelids to stay shut, trembling
with the effort. The room was as cool as December, and
Bondurant caught a faint whiff of dirt and decaying
leaves.

Sammy's voice was at his ear. "Bye, Mr. Bondurant.
See you around."

One of the chairs fell over, then silence.

After ten minutes, Bondurant opened his eyes, his cheeks wet with tears. In the dim light of daybreak, he looked around the circle of vacant chairs. He reached into his pocket and touched the flask, swearing for the hundredth time that he was through. Then he looked at the door.

Against its metal face he saw an image of the old man in the gown. The man's lips moved, but no sound came out. As the shape dissolved under the sunrise, Bondurant thought he knew what words the ghostly lips had formed·

We're getting closer.

TWENTY-NINE

"Are you comfortable, Miss Rogers?"

Starlene nodded at the mirror on the wall. An apparatus that looked like a high-tech chandelier lowered from the ceiling, stopping several feet above her head. The humming rose in intensity, vibrating the cot to which she was strapped. Her skin itched beneath the electrodes stuck to her temples. The pinprick of pain had faded where Dr. Swenson had injected the radiopharmaceutical that would allow Kracowski to track her brain's chemistry and blood flow.

Randy had fastened the restraints, ignoring her questioning eyes. Now she was alone in the room. She gripped the sides of the mattress and waited for Kracowski to flip the switches that would send the currents racing through her brain, the weird waves that would oscillate through her molecules and send her into the unknown.

Kracowski's voice came from the speakers again. "Remember that this is strictly voluntary."

"I know," she said. "Just like it is for the kids."

"This is not a good time for a debate on the merits of traditional counseling versus Synaptic Synergy Therapy. My results speak for themselves."

"Are you talking about your therapeutic results or . . . you know, all that other stuff?"

"Ah, the phantasmagoria effect. Don't you Christians believe the souls of the dearly departed are immediately vacuumed off to hell or heaven?"

"Only people who actually *have* souls."

"You are a doubter, Miss Rogers. I've had many doubters. In that respect, I am not unlike your beloved Jesus of Nazareth."

"Except Jesus did what He did for the good of others, not to boost his own ego."

Laughter crackled over the speakers. "If Jesus had computers and a better understanding of electromagnetic fields, He would have invented SST himself."

The lights in the room dimmed, and Starlene tried to relax. Her sleep had been short and interrupted by nightmares. Each time she had awakened in her cottage, sweaty and tangled in sheets, she prayed the fear away. The Miracle Woman had drifted through her fleeting dreams, holding out those tragic eyes. The dread of the treatment had also kept her restless and anxious.

But it was too late to back out now. If she wanted to understand what Wendover's children were going through, she had to endure the same treatment. She stared at her reflection in the mirror and told herself to be brave.

"Yea, though I walk through the valley of the shadow of Kracowski," she whispered to herself, "I will fear no evil."

The humming grew louder and the floor pulsed. A faint tingle trickled across her skin and the walls became softer. Above, the ceiling spun and lifted away, but instead of morning sky there was only a black void. Starlene's heart accelerated, racing to the rhythms of Kracowski's machines.

She concentrated on her face in the mirror, but the glass warped and melted away. Now the walls were gone, and so was the bed she had been lying on. She panicked and reached up to her temples to yank away the electrodes. The restraints had vanished, as well as the electrodes.

She tried to stand but her legs were warm taffy. The floor opened beneath her and her stomach tightened in anticipation of falling. Starlene closed her eyes but still saw the floor yawning like a hungry mouth, and in the dark throat of the basement, faint wisps of light floated upward.

Starlene screamed at Kracowski, but the sound was swallowed by the roaring of reality's death. The wisps solidified and the Miracle Woman stood on nothingness, holding out her palms, showing her dead eyes. Around the Miracle Woman came others, formed from the milk of afterlife, all wearing the lost and crazed look of the eternally restless.

The Miracle Woman's lips moved, and her words came not as sound, but as thought. "Starlene Rogers."

Starlene pushed toward where she thought the door was, but the door had disappeared along with the rest of the room.

The Miracle Woman smiled, and things fluttered around her tongue. Her thoughts came to Starlene like wind through graveyard grass. "The door is below you."

Starlene turned and came face-to-face with the old man in the gown, the one who had walked into the lake. He spoke-thought into her skull. "I can make you better."

"I don't want to be better," she thought or screamed or whispered, and she clawed frantically at the air, trying to move in whatever direction she could.

"My motto is, 'Heal you or kill you,'" said the old man. "I win either way."

A young guy, thin and ragged and pale as a maggot, drifted down from above. A sleeveless institutional gown draped him like a funeral shroud. He waved a hand at Starlene's hair, seemed surprised when his flesh passed through her, and said, "Can we keep her?"

The Miracle Woman said, "She's not ours yet."

The young man whimpered. "The doctor said we could. I promise to play nice."

"Since when have you ever believed your doctor?"

"Since yesterday."

"You weren't alive yesterday."

The old man said, "And you never took your medicine. No wonder you ended up like you did."

The young man looked down at his wrists. Long scars, gray against the white threads of his skin, ran from the base of his thumbs to his elbows. "Can I take it back?"

Starlene pressed her hands over her ears, but still she heard the words from those impossible mouths.

The old man said to the suicide victim, "You'll have to do better than that. You've been very, very bad."

"Leave him alone," said the Miracle Woman. "Haven't you harmed him enough already?"

"I was only trying to help."

"I know. That's the worst part. You never saw the patients as human beings. You saw them as numbers, experiments, sets of diagnoses. As problems to be solved."

The old man drifted nearer to Starlene. He put a hand out, like a Catholic priest bestowing a sacrament, and his cold touch penetrated the bones of her skull. She couldn't twist away, no matter how she struggled. Behind him, in the shadowy ether, more shapes hovered, their faces blank.

"If only I had another chance," the old man said. "I know what to do now. I know where I made my mistakes."

"Keep away," the Miracle Woman said. "This one needs a different kind of healing."

The Miracle Woman closed her hands, hiding those hideous, wounded eyes. She grew brighter, her words falling more softly in Starlene's head, no longer shrieking.

"Have faith," came the gentle voice. "They can judge your mind, but they can't judge your soul."

The shapes began spinning, as if Starlene were at the center of a double Ferris wheel that turned in two directions. The Miracle Woman blurred, the shapes became dots of smeared light against black, and the humming swelled into a chorus of moans. Starlene reached for her own eyes and found they were still closed, and the lights became thin streaks circling and circling, until at last there was only darkness.

Her pulse pounded in her neck. A soft light bathed her, and she shuddered in fear of more encounters with the things that walked the deadscape. The light became stronger and another disembodied voice pierced her skin.

"Miss Rogers, are you okay?"

Kracowski.

She opened her eyes. The ceiling was back in its proper place, the mechanism quieted. The mattress beneath her was solid. She tested the substance of her fingers and found they were again made of flesh.

She drew air into her lungs and looked at the mirror, toward where Kracowski would be standing behind it. "What happened?"

Through the microphone: "How are you feeling?"

"I don't know."

"You're better, of course."

"Better than what?"

"You've been aligned. You're harmonized. I have healed you."

"But I wasn't broken." She gripped the mattress, unable to trust herself to stand even if the restraints hadn't held her.

"That's what's so wonderful about SST. It heals even those who aren't aware they are in need of healing."

She closed her eyes, and the images from the deadscape flickered at the back of her eyelids. She stared at the mirror instead. "How long was I out?"

A pause came from the speakers. Then Kracowski said, "You were dead for three seconds."

If three seconds of death were that unbearable, Starlene wasn't sure whether the afterlife was a promise or a threat. Already the memories were scrambled and weak, and she couldn't trust what she had experienced.

Randy entered the room, and their eyes locked. For the

briefest of moments, she thought she heard him speak, but then realized his lips hadn't moved.

She'd read his thoughts.

Something about the Trust and how McDonald needed to get rid of this particular problem known as Starlene Rogers. Though she was a cute little thing and would be fun for a tumble, she asked too many goddamned questions. She was trouble, he just knew it.

She rubbed her forehead after Randy released the restraints. She tried to read him again, but it was as if a fog had rolled in between them. She had almost convinced herself she had imagined the entire thing, the shock and the deadscape and Randy's thoughts, when Kracowski and McDonald entered the room.

She picked up McDonald's thoughts. He was wondering if the force fields could be aligned to scramble neural patterns so people like Starlene could be lobotomized without leaving scars. A brain death that left no evidence would be a useful tool.

And, McDonald thought, before another fog rolled in, maybe Kracowski could be scrambled once he'd outlived his usefulness.

Starlene closed her eyes and waited for Randy to remove the electrodes.

THIRTY

Freeman peeked out the window. The kids were in gym class, and Freeman had faked a sprained ankle. He'd been sent to the rec room again, where he was supposed to rest and watch whatever uplifting program PBS was broadcasting. Instead, Dr. Phil was brow-beating a couple into a changing day in their lives. He turned down the sound on the television so the noise wouldn't distract him.

He reached into his pocket and pulled out the yellowed newspaper clipping. A tiny piece of it broke away as he unfolded it. The photograph had faded a little over the years, but it still had the power to reach off the page and squeeze Freeman's throat.

Dad's mug shot.

The headline above: "PSYCHIATRIST ARRESTED IN WIFE'S MURDER."

And then came the deck: "Mills Was Respected in Mental Health Circles."

Like all small-town papers, the *Neuse River Tribune* delivered sensationalism with a community touch. The article hinted at the gruesome nature of the crime with phrases such as "mutilated corpse" and "unsuspecting victim," but also included eyewitness testimony:

"Dr. Mills was the nicest man you ever met," said

Doris Jenkins, who had lived next to the Millses for four years. "He was quiet and always waved hello. You never would have expected something like this."

Doris Jenkins, as Freeman recalled, had been an old witch who shook her broom at the kids whenever a stray football bounced into her roses. In her account to the press, she neglected to mention she'd never waved back. Now she was frozen in ink as the voice of authority. Whatever.

Freeman read the article all the way through, though he knew it by heart. His name was in the last paragraph. The poor kid who hadn't spoken since witnessing the terrible tragedy. The kid who was in an emergency foster placement until Social Services could figure out what to do with him.

The kid who grew up to be *him*.

Freeman carefully folded the article and returned it to his pocket. There had been other articles, page two follow-ups, and coverage of the trial before the DA pled Dad down because it was an election year and all the expert shrink witnesses were ready to declare Dad a basket case. But Dad had never again made the banner headline. That murder was the best the old bastard ever got.

Freeman closed his eyes and leaned against the mildewed sofa cushion. He could go to sleep here, with the sun dappled across his face from the window, nobody to bother him. Mercifully alone.

Something landed on his stomach.

He cocked an eye and saw Vicky standing over him. She wore brown today, a sweater that suggested two small shapes on her chest beneath it. Her skin was pale and vibrant, her eyes black. She nodded at the floor beside him.

A penny lay on the stained carpet.

"How did you find me?" he asked.

"How do you think?"

He tried a triptrap but he was on a definite downer. "Do you have to follow me every second of the day?"

"Can't help it." Vicky touched her head. "You got inside here, and now I can't get you out."

At least he was in her brain and not her heart. ESP he could understand, because it made sense if you thought about electricity and radio waves and how the brain was just a bunch of wet wires. But that other stuff was way too freaky. It seemed bigger than the brain.

Freeman sat up with a fake groan. "What do you think they're doing to Starlene?"

"Can't you triptrap her?"

"I'm beat. Even a genius like me can't turn it on all the time."

"Depressed?"

Freeman put a hand over his pocket, where the clipping was safely hidden. "Yeah, a little."

"Memories are hell, aren't they?"

He looked at her. "You're not going to make me talk about it, are you?"

"I just want to help."

Freeman grabbed two fistfuls of ratty couch cushion and squeezed. He wasn't going to get mad. It wasn't her fault. She was like all the others, the shrinks, the cops, the social workers, the whole goddamned system, all of them wanting to help when they could have helped most by leaving him the hell alone.

He rolled to his feet and faced away from her. Through the rec room window, he could see the front fence. Dewy strands of barbed wire glistened in the sun. Beyond that stretched the mountains out and up, solid rock. If only he were on those gray peaks, above it all, where they couldn't get to him. Where he couldn't even get to himself. Like Clint in *The Eiger Sanction*.

"I don't want any help," he finally said.

"I figured that out the second I laid eyes on you."

"Then why are you bugging me?"

"Because we need each other if we're going to get out of this mess."

"We don't even know what the mess is."

"Dead people. It's about dead people."

"I hate dead people," Freeman said.

"You hate everybody."

"Come here and look."

"Don't change the subject. We were starting to get linked there."

"Yeah. And I don't want you triptrapping into my head without permission."

He pointed outside. The autumn sun had risen fully and capped the ridges in molten gold. Thin strands of clouds hung like silver monk's hair in the lavender sky. The tree-covered slopes were the colors of pumpkins and plums.

"It's beautiful," Vicky said.

"And, in case you hadn't noticed, it's on the other side of the fence."

"Ten miles away."

"A million miles."

"What are you hiding from me, Freeman?"

"I'm not hiding anything."

"Don't lie. There's dark water beneath the bridge."

"I told you I didn't want your help, and I don't want to talk about it. Now stay out of my head."

"Why did you try to kill yourself?"

"I thought you already knew everything."

"It's something to do with your parents, isn't it?"

Freeman spat a laugh. "Sure, blame it on the parents. Are you studying to be a shrink or something?"

"I say that because my parents wanted me to disappear. My dad was too busy for children, and Mom was too busy trying to please Dad. He was out of work a lot, I think because he drank too much. One day I was eating breakfast, a bowl of corn flakes, and Dad was reading the newspaper. Mom gave him a cup of coffee and went back into the kitchen.

"Dad said something about a job market, and what did

I know, I was only five years old. I said, 'Daddy, if you need a job, why don't you just go down to the job market and buy one?' He slammed his coffee cup on the table and looked at me.

"'You're just another goddamned mouth to feed,' he said to me. He didn't yell it or anything, just said it like he was asking me to please pass the butter. Mom hurried in from the kitchen, wringing a dish rag.

"'What's all this ruckus about?' she said. Dad looked past me and said, 'Make her disappear.' Mom didn't understand, then Dad threw the cup against the wall and said, *'Make the little bitch go back where she came from.'* He got up from the table and left the apartment. Mom looked at me like it was my fault Daddy was mad. My stomach started hurting and I ran to the bathroom and threw up. The corn flakes scraped my throat on the way out. But I felt better, leaning against the toilet, and I thought I could make everything okay if I could only disappear."

Freeman continued staring out the window, feeling like a priest stuck in a confessional booth, wondering how priests handled all the heavy crap that got dumped on them.

"I barely ate any lunch that day, two bites from a bologna sandwich," Vicky continued. "I threw that up, too. Maybe if I got small enough, Daddy wouldn't notice me and then Mom would be happy. But Daddy never came back. And Mom blamed me. I've spent the rest of my life trying to make myself invisible."

A squirrel skittered along a branch in a tree outside, jumped to the next tree, and got lost in the leaves. Freeman exhaled. His breath tasted like old coins. He couldn't help it, his eyes were drawn to hers.

He knew the pain in her eyes. He'd seen it in the mirror enough times. Maybe he didn't have the market cornered on self-pity and hurt. Maybe he wasn't the only one in the world who was all alone.

He touched her shoulder. Her skin was warm. A frown

played against the bones of her face. She brushed her blond hair behind one ear, the unconscious gesture that tickled Freeman's guts.

"So now you know my secrets," she whispered.

"I don't think so," he said. "I believe that's the first time you've ever lied to me."

Her eyes widened. "I swear it's all true."

He caressed her cheek with the back of his hand. The act felt weird. Natural. "No, not the part about you wanting to disappear. I mean the part about me knowing your secrets. I'll bet you got plenty."

Her lips parted, Freeman was suddenly triptrapping, no, she was triptrapping him, and then they were triptrapping together, and she was almost into the part of his head where that long-ago night lived, tucked away in its dusty trunk, chained and double bolted, and he was pushing her thoughts away, and still they came on, into him, through his skin, through his blood, touching his heart, and he found that his arms were around her, pulling her close, those mysterious curves pressed against him, and their lips drew so close that he could feel the wind from her breath.

Behind Vicky, the door to the rec room opened, and Freeman froze, his face inches from Vicky's. She smelled of shampoo and meadows and sunshine.

Isaac poked his head through the door. "What are you guys up to?"

Freeman released Vicky and stepped away from her. "Nothing. She had something in her eye."

Vicky looked at Freeman and grinned. "Gym over?" she said to Isaac.

"Some of the kids said Starlene Rogers went into Thirteen," Isaac said. "Kracowski's giving her the treatment."

"No way," Freeman said. "Nobody's that dumb, even a grownup."

"I wonder if she saw the deadscape," Vicky said.

"You guys and your deadscape," Isaac said. "You're nutballs, did you know that?"

"So they keep telling us," Freeman said. "Let's go see what happened to Starlene."

"Wait," Isaac said. He stooped and picked up the penny from the floor. "Look what I found. Tail's up."

"That means bad luck," Vicky said.

"Is there any other kind?" Isaac said.

Allen came in, frowning, as if they were up to something sneaky just because no grownup had been supervising them. A bell rang in the hallway.

"You kids better hurry on to class," Allen said, disappointment in his voice. Probably wished he'd caught them smoking or something.

They walked past him, Isaac flipping the penny in the air. Freeman wondered how many more pennies Vicky had stashed away in her pockets and if he had enough thoughts for each of them.

THIRTY-ONE

A man in a uniform stopped Kracowski's Nissan at the front gate. The guard had a clipboard tucked under one arm, his neck so closely shaven that the skin was raw. Kracowski let his window down and looked at his twin reflections in the guard's mirrored sunglasses.

"What's the meaning of this?" Kracowski said.

"Name, sir?" The guard's tone was even, almost bored.

"You've got to be kidding." He pointed to the small walkie-talkie clipped to the guard's belt. "Let me speak to McDonald."

The man shook his head, the shades giving nothing away. "We have no McDonald. Please give me your name, sir."

"I have a better idea. Why don't you give me *your* name, so I can have your ass reamed for not knowing who I am?"

Kracowski squeezed the steering wheel. *McDonald and his damned spy games.* How many other agents of the Trust had been scattered around Wendover that Kracowski didn't know about? Probably a couple in the basement, beyond the range of his surveillance system. McDonald himself had insisted on staying at one of the counselor cottages, the one vacated by the frightened cleaning lady.

At least the guard didn't appear to be armed. It's a wonder the man didn't have a submachine gun strapped to his shoulder. Couldn't have any kids sneaking out, not with McDonald's secret superiors calling the shots. The electric fence was bad enough, but Kracowski resented this final humiliation.

"I'm only following orders, sir," the guard said.

"Whose orders?"

"I'm not at liberty to say. I need to check your name against this list to make sure you're authorized."

"*I* do the authorizing around here," Kracowski said.

McDonald came from behind the stone fence and walked to Kracowski's car, a steaming Styrofoam cup in his hand. "What's the problem?" he said to the guard.

"No problem, Mr. Lyons. I'm just explaining our security precautions to this man. No one in or out unless they're on this list."

McDonald tapped the guard on the shoulder. "Good. I can vouch for this man."

"Yes, sir."

To Kracowski, McDonald said, "Unlock the passenger door."

"Don't be ridiculous. I'm on my way home. I was up very early this morning."

"Yes. Arrived at 6:04 A.M., you were in your office with Paula Swenson until just before dawn; then we conducted an SST treatment on Starlene Rogers. You had lunch in your office: tuna salad, yogurt, and diet Sprite."

"Now wait a minute—"

"Unlock the door."

"Or what? Your rent-a-thug will write me a parking ticket?"

The guard's blank expression didn't yield. McDonald said, "This thing has gotten bigger. I just thought you'd like to be brought up to speed."

"I thought this was on a 'need-to-know' basis. You keep changing your catchphrases on me."

"Don't be a smartass, Doctor. Don't forget who holds the keys to your future. To your career. To your *ass*. One word from me and all your electronic toys go bye-bye."

Kracowski looked in the rearview mirror. The stones of Wendover glowed in the sun, the windows bright with the afternoon. In those rooms were children who needed his treatment. He had the power to make a difference in so many lives. And this group home was only the beginning. If his theories played out as he believed, then his name would be synonymous with a new revolution in the field of behavioral health. Freud, Skinner, Kracowski. A holy triumvirate.

But every revolution had its bloodshed, every freedom its price. ESP was the genie that came out of the lamp of knowledge, and the deadscape was the mystery hiding behind that one. If the Trust pulled the plug now, Kracowski might never make the final breakthrough. He unlocked the door and waited for McDonald to slide into the passenger seat.

" 'Lyons,' huh?" Kracowski said once his window was up. "Or is McDonald a fake, too? I'll bet your own mother doesn't even know your real name."

"That's 'need-to-know,' and right now, you don't. Drive."

"Where?"

"Your house."

Kracowski pulled through the gate. McDonald waved at the guard, who resumed his post, as stolid as the stone columns that supported the gate.

"Why have you put Wendover under siege?" Kracowski said. "And don't you think the locals are going to get a little suspicious with all these changes taking place? They don't get many secret government agents in these parts."

McDonald said nothing. He reached over and took Kracowski's brief case from the back seat. "What's the combination?"

"You can't be serious."

"Listen, I'm not stupid enough to think you leave all your data on Wendover's computers. I want everything you have on Starlene Rogers."

"I'm not keeping any secrets. You're the one blowing smoke all over the place."

"Don't waste your breath. We searched your home computer, and we know all about the early experiments. The ones you hoped had been forgotten, snowed under by the bullshit system."

"No charges were ever filed against me, and Bondurant—"

"Bondurant's a drunken jackass. He's only useful in the event something goes wrong and we need somebody to finger. He's a born victim, anyway. But I guess you figured that out a long time ago."

Kracowski licked his lips and kept his eyes on the gravel road. To the right was farmland that sprawled out in uneven humps, broken by creeks and patches of woods. Wendover was three miles from Elk Valley, which was useful when the clients ran away, because they always followed the main road straight into town. They became like animals that had been caged too long, their survival instinct lost.

"The combination," McDonald repeated.

Kracowski told him. McDonald flipped open the briefcase and rifled through the papers. He took the computer disks and tucked them into his pocket. "You're the trusting sort, aren't you? I figured you'd have a false bottom."

"I told you, I have nothing to hide."

"What about the data hidden on your hard drive at home?"

Kracowski looked in the mirror. Far behind them was a black sedan with tinted windows. Most people who used this road drove pick-ups. Kracowski rounded a bend and lost sight of the sedan.

"It's all theoretical, anyway. I would never have been able to prove it. Ghosts don't exist, McDonald."

"You're starting to come up with some catchphrases of your own."

"You can steal my disks and download my files and prowl through all the case histories, but you won't find a single shred of evidence that supports life after death."

"Except for the evidence I've seen with my own eyes."

"Eyes can lie, can't they?" He looked in the mirror. The sedan was still behind them, gaining fast. The farmland had given way to a planned development, big houses with landscaping and split-rail fences. The gravel road turned to asphalt and Kracowski pushed the accelerator.

"Slow down," McDonald said. "This isn't a James Bond movie."

"We're being followed."

"No, we're not. We're just both heading for the same destination at high speeds."

They reached the outskirts of Elk Valley, a smattering of gas stations and fast food restaurants mixed with ski rental outlets and roadside produce stands. The sedan dropped back to the speed limit as soon as Kracowski did, but maintained the distance between the two cars. Kracowski took a left and soon they were on the private road leading to the doctor's estate.

The house came into view between two magnificent oaks. It was a Colonial, white siding with black shutters, far more space than Kracowski needed living alone. He'd bought the property because of its eighty acres of pasture and forest, his boundaries reaching over the ridge so that no one could build above him. The mountains had always given him a sense of security, as if the dirt and granite would repel all invaders.

Kracowski parked by the barn and waited for McDonald. He'd decided that he would bide his time and see what kind of game the man was playing. McDonald waved to the sedan, which pulled to the front of the house. Two men got out of the car, the driver was dressed like the gate guard at Wendover, his familiar looking passenger in a rumpled gray jacket and tie. The back door of the sedan opened and Paula Swenson stepped into the sunshine. She wore sunglasses like the driver's.

"Time to meet your new partner," McDonald said, getting out of Kracowski's car.

McDonald led the way to Kracowski's house, fumbled in his pocket and came out with a key. Within seconds the door swung open and McDonald stepped aside so the others could enter.

"I thought you secret agents employed more sophisticated methods to gain illegal entry," Kracowski said.

"I've had a key almost as long as you have," McDonald said. "Thanks, Paula."

Paula almost smiled at him, then her face went blank again. Kracowski stared at her, for the first time wondering if what he had mistaken for admiration and affection in her eyes was actually animal cunning.

"Nothing happens by accident," McDonald continued. "You may think you moved here of your own free will, because of the important research you needed to conduct at Wendover, but didn't you ever wonder at how easily the red tape fell away? And why the Department of Social Services wasn't constantly breathing down your neck?"

"I should assume my house has been bugged?" Kracowski looked at the corners of the living room with new interest. "With tiny cameras planted all over the place? Where are they? In the mantel clock, maybe?"

"You're too trusting, Richard," Paula said. "You shouldn't have let me move in until you got to know me better."

Kracowski studied the two men from the sedan. The guard wore an unreadable expression that looked as if it would break before smiling. He'd taken off his sunglasses, but the eyes were as blank as windows.

The man in the gray jacket, on the other hand, had eyes that rolled in their sockets as if constantly on watch for phantoms. His face was wrinkled and pale, dark hair trimmed unevenly close to the scalp, sprouting out at the sides like some grotesque clown's. He smelled of institutional soap. His teeth worked together, chewing air.

"I want you to meet the man who is going to help you prove the existence of life after death," McDonald said. "Someone who was working for us in a similar capacity before he had . . . personal issues."

The anxious man nodded at the fireplace and picked a glass paperweight from a dusty hutch. He held it to one eye and squinted through it, his pupil made large and obscene.

"Dr. Kracowski, say hello to Dr. Kenneth Mills, esteemed clinical psychologist."

"A pleasure to meet me, Doctor," Kenneth Mills said. He turned abruptly and flung the paperweight into the fireplace, shattering it. Broken glass sprayed across the carpet. Neither McDonald nor the guard flinched. Swenson fumbled in her purse.

Mills grinned, showing sharp incisors to Kracowski. "I look forward to working with you. By the way, how's the boy?"

"Boy?" said Kracowski, blown off balance by the man's tempest.

The grin grew wider and sharper. "My son. Freeman."

THIRTY-TWO

Starlene touched the wall again just to be sure that the world was solid and real. She was still dizzy from the treatment, though the ghosts had faded the moment Kracowski had shut off the energy fields. Or were the ghosts still there, only she couldn't see them? What sort of boundaries did ghosts observe? Was the deadscape confined to the basement of Wendover, or were the spirits at this moment running their invisible hands across her flesh?

She felt safer here, in her cottage a hundred feet away and not in the musty bowels of the group home. She shared the cottage with another counselor, Marie, who was on vacation. Too bad, because Starlene could use some company, even if Marie was of that peculiar Baha'i faith. Marie's placid chatter would have been a welcome distraction from the memories of the ghosts.

Starlene picked up the phone and called the main building. "Randy?"

"Yeah," he answered, in the same cold manner he'd displayed toward her since the incident with the man at the lake. "What's going on?"

"I need to talk to you."

"You know I'm on duty."

She was careful to keep her voice level. She hated signs

of weakness or desperation in others, and she especially despised them in herself. "Can't one of the other counselors cover you for a few minutes?"

Randy sighed and put a hand over the mouthpiece. She heard his muffled voice as he called out to someone. Moments later, he was back on the line. "Allen will cover. We're in between classes right now, so we should be okay. You at your cottage?"

"Yes."

"Wait there. This had better be good."

She hung up and thought about calling her minister, to ask how ghosts fit in with God's plan for the world. What would Jesus do? If Jesus saw a ghost, what would He do? But the minister wouldn't understand, because his miracles were confined to the pages of the Bible.

She sat on the worn vinyl sofa that might have been here since the 1950s. The rest of the furniture was just as outdated, except for the few feminine touches she and Marie had injected. She picked up the cat-shaped throw pillow and hugged it to her chest. Something fluttered in the kitchenette and Starlene lifted her feet from the floor and tucked them under her knees.

A mouse. Probably only a mouse.

A knock came, and at first she thought it was Randy, although Randy usually pounded with the bottom of his fist instead of tapping.

"Come in," she said.

Another knock, softer than the first, and Starlene realized the knock had come from inside the house. The bathroom. *No one was in there.*

No one.

She could sit there scared half to death, waiting for Randy to come rescue her, or she could open the bathroom door and prove to herself that a ghost hadn't followed her from Wendover. Except you couldn't prove that ghosts didn't exist. Even when you had or hadn't seen them with your own eyes.

She put her feet on the floor. A Bible sat on the battered coffee table, the King James version, the Gospel. She picked it up. Bibles worked against evil, didn't they? Or was that only crosses? But what if the ghosts weren't evil? They had to be evil, or else God would have given them a proper place in heaven.

She pressed the Bible to her chest and went down the short hall to the bathroom. This was a job for Ecclesiastes. She sought scraps of remembered verse, something fortifying and enlightening. The knock came again, like an insistent whisper.

Starlene clutched the door handle. The metal was cold as a morgue slab. She wanted to run, Randy would grab her and hold her, she could cry on his shoulder and everything would be okay and all the bad stuff would go away and—

Running would show a lack of faith.

God in His mercy would never allow harm to come from the other side of the grave. And surely the dead were beyond sin. Even a soul damned for all eternity should have its license to harm revoked.

Maybe these souls were *good* souls, Christian folk who had gotten lost on the way to Rapture.

The knock came again, vibrating the air of the room. The deadscape experience had been subjective, a strange and short nightmare, a contrived memory that would have faded with time. This was real. This was happening. Before she could talk herself out of it, she twisted the handle and let the door swing open.

The boy was on his knees, his face as white as the porcelain sink. The hand that had tapped at the door was poised in the air, quivering. His dark eyes were wild and lost, his lips trying to form words. The sun cut an orange slash between the curtains, the light parted the boy's hair, specks of dust spun in the air.

"Deke," she said. "Where have you been?"

His mouth gaped. He was a beggar asking for impossible things. She wanted to reach out to him, but was afraid of what he might do. She had read his case history, and had even built part of it. Sociopathic behavior couldn't be flipped on and off like a light switch, no matter what Kracowski believed.

The door to the linen closet was ajar. Deke must have hidden there since he'd gone missing the day before. The cottage windows were easy to break into. Starlene had forced her way inside several times after misplacing the house key.

His silence was eerie, so she spoke in her authoritative counselor voice. "What are you doing here?"

Deke still didn't speak. Sweat beaded the boy's skin, and though his face looked young and frightened, his eyes were those of a ninety-year-old man's staring down a terminal disease. The bathroom smelled sticky sweet with vomit. And something else.

Starlene stepped forward, pores tightening on the back of her neck, the hairs like electric wires.

Deke shook his head. "It wasn't me," he whispered, one eyelid twitching, his fingers trembling.

Then Starlene saw what was in the bathtub.

She put her hands over her face, trying to block the red images that spattered her mind. She backed down the hall, begging her legs to work, shouting at her feet to stop being so heavy, wanting nothing but the door and the lawn and a sane sky overhead and no more ghosts and no red things in the tub and—

Hands clutched at her before she reached the front door, two or a thousand. She screamed again and slapped the hands away.

"What in God's name?" Randy said.

"In there," she gasped. The words tasted of Ajax cleanser. Randy disappeared into the bathroom, then came back out moments later.

"Whatever it was is gone," he said. "Spider? Or a mouse? We get a lot of mice out here."

How could he not have seen it? Smelled it?

"The tub," she said.

"Nothing in there."

"Where's Deke?"

"Deke? You know he's gone missing, don't you? Are you okay? You don't look so hot."

She pushed past him into the bathroom, bracing for the nightmare vision that awaited. The tub was empty, except for a bottle of shampoo that had fallen from the shelf and her damp towel hanging over the shower rod. No mutilated corpse, no gleaming bones, no blood running in rivulets down the shower curtain.

And no Deke.

She yanked open the door to the linen closet.

Nothing but towels, extra toilet paper, first aid supplies, and tampons. No hideaway teenager.

No dead body.

No ghost.

She turned and went into the living room. Randy followed, waited until she'd taken a bottled water from the refrigerator and downed half of it, then he said, "Not again."

She sat in the thrift-shop armchair and picked at the cotton. "What do you mean?"

"You saw the man again, didn't you? The one from the lake, the one you nearly drowned yourself over. The invisible man."

"No." The carbonated water's bubbles bit her throat.

"Look, Starlene, you don't have to lie to me. I thought we had something going between us. A little thing called 'trust.'"

"Trust lasts about as far as you can throw it."

"Trust me. Tell me."

"So you can laugh at me again?"

"I don't think it's funny. I'm worried about you. You need to get some help."

Her laughter was as brittle as thin ice. "Help? Maybe I've had too much help."

"Tell me what you think you saw." He sat on the plaid couch. The pattern clashed with his checked shirt and sandy eyebrows. His face was square, precise, not the kind of face that would forgive foolishness. Randy was a rock.

So was God a rock. And the deadscape was a hard place. And she was caught in between.

The ghosts weren't imprisoned in the basement of Wendover. They had been set free by electromagnetic energy or evil forces or the will of the Almighty. The dead had taken up their robes and walked.

"Deke is dead," she said.

"He ran away. He's done that before. Usually he goes to town and breaks in somewhere and steals some beer, and the police find him sleeping it off behind a Dumpster. We'll find him."

"You won't find him. He didn't run away. He ran *here*."

Randy leaned forward. "Here?"

"I saw him in the bathroom."

"Saw him? But he couldn't have escaped. You've only got one door."

"Maybe he didn't need a door."

"Honey, we need to get you to the main building. You need to see somebody."

"You mean, besides somebody who doesn't exist?" The image of Deke on his knees, skin like snow, one hand holding—

Silver and red.

She closed her eyes. "I'm okay. I stayed up too late, that's all. I need a nap before my shift."

Randy's gray eyes narrowed. The square slab of his face softened. "You sure you're okay?"

"Yeah. Really. If a shrink can't sort things out for herself, she's not got much of a career ahead, right?"

His face split into a smile. "That's my girl."

He patted her hand, leaned forward, and for a moment Starlene thought he was going to kiss her, but he gave her a brief hug and stood. "When do you go on duty?"

"Four."

"I'll buy you a cup of coffee, then. Enjoy your nap."

"Randy?"

"Yeah?"

"What are you hiding from me?"

"Nothing."

"You work with Kracowski a lot. What's he up to?"

"I don't know anything. Remember when I told you not to ask too many questions?"

She nodded, pressed the cold water bottle to her forehead, and reached for the Bible on the end table. The wall between them was as invisible as a faded ghost, but might as well have been miles thick. How far could you throw trust? "Sorry I scared you."

"We'll find Deke. Don't worry."

"I'm not worried."

"The Lord is my Shepherd—"

"I shall not want."

He was gone, and the cottage was silent besides the hum of the refrigerator and the soft rattle of leaves against the foundation.

She would have to face it sooner or later. She would have to look in the mirror, to see if her eyes were bright and her skull cracked and her brains sliding from her face. She would have to stare herself down and give herself a good scolding.

The bathroom door stood open. The linen closet was as she had left it. The tub was empty. Deke no longer haunted her.

She twisted the tap on the sink, splashed cold water on her face. The woman in the mirror was pale, eyes wild, but she had seen worse. She patted herself dry with a towel, then saw the disposable Gillette razor she'd used to shave her legs the day before.

The handle lay beside the toilet, the head torn, plastic bands curling. The blades were gone.

THIRTY-THREE

Freeman couldn't concentrate on the history lesson. Ever since group homes had been turned into charter schools, with shrinks and teachers teaming up to make a bad situation worse, education had become yet another weapon the system used against you. Take the history teacher, for example. He might as well have "This space for rent" stamped across his pasty forehead, but he got to decide who was smart and who had a future and which kids were failures. All because he wore a necktie.

Leave it to a loser to be able to pick out the other losers. The teacher's voice was like chalk on a blackboard as he talked about patriots sneaking onto somebody else's ship and dumping tea into the Boston harbor. Creepy little vandals. And now they were hailed as heroes.

People sure didn't know much about heroism back then. The patriots even dressed up as Indians, that's how pathetic they were. The teacher was calling them Freedom Fighters. If you did that kind of thing today, you'd be called a terrorist and locked up for observation with no attorney. Or shot on sight.

Well, the winning side always wrote the history books and freedom was subjective. Being confined in a group home with barbed wire around the perimeter, right here

in the Land of the Free that God had blessed above all
other countries, didn't seem a bit contradictory to the
teacher. Having Social Services telling Freeman where to
live wasn't exactly what the Constitution meant by the
"pursuit of happiness." The First Amendment didn't pre-
vent shrinks from getting an endless ride inside his head.
To Freeman, it seemed the only people who got to do
what they wanted were the grownups and the ghosts.

At least Vicky was in this class. He tuned out the
squeaky teacher and looked at the back of Vicky's head.
The sun was in her hair, and the air around her almost
shimmered. She sat in the front, by the window, a consequence of alphabetical order. Freeman was always stuck
in the middle of the class. At least he had a good view of
the mountains from here, and the fence that kept the
world a safe distance away.

Vicky dropped her pencil, bent from her desk, and
winked at him. He tried a triptrap, caught something
about doughnuts, so he smiled. Then the door opened and
a man in a blue suit and sunglasses entered the classroom
and whispered in the teacher's ear.

Suits meant something at Wendover, so the teacher listened, then said, "Class, we've had an emergency and
everyone needs to report to the dorms."

The class erupted with murmurs of glee and gossip.
Isaac slapped his book closed and stared at Freeman as if
this were all his fault. Isaac was way too serious about
learning. Or maybe he was scared by the "emergency,"
because, even if he thought Freeman was bullshitting
about the deadscape, Isaac had to admit that things were
getting pretty weird around this place.

As the kids filed out, Freeman went to Vicky's desk.
"What is it?" she whispered.

"What do I look like, a sawed-off Nostradamus or something? Ask Dipes, he's the one who can see the future."

"Oh, so you're in one of your patented mood swings. And you're going to make sure everybody suffers a little."

Why was she mad at him? He thought they were friends, maybe even more than that after this morning, when they had shared a "special moment."

Girls. Who could ever figure them out?

"It's okay to be afraid," she said.

"I'm not afraid," he said, even though the man in the suit and sunglasses was headed straight for him. The Suit had the Trust written all over him, from his buzz cut to his creased jaw to his shiny shoes. Even his cologne was by the book, making a weak attempt at feigned personality.

"I'll be thinking about you," Vicky said, and then the man had a hand on Freeman's shoulder and Freeman thought about ducking and running for the door, but what was the use? The room was a prison and Wendover was a prison and the world beyond the electric fence was just a bigger prison, because he'd been condemned to a life sentence inside his own skull.

"I owe you a penny," Vicky said, and lightning flashed across his soul and his skeleton rattled and ten thousand elves in cleats stomped across his skin. She had trip-trapped him.

The Suit said, "Mr. Mills, you need to come with me."

Not a question. Not a request. Just a fact of life.

The Suit led him past the teacher, who was rattling some papers in a bottom drawer. Freeman couldn't resist a Pacino wisecrack. "Guess this means no homework?"

The teacher got busy erasing the chalkboard, even though nothing was written on it. Freeman looked back at Vicky, who flashed him a thumbs-up. The inside of his brain itched and he had no way to scratch it.

In the hall, The Suit stood even taller, his leather shoes squeaking as he marched Freeman in a familiar direction.

"You can take your hand off me now," Freeman said, trying to be Eastwood–cold. "I'm not running."

The Suit said nothing, having used up his requisition of syllables. What did they teach these guys in Secret Agent School, anyway? Besides how to keep from smiling. Back in the good old days, before Mom died, men like The Suit would sometimes stop by and visit his dad. Even at age six, Freeman knew these guys were bad news. They all smelled of hidden ammunition and secrets.

"I know the way," Freeman said. "Room Thirteen. I've spent some of the best moments of my life there."

They passed Bondurant's office and a couple of classrooms. The door to Kracowski's lab was closed. Freeman wondered how many people would be on the other side of the two-way mirror this time. No doubt the mad doctor had rounded up some spectators for his favorite rat's next run at the maze.

The Suit tapped on the door to Thirteen. The wing of the building was empty. You could almost hear dust collecting in the corners. The electronic lock beeped, then the latch clicked like an executioner's pistol.

"Hello, Freeman," said Randy.

Freeman disliked Randy, not just because he was a jock, but because he had the chin of a Secret Agent type. He wore his chin as if it were a boxing glove. Randy had the double disadvantage of being a counselor.

"Let me guess," Freeman said, climbing onto the cot while The Suit waited by the door. "Either I've just been selected as the next contestant on *Fear Factor* or the doctor's going to put the screws to me again."

Kracowski's voice descended from the hidden speaker in the ceiling. "We would never do anything to hurt you, Freeman."

He flipped a bird at the mirror. "Hitler was sincere, too. And those guys who dumped the tea in the harbor. And God. And all the other bastards back through history who messed with innocent people."

"I'm sorry you feel that way. I thought the last treatment would have helped you overcome your anger."

"Oh, I'm not angry. I've never been better."

Randy rubbed Vaseline on Freeman's temples and attached the electrodes. Then he tapped the flesh on the inside of Freeman's elbow, drew out a syringe, and injected an iridescent, syrupy substance.

"Seriously," Freeman said. "You don't have to sell me on the idea. I *believe* I'm better."

"No, you don't." Kracowski took on that familiar tone of all the shrinks who had ever subjected Freeman to their utter sincerity. The tone of smugness, rightness, absolute certainty. A tone that God Himself might use if He ever bothered to speak.

"Do we need the straps?" Randy asked the mirror.

"How about it, Freeman?" Kracowski asked.

"I promise to behave."

"We only want you to be better."

"I know. You and all the other brain police. Did it ever occur to you that I'm *happy* being a suicidal manic depressive? And if you just want to help me, why do you make me take ESP tests?"

Randy put a hand on Freeman's chest and forced him onto his back, then unreeled the canvas straps from beneath the bed. Freeman stared at the ceiling tiles, trying to picture the strange gizmos and wires of Kracowski's machines. The walls must be filled with them, too, the electronic bloodstream of the SST equipment. All connected to those big tanks and computers in the basement, which was the heart of the mad doctor's monster maker.

While the brain lay behind that mirror.

Freeman craned his neck to stare at the cold glass as Randy attached padded cuffs to his ankles and wrists. Clint Eastwood would never let them see him flinch. Clint would think of something clever to say, as if living or dying were pretty much the same to him.

"What do you have in mind this time, Doc?" Freeman said. "Want me to bring back a little souvenir from the deadscape? Maybe your Momma's underwear?"

"Freeman, you need to relax in order for the treatment to be effective. This is important."

Randy made a final check on the restraints. He pulled a hard rubber mouthpiece from a drawer and pressed it into Freeman's mouth. That meant a major shock was coming. Freeman waited until Randy was gone and the door had closed, then pushed the mouthpiece out with his tongue.

"Who you got over there with you, Doc?"

"Just a few . . . friends."

Freeman tried to think of something wise-assed to say, like "With friends like yours, who needs enemies?" but that was too corny, and besides, the Vaseline made his skin itch and his chest ached and he realized he'd never been this scared in all his life. Not even when Dad had locked him in the closet for two days. Not even when Dad cornered him with the blowtorch. Not even when he came out of one of Dad's treatments and carried the knife into the bathroom where Mom—

No, that never happened.

Then his thoughts turned to broken bits of alphabet as the juice hit and the lights dimmed and his ears crackled and buzzed. The scream didn't come from inside his throat. Instead, it clawed its way from the center of his brain, writhing like a fanged worm, chewing up his hippocampus and thalamus and vomiting pain against the curved plates of his skull.

His bones turned to air and his eyes clamped shut but still he saw the blackness beyond color, a black that had never existed in nature, a dark solid mass that crawled into his lungs and smothered his heart and seeped into his bloodstream.

Then the darkness eased, giving way to a mottled gray,

and people walked toward him across the land of smoke and sorrow.

The Miracle Woman led them, a Moses of the damned, naked and blind and beautiful. All those shuffling behind her, the stooped, the wild-eyed, the scarred, were just as lifeless; impossible things, spirits that clung to bodies that by rights should have long been abandoned.

Freeman tried to yell at the doctor to shut off the god-damned machines and get him the hell out of there. But he knew, through some instinct older than consciousness, that this world was connected to the other *real* world only by the human bridges that were subjected to SST. Those who could read minds beckoned the ones brought from the dead by Kracowski's weird machines. Freeman was cut off from the real world until Kracowski pushed his little God buttons and made everything normal again. He was all alone now, as alone as Clint in the Italian desert scrapping for a fistful of dollars.

He shifted himself, the straps gone, the mirror gone, Thirteen gone. He found he could move as if swimming in thick water, though he could see through his own skin and he weighed a thousand pounds. His feet were lost in the strange mist that covered the deadscape like an ever-shifting skin. He tried to run but the Miracle Woman raised a hand, and though her eye sockets were torn and empty, the mouth wasn't scary at all now. The mouth was sad.

Freeman looked past her at the pale and aimless legion. He saw the old man in the gown, the one who had shuffled past him on Freeman's first day at Wendover and had recently walked on water. A stooped woman nodded constantly, as if her head were on a spring, gaunt fingers yanking her long hair. A thin, ebony-skinned man in coveralls bit his fingertips. One of the ghosts, a man with a broad and blank face, did a dervish dance, clumsy despite his lack of substance. He, too, wore an institutional gown.

Freeman backed away, trying to figure out the laws of

this new universe, commanding his transparent flesh to run. He wasn't breathing, but still the air tasted of ash. Behind him the smoke stretched as far as he could see, and layers of gray clouds marked the seams of the sky. He reached up and the threads of his hand mingled with the deadscape.

He was part of the deadscape.

He was one of them.

Dead.

A member of that sick and shuffling crowd, those who wore masks of pain and hopelessness and confusion. Chained to their humanity, though being human must have been the most horrible punishment ever inflicted upon them. Not even death had released them from their agony. They might have walked the deadscape for centuries, but time had no meaning here, which would make it the cruelest death sentence of all. Could God be that cruel?

The ebony man bit off his pinky and spat it into the mist. The dervish spun and his lips parted in a silent chant. The Miracle Woman came nearer, her palm lifted in supplication, the torn eyeball in it staring at Freeman as if he owed her an explanation.

Freeman wanted to disappear, wanted to jump back into the real world with its ordinary despair, but his feet were part of the mist, his skin sewn into the fabric of this ethereal tapestry.

The Miracle Woman stood inches away from him, the silent ghosts looking on. She moved her hands to her face. Freeman tried not to stare at her white breasts and curves, and the mysterious dark patch between her legs. Then she moved her hands away and her eyes were in her head, she blinked and smiled.

"I'm not going to hurt you," she said. Except her lips didn't move. This was a triptrap from the dead, and as creepy as hearing the thoughts of another human being was, it was nothing compared to the cold, sharp words that came from the Miracle Woman.

A triptrap from the dead.

Then more thoughts gushed through him, *into* him, a multitude of voices drove spikes through his soul. He felt their pain, he absorbed their bleak pity, he ate their psychic sickness.

"A white, white room in which to write."

"The answers are hidden in the television."

"I am a tree I am a tree I am a tree and I leave."

"The voices in my head are telling me to listen."

"Yes, doctor, I AM feeling much better, thank you."

More voices, other phrases, scraps of broken sorrow.

And the Miracle Woman: *"You don't belong here yet."*

Freeman wanted to shout that he'd never asked to be here, he'd never volunteered to have ESP in the first place, he'd never wanted any special gifts, he just wanted to be a normal boy with a Mom and a Dad and a dog and a house that didn't hurt and no weird games with Daddy and no experiments and no Department of Social Services and no Wendover and no Kracowski and no Trust and no more people trying to heal him when he'd never been broken in the first place, but then the voices all ran together and he knew what it was like to be insane, because the deadscape was nothing if not a land of the insane, and it certainly wasn't *nothing* because he was here now and it was real and this was everything and forever and God made a place like this for people who couldn't help themselves or maybe insane people made God and the voices in his head and the triptrap dead and yes doctor daddy daddy daddy had a white, white room in which to write I'm feeling much better now television in my tree God is an antenna is a computer is a doctor I'm feeling much better now blade in my brain and cut out the bad part and shock me doctor I'm feeling much better now leave me alone daddy daddy daddy and why are you dead Mommy—

"You don't belong here yet."

The Miracle Woman's words were softer now, caressing, and the other voices faded like a radio dropped down a hole and the smoke shifted, became more solid, and the ghosts dissolved, and the Miracle Woman smiled, and the gray gave way to the darkness.

And Freeman was alone in the darkness.

How long was forever?

Just as he reached for his chest, to see if his heart was still beating, another voice reached him like a golden shaft of light.

It was Vicky, and she said, "Told you you're not alone."

THIRTY-FOUR

"My, how you've grown," Dr. Kenneth Mills whispered to the dark-tinted window.

In the room on the other side of the glass, Freeman stared blankly at the ceiling, lips forming nonsense syllables as he struggled against the restraints. Kracowski watched Dr. Mills's face. No protective parental instinct flickered on those intense features. The only resemblance between father and son was the wild panic in their eyes. At least Freeman had the excuse of an electric shock jarring his flesh against his skeleton.

Dr. Mills had no excuse. Unless madness was an excuse. Mills's defense attorney had certainly used madness as a motive. So Mills had only served six years in a state psychiatric hospital, and McDonald's people had enough pull to have him pronounced "cured" and fit for society. Even spouse mutilators were redeemable in the modern mental health care system.

Kracowski pulled a sheet of data from the printer and matched it against the graphs on the computer screen. Freeman's EKG was strong, with a few aberrant spikes, but nothing that would indicate serious damage. The magnetic signatures of the middle frequency ranges showed decreased amplitude, and the PET scan painted Freeman's brain in warm colors.

"You've expanded my theory in dramatic fashion," Mills said.

McDonald frowned from the corner of the lab. Kracowski pretended to study the data. Mills bent forward, his breath making a mist on the glass. The walls vibrated slightly from the machinery that created the calibrated array of electromagnetic waves.

"But your data are still unreliable," Mills said. "You should have stuck to my ratios of magnetism to electricity. And you've totally ignored the subjective elements of my theory. Focus on the hippocampus, where you can scramble memories before they're even made."

"This wasn't part of the deal," Kracowski said to McDonald. "I thought you were going to give me more time, not bring in somebody to meddle."

"I didn't hear you object when we opened our files and gave you all the research," the agent said. "Who else would have funded you and given you access to our brave little volunteers? Unloved children don't exactly grow on trees, you know."

"That was the hardest part for me," Mills said. "Finding subjects. In the end, I found it was easier to grow my own."

In Thirteen, Freeman writhed against the canvas straps, back arched, face contorted.

"Ooh, that must have been a good one," Mills said. "I like the way you've increased the voltage in your version. That risky bilateral shock is bound to wipe out some short-term memory."

Kracowski's hands tightened on the sheet of paper. Synaptic Synergy Therapy was *his* idea. Mills had made some advances in the ESP theory, adding classic brainwashing techniques to the delight of his backers, but Kracowski saw the mistakes Mills had made. Mills counted on subjective influence, human interaction, the power of suggestion. All smoke and mirrors.

Kracowski had reduced the process to pure science. Cold numbers and waveforms and logic. Quantum thought. Truth. He'd accomplished in only two years what Mills had fumbled around with for nearly a decade.

"Dr. Mills, I'm afraid I have to disagree with you," Kracowski said.

Mills turned from the window as if reluctant to miss Freeman's agony but compelled to win any argument, no matter its nature. "How can you disagree with *results*?"

"Your work was impure. Your adherence to traditional psychiatric techniques affected your outcomes."

"Wrong, Dr. Kracowski. The Trust wanted ESP, and I gave it to them. Freeman. The first human in the history of the world to have the gift induced through scientific means."

"But you were only able to generate it in one patient." Kracowski looked over Mills's shoulder at Freeman, then glanced at the clock. "I have a dozen case histories that prove my therapy has widespread applications. For improving the overall operation of the brain, not just focusing on a single power. *I'm* the one who is discovering scientific proof of life after death."

McDonald watched as if the doctors were two bugs battling in a Mason jar. He finally spoke. "You forget who your boss is. That's a mistake you can't afford to keep making. *We* decide what is proof, and *we* decide who is alive and who is dead."

Mills grinned at Kracowski like a fanged jack-o'-lantern. "He's right. He's always been right."

McDonald took the paper from Kracowski's hand and scanned the data. "Nothing too unusual here."

"How long?" Mills asked.

Kracowski checked the computer. "Ten minutes, fourteen seconds."

"I have to confess, Dr. Kracowski, maybe you *have* made some advances. Under my formula, Freeman would be dead by now."

Freeman had been lucky to survive in the first place. Mills's experiments went too far. All because Mills relied on emotional turmoil in the subject. All because Mills needed that final shock to push Freeman over the edge. Mills's case files on his son were filled with enough trauma to fill a dozen mental wards. And those sessions in which he force-fed his own sick thoughts into Freeman's brain—

"Stop at eleven minutes," McDonald said.

Kracowski rankled at the agent's self-righteous tone. As if McDonald had even the vaguest understanding of the work. At least Mills understood that discovery was more important than the resulting effects of that discovery. McDonald only wanted something he could show his superiors, a weapon so abstract that it could never be applied toward military objectives. Knowledge had never served a positive political purpose, and wisdom had rarely intersected with knowledge, at least where political power was concerned.

"Why do you want to stop at eleven?" Mills turned back to the window, savoring the torture etched into his son's face.

"Supposed to be a mystical number," McDonald said.

Kracowski pressed his lips together to keep from speaking and watched the digits blink upward.

"What do you suppose he's seeing?" Mills said.

"For his sake, I hope it's the future and not the past," Kracowski said.

THIRTY-FIVE

Not alone. Not alone. Not alone.

Freeman peered into the dwindling gloom. Vicky was in here somewhere, trapped in this same gray deadscape. Her voice came to him again.

"Triptrap, Freeman. Reach out to me."

How could he reach with arms that were heavy as mud? The ghosts had dissolved and the darkness pressed in on all sides. He wanted to speak but his throat was clogged with black oxygen. Then he remembered he didn't have to speak. Not out loud, anyway.

"Where are you?" he thought.

"The Green Room," came Vicky's voice. "They made us go to our beds."

"I saw them. The dead people. The Miracle Woman—"

"I know. I was with you the whole time."

"How did you do that?"

"My brain works better now. Even when I'm not in Thirteen. They must have really juiced up the machines and maybe it's spilling over or something."

"How am I supposed to get out of here?"

Freeman turned his head, looking for any sort of dismal sunrise in this land of midnight. He hoped he wasn't dead. He didn't want to spend another second in this place, much less an eternity. A hum drifted from the unseen distance, growing louder, as if a monstrous swarm of insects was approaching.

"Vicky?"

The sky broke apart and became part of the swarm. The darkness spun, the horizons narrowed, a frozen wind arose from somewhere below. Freeman shouted, but his words were lost in the surreal tornado. As he felt his body being lifted, he grabbed for the darkness that had seemed so solid only moments before.

He found himself on the cot in Thirteen. His stomach fluttered and his head throbbed. He opened his eyes to a blurred world of soft light and moving shadows. People stood around the bed, and for a moment, Freeman thought they were ghosts, and he closed his eyes again, but then someone loosened the restraints.

He heard a voice that sent an icy stake through his heart, a voice that was worse than death, a voice that sent him shivering and made the memories spill from that dark space under the bridge.

"Hey, Trooper."

Dad.

Freeman's eyes snapped open as if awakening to escape a nightmare, only to find the nightmare was there in the flesh, standing at the foot of the bed.

Dad.

The fucking troll. Out of the loony bin. How had he found Freeman?

No, the question wasn't *how* he had found Freeman. The question was, what had taken him so long? Because Dad had promised to finish the job. After Freeman had testified in the judge's private chambers, Dad had stood up in court and screamed at his son, frothing at the mouth as if to verify a self-diagnosis of sociopathic schizophrenia. Freeman had known, even as a six year old, that Dad never lied, at least not about enjoying his only son's pain.

"I'm going to triptrap you to death," Dad had shouted

that day six years ago, and now Dad repeated it so softly that only Freeman heard. He added, "Because we both know what really happened to your mother, don't we?"

"What was that?" Kracowski said.

"A secret joke between Freeman and me," Dad said. "Right, Trooper?"

"Trooper" had been Dad's pet name for Freeman, usually used in public when Dad was pretending to be affectionate. But Freeman knew the real meaning behind the name, because Dad loved to torment him with it. Like the time he'd hooked Freeman to the machines in the closet and said, "I'm melting your brain like I melted your toy soldiers. You're a trooper. You're going to be a soldier in a different kind of war."

Freeman rubbed his wrists where they'd chafed against the restraints. Kracowski checked Freeman's pulse, then shined a penlight into each of his pupils. Freeman stared back at the light, hoping it would burn him blind so he wouldn't have to look at his father.

"No outward sign of neurological damage," Kracowski said.

Dad pushed the doctor away. "Well, we've got plenty of time yet, don't we?" He stared down at Freeman, his chin sharp, his teeth too white and narrow, his eyes bulging.

Then Dad triptrapped him, just like the old days, only Freeman was smarter now and Dad was a little out of practice. Dad's strange broken thoughts bounced off the shield that Freeman had thrown up and Freeman felt a surge of triumph.

I can knock down the troll, Freeman thought. *He's not going to eat me for his dinner.*

But the euphoria died as Dad cracked the blockade and roared into his mind like a hurricane of knives. To the bystanders, Kracowski and Randy and McDonald, it probably looked like Dad was leaning down to kiss Freeman on the forehead. But Dad was really getting close so that his frontal lobe could spew its poison through the bone of Freeman's skull. Dad let loose, as if he'd been storing up his anger for years while locked behind bars in a Dorothea Dix psychiatric unit, pretending to slowly get better, acting as if the medication was working and believing that, yes, Kenneth Mills had committed a terrible wrong, but now Kenneth was all better, and with the benevolent blessings of the government shrinks who'd pronounced him sound and sane, Kenneth Mills was now ready to pick up where he'd left off.

And ready to see just how much damage Freeman could withstand.

Dad's words tumbled forth in fractured phrases. "How dare you . . . thought you'd escaped me, didn't you, you little shit? Kracowski's trying to steal my thunder . . . but we both know *I'm* the only one who can control minds around here. The crazy fucks . . . babbling about spirits and the deadscape . . . hey, you really *do* think you saw ghosts . . . you're a chip off the old block, aren't you, Trooper? Madder than a fucking hatter."

This was just like the old days, when Dad hadn't been afraid to juice himself in the interest of science; though Freeman was the star pupil. Kracowski called it SST, but Dad hadn't needed a fancy acronym. Dad had simply called it "triptrap."

"How is he?" McDonald said.

"He's perfect," Kracowski replied.

"No, I mean, did we learn anything?"

Dad turned his attention from Freeman to Kracowski. Kracowski shook his head at McDonald. "I can't tell yet. My treatment is designed to work in an emotional vacuum. I'll have to see how the subject responds to this disturbance."

"Disturbance?" Dad screamed at Kracowski. "You're the one that's disturbing. I was right on the threshold of a breakthrough. All you've done is come in and stir the stew, but it's my recipe."

Freeman sighed with relief because Dad was out of his head for the moment and he could breathe and think again.

Dad pointed a finger at McDonald. "Your guys could have freed me a lot sooner. But, no, I guess I was disposable because you found Kracowski and figured one scientist was as good as another. Only you found out that you needed me because Kracowski here has these little moral qualms and will only push the buttons so far—"

McDonald crossed the room and backhanded Dad across the cheek. The blow was so intense that even Freeman felt it, the raw pain flickering across his mind like a lightning strike.

Dad fell to his knees, rubbing his cheek where he'd been struck. Dad smiled. "Not bad. With a goon like you in charge of this operation, maybe the Trust will take over the world yet."

McDonald stared at the mirror, expressionless. "We tried to protect you, Mills, but murdering your wife was something even the Trust couldn't bury, not the way you did it." His eyes darted to Freeman. "Right there in front of witnesses."

"It was in the interest of science," Dad said. "I had to keep pushing him. You have to admit, even though Kracowski's had a little success, Freeman still outshines them all. He's a regular triptrapper from hell, the world's first workable spirit spy."

"Results will speak for themselves."

Freeman tried his tongue. "Sorry. I don't know what your game is, but I'm not playing anymore. You can shock me until my brain fries, like those eggs in the anti-drug commercials, but you're never going to break me."

Freeman sat up and glanced at Dad, then looked back at McDonald. "*He* couldn't burn me out, and Kracowski doesn't have the slightest idea what it's all about."

"Synergy," Kracowski said. "Tapping the brain's potential."

"Wrong," Freeman said. "It's about control."

McDonald's lips tightened in a movement that would have passed for a smile on someone else's face. "Control. The boy's not so dumb after all."

"Except you got it wrong, too." Freeman said. "You can build bigger bombs and faster planes and deadlier chemicals, but there's one thing you'll never control."

Dad had risen and leaned over Freeman again. Freeman turned away but Dad was already up from his troll hole and standing on the bridge, eating Freeman's thoughts.

Dad straightened and laughed. "The little trooper thinks you're not after ESP at all, McDonald. He thinks you're wanting the *ghosts*. Is that why they call you secret government types 'spooks'?"

McDonald said nothing. Randy waited by the door, arms crossed. Kracowski looked down at the floor as if trying to picture the strange spirits that swirled in the mists of the deadscape.

Freeman waited until the shock of Dad's invasion faded, then reached out for Vicky. Anything was possible. The mind was an incredible machine, so incredible it could even be a weapon. But right now, all he wanted was one slim bridge between himself and somebody he could trust.

He triptrapped, but his thoughts couldn't reach beyond the room. Vicky had abandoned him. Despite her promises. But, then, hadn't he learned a long time ago that you couldn't count on anybody?

He was alone again, except for the mad, dead voices that still whispered from the corners of his soul.

THIRTY-SIX

Starlene wanted a shower to blast the creepy feeling from her skin, but she couldn't face the bathroom, no matter what Randy said she hadn't seen. No matter that ghosts didn't exist and that only God had the ability to inspire visions. God's visions were fire and thunder, not feverish thugs and bloody corpses.

She went into the little bedroom she shared with Marie. Due to their rotating shifts, the two of them rarely stayed here at the same time. They both had places offsite, so the room was only sparsely decorated, and didn't reflect their true personalities.

Starlene picked up a book, something thick and dull by the Southern novelist Jefferson Spence. She couldn't concentrate on the meandering sentences, and after the author's second clumsy allusion to snowy fields of cotton, she closed the book and looked out the window.

A soft mist hung over the lake. She half expected to see the old man in the gown drift up from the water. Clouds had begun to gather over the mountains, pushed by a slow wind. The shadows of clouds crawled across the slopes, resembling great black beasts. The air was heavy with moisture.

A knock at the door caused her to drop the novel. It barely missed crushing her toe. She paused in the hall, making sure the knock hadn't come from the bathroom. No, it was at the front door.

Bondurant nodded at her when she opened the door, then staggered into the room before she could ask what he wanted. His face was blanched and his hands trembled. He adjusted his glasses on his long nose and licked his lips.

"You look terrible," she said.

"Like I've seen a ghost?"

"Worse. Like maybe a mirror."

"Can I sit down?"

"That depends. Are you ready to tell me what's going on?"

He shrugged and looked behind him, then peered at the corners of the ceiling. "Have to be careful. You never know who's listening."

"Are you looking for invisible people?"

"Bugs."

"We sprayed for those last month, remember?"

"I'm not talking about those kind of bugs. I'm talking electronic bugs." Bondurant coughed, and the odor of liquor filled the room. Purple welts beneath his eyes gave him the appearance of a punch-drunk insomniac. Starlene didn't know how much faith she could put in anything he said.

"Got anything to drink?" he asked, checking out the countertops in the kitchenette.

"Aren't you on duty?"

Bondurant sighed and sat on the edge of an armchair. He didn't remove his coat. "What happened when Kracowski zapped you this morning?"

"You know. You were there."

He waved one hand in the air. "I saw him press some buttons and flip switches. I saw you in Thirteen. I saw you gasp and scream and stop breathing. And then it was over. But I want to know what *happened*."

"Mr. Bondurant, I've questioned that treatment ever

since I started working here. Are you telling me you're just now starting to have some doubts?"

"What did you *see*?" He leaned forward, his face contorted, and she backed away and stood by the door. He didn't rise from the chair, or she might have fled. "You're in on it, too, aren't you?" he said.

"In on what?"

"The whole thing. I thought you were a Christian."

"I *am* a Christian. And I have no idea what you're talking about."

"They're meddling in God's domain. Only God can draw the line between the living and the dead." He talked faster, spittle flying from his mouth. "Only God says who gets into heaven and who must walk through the fires of hell. So why is God, in His almighty wisdom, letting that heathen freak bring back the spirits of those who have already faced the Judgment?"

"Look, a lot of weird stuff is happening around here, but I don't think you need to drag God into this. Put the blame where it belongs."

"That's the whole problem. They've pushed God out of everything. The Supreme Court has locked Him out of the schools, the government pushes for a United Nations that only serves atheists, and now they've taken over Wendover, where I've turned so many lost souls toward the light of our Lord." He pounded a fist against the padded chair.

"You've seen them, too. Not just the Miracle Woman, but the others."

Bondurant's lips moved, but no words came out. Color returned to his face, a shade of deep crimson that was less alarming than the previous gray.

"It's all wrong," he said.

Something fell to the floor in the bathroom.

"That's one of them now," she said. "What happened to Deke?"

"I don't know."

"Don't lie to me."

"Please, Miss Rogers. Don't make me—"

"Something's in the tub." A scratching had arisen in the bathroom, echoing off the ceramic tiles. Water, or some other liquid, dripped in an uneven rhythm.

"I didn't let them in," Bondurant said. "They said nobody would get hurt. They said they'd only be here for a year or so, then they'd go away and Wendover would have all the funding it needed."

"Who are *they*?"

Bondurant shrugged, then slumped, defeated. The stirrings in the bathroom grew louder.

Starlene opened the front door and looked at the cold stone hulk of Wendover across the grass. "We have to get the kids out."

"You don't understand." Bondurant fidgeted with his rumpled tie. "Nobody gets out. Not anymore."

"You can sit here and wait for whatever happens next if you want. Me, I'm going to help the children I pledged to serve."

Bondurant laughed, drowning out the moist noises from the tub. "Little Miss Do-Gooder. You and all the other people who think they can save the world through kindness. There's only one way to save the world, and that's by hammering the misfits into shape. You can't love these brats into being productive members of society. All you can do is put the fear of God in them, by force, and let them burn in hell if they don't choose the right path."

"Tell that to the thing in the bathroom." Starlene left the cabin, slamming the door behind her, and walked toward the small gravel lot that was tucked behind the trees. She could fit maybe fifteen kids in the bed of her pickup, then come back for the rest. She didn't have a plan yet. She'd probably have to drop them off at the police station. Randy would help her. She had to find Randy.

Bondurant called to her from the cabin door. "Don't leave me, Miss Rogers."

She didn't turn around. The wind picked up, and more clouds had gathered in the sky. The surrounding forest was alive with movement. Bondurant shouted something else but she couldn't hear it.

Starlene reached her truck and locked herself inside, then started the engine. She put the truck in gear and glanced in the rear view mirror. She gasped and yanked her foot from the clutch so fast the engine died.

She turned around. Nothing in the bed of the pickup.

Not now. But, moments before, Freeman had stood there, clutching the same red wedge of razor that Deke had held in the bathroom. She shivered, restarted the engine, and drove to the main building.

THIRTY-SEVEN

Kracowski stood impatiently while McDonald gave Dr. Mills a tour of the basement. He resented this invasion. Bad enough that McDonald meddled in the experiments, but now he'd brought in a rival whose instability bordered on the psychopathic. Research of such a delicate nature was best pursued with a cool head, and Mills's mood swings occurred almost as rapidly as his son's. At least Freeman was stuck under observation in the Blue Room for the moment, with Randy standing guard.

Mills whistled in wonder as he inspected the machinery that created Kracowski's energy fields. He said to McDonald, "If you had given me this kind of backing, you'd have had your breakthrough years ago."

"Back then, all we wanted was mind control," McDonald said. "ESP was a byproduct."

"Isn't that just like the government?" Mills said to Kracowski. "You give them the answers, and then they find new questions. At twice the cost."

Kracowski said, "How do you know he's even *with* the government?"

McDonald laughed. "Do you want to see some identification? I've got a card in every pocket, each with a different name and agency. You have a serious problem with trusting others, Doctor. You ought to see somebody about that."

"I can make a few recommendations," Mills said.

Kracowski didn't like the way the men joked. This research was far more important than whatever espionage or brainwashing techniques were discovered. He didn't expect McDonald to grasp the significance of the discovery, but surely Mills could appreciate the near-divine implications of life after death. Unless the man's madness had removed him so far from the ordinary world that miracles were of no consequence.

"What's the next step?" Mills asked.

"Off the cliff and into the void," McDonald said. He tapped one of the tanks of liquid helium with the base of his flashlight. "We need to push some of the children a little bit harder and see if they crack."

Mills rubbed his hands together, eyes dark in his pale face. The dim shadows of the basement made his cheeks look even more gaunt and fleshless. "Despite your theory of harmonization of the brain's electrical patterns, Kracowski, I believe the effect works best when the brain is stimulated. Turn up the heat, and the kettle starts to boil."

"So I gather, from reading what you've done to your son."

"Don't judge me, Doctor. He was the perfect subject, and one day he'll understand that. Freeman will see that I sacrificed his emotional security for the good of the free world. And, ultimately, for the good of the human race."

"Love of the world versus love of your own offspring. You'll have to write that one up for the trade journals."

"That's enough," McDonald said. "You guys can fight turf wars on your own time. Right now, I've got a mission to complete."

McDonald switched on his flashlight and headed down the main corridor, into the cold, musty bowels of Wendover. Mills held out his elbow in a mockery of escorting Kracowski. Kracowski brushed past him and followed McDonald.

The building's wiring was corroded in this section, eaten by rodents, and had not been restored when the building was renovated to serve as a group home. Kracowski had never expected these rooms to be used.

The agent reached the first cell. The heavy steel door was brown with rust. The door was solid with the exception of a sliding mechanism for delivering food trays. McDonald shined the light into the cell. Bits of mortar between the cinder blocks had been scraped away by one of the cell's former tenants. Kracowski winced at the thought of the raw, bloody fingers scrabbling themselves to the bone.

"They knew how to treat them back in the old days," Mills said. "None of this coddling and medication and turning out onto the streets. If they wanted to board their alien starships or dance with angels, they had to claw through the walls first."

Kracowski didn't like being down here, and not just because of the alleged manifestations. He wasn't yet fully convinced the dead could cross back into this world, but he knew actual pain and misery and lunacy had existed in this cramped room. Perhaps emotions could cement themselves into the walls and become a part of a building's molecular structure. He'd have to investigate the theory once he was done with McDonald and SST.

"This will do just fine," McDonald said.

Kracowski didn't like the way the man's words were swallowed by the stale air. "What do you mean?"

"The next stage."

"I thought we'd agreed I would do more treatments in Thirteen. At least for a few more months. We need to check our subjects against the control group or we won't be able to verify our results."

"I think Dr. Mills was on the right track. Which of your subjects has exhibited the most potential?"

"Freeman." Kracowski looked deeply into Dr. Mills's eyes, but saw no hint of regret there. "He's also the most emotionally disturbed of the patients."

"Exactly," McDonald said. "And the others showing a . . . talent?"

"Vicky Barnwell. Edmund Alexander. Mario Rios."

"We've read the case histories. All problem children."

Mills grinned. "Not a bad test pool. A manic depressive, a bulimic, a molestation victim, and a plain old basket case. A test group with gender and ethnic variety, no less."

"I think we need to put a little pressure on," McDonald said. "See how they respond. The field is stronger down here, if I understand your descriptions correctly."

"But I can't control and isolate the focus of the fields outside of Thirteen," Kracowski said. "We'll lose our standardization."

"You can publish your little theories in all the shrink journals in the world for all I care, as long as you leave extrasensory perception out of it. And if you start babbling about ghosts to your esteemed colleagues, you'll soon find yourself on the soft side of a padded wall. When the Trust needs to shut someone up, it's easier to declare him insane than to kill him and risk a bad cover job. Right, Mills?"

Mills gave a sick grin, then turned his attention to the clogged stainless steel toilet in the corner of the room. "I think I'd rather have a bucket, myself."

"So, do these walls bring back memories, Doctor?" McDonald asked Mills. "How does it feel to be called a lunatic?"

"Sticks and stones," Mills said. "But I learned something. The line between the sane and the insane is invisible. It all depends on which side of the bars you're standing."

McDonald tried the door. The hinges scraped as he

swung it nearly closed. The blue glow of the machinery was mostly cut off from the outside, and the only light in the cell was from McDonald's flashlight. Kracowski shivered, imagining the horror of being shut up in solitary confinement here.

Mills noticed his discomfort. "Claustrophobic, Doctor?"

"Have you ever heard of 'empathy'?"

"I've successfully avoided that weakness. It tends to make you worry a little too much about other people."

"So all you care about is yourself," Kracowski said.

"Wrong. You're the one who's in this for personal gain. I'm after something that's bigger than all of us."

A soft shuffling arose in the hall outside. McDonald opened the cell door and shined his light in a sweeping arc. "Who's there?" he called in his authoritative voice.

No one answered. Kracowski stood behind McDonald and peered into the shadows. The hum of the machinery grew louder, and the glow from the main basement area pulsed like a heartbeat.

"That's not supposed to happen," Kracowski said. "The program is triggered by the computer in my office."

"I know who it is," Mills said, sitting on the corroded and moldy cot.

Kracowski grabbed at McDonald's flashlight. The agent elbowed him away. The hum increased in intensity, like a jet engine warming for takeoff.

"Something's wrong," Kracowski said.

"She wants to play," Mills said.

McDonald directed the beam onto Dr. Mills's face. The man's eyes were as large as Ping-Pong balls, the irises glittering with a faraway and secret pleasure.

Then Mills broke into laughter, the kind that Kracowski had heard during his internship at Sycamore Shoals Hospital; on the upper floor, the terminal cases, those who had crossed over into a land beyond reason; a land where only a few were invited, and from which no one ever returned.

McDonald crossed the room and yanked at Mills's shirt. "Tell me what's going on, damn you."

"It's better than I ever dreamed," Mills said.

Kracowski stepped into the hall and looked toward the row of circuit boards and the holding tanks. The boards lit up in random splashes of green, red, and yellow. The main dynamo whined like an animal caught in a steel trap. The air was warm and the smell of hot copper filled the basement.

"She's the ghost in the machine," Mills said. "Remember that old album by The Police? Spirits in the material world. Eee-yo-oh. Eee-yo-oh."

McDonald grabbed Mills by the shirt and pulled him from the cell. The agent shoved Mills against a wall and pressed the flashlight under his chin. The strange angle of the light made Mills's eyes look even more bulging and deranged.

"Tell me what's going on," McDonald shouted above the roar of the machines.

"She's taken over," Mills said. "Didn't you read my paper on mechanical anomalies?"

Kracowski recalled some talk years ago of studies conducted at Princeton University, of how random number generators could be influenced by telepathy. Back then, he had ridiculed the notion along with the rest of the professional establishment. Such nonsense had been the realm of the Rhine Research Center and other New Age illusionists. Now, the nonsense was real and crawling up his spine.

Kracowski felt a faint pull against him and realized the intense magnetic field was tugging at the metal in his zipper, his belt buckle, the pen in his pocket, and the eyelets of his shoes.

"She's here," Mills said.

Kracowski looked down the hall toward the black heart of the basement. Nothing stirred, though the shadows had an undulating, liquid quality. What had Freeman and the others seen in that darkness?

"Suffering," Mills said. "I never knew it would taste so sweet. Freeman's misery was a joy, but *this* . . ."

McDonald shoved Mills. The deranged doctor shook off the blow and smiled. "Ordinary pain. You can't touch me with ordinary pain."

Kracowski stopped McDonald from delivering another blow, this one to Mills's face. "It won't do any good."

McDonald looked toward the equipment, face wrinkled with worry. "We can't replace this stuff if it melts down."

Kracowski checked the meters on the closest amperage box. The needle flickered in the red zone, but the flux was erratic, not the way electricity behaved under normal circumstances.

"It's the Miracle Woman," Mills said.

McDonald looked at Kracowski. Kracowski shook his head. Mills was done, cooked. Whatever secret agency McDonald worked for, it had made a mistake by bringing the doctor out of the institution. Or maybe the mistake had been made years ago, when Mills first decided that the mind could be mapped and directed, and from there, believed that the spirit could be enslaved.

Kracowski felt a sudden rush of shame for his own foolish ambition. Even if God didn't exist, there was a domain that was off limits to those who lived and breathed. That domain had been invaded with all the carelessness and brute force exhibited by Attila's hordes, Hitler's tanks, and Stalin's KGB.

McDonald pressed his face close to Mills's. "Talk to me. Tell me what's going on or your ass will be in a strait jacket so fast and so tight you'll shit your pants before the Thorazine kicks in."

"Don't you know what this is all about?" Mills shouted. "I'm with her. I'm inside her. *She's dead and I'm reading her mind.*"

His cackle ran through Kracowski's ears and into his bones, where it settled with a chill as deep as the grave's.

"Okay. Fine." McDonald's face was blank, as if he were used to Mills's maniacal spells. "Let's start with the Barnwell girl."

THIRTY-EIGHT

"Dr. Kracowski asked me to get him," Starlene said to Randy.

"I'm sorry, honey, I can't let you do that," Randy said. "I can't release Freeman to anybody but the doctor himself."

"You can't keep him locked up all day."

"He's got some books. Besides, these brats keep themselves amused with their own little mind games."

"Randy." She looked into his eyes, but none of the former passion burned there. "Tell me what's going on. Please."

"You know more than I do. You're the one who keeps having visions."

"Don't be like that."

"Look, everything's gotten too complicated. I shouldn't have been interested in you in the first place."

She pretended to be hurt, and bit her lower lip while gazing past him to the door of the Blue Room. One keyed lock and one operated by an electronic combination. Randy wore a ring of keys on his belt, but how could she trick him into revealing the pad's combination?

"You know about Room Thirteen," she said.

"You lived through it, didn't you?" He looked down

the hall toward Kracowski's labs, which were around the corner.

"Did Dr. Kracowski make you have a treatment?" She touched her head as if suffering a migraine.

"That's none of your business."

"Dr. Kracowski's hiding things from you. You can't trust him. Did you know about the ESP?"

"Now you're getting paranoid. Maybe you need to take a few days off."

"In case you haven't noticed, Wendover has turned into a concentration camp. Barbed wire and armed guards."

"They're not armed."

"Not that you can see. But Kracowski does compare unfavorably closely with Josef Mengele, wouldn't you say?"

"Kracowski never hurt anybody. He *heals* the kids. Improves them. I've seen it with my own eyes, many times. This work is important, and it doesn't help that you're sticking your nose into everything."

"Sure, he *healed* me, all right, when I had the SST. Do you want to know what I saw?"

Randy swallowed hard. "I . . ."

"Or can you read my mind?"

"Wait a second. I said I never had a treatment."

"I almost believe you. How many treatments does it take before you can read minds outside of Thirteen? I could only do it for a few minutes, then the effect faded. But I saw a whole hell of a lot while the juice was running through me."

"I don't believe that stuff. Ghosts aren't real. God would never allow such a thing."

"Yet He allows people to read each other's minds?"

Someone was coming down the hall, the footsteps of hard shoes echoing in the next wing. A door opened and the steps trailed off up the stairs.

Starlene lowered her voice. "I never believed in ESP and I only believed in one sort of life after death. I didn't ask for any of this. All I wanted was to help the children."

"You can help Freeman by leaving him alone. Dr. Kracowski knows what's best. This is bigger than any of us."

"Are you sure you haven't been through some brainwashing? Whatever Dr. Kracowski's up to, I'd bet that turning you into a zombie would be child's play. Maybe ESP can be manipulated to work like a one-way street, put thoughts in there but not let them out."

Randy grabbed her arm. "I'm serving the Lord, too, the same as you. You spread His glory through love and understanding and I do it by helping our mission of improving the human soul."

"You were handpicked by Bondurant, no doubt. That's his brand of salvation."

"God made Jesus suffer."

"Oh, so you think you're God, too? Or is Kracowski the real God and you're just one of the prophets?"

The small walkie-talkie on Randy's hip hissed. He pulled it from his belt and turned away from Starlene. He spoke in low tones, then took several steps down the hall so she couldn't overhear. Starlene took the opportunity to make a closer examination of the lock.

Randy put away the walkie-talkie and stuck his key in the Blue Room door. His hand flew over the electronic lock's keypad, too quickly for Starlene to memorize the sequence. "You'd better go now," he said.

"I want to help."

"You can help by getting out of the way."

The door swung open, Randy's key still in the door. Freeman stood waiting. Behind him, the row of cots were neatly made. No one else was in the room.

"I'm ready," Freeman said to Randy. He glanced at Starlene. "You'd better stay out of the way, like he said."

"I only want to help," she said.

"I've been helped so much I'm sick and tired of it. I'm about helped to death. At least the people in the Trust are sincere about what they want."

"The Trust?"

"Be quiet," Randy said to Freeman.

"Oh? She doesn't know? I thought you guys were soul mates." Freeman gave a smile that was even more elusive and sardonic than usual.

"What's he talking about, Randy?"

"I thought having a psychology degree automatically made you a know-it-all," Freeman said to her. "Certainly worked for my Dad. He has three of them so he knows *more* than everyone."

Freeman pointed to Randy's walkie-talkie. "And that's a great way to keep a secret. Except from people who can read minds."

Randy stepped forward, mouth twisted in anger. Freeman scooted back into the room.

"Come here, you little smartass," Randy said. Freeman winked at Starlene and ran between the rows of cots. Randy yelled and gave chase. Starlene waited until they were at the far end of the room, checked the hall in both directions, then went inside and pulled the door nearly shut. Freeman was cornered now, and Randy climbed over a cot, watching the boy's eyes.

"Head him off that way," Randy shouted to Starlene. She closed in to trap Freeman. Randy lunged at Freeman, who tried to dodge, but Randy was too fast and strong. He wrestled the boy face-down onto the cot. His walkie-talkie fell from his belt and bounced to the floor as they struggled.

"My back pocket," Randy said to Starlene. "Restrain the little shit."

Starlene pulled the handcuffs from Randy's pocket. Freeman kicked and squirmed, the pillow pressed against his face so that his screams were muffled. Randy put a knee on the boy's back, then stuck one hand behind him, reaching for the cuffs.

"Here," he said. "Hurry."

Before Starlene could think, she snapped one of the cuffs on Randy's wrist. He turned toward her in surprise and, as he hesitated, Starlene closed the other cuff around the cot's metal frame.

"Damn you," Randy said, swinging his free hand at her. The blow caught her across the cheek and she fell onto the concrete floor. Randy fumbled at his belt where he'd kept his keys. When he realized he'd left the keys in the door, his face contorted into a mask of rage.

Freeman rolled off the cot while Randy tried to free himself. Freeman wiped blood from his lips and helped Starlene to her feet. She rubbed her face. Her skin hadn't split, but her pulse roared beneath her skin.

"I feel your pain," Freeman said.

"So do I," she said.

Randy jumped from the cot and clawed at them, tugging at the handcuff. The cot was bolted to the floor, though its frame rattled with his effort. "I'll kill you both."

"Great," Freeman said. "I can't wait to be a ghost so I can come back and haunt your ass."

Starlene took Freeman's hand. "Let's get out of here."

"Where are we going?" he said.

"I thought you could read my mind."

"Well, I figured you were trying to rescue me, but you don't have any kind of plan, do you?"

They reached the door. The hallway was still empty. Starlene looked back at Randy, who'd stopped pulling at the handcuff. He was busy unhooking the springs of the cot. He'd have to work his way down, removing one spring at a time, but soon he'd reach the end and be able to slide the cuff through a gap in the folded corner of the cot.

"Damn," she said. "Well, I guess our secret will be out soon."

"One thing about this place," Freeman said. "Secrets don't stay secret very long."

"So I've learned," Starlene said. She slammed the door closed, yanked the key back and forth until it broke off in the lock, then stuck the key ring in her pocket. "Hope that locks the jerk in. What now?"

"We need Vicky," Freeman said. "She's smart and she knows her way around Wendover."

"What about the other kids?"

Freeman looked at her with his piercing eyes. "You ought to know by now, you save the world a little at a time, not all at once. Even your old pal Jesus H. Christ figured that one out."

Starlene let the sarcasm pass. "To the Green Room?"

"She's not in the Green Room. She's in Thirteen."

"What's she doing there?"

"Dying," he said. "That's what we're all doing. Some of us faster than others."

As they ran down the corridor, Starlene wondered if Freeman could read her mind enough to know how terrified she was.

THIRTY-NINE

He should have known better.

If he had played the game and kept his thoughts to himself, this never would have happened. He should have stuck with the loner act, the Clint Eastwood bit, or the tough guy swimming against the current, like Pacino in *Serpico*. Sure, he was special and he could read minds and it was only a matter of time before the Trust broke him. But now he'd crossed the line, stepped up as yet another miserable Defender of the Weak and Protector of the Innocent. Just what the world needed. Another freaking unsung hero.

Freeman ran beside Starlene, triptrapping outward to see if any of the Trust's goons had been tipped off by Randy. But too many of them were shields. When it was working, his ESP was as reliable as radar or sonar, but he could never be sure about the thoughts floating around that he *wasn't* intercepting. When he was on the up cycle, the gift was golden. And he was definitely up now, the hairs on his neck like antennae, his skin alive with the force radiating from the basement.

He'd read Starlene easily enough, but she'd just undergone a treatment and was susceptible. Soft on the brain. Vicky was even softer because she'd been through several of the treatments. The freaky thing was that the treatment did different things to some people, and to others, nothing at all seemed to happen. Maybe it was a natural talent, a third eye or sixth sense or some other baloney. Maybe Freeman would have been able to do it anyway, even without the years of Dad's experiments.

Either way, he wished that God would take the gift back, because it had been nothing but a pain in the ass from the very beginning. But God hid away up there in the sky where only people like Starlene could believe in Him. No matter how hard Freeman tried to read *God's* mind, he drew a blank. God, if He even existed, probably had the thickest shield in the universe.

After all, if God could read everybody's mind at the same time, He'd probably gone bonkers way back around the time of Adam and Eve.

The thing about being in a manic phase, a thing that he'd only recently been able to catch himself at, was that his thoughts rambled on about stupid stuff like God and love and other people and being afraid he'd never go to sleep again and stupid, stupid, stupid worries even when he ought to be concentrating on more important things. Like surviving.

Freeman squeezed Starlene's hand as they slowed. She made an unnecessary hushing motion with her finger against her lips. Thirteen was around the next corner, and Kracowski's lab two doors down from that. If Vicky was undergoing an SST, then for sure the Trust would have a guard on hand. Freeman expected a walkie-talkie to crackle with Randyspeak at any moment.

"Is she in there?" Starlene mouthed silently at him.

He closed his eyes and concentrated. He'd heard Vicky clearly while he was locked in the Blue Room, triptrapped through the space between them as if they'd been talking via a cellular telephone at close range. But now, he picked up nothing. That could mean several things: she was

shielded somehow, or she had slipped into unconsciousness and couldn't transmit her thoughts. Or she was dead.

Freeman was overwhelmed by a sudden image of
Vicky lying pale and breathless on the cot in Thirteen, the
straps tight around her as her color faded. He shuddered
the picture from his mind and concentrated harder.

Nothing.

He shook his head at Starlene. He couldn't even read
Starlene's mind now. Something was happening. Maybe
the puppet masters had changed the rhythms of their experimental waves. Maybe Dad had come up with some
new gizmo that blew Kracowski's brain cooker right out
of the water. Maybe Freeman's manic phase was over, in
which case his number one survival skill would be down
for the count when he needed it most.

Starlene knelt and peeked around the corner, Freeman
holding onto her shoulder in case he needed to pull her
out of the way of a bullet or something.

He silently scolded himself. Here he was again, playing Protector of the Innocent. This was getting to be a
way bad habit.

She turned and whispered, "Nobody."

Freeman took a look for himself. The hall was empty
and quiet. Except . . .

Freeman whispered back. "I thought you said 'nobody.'"

"I did."

"Then what about the geezer in the gown?"

Starlene looked again. "What geezer?"

"Uh oh."

The old man stood in the hall plain as day. It was the
man from the lake, hunched and gray and wrinkled. He
moved toward them without a sound, his eyes staring past
them as if a hole to heaven had opened up on the opposite wall. Freeman fought an urge to reach out as the man
drifted past, his gown and skin shimmering with a faint

silver dust. The man disappeared into the wall, leaving no trace on the crumbling stucco.

"So, you didn't see him?" Freeman said.

"See who?"

"Never mind."

"Do we try the door?"

"Well, considering we have a minute at the most to get out of here before Randy tips off the entire free world—"

"You want to rescue Vicky, because you're always thinking of others," Starlene said.

"You don't have to be mean just because you're a shrink."

"Sorry. But you're going to have to trust me if we're going to get out of this mess."

"Trust. That's a good one."

"Well?"

"Sure. Just don't try to 'understand' me or 'heal' me or shower me with 'tough love.'"

"Deal."

"Let's go for it, then."

They rounded the corner and crept to Thirteen. "Damn," Freeman said. "I forgot they use these stupid keypad locks everywhere."

"Why didn't you read somebody's mind when they were punching in the numbers?"

"Look, you try lying there getting shocked and skull-fried and being sent on a journey to the land of the dead and see how practical *you* are."

Starlene paled as if recalling the visions from her own treatment. "Yeah, I see what you mean."

"What do we do now?"

"Knock?"

Freeman shrugged and tapped at the thick door. A series of beeps flashed from the electronic lock, and the handle turned. The door opened. And Freeman was face to face with the last person he ever expected to see again.

Except, you couldn't really call what he was looking at

a *face*. It was red and raw and exactly as he remembered it, only worse.

He tried to scream, but you need air to scream, and his lungs were solid steel and his throat was stacked with bricks and his skull was pounded by eighty-eight invisible hammers and he wanted to fall but his limbs wouldn't even cut him that much slack. All he could do was stand and stare and wish himself away.

The thing that stood before him reached out wet rags that must have been arms.

A hug.

Just like Mom used to make, back before Freeman had ripped her to shreds with a steel blade. Back before Dad had screwed with his brain and turned him into a mother-murderer.

Suddenly he was six years old again, and in the memory at least he could cry, unlike now, because he'd opened the bathroom door and Mom's eyes were closed and her naked body was hidden beneath the bubbles. Soaking, she always called it, because she said it was the only time she didn't have to answer the phone or obey Dad's orders.

And in the memory the knife was cold in his hand and Dad's voice was in his head, so loud that there was no room for any of Freeman's own thoughts, which made him glad in a way because that meant he couldn't help himself and it wasn't his fault.

But of course it's your fault.

Freeman tried to blink but his eyes were wide and dry and the memory was gone. The words had come from the thing standing before him, the thing he had once loved more than anything in the world back when love and trust and hope were more than just useless shrink words.

A dark maw opened in the middle of the mutilated face. She was trying to speak. Oh God, she was trying to speak, except she didn't need a tongue to say what she needed to say. Who needed a voice when you could trip-trap right to the source, get in there with the lies and the tricks and the deception and, right at the core, find the tiny secret hope that Freeman harbored, a nut that no shrink had ever been able to crack, that no triptrapper had ever glimpsed, that even Freeman himself rarely probed?

A hope of false innocence. A sincere and unshakable belief in a lie. A faith in an utter and utmost betrayal. His own private troll beneath the bridge.

He'd always told himself, even though the nightmare rose in its crimson wounds every time he shut his eyes, that it had never happened, that it was just the way the newspapers reported it, that Dad was the real killer.

Dad, and not Freeman. Freeman had *loved* his mother, no matter how many brain games Dad played, no matter how much shock treatment Freeman had endured, no matter how many mental mazes the old bastard had run him through. When you love somebody, you don't hurt them.

When you love somebody, you take care of them. You don't—

But the thing before him didn't look to be in a forgiving mood. The maw parted and closed with a moist sigh of contentment, the arms edged closer, and Freeman was frozen by a chill a thousand graves deep.

The words were in his brain, in that same voice that used to sing him nursery rhymes and tell him bedtime stories.

You don't get second chances.

The paralysis broke and tears streamed from his eyes and he wanted to say he was sorry but what good was that useless word when you don't get second chances?

That was one of Mom's mottoes: do right the first time, avoid suffering regrets at any cost, love with all your heart, because *YOU DON'T GET SECOND CHANCES*.

He could breathe again and he was about to scream for real, he was shaking so hard his bones could wake the dead, and the memory of the warm blood against the silver blade slashed through the little secret hidey hole in his head, and he knew he was guilty. And that she'd never forgive him, even if she lived a billion eternities.

Before he could scream, Starlene's hand clamped over his mouth. He hissed against her palm and tried to squirm away. That was when Bondurant spoke.

"I told you he was troubled," Bondurant said. "May God have mercy on his soul."

Freeman's eyes snapped open. The mother-thing was gone.

Or had never been.

But this was the deadscape and Freeman couldn't tell anymore who was alive and who was dead. Or if it made any difference, because Mom hadn't died in the dead-scape.

Maybe you carried your dead with you, forever.

Bondurant stood in place of the nightmare, licking his lips and squinting through the fog of his glasses. His jacket was wrinkled and the knot of his tie was loose. No matter how scary and ugly the director was, Freeman was glad to see him. Anybody but Mom.

"Mr. Bondurant," Starlene said, pushing Freeman in-side and closing the door behind her. "What are you doing here?"

"I have the keys, remember?"

"We, um . . ."

"Say no more," Bondurant said. "Can't you see your liberal views are carved in your face in big letters? Save the children. Sacrifice. Do good instead of evil."

Freeman shuddered. That was exactly the sort of phi-losophy Mom would have had, if she'd been a social worker instead of a lawyer. If she hadn't fallen under Dad's control. If she were alive instead of dead.

"Well, I've got a job to do," Starlene said. "And if you're with Kracowski and McDonald, then I'm afraid I'm going to have to do some evil to *you*."

Bondurant shook his head. "Sweet, sweet Starlene. I could have put that fire of yours to such use." He glanced down the hall toward his office. "But, see, I'm a changed man, and God's servants don't get much choice in the duties for which they are chosen."

"Oh, dang," Starlene said. "Don't tell me you've had another vision? Well, I hope this one involves a chariot in the sky, because that's the only route out of this place. Or haven't you noticed the armed guards and the barbed wire?"

"God is testing us."

"One thing I know is that God doesn't send you anything you can't handle."

"Where's Vicky?" Freeman cut in. "I know she was here because I saw it inside her head."

Bondurant looked down at Freeman. "She was here. One of the guards took her away."

"They didn't say where?"

Bondurant tilted his head back as if Michelangelo's ghost had painted a mural on the ceiling. He let out a laugh that was too loud for the room.

"Where is she?" Starlene said.

"Where we all go, sooner or later," Bondurant said between cackles.

Starlene pulled Freeman back as if the crazed director were playing on a strange television quiz show, one where the wrong answer meant instant death. "Heaven?"

Bondurant rolled his reptilian eyes toward the floor and stopped laughing. This time his voice was a deranged imitation of Vincent Price's. "The other place," he said.

"The basement," Freeman said to Starlene. She yanked open the door and they ran down the hall.

Bondurant's melodramatic voice boomed after them like B-movie thunder. "Take the stairs. That's the fastest way to hell."

FORTY

The girl would be the first victim.

No, not victim . . . a PATIENT, Kracowski reminded himself. But with Dr. Mills involved now, there was no other way to think of her. Vicky Barnwell had passed from his caring and kind treatment into the clutches of a madman. Even in Kracowski's most self-deluded moments, he never completely forgot that the well-being of his patients was of at least secondary importance. His system was designed to heal them as much as it was to research brain function.

Mills exhibited no such concern. Mills wanted to push everything to the limits, even when those limits stretched into the bizarre. Mills exhibited far too much glee as he placed the gaunt girl in the cell. She hadn't spoken when the guard escorted her down the dim hall. She simply looked each man in the face, staring a moment longer at Kracowski than the others, and didn't resist when Mills took her arm and led her inside.

Mills closed the door and twisted the corroded slide lock into place. McDonald waited until the guard left, then said to Mills, "Let the games begin."

Mills moved to the circuitry board and the remote network computer he'd hastily installed. Two large curved panels, housing a series of superconducting magnets, stood just outside the cell door.

"Let's see what this baby can do," Mills said. Kracowski couldn't tell whether "baby" referred to the girl or the equipment.

"See, where you went wrong was in the direct application of the electrical charge," Mills said as if lecturing a mediocre student. "If you'd read my paper on magnetite in the brain and the resultant effect of misaligned electromagnetic waves—"

"I've read all your work," Kracowski said, "and I learned from your mistakes."

Mills paused in his entering of the commands. He put a forefinger to his temple. "You didn't read what I carry up here. Unless you've learned to read minds, but I'm willing to bet that you haven't subjected yourself to your own treatments. That's the difference between us, Doctor. You can't take that final leap of faith."

"I don't need faith. I believe in *myself*."

Mills said, "By the way, McDonald, you're not carrying a firearm, are you? Or any other large metal objects?"

McDonald didn't answer.

"Because the magnetic force will reach five Tesla, which is three times stronger than a typical magnetic resonance imager in a hospital. There have been reports of metal objects flying through the air in the vicinity of the fields. Sometimes it's a mop bucket, sometimes an ink pen. On at least one occasion, a policeman's pistol was pulled from its holster and flew to the head of the magnet's coil. The gun discharged. Fortunately, the bullet didn't pierce the holding tanks."

"That would be bad?" McDonald said.

"Well, the liquid nitrogen in the outer tank is 320 degrees below zero. If you don't freeze to death first, the oxygen in the room will be reduced so drastically that you'll suffocate. And the liquid helium in the inner tank is only a few degrees above absolute zero."

"That's cold, right?"

"You'll turn into an ice sculpture and probably shatter at the slightest air current."

"I never knew science could be so much fun."

"Stick around and I'll show you the meaning of 'fun.'"

McDonald put a hand inside his jacket and came out with an automatic pistol. "Glock .45. Triple safety. It won't go off accidentally. What about the steel door?"

"The field isn't strong enough to pull the door from its hinges."

McDonald looked at Kracowski, who shrugged. Kracowski said, "I'd never push the Tesla that high, and I always used lead shields to limit the exposure. But, then, I'm just an innocent bystander."

"Nobody's innocent," Mills said. "And it's time to go for some serious results."

McDonald placed his firearm in a cell two doors down the hall. "Most of the components are plastic. Is that far enough away?"

"The magnet is focalized enough that it probably wouldn't have mattered anyway. I'm being overly dramatic. The real force will be directed at the subject inside the cell."

"Her name is Vicky Barnwell," Kracowski said.

Mills flipped through a folder. "That's funny. You termed her 'Patient 7-AAC' in your records. Her ESP score was pathetic, though. We'll see if we can fix that."

"I'm sure you'll do better. Compared to you, I'm just a guy who sweeps up after the lab closes."

"Then watch and maybe you'll learn something, and one day you can play 'genius,' too."

Mills entered the rest of the commands, then keyed the machinery into action. The tanks hummed and Kracowski tried to visualize the process of the electricity running through the miles of coil wire in the superconducting magnet, the helium lowering the temperature and reducing the wire's resistance. The draw on the electrical grid caused the scant lighting to grow even dimmer, until the room was cast in orange and deep blue. The whine of the machinery grew louder, and McDonald moved behind Mills's computer as if that would provide some protection in case the tanks exploded.

Kracowski looked at his wristwatch. Electromagnetic fields could impair the functioning of watches, but Mills had done a good job of isolating and controlling the direction of the field. Whatever his other flaws, he was a brilliant physicist.

Thirty seconds went by.

Kracowski expected any number of things: for Vicky to scream, for Mills to jump up the juice, for McDonald to ask what was going on. But no theory could have predicted what happened next.

Vicky pounded on the inside of the cell door with the bottom of her fist. In a calm voice, she said, "Hey, you guys. Better come see this. There's somebody in here."

FORTY-ONE

Footsteps approached from the far end of the hall. *Somebody was in a hurry,* Freeman thought. He and Starlene pressed into the corner. The stairwell was close enough to make a run for, but it was keyed like most of the other doors, and they'd have to go through Randy's assortment to find the one that fit.

"Hey, Freeman, is that you?" Isaac said in a loud whisper.

Freeman was about to answer, then wondered if Isaac had been turned into a mole for the Trust. Stranger things had happened. You couldn't trust a guy just because he was a kid instead of an adult.

"I saw it happen," Dipes said, sniffling from a cold. "I mean, I saw what's going to happen. And it's not nice."

Freeman peeked around the corner. Isaac and Dipes stood there in sweatpants and T-shirts. Isaac's curly hair was damp, and they were both panting from exertion. Isaac nudged Dipes and said, "He saw you guys hiding in the corner by the stairs."

"So *you* can read minds, too?" Starlene asked Dipes.

"Sort of," Isaac answered for him. "He saw it ten minutes ago. It took us that long to sneak away from the gym and get here."

"Is that where the other kids are?"

"Yeah. Except Vicky. Some goon came and got her. A new guy, wearing a uniform. And Deke's still nowhere to be found."

"What else did you see?" Freeman asked Dipes, then added for Starlene's benefit, "He's clairvoyant, or whatever you call it when you know the future. Like Nostradamus or Edgar Cayce, except Dipes doesn't talk in stupid riddles."

Starlene nodded as if such a talent were only natural in a world where kids had ESP and ghosts walked around like they owned the place. At least she seemed to be losing some of that grown-up tendency to deny everything that didn't fit into her narrow worldview. Freeman decided maybe there was hope for her after all.

"Can we trust her?" Dipes said. Isaac put a hand of encouragement on his shoulder.

"She's promised not to shrink us," Freeman said. "She just wants to help."

"Couldn't have said it better myself," Starlene said. "So, what's going to happen that we need to be scared of?"

Dipes looked at Freeman. "Ghosts."

Isaac said, "You guys keep going on about ghosts. I'll believe it when I see it."

"Believe it," Starlene said. "What ghosts in particular are you talking about, Edmund?"

"Edmund?" Isaac said, looking at Dipes. "That's a pretty cool name. Like in a British book or something. Why didn't you tell us?"

He shrugged. "I like 'Dipes' better, 'cause Edmund's what my folks called me."

"What ghost did you see?" Starlene repeated.

Dipes pointed a finger at Freeman's chest. "Yours."

"Great," Freeman said. "Well, maybe you saw only one kind of future, and there's bound to be a gazillion different futures."

Isaac's dark complexion grew a shade paler. "Sure.

Like opening doors on a video game. Depending on which room you go in, different stuff happens."

"We better go in one of them, and soon," Starlene said. She went to the stairwell door and began trying keys. "They'll be after us."

"Are you scared?" Dipes asked Freeman.

"About maybe dying? Nah. There are *way* worse things than that."

"Like what?"

Freeman didn't want to dwell on it. For one thing, if he died, that meant he'd have to see Mom again. For another, he didn't plan on dying. Even Clint Eastwood managed to make it to the final credits nine times out of ten.

Except in those movies where Clint was the Defender of the Weak, Protector of the Innocent. Then it was practically a hero's requirement to take one for the team. He looked at Starlene's face. Tears made twin lines down her cheeks.

Damn, Freeman thought. *She must really sort of like me a little bit.*

"It's worse to live like you're waiting for second chances," Freeman finally said. "That's worse than being dead."

Starlene found the right key and swung the door open. She wiped her nose and regained her composure.

"You guys better stay here," Freeman said.

"No way," Isaac said. "They're going to pick us off one by one if we don't do something."

"Yeah," Dipes said. "I saw a future where this place was empty. All the kids gone. Except for the ones in the basement."

"The basement?"

"Yeah. Where the ghosts live."

Freeman followed Starlene down the dark stairs.

Isaac took Dipes's hand and came after them. "So we better stick together. Plus, this may be my only chance to see a real live ghost."

"Just hope you're not looking in a mirror at the time," Freeman said.

They felt their way down. A dim emergency light filtered up from the base of the stairs, the glow painting the cobwebs a sickly yellow. The air was thick with dust and the rot of old masonry. The walls of the stairwell were stone, and a damp chill settled into Freeman's bones as they descended. They gathered at the basement door and Starlene began trying keys.

"What's the plan?" Freeman whispered.

"Get Vicky and get out," she answered.

"Out, where?"

"We'll make up that part when we get to it."

"Good plan," Freeman said.

"Can you read Vicky's mind? Or, what do you call it, 'triptrap' her?"

"I've had other things on my mind. Like being a ghost."

"Try again," Isaac said.

Freeman shut out the sound of the water dripping behind the walls, forgot the fear of death that tickled his skin like knife tips, ignored his heart pounding as if trying to hammer its way through his rib cage, blocked whatever thoughts were racing through the minds of Starlene and Dipes and Isaac.

He sent his mind out, in that process that was still freaky even though he'd done it hundreds of times. Triptrapping, walking across that mental bridge. He concentrated, picturing Vicky's face, the lips that said such kind words, the pretty eyes that looked all the way through him . . .

He had to back up because he was getting distracted. He couldn't afford to think of that other stuff, that mushy, kissy lovey-dovey crap. Clint Eastwood didn't have time for it, except in his worst movies, and neither did Freeman.

He triptrapped again, concentrating harder this time. He was rapid cycling like crazy, going from manic to depressed, up to down, white-hot to blue, throbbing like a police car's lights. Something weird was going on, the erratic electromagnetic pulses were scrambling his synapses. He was swinging from mania to depression so fast that the two almost merged into a bizarre new emotional state.

You've been here before. Maybe it's just your imagination, though, but that's the kind of obsessive thought you have while depressed, or maybe you're up and you think this is some kind of holy gift.

Maybe you're supposed to use this power to be a Protector of the Innocent. Don't be a damned fool. Nobody's innocent, and nobody's worth protecting. Or is that just depression talking?

You're innocent. You didn't kill her.

If you try hard enough, you can make the world stop. You can make your brain go away. You're bigger than God.

Forget about all that and CONCENTRATE. This is about saving Vicky, not you. For once in your sorry life, it's NOT ABOUT YOU.

And then he broke through, bridged with her as she was trying to reach him, and for the most beautiful, terrible moment they were linked, their sentences cramming together and overflowing like two glasses of water poured into a third, thoughts circling and dancing and taking on meanings beyond words.

Then Freeman saw what Vicky was seeing, and wished that the gift had stayed in the hands of God or Satan or Dad or whatever else cruel bastard had given it to him. Because Vicky was in the deadscape, big time.

FORTY-TWO

"You have to get right to the source," Kenneth Mills said. His voice rose as the power to the superconductors increased. Kracowski looked at the rows of specially built fuse boxes that were stacked on the wall behind the tanks. He didn't know what would happen if the whole operation shorted out, but that might be preferable to observing the results of Mills's mind games.

The girl pounded on the door again. "You better come see."

McDonald approached the door, hesitated, then asked Mills, "Should I open it?"

Mills cracked a grin that resembled that of a sadistic clown's. "Sure, step right on in. Let's see what the treatment does to *you*." Mills's eyes were closed, and he leaned back from the computer keyboard like Captain Nemo playing a demented organ melody.

"Ah, I can see it," Mills said. "I knew I could do it. See, McDonald, you and your Trust thought I was wrong, that I was used up and broken. You were ready to throw me away, but you *need* me. I'm the only one who can make it happen."

"Don't keep me in the dark on this thing," McDonald

said. "Kracowski made tons of notes. Why do we have to keep guessing with you?"

"Kracowski wants other people to know what a genius he is. All I want is to find out for myself."

Mills opened his eyes as if finishing a prayer, then altered the programming. "See, Kracowski, you don't need to shock them if you want to kill them. Kill them and let their hearts keep beating. That's the way to get inside the dead."

Kracowski had administered death in doses that lasted for fractions of seconds. Mills appeared capable of killing millions without hesitation. After what he'd done to his own wife and son, Kracowski wouldn't be surprised if the man would wipe out the entire human race just to prove himself right. Mills would even kill God if he had the means and opportunity. He already had the motive.

"Take a look for yourself," Mills said. "It's beautiful. Dead is beautiful."

Kracowski looked at the readings on the computer screen. The amplitude was erratic, scrambled into a wave pattern he'd never seen before. Not even the radical physicists, those who linked electromagnetism with UFOs and world war and brain cancer and killer viruses, had directly connected the silent radiation with the human spirit. Mills was pushing it with no idea what the result would be, playing a guessing game that might be far more tragic than the splitting of an atom.

Even nuclear reactions obeyed the laws of nature, and Mills was playing in the field beyond nature.

Kracowski cursed himself for not being able to look away. He was just as curious as Mills.

"Open the door," he heard himself saying.

McDonald put a hand on the thick handle of the slide lock. He eased the lock free and winced, as if expecting the walls to fly loose from the floor. When nothing happened, he took hold of the door handle. He paused, then knelt to the slot in the door, pulling the rusty mechanism where food had long ago been shoved to the cell's inhabitants.

Vicky's voice came from the slot, louder than before. "They're eating the light," she said, the words made even more haunting by her calmness.

Mills laughed. "Dark tastes better. Less filling. Don't have to make yourself vomit after."

McDonald said, "What the hell's going on in there?"

Mills traced a strange pattern in the air with the tip of his finger. Painting an invisible Picasso, or maybe conducting a frenzied Phillip Glass piece for full orchestra. Communing with fleshless things. Or stroking the molecules of heaven.

"Damn you," McDonald said to Mills. "Talk to me, or I'll have your ass stuck back in the loony bin."

The agent worked the lever on the food slot and peered inside the cell. Kracowski wondered if McDonald would be able to see anything because of the darkness. McDonald shook his head as if trying to clear his vision, then pressed his head closer to the slot. He squealed in sudden pain, as if acid had been dashed in his eyes, and rolled to the floor.

McDonald huddled with his knees against his chest and moaned unintelligible syllables. He shuddered, eyes fixed open, staring past Mills and Kracowski. Mills hurried around the computer table and grabbed the man by the jacket, shaking him. "Help me get him away from the fields," he said to Kracowski.

Kracowski glanced at the computer screen, where the resonance image of Vicky's brain flashed in bright purple, green, and gold, the colors one saw when pressing fingers against closed eyelids. An infrared video camera depicted an aurora surrounding her body. Other cloud-like shapes flickered against the darkness, clusters of energy that weren't connected to the girl's physical form.

"What did you see?" Mills shouted at McDonald, spittle flying into the dazed man's face.

"Nuh—nuh—nuh," he grunted in reply.

Mills pushed McDonald to the floor. He shouted at Kracowski, "Don't touch anything. I'm going in."

Mills yanked the cell door open. But he didn't go in. He couldn't.

The room was gone.

Kracowski forgot the computer, the straining machinery, the burning fear in his stomach, the hopeless sense that everything was too far out of his control, because none of that mattered. In the face of a miracle, even the extraordinary was meaningless.

FORTY-THREE

Freeman was with Vicky, bridged, as the floor disappeared beneath her feet in the cell. The darkness of the small room gave way to gray as the writhing shapes appeared like an invading army on the horizon. Faces stood out among the coalescence, sets of eyes that had seen as much horror in death as in life. Faint fingers clawed the air, tongues and teeth gnashed in silent anger.

Ghost bedlam. These spirits had shouted their broken words against the cell walls, painted their pain in the stone and steel and concrete of the basement, bounced their mad thoughts against the unyielding fences of reality. These were the patients who had been damned and doomed to live out their confused lives in the narrow basement rooms. Now they were forever committed to Wendover's regiments of the dead.

Freeman couldn't blame them for being angry at those who had disturbed their slumbering escape from this vicious world.

"They're eating the light," Vicky said.

"I know," Freeman said. He felt the vibration as she pounded on the cell door.

"Kracowski's machines brought them back. Here where they hurt the most."

"They're still lost, though. Listen . . ."

Outside Vicky's cell came a roar like a metallic tidal wave. The other cell doors in the basement had yanked themselves open and slammed against the walls. Either the magnetic force had pulled the doors from their locks or the rooms' former inhabitants were staging a massive jail-break.

Disconnected and mad thoughts spilled into the open line that existed between him and Vicky, a triptrap with the spirits that froze the inside of Freeman's skull like a hundred hits of ice cream. He recognized some of the voices from his earlier journey into the deadscape, but familiarity didn't make them any less insane. He tried to block them, but they came regardless:

Notes in the television, doctor.

I am a tree and I leave.

Crazy as a bugbed.

A white, white room in which to write.

Freeman focused on Vicky again as the shapes drew closer. "What do they want?" she thought at him, *inside* him.

"Maybe they're just coming back because they don't have anywhere else to go. Maybe these cells were all they ever had, the closest thing to home. Sad as it sounds, maybe they *belong* here."

"Don't be scared."

"I'm not scared," Freeman thought.

"Look, I told you, you can't lie to somebody who's reading your mind."

The spirits closed in, drawn by the invisible field, their eyes glittering, mouths gasping for air they couldn't breathe. Freeman thought about breaking the bridge, pulling away from Vicky, and shutting off those crazy dead voices. Then he felt ashamed for his selfishness, and linked to her again with all his concentration.

The ghosts were so close that their cold mist shrouded Vicky, the impossible flesh giving off a faint effervescent light. The endless darkness around them and behind them grew even blacker, as if drawing energy from the stray photons in the basement.

"They don't know who to blame," Freeman thought. He felt a hand on his shoulder. Afraid it was one of the deranged ghosts, he turned. Isaac stood behind him, with Starlene and Dipes. In reality, the one with hard walls, not the just-as-real but less-solid deadscape. He crouched and closed his eyes, found Vicky again.

"Where did you go?" she asked.

"Not very far. This is weird."

"Clint in *High Plains Drifter,* huh?"

"That'll do."

She pounded on the door again. Freeman heard Dad's muffled ranting on the other side of the door, then the door cracked open and a wedge of light sliced into the cell. Dad's face appeared, his grin like a gash, eyes bright and watery.

"Vicky, meet my Dad," Freeman triptrapped.

Freeman felt a little of his carefully hidden secrets slip out, heard Vicky gasp as she caught a glimpse of the tortures inflicted upon him, the dark days in the closet, the ESP tests, the brainwashing experiments, the needles and cattle prods and shock treatments, the infamous incident with the blowtorch and—

Luckily, Freeman shut down before she walked the halls of his memory with him, blade in hand, to visit Mom in the bathtub.

Vaporous hands reached for Vicky, passing through her. Freeman felt the contact on his own skin, then realized it was Starlene, tugging him into the basement from the stairwell door. She pulled again and Freeman lost contact with Vicky.

"What's going on?" she asked, as Freeman shook himself back to the physical world. Dipes and Isaac looked at him as if he'd returned from Mars and they were awaiting tales of green aliens.

"Vicky," Freeman said. "She's in trouble."

They could hear Freeman's dad at the far end of the basement, laughing like the world was ending. Freeman tried to triptrap back to Vicky, but something had changed. Either Kracowski or Dad had screwed with the field again, or else Vicky had gone under.

He remembered the icy touch of that dead hand passing through her skin, and imagined it squeezing her heart. Did this mean he was down, depressed, out of the loop? He couldn't afford that now.

"Come on," he yelled at the others, running down the dim corridor. The glow of the machinery beckoned him, and he tried to recall the layout of the basement using Vicky's memory. Dad had obviously renovated the setup a little, taken control, put a new spin on Kracowski's treatment.

The others followed him. He tried to put on his Clint Eastwood face, twisted his mouth a little and squinted through one eye, but the act felt stupid. De Niro in *Goodfellas* or Pacino in *Carlito's Way* didn't work. Not even Nicholson in *The Postman Always Rings Twice* would fly in this situation. No time to pretend to be a flawed hero. Besides, heroes weren't supposed to be this scared.

He rounded the corner just as Dad threw the cell door open. A sick light leaked from the room where Vicky had been trapped, the results of Dad's and Kracowski's experimental solution now free from the flask, the genie out of the bottle, Pandora's box unsealed.

The tortured souls of the insane fell through the door into the real world, a world they had never understood. A world that had shocked and strapped and chained them, a world that denied them and jailed them and forgot them. This time, they had someone to blame for their pain.

They swarmed over Dad, a dozen milky hands grabbing at him, touching, investigating, trying to make sense of this fleshly invader of their hidden land. They rode the electromagnetic fields into the basement, drawn to the machines, staring at the curved panels, the tanks, wires, and circuitry as if they were tricks in some new psychological assessment test.

Dad put out tentative hands against the ghosts, white Rorschachs, testing their solidity, no doubt making mental notes on this new species. It was a species he'd love to claim for his own. Freeman knew the agony written on the faces of the dead had no effect on Dad. The suffering of others meant nothing. Pain was a means to an end, and if some poor pathetic souls were wrenched from eternal rest, that was the price of understanding.

Not human understanding, Dad's understanding.

Dad had to know every goddamned thing in the world; he had to know why people lived and why they hurt and why they dreamed and what made them tick and what made them break. Freeman knew all that very well. Dad had broken him plenty.

A rage filled him as he crept down the hall. The equipment throbbed and hummed, and Dad's voice rose over the electronic chaos. Dad was talking to the ghosts, shrinking them, pushing them to the edge. Even the dead had to endure his scorn.

"Come on, you crazy dead fuckers," Dad screamed. "You're supposed to *hate* me. You know why? Because I'm the one who brought you back. Hahahahaha."

Freeman ducked behind a row of metal cylinders and peeked around, unsure what to do next. Starlene caught up with him, Dipes and Isaac close behind, all of them panting.

"Don't look at *him*," Dad shouted, as the ghosts drifted toward Kracowski. "I'm the one who did all the work. It was my idea. You belong to *me*."

Kracowski pressed back against the wall, face blanched and blank, hands in his lab coat.

Dad chopped at the air like a stunt man in a kung fu movie. His arms passed through the ghosts, the ether barely stirred by the motion.

"Damn, Kracowski," Dad said. "The field is cooking

with gas now. Just think, if we can make one big enough, we might fill up the whole fucking world with ghosts."

Kracowski, his words nearly without air, said, "What have we done? Good God, what are we doing?"

Dad laughed, blew a breath at the nearest ghost, a wiry figure who made a drawing motion in response. Freeman guessed it was the writer, the one who was forever fixed on that phrase, "A white, white room in which to write." Beside The Writer stood an old woman with a large iridescent scar across her forehead.

"The dead and the living, walking side by side," Dad said to the stunned Kracowski. "Who knows where it will end? What do you think, McDonald? Think your little secret society will find a way to take over the world using these things?"

McDonald said nothing in response. Drool leaked from one corner of his mouth, his pupils of different sizes. He crawled on his belly as if he'd lost the use of his legs. And his mind.

"The Mills Effect," Dad said, turning his attention back to Kracowski. "What do you think? Catchy, huh?"

Dad slapped at the ghost of an old woman, who was hunched and wrinkled and ragged, whose translucent face registered a sneer of suspicion. "How about it, bitch? The Mills Effect. Do you like being the byproduct of my out-of-this-world genius?"

Starlene, leaning over Freeman's shoulder, whispered, "He's gone over the edge."

"He was born over the edge," Freeman said. "Trouble is, he wants to drag everybody else over with him."

"How do we get Vicky?" Isaac said.

"McDonald's down for the count, and I don't see any guards. I guess McDonald didn't want any witnesses."

"Then we go for it?" Starlene asked.

"What about it, Dipes? What kind of future are you seeing?"

"I see four," Dipes said.

"Four. Choices, choices. Do any of them have happy endings?"

In the silence, they heard Freeman's dad shouting at the ghosts.

"What about it, Dipes?" Freeman asked.

"I think we better leave now. I don't see the future where we leave, but it's got to be better than the ones I *do* see."

Freeman watched as a shape appeared on the basement wall beyond the bright metal of the holding tanks. The shape flickered like a magic lantern, grew nebulous flesh, peered blindly at Dad and Kracowski and the machinery and the other ghosts.

Then the Miracle Woman came up from her cold and faraway land, drifted from the stones where she slept, stepped into the dim and restless reality that Freeman had never before so strongly doubted.

At that moment, Freeman understood the real world was nothing more than the collective nightmares of the sleeping dead.

FORTY-FOUR

Francis Bondurant sat on the cot in Thirteen, staring at his reflection in the two-way mirror. What had these kids seen, lying here blasted by Dr. Kracowski's forbidden fields? Had they come face-to-face with the Devil himself? The way they shook and whined and gurgled, Bondurant wouldn't be surprised. After all, the troubled little sinners deserved that sort of punishment.

He fumbled with the restraint straps and the cold buckles. Then he picked up the wires ending in the padded electrodes that Randy and Paula stuck to the kids' heads. Kracowski's torture was complex, his tools of inflicted salvation full of arcane symbols and machines and invisible waves. But wasn't science the realm of Satan? Didn't lust for knowledge cause that first bite into Eden's apple?

Bondurant looked at his own image again, at the man staring back at him. That was a righteous man, a true servant of God. If his flask weren't empty, Bondurant would have toasted the man. The world needed more like him. Fair, stern, and charitable, but if the Lord so willed, he knew how to deliver a Joshuan trumpet blast.

As he watched, the face shifted, the image rippling against the glass as if the mirror were under moving water. The eyes staring back at him became dark and hollow, his thin red cheeks swelling into wrinkled puffs of gray flesh. The image finished its transition and Bondurant found himself looking at the old man from the lake, the worn and weathered creature who had long ago left his skin and bones behind. The man's cracked lips moved, and though no sound came from his mouth, Bondurant heard his words.

"Instrument of the Devil, eh? Isn't that a little bit melodramatic, Francis?"

Bondurant started to speak, then found he didn't have to, at least not aloud. For the man knew what he was about to say before the thought reached Bondurant's tongue. "How do you know my name?"

"Your office used to be my office."

"Y–you don't belong here."

The man's silent laughter crept through Bondurant's forehead. "I belong here more than you do, Francis. I was at Wendover before it was Wendover. I was head of the ward."

"You drowned in the lake."

"You can't very well drown when you're already dead."

Bondurant's chest grew cold. "Are you . . . Satan?"

"Not quite." Again the inaudible laugh came, a soft sound that held as much sorrow as joy. "Though some of my patients thought so. Then again, other patients thought I was God."

"Our blessed Father in Heaven."

"Yeah, Kingdom Come and all that. Well, Francis, take it from one who's been there, it's all a crock of shit."

Bondurant shook his head.

The wisps of the old man's features faded a little, then sewed themselves more solidly together on the mirror's surface. "If there was a God, then I would have looked Him in the eye when I died. Because there's one thing I've always wanted to ask Him. And I'll bet you've wondered the same thing. You know what that is?"

"No," Bondurant thought, staring at the floor. He

couldn't endure the black nothingness of the old man's eyes anymore.

"I'd ask him, 'Why do bad things happen to innocent people?'"

Bondurant thought of the children who'd been entrusted to his care, the abused, the orphaned, the lame, the unrepentant. He'd allowed the children to talk about their problems, submitted them to group therapy and individual counseling, let them speak their worries in confidential rooms. The sorry little sinners should have spilled their guts on their knees in Wendover's chapel instead. Just them and the Lord, heart to heart. The wicked would burn and those who saw the light would be saved. That was the way of God's Earth, and all else was smoke.

The old man's image shimmered again, drifted from the surface of the mirror and became whole. He stood in his dirty gown and bare feet like a wandering monk. A beggar. Or was this man sent by God Himself to deliver a message to Bondurant?

The room was quiet except for the faint hum of the machinery beneath the floor. Kracowski was playing games in the basement, him and McDonald and that new one, Dr. Mills. Wendover had been given over to dark forces. Bondurant's only hope now was for personal salvation. All the rest was lost.

The old man shuffled over to Bondurant, his feet making no sound. With each step he became more solid, until Bondurant could smell the soiled gown and the toothless breath. He put an icy hand on Bondurant's chest and gently pushed him back onto the cot.

"Rest, Mr. Bondurant."

Bondurant wanted to struggle, to jump up and run screaming from the room, but the hand was insistent. Was this the hand of God? Bondurant grew dizzy and weak, confused. If only he had a bottle.

"I want to help you," the man said, raising one of the restraint straps. "With this problem of yours."

Bondurant lay helpless as the old man folded the straps over Bondurant's legs and chest. His wrists and ankles were then locked in padded cuffs. The old man applied the blue gel to the electrodes and attached them to Bondurant's head.

"Will it hurt?" Bondurant asked.

"Suffering is the way to healing," the old man said, his eyes like dark seeds under the thick eyebrows.

"Who are you?" Bondurant wasn't sure he wanted to know the answer. But he was on the edge of something important, some connection between himself and Wendover's past. Or maybe he was sobering up. An uneasiness rippled through him, the gel tickling his skin.

The old man knelt so close to Bondurant's face that his words made a breeze on his cheeks. "I'm the doctor. I make people better."

He gave a grin that looked far too much like a tray of scalpels. Then he turned and shuffled toward the mirror. He met the surface, shimmered, then melded into the glass and disappeared. The ceiling microphone came on with a hiss. "I prefer the old-fashioned techniques," the old man said, "but I suppose one must change with the times."

A thread of juice stitched across Bondurant's skin. A hum arose in the walls, soft and sinister, as if a nest of winged things had been disturbed. The cot vibrated slightly, and Bondurant clenched his fists. The first shock pierced his skull and he bit his tongue, tasting blood.

Riding that jolt of electricity were scattered thoughts, nightmare glimpses, visions that Bondurant immediately knew had been witnessed by the old man's living eyes:

A needle, pushed into a woman's frail arm, dosing her with enough insulin to knock her into a coma.

More electroshock, an assembly line of frightened patients in white, all led from the treatment room like drooling sheep.

A scene from the basement, the inside of a cell, orderlies

carrying the corpse of a woman with bloody sockets where her eyes had been.

An ice pick, slid up a nostril and turned inside the upper curve of skull, severing the frontal lobe.

Another operation, this time a saw rasping through the skull to take the lobe via the forehead.

Bondurant screamed for mercy, but the dead doctor only turned up the juice. Then the force field radiated from the walls and slapped him into darkness.

The old man's voice followed him. "See? A doctor's work is never done. Even death can't ease their troubled minds."

Bondurant wasn't listening, even though the words reverberated inside his head. Amid the black, suffocating stillness that surrounded him, pale shapes slithered through the cracks of nothingness. He closed his eyes and wept like a baby until the doctor came to comfort him and remove the straps.

FORTY-FIVE

The Miracle Woman called to Freeman, drifted past the other spirits toward where he crouched at the mouth of the hallway. The glow from the machinery swirled around her and through her, as if her impossible flesh were lit by a cold fire.

"Do you see her?" Freeman asked the others.

"Who?" Starlene asked.

"Her." He pointed at the naked woman, whose long, dark hair flowed over her shoulders. She looked like one of those Venus on the Half-shell drawings done by some acid burnout from the Sixties. Except for the part about the bloody eye sockets. Not even a drug overdose victim could have imagined those.

"I don't see nothing," Dipes said.

"Not even the future?" Isaac asked. "Well, I see Kracowski and that new guy, the crazy one. And the weird guy flopping around on his stomach like a beached fish."

"You don't see the ghosts?" Freeman asked. The Miracle Woman floated closer, her hands closed. Freeman hoped she wouldn't open her palms and look at him. He couldn't handle that right now. All he wanted was to reach Vicky.

"We can save her," the Miracle Woman said. "Follow me."

Freeman froze. She drifted closer, skin fluttering like psychedelic rags, her torn face wearing a faint smile. "Trust me," she said.

Freeman clamped his hands over his ears. "No. Get out. You're not here. You're not real."

"Trust me, Freeman."

"No. You can't triptrap a dead person. That wasn't part of the experiment. That wasn't what he turned me into."

"Your father hurt you. But he also *made* you. See, he gave you a gift. It doesn't matter what his intentions were. Now it's yours, and you're the one who has to use it."

"I don't want it."

"Do you want to save Vicky?"

Damn her. Why couldn't she just stay dead? Why couldn't she leave him alone? She was just like all the others.

"Trust me," she said, and a soft tickle caressed his cheek. He thought it was her finger, and he opened his eyes.

It wasn't her finger, it was his tears.

"Trust me," she repeated. "Starlene said God doesn't send you anything you can't handle."

"Why do you want to help?" he said, this time aloud instead of through his thoughts.

She flashed a triptrap of her own, and he saw the past through her eyes, the old man from the lake standing over her, she was strapped in Thirteen, helpless, and the old man applied the electrodes and Freeman twisted in agony as the electricity sliced through their mutual nerve endings, the old man wearing a lab coat now, a tie, taking notes, serious, concerned, injecting her with something that made Freeman's brain cloud, the old man and an orderly leading her into the basement, only it was cleaner back then, though still dark. She was put in a cell, the same one in which Vicky was now trapped, and at last Freeman knew.

The Miracle Woman had died in the cell. She had torn her own eyes out, not wanting to witness any more of the doctor's treatments. She bled to death in silence, able to weep only blood. As Freeman felt her blood pour down his own face, as the hot pain smothered like a molten mask, as she bit her tongue to keep from crying out and drawing the attention of the orderlies, who might save her for yet more misery, Freeman understood that he didn't have an exclusive hold on suffering.

She freed him from her memories and Freeman clutched his head, dazed.

"Are you okay?" Starlene asked.

"Yeah." He wiped his cheek before the others noticed. "But I've got to do this alone. She told me so."

"He's right," Dipes said. "That's the way I saw it happen. We're supposed to go over there, into that room. Freeman goes on alone."

Starlene paused a moment, squeezed Freeman's shoulder, then said, "Okay. But we won't be far away."

Freeman waited while the three hid in the nearby cell. The triptrap with the Miracle Woman seemed to have taken hours, but the milieu before him in the basement had not changed. Dad stood by the open door to Vicky's cell, mumbling in his crazed voice about validity and breakthroughs and control. Kracowski hung back near the large holding tanks as if wanting to hide in their shadows.

The Miracle Woman had disappeared, and Freeman knew she was in Vicky's cell, keeping her company, or driving her insane. Because, when you triptrapped a crazy person, then you got crazy, too. Freeman couldn't reach Vicky, at least with his mind. So he would have to reach her the normal, old-fashioned way.

He swallowed hard and stepped out into the open area of the basement. "Hey, Dad!" he shouted.

Dad turned, his eyes growing even wider, the grin changing into something sharp and sinister. "Well, this is just perfect. A family reunion, right when I'm about to become the most brilliant person in the universe."

"What do you want a stupid girl for? She doesn't know anything about the power of the brain."

"She was available," Dad said. "Didn't I teach you about test runs?"

"You taught me plenty, Dad. No pain, no gain, right?" He pointed toward Kracowski. "He had the crazy idea that you need to control things, put limits on it. But we know better, don't we, Dad?"

"That's the old Trooper. Pedal to the metal, wide open, full speed ahead. What do you think of this one?" Dad passed his hand through the soft skull of one of the ghosts. "Can you see his thoughts? He put tin foil in his ears to block out the radio signals being broadcast by secret government agencies. Seems like that's the kind of message you'd *want* to receive, isn't that right, McDonald?"

McDonald groaned from the floor, then tried unsuccessfully to rise.

Kracowski emerged from the shadows, bolted to the computer, and tapped some keys. Dad screamed at him. "Leave it alone, you idiot. Don't you want to be part of the breakthrough?"

"Not *your* breakthrough," Kracowski said. "This isn't the experiment."

Dad jumped at Kracowski, shoving him away from the computer. Kracowski threw a weak punch and missed. Dad knocked Kracowski down and checked the readings, then began frantically working the keyboard.

"You screwed up my ratios, damn you," he said.

Kracowski, wiping blood from his mouth, said, "I had to have an override. Once the Trust got too far involved, I figured things might go bad."

Dad's twisted face was green in the glow of the screen's phosphor. "Bad? *Bad?* I'll show you goddamned *BAD*."

The whine of the machinery intensified, and Freeman

knew it was time to make a move, while Dad was distracted. He raced toward Vicky's cell, wading through the ghosts whose cold flesh had grown more solid. The field throbbed as it gained in strength, the walls vibrated, the cell doors clanged against stone, the ghosts' thoughts slipped across Freeman's mind. He wondered if this was what it was like to hear voices, to be a full-blown schizophrenic.

Maybe schizophrenia was more than a condition of the mind, an imbalance in brain chemistry. Maybe it was a reality for some people. Maybe the voices weren't imaginary.

"Where are you going, you little shit?" Dad yelled at Freeman.

But Freeman was past him, running through the door into Vicky's cell, diving into the dark, endless void, screaming as he fell upward and downward and sideways all at the same time. The door slammed closed beyond him with a metallic finality.

FORTY-SIX

"Vicky?"

Freeman reached out for her, both with his hands and his mind. The darkness crawled down his throat, solid as a snake. It blinded him and clogged his ears, surrounded him like a second skin.

The fields shifted again, and from the way the world beyond the darkness shook and trembled, his outside reality was going to break into fragments any second now. If that happened, if everything he'd known and hated and feared and tasted was going to disappear forever, he wanted to be with Vicky when it happened. *Inside* her.

Her words came from the bleak black beyond: "Because you don't want to be alone."

"No, it's more than that." The triptrap worked, and the bridge between them threw off a faint light. She stood at the far end, glowing and pale, scared, ten million miles away.

"They're breaking it down."

"I know. Once Dad got involved, it was bound to get screwed up."

"Come to me. I'm losing you."

Freeman's heart pounded like a funeral drum near the end of a dirge. If there was a reason for this gift, if it was ever going to do anything for him besides cause him trouble, this was the time. He needed it, whether he was manic or depressed or insane or just a scared little boy. He wanted to touch and know one person before his whole universe blew apart. Who cared what Clint would do? Clint Eastwood had his own life, and no matter what happened to the character in the fantasy world of film, the actor Clint moved on after the final credits.

Freeman didn't think he'd be so lucky.

Desperation drove him, excited him, juiced his brain more than any machine ever had. He was on an up like nobody's business.

The bridge got a little bit brighter, and Vicky was now only a million miles away. He could see her clearly in his mind: blond and pale with fervid eyes, more beautiful than ever because she was reaching back to him, and this time he didn't have to build the bridge alone.

The light from the bridge pushed back the darkness, and they moved closer together.

"Come to me, Freeman," she triptrapped.

Freeman focused on the image of her face, and that brought her more fully into him; he tasted her past, and walked through her pain, and knelt with her as she forced herself to vomit. He absorbed the simultaneous emotions of love and hatred of her father, the man she wanted so desperately to please that she was willing to make herself disappear.

As he felt that soul-deep sorrow, the bridge dimmed, and she faded back into the darkness at the far end. He was losing her. She'd wanted to disappear, and this was her chance.

"No, that's wrong," he said.

"Don't tell me what to feel."

"You don't have to go away. It's not your fault. And you're not fat."

"Freeman Mills, you're starting to sound like a shrink again."

"It's in the genes. I know what I'm talking about. Hold on."

"But it would be so easy. Nothing but nice, safe dark. Just slip under like a stupid old whale and let all the problems be gone. Instant weight loss."

"Remember when you gave me hell about feeling sorry for myself? Well, that's what you're doing now. You're being selfish. Believe me. I've been there."

He triptrapped a memory toward her, the one where he found the razor in the bathroom at Durham Academy, left there by a careless counselor, and he twisted the blade free and put it to his wrist without a single thought except escape.

He felt her shudder as the metal sliced and the blood spurted, as Freeman looked down at the wound and realized this wasn't the way he wanted to go, not as the edges of the world went gray and his thoughts slipped to the floor, not this way, not like Mom—

He froze, his thoughts hanging like icicles. He'd opened that dark space under the bridge, the place where he'd hidden the bad things.

But Vicky had seen a glimpse through that brief crack, and now she probed, her curiosity making the connection stronger.

"'Not like Mom' what?" she asked.

"Don't even think about it," he said. "Don't even try."

"Look, a second ago, or whatever passes for time in here, you were wanting me to share everything, get inside, do the one-mind thing. You get my blubber and I get your scars. And now, when things get a little too personal, you back off. What's it going to be, boy?"

The bridge grew dimmer. He was losing her, shutting her off, crawling back inside himself. Where he would be alone. With the memories.

Then he knew what hell was like. It wasn't a hot place where a pointy-tailed beast poked you with a pitchfork. Hell was inside your own head, where the doors were closed, where hope never knocked, where darkness and pain and self-pity were the only companions. Forever. And, as the crazy dead folks could tell him, forever lasted a long time.

He reached for her again, triptrapped until his brain burned, rode the up, and this time the glow radiated from his head and through his nervous system, warming him, bringing him more fully alive than he'd ever been.

He *wanted* this. More than he'd ever wanted anything.

"This must be faith," he said. "Believing in something. No wonder Starlene gets so high off this stuff."

"Believe in me, Freeman. Believe in *us*."

The bridge flickered to life, grew strong, cut a long golden ribbon through the black deadscape. Vicky was closer now, so near Freeman could reach out and touch, even though his flesh was lost and left behind. This was a touching of the soul.

Her thoughts flooded him, her love seeping into him like a warm and gentle electricity, a power of life and yearning. They probed each other's dark spaces, threw out their fears and regrets as if they were old clothes in an attic trunk, opened the doors inside and walked together into strange rooms.

The bridge was heaven-white now, shining, the gap closing, the triptrap taking on something beyond mere mystery.

He let some of that light into the dark place under the bridge, the place that no one was allowed to see, a memory from the day that Dad took over his head and made him kill Mom. Six years fell away like nothing in the land where time had no meaning.

Vicky was with him as Dad juiced him and triptrapped him, filled his brain with thoughts, an experiment of Dad's mind control theory, just another day at the office for the world's most daring pioneer, and Freeman had no choice but to leave the closet in Dad's lab and walk through the kitchen and take the knife from the drawer

and go down the hall, Dad working his legs, commanding his muscles, making Freeman *want* to do this, re-
minding him that Mom demanded perfection even more
than Dad did, with her "no second chances" philosophy,
convincing him that Mom was the enemy, *she* was the
one who deserved to be punished for bringing Freeman
into this sorry world and for letting Dad inflict all those
cruel tortures on him.

Vicky opened the bathroom door with him, Mom
never locked it because everybody knew that soaking
time was her private time, and everyone needed a place
to escape now and then, especially when Kenneth Mills
was playing mind games, and the knife was in his hand
and the steam on his face and Mom had her eyes closed
as she lay in the tub, the soap wreathing her neck, her
body beneath the bubbles, and just as he lifted the knife,
she opened her eyes and smiled and the smile stayed
frozen there as Dad ordered him to bring the knife down
and the water turned red and she tried to say something,
but he brought the knife down again and the blood trickled from her lips and Vicky screamed with him, screamed
from the outside in, and Dad laughed in awe of his own
power, because if he could make other people murder the
ones they loved, then the world was his.

Vicky stayed with Freeman as he brought the knife
down again and again, and even when his arm was tired,
he couldn't stop, Dad made him do it some more, and the
tears ran down his face along with the spattered blood,
and the soap bubbles cast their rainbows in red, and Dad
was all over his brain, whispering things, putting sick
thoughts in there, promising him that this was only the
beginning, no one could stop them now that Dad knew
the way in, and the Trust didn't matter, the Trust wouldn't
understand, this type of control belonged only to those
who knew how to use it.

Vicky stood with him when the knife finally clattered
to the tiles and Dad came into the bathroom, and for the

first time ever Dad was proud of his son, proud because he could make his son just like *him*, and Dad picked up the knife and wiped it clean on a towel and then the guys from the Trust came by and took away all of Dad's machines and made an anonymous phone call to the police and the rest was almost history except history not only repeated itself, it never went away.

Freeman expected Vicky to draw back now that she knew. He deserved to be alone. That type of monster should be thrown to the darkness, not pitied or mourned or loved. Such a monster should be condemned to the black, cold world beneath the bridge, where it could wallow in its own hate until it drowned.

"I . . . I didn't know," Vicky said. The bridge dimmed.

"Go away."

"Why didn't you tell me?"

"Get out of my head, damn you."

The bridge faded, fell to threads, dissipated like a ghost that had died a second time.

"No," she said.

The light swelled. The link grew stronger as she came on again, sent herself out to him, grabbed with all the hunger for things Freeman called hope.

She opened herself to him, offering everything, pouring into him, and he had no shield for this, because he didn't expect it, and had never known such a force could exist.

The bridge was as hot as the sun, even more blinding than the surrounding darkness, but Freeman could see clearly, their souls had substance, they walked toward each other across the bridge, slow motion, every step a miracle, and Freeman made himself stare straight ahead, to not look over the side of the bridge where the darkness ran like rivers in every direction and dead things flitted.

"It's not your fault," she said. "I understand."

He'd heard that before. It wasn't his fault. He was the perfect victim. He just happened to be in the wrong place at the wrong time, his soul trapped in a body born to a man who wanted the power that only God should have. The power to shape the souls of others. To crush them and burn them and ruin them. The power to inflict the worst kind of pain.

"It wasn't . . . I didn't mean to," he said.

Vicky's image approached. "It will be okay, as long as we're together."

"I don't think we're going back. To the real world, I mean. I think Dad is killing us. Back there in the real world."

"I'm not afraid anymore."

"Me, either."

"Touch me."

They closed that final distance, the tug of their souls exerting spiritual gravity, so close, so hopeful, desperately close, a flicker and heartbeat away from joining in a union stronger than that of atoms.

Then the troll appeared.

Dad stood between them, with his black soul and his twisted brain and his sharp teeth, ready to gobble them up.

FORTY-SEVEN

Starlene huddled in the dark cell, her arms around Dipes and Isaac. The walls quivered, the metal doors clanged in the corridors, and bits of ancient plaster fell from the ceiling. Whatever Kracowski and Mills were doing, it was tearing the building apart.

"What's happening, Dipes?" Isaac said. "I mean, what's *about* to happen?"

"It keeps changing," Dipes said. "First everybody was dead and wandering around, then we were standing outside the fence, looking back at the building."

"All of us were outside?" Starlene asked.

"No. Not Freeman and Vicky."

"That's what I was afraid of." Starlene wasn't sure that God would want people to know the future, because they might try to change it. But maybe God's plan included taking responsibility for the future. God didn't send you anything you couldn't handle, even telepathy and clairvoyance and precognition.

She wondered if God would want her to reach out with her mind, to triptrap like Freeman and Vicky. Surely He wouldn't stop her if it was His will. But, if He didn't approve, would He blame her for trying? It might be a sin that had never come under consideration. She offered a

quick prayer, linked with God in that strange and power-
ful way that was the biggest mind trip of all.

She asked her question and the answer came. Her heart
was clear. Her soul was pure enough. She called on the
memory of that brief moment in Thirteen, when she
could read the thoughts of those around her.

Nothing.

Isaac peeked out the cell door. "That new doctor's
doing something to the machines."

Starlene closed her eyes and concentrated. All she
heard were her own panicked thoughts and the vibration
of the building roaring in her ears. Powder poured from
the crumbling masonry. She hugged the boys even more
tightly.

"We'll be okay," she said. "God told me so."

Isaac said to Dipes, "What did God tell *you*?"

"God's not talking to me," Dipes said.

Starlene tried one more time, asking God for strength
if it be His will, and the voice came to her from the rear
of the cell. She turned to the dark corners and saw the
Miracle Woman, ethereal, whole, smiling.

"I, too, prayed to God," the Miracle Woman said.
"Every night. Even after the doctors gave me injections
and I was out of my mind."

"You died here, didn't you? In Wendover?" she said
aloud, even though the Miracle Woman's words came
into her head without the benefit of sound.

"Who are you talking to?" Isaac said. "One of your
ghosts?"

The Miracle Woman grew more solid, radiant. Clothed
in what looked to be a gown of sheer silver.

Isaac gasped. "I *see* her."

"Have a little faith, Isaac," the Miracle Woman said.
"Miracles happen every day."

"Are . . . are you an angel?" Dipes asked.

She smiled. "Whatever you believe. Someday you'll
understand, but not too soon, I hope."

"You're here to help us," Starlene said.

"I'm here to help *us*," she said, her voice hollow yet soothing. "The ones who have been disturbed from our rest."

"What do we do now?" Starlene said.

The Miracle Woman smiled again, her eyes kind, suffused with a strange light that reminded Starlene of a candle behind smoked glass. "Look inside. Then you'll know. And, Edmund, the answer is at your fingertips."

The Miracle Woman faded back into darkness.

"A lot of help that was," Isaac said. "Like some sappy line from *Touched by an Angel*, where your problems get solved just in time for the commercial break. And nobody's hair even gets messed up."

Starlene looked out the cell door at Mills feverishly working the computer keyboard, punching in commands. The chaotic wisps of spirits swirled around him, a maelstrom of scattered soul-threads. Kracowski, his lower lip swollen and his scalp bleeding, crawled to McDonald. The utility lights above the holding tanks pulsed unevenly, as if the drain on the electrical grid was threatening a meltdown.

Then Dipes said, "Hey, look what I found," and pressed something into her hand.

A pistol.

FORTY-EIGHT

"You little shit, you never did appreciate what I gave you," Dad said.

Freeman shivered, and the deadscape beyond the bridge became more tempting than ever. He could drown in that lightlessness and not care. He could face dying, he didn't mind going into the dark, as long as he was with Vicky. But not with Dad hanging around, smart or crazy enough to split himself, keep one half back there in the real world and the other here in the deadscape.

"So you think you're going to take this little sack of vomit with you?" Dad triptrapped them both. He turned toward Vicky, his soul sharp around the edges, his form ten feet tall, his fingers ready to rip into anything that smacked of unity.

"Leave her alone," Freeman triptrapped.

"Ah, finally growing some balls, Trooper? You were so easy to control, you pathetic little puke. I tried it on other people, even your mother, but nobody rolled over like you did. You opened up your mind and invited me in, dared me to play with it."

"That was a long time ago. I was just a little boy. How could I know what was going on?"

Dad's laughter tore across the deadscape, making the

darkness rattle, pulling the cloak of eternal night closer around them. "Still trying to blame others, huh, Freeman? All your miserable life, you've been telling yourself it's not your fault. Well, Shit for Brains, it *is* your fault."

Dad turned back to Vicky, and the force of his triptrap seared through both of them. "So he finally told you, didn't he, lard-ass? It's all true, except for that part where he said I was the one who made him do it. Truth is, you always wanted to kill her, didn't you, Freeman? It was your idea, and you built this little fantasy where I was the one who made you do it. You can't out-shrink me, can you, Trooper?"

Freeman wished he could slip back into his flesh and suffer some ordinary pain. He didn't want to die like this, with the guilt pressing on him, a blame that would follow him beyond death forever.

Vicky's thoughts swept into him, crowding Dad's. "Hang on, Freeman. Whatever happened, it's over now."

"*Over?*" Dad triptrapped a psychic tornado. "It's only beginning. Mind control doesn't have to end just because your heart stops. Thanks to Kracowski, I can mess with you for the rest of eternity."

In a flash, Freeman saw a vision of what Dad had in store, a timeless future where Dad raped Vicky and made Freeman watch, where he shoved doughnuts into her mouth, where Dad brought Mom back to life so Freeman could kill her over and over again, where the insane dead people threw their tortured thoughts into Freeman's head, where all the pain of all the souls in the world could be his. A hell in his head.

The vision fell away and he was back on the bridge, Vicky receding on the far end, the bridge flickering and fading beneath them, Dad's dark soul swelling, merging with the greater blackness beyond, joining the deadscape, becoming it, taking on a power that surrounded everything, that built a universe where there was no room for light or peace.

The edges of the deadscape quivered, monsters moaned from their hidden holes, ghosts whispered sorrows, despair rained in gray and washed the bridge away. The darkness ate at Freeman, nibbled him with its teeth, and he was tired, ready to surrender, because Dad was right.

It *was* his fault. And he deserved every kind of punishment that Dad could dream up.

As he closed the eyes of his soul, a bolt of lightning juiced through him, an electroshock of energy.

"We can beat him," Vicky said, flooding his head, filling him up. "Together."

Filling him up and up and up.

FORTY-NINE

Starlene pressed her damp palm around the gun. Was this the answer to her prayer? A sign from God?

God didn't send you anything you couldn't handle.

What could she do? There didn't appear to be a safety switch. She knew how to point and pull the trigger, but could she actually *shoot* another human being?

"I see another future," Dipes said.

"Great," Isaac said. "Please tell me in this one we all live happily ever after, even the Jews."

"That never happens in *any* future."

"Well, how about this? Starlene makes like one of Charlie's Angels and blows away the bad guys."

"Sort of. Except, we better get out of the basement."

"Because it's going to collapse, right?"

"No. Because it's *all* going to be a deadscape."

Starlene said, "You guys head for the stairs. I'll be right behind you. I have to do something first."

Isaac grabbed Dipes's hand and Starlene pushed the two of them into the corridor. The basement was a crazed kaleidoscope of lights and noise. She waited until she saw the stairwell door swing closed, then slipped to the opening of the main area, where the lights strobed and the machinery whined. She peered down the corridor and saw

Kracowski slumped to the floor, holding his head in his hands. McDonald lay inert by the cell where Vicky and Freeman were locked away. The large curved panels, like something off a space station, shook with whatever Dr. Mills was pumping into them. Mills himself stood behind the computer, eyes closed, a twisted smile on his lips.

"What now, God?" she asked, holding the gun in front of her.

A hand fell on her shoulder, she turned, half-expecting to see the face of God, or maybe the Miracle Woman, but it was Randy. His punch landed and her mind screamed blue and she heard the distant clatter of the gun falling to the floor just before her head cracked against the cold concrete.

FIFTY

Warm.

That was what this union was; that was what hope and faith felt like. Vicky was right. Together, you could beat back the darkness. Together, you never had to surrender or apologize.

"Oh, that's just hilarious," Dad said, twenty feet tall now, grim smoke pouring out of his soul. "You murder your goddamned mother and then think you get away with a slap on the wrist because now you have somebody to share the blame. That's not the way it works, Trooper."

"You don't know everything," Freeman triptrapped, angry now, feeling the warmth expand, watching as the bridge grew brighter beneath Dad's monstrous shape. "You think you're God but you're just as much of a loser as I am. Worse, even. Because I never asked for this and you searched for it. You begged for it and sold your soul for it. You pulled out every trick in your sick little book, but it's nothing but a meaningless mind game. And now the game's over."

"He lied," Vicky said. "He never gave you a gift. He gave himself the gift."

"Shut up, bitch bones." Dad quivered, his mouth alive now with dark shapes that fluttered like winged creatures.

"I'm the one who controls things around here. This is a world *I* built."

"Then you can fucking have it," Freeman said. "Because we're getting out of here. In the deadscape, nobody has to follow your rules."

He focused, shielded himself from Dad's thoughts, sent himself out and up, and Vicky joined him, the strength of their combined triptrap going through the deadscape and back to the real, living world and through the walls of the cell into the basement:

Dad, in the flesh, at the computer.

Kracowski in pain, stomach tight, mind sick with regret.

McDonald, rolling over, mad with the visions of things he'd never expected.

Randy . . .

Randy?

Randy, shielded, going to McDonald, a mission to complete.

And Starlene.

Freeman and Vicky went into Starlene's head, saw only gray. And then black.

And they were back in the deadscape.

Dad stood between them again.

Freeman tried another triptrap, this time not beyond the deadscape but *into* it. He called to those who hid behind the darkness, those who orbited this freakish universe. The dead. The ghosts. The true rulers of this bleak land.

Vicky joined him, and the broken, sad thoughts spilled into them, the dreams and screams of those who had died in the basement, those whose souls were stitched into this fabric, those who belonged here.

A form came up from the blackness, the Miracle Woman, her light faint but unyielding, and Dad was confused for a moment, as if the playground had changed without his knowledge.

"That's right, you bastard," Freeman said, taking advantage of the lapse. Coming on like Clint Eastwood in *Unforgiven*, his greatest role, giving in to his dark side and riding hellbent for revenge. "If you want to play God, then you may as well meet those whose souls you own."

The Miracle Woman ascended to the bridge, as soft as a snowflake, and the bridge grew brighter. Her eyes were healed, her face clear, her soul pure. And as she joined the bridge, it grew brighter, the world tilted yet again and a storm roared from the dark corners of the deadscape. A keening of a strange wind arose and swirled around the bridge.

The Miracle Woman's shape dissolved, shifted, the soul realigned. And Mom stood in her place.

Mom.

"Don't turn away," Vicky told Freeman, and he looked into Mom's eyes, Mom who bore no scars, Mom who held no regrets.

"It's okay, Freeman." Mom smiled at him. "Vicky's right. It wasn't your fault."

Dad swelled with rage, a hideous black disease, and hovered over Mom as if ready to collapse on top of her, drag her back into dim memory. *"What the HELL are you doing here? WHO TOLD YOU TO COME BACK?"*

"Oh, didn't you know? Something I learned after you killed me. You carry your dead with you, Kenneth."

Freeman triptrapped her, and saw the truth of it: Dad had experimented on Mom, made her a victim, too. *Dad* was the one who went into the bathroom with the knife, *Dad* was the one whose perverted flesh wanted to taste that ultimate power. Freeman triptrapped Dad, who was weakened now, and saw what Dad had hidden away, that Dad had planted the memory of Freeman committing the murder, muddled in his hippocampus, and built a corrupt story.

Mom grew larger, became the Miracle Woman again, white and hot and angry, and all the ghosts of the deadscape spilled from their secret spaces, swarmed into the

Miracle Woman, became a large shining globe, brighter than a billion stars, and now it was Mom, as big as the world, burning Dad, scorching him, and Dad's soul screamed and scattered and a scrap of thought flew into Freeman's mind, and Freeman and Vicky held together in the face of this strange explosion, the Big Bang of a separate universe, the simultaneous birth and death of a place that couldn't exist.

Freeman triptrapped, Vicky with him, everywhere at once, the gift grown large, and he saw Starlene blink awake, look through fogged eyes at Dad standing over the computer, her hand clawing for the pistol, then she had it and she raised to her elbow and fired at the computer, hoping to destroy it, but the shot went wide and glanced off Dad's shoulder and struck a large tank that stood against the wall.

As the tank hissed from the puncture, Freeman and Vicky triptrapped Starlene and told her together:

Run up the stairs and quick, don't worry about us, we'll be just fine, we're together and the bridge doesn't have to break and there's always hope with a thousand roads to healing and good-bye—

Then Dad's final thought cut in and Freeman wondered if Dad would ask to be forgiven.

Dad said, "You carry your dead with you, Trooper," and then he was gone, his brain frozen, and the deadscape shimmered, became something strange and wonderful, and he suffered the slightest fear, but then Vicky's hand, her *real* hand, was in his as the cold settled around, the cold that seeped under the cell door, a cold that stole their breath and took away their pain. Together they said a final farewell to flesh and walked into a landscape of their own.

FIFTY-ONE

Starlene stood at the gate of Wendover, looking back at the cold stones and unblinking windows of the building. The children had been evacuated and now milled around as if it were a holiday, playing under the trees, throwing pine cones at each other, yelling as the trucks drove past and around the building. The clouds had broken up and the world was bright with autumn, full of the promise of change.

"What did you do?" Isaac asked her.

"I'm not sure. All I know is I pulled the trigger and Freeman and Vicky told me to run. I was in the stairwell and I thought they must have escaped and gone ahead, because it sounded like their voices were far away. Some kind of gas was hissing from the tank, so I closed the door to the stairs, then came out and saw you guys, and the guards were bringing the other kids out of the gym."

"The door," Isaac said. "It locks automatically."

Starlene felt the blood leave her face. "They were trapped—"

"It wasn't your fault," Isaac said. "Blame it on the idiots who put the brain cookers down there."

Dipes shook his head. "I didn't see this one. Not with Freeman and Vicky and all the rest of them down there."

"Where are they?"

The boy smiled. "I can't see anymore. Once the machines shut down, the future was gone. But I think they're going to be okay Something about second chances."

Had she killed them? How could she ever forgive herself? Starlene wiped at her eyes, ignoring the clenched fist of pain around her heart, making herself be strong for the children. "I hope you're right."

"Well," Dipes said. "Some futures, nobody knows about."

"God knows," Starlene said. "God knows everything."

Paula Swenson was talking to Bondurant in the driveway, and a shaken Bondurant nodded and rubbed at his head. He pulled a silver flask from his pocket and Swenson smiled in approval as he took a gulp. He shivered, his eyes bloodshot and his skin pale.

Starlene approached them. She overheard Swenson say, "You were drunk the whole time, got it? They're going to ask you questions but you don't know anything."

"I don't know anything," Bondurant said. "Believe me, I don't know anything. You can say that again. I don't know anything." He tilted the flask again, and it flashed in the afternoon sun.

Swenson turned to Starlene. "You have no idea what you've done." Her voice was cold, harsh, and she was not at all the giggly, girlish thing she'd been before. Starlene saw a pistol tucked into her waistband.

"I think I have some idea. But I guess I'll never know the rest."

"You already know too much. We can get rid of the machines, and we've got the data on file, so at least Kracowski's work won't be wasted."

"You're in it with them, aren't you? What Freeman called the 'Trust'?"

"The Trust doesn't exist."

"What I'm wondering is how you're going to explain this to the authorities."

Swenson gave a tired smile. She looked old, wrinkled around the eyes. "You mean, how did six people freeze to death on a warm September day? I guess we'll have to call in a few favors. And count on you to keep your mouth shut. Or maybe we'll just blast your memory to pieces. You wouldn't want to end up in a mental ward, would you?"

"You wouldn't dare."

"Oh, I forgot. You're the self-sacrificing type. Religious. Into the whole martyr bit. Well, let's try another way. You don't want anything bad to happen to these kids, do you?"

Starlene looked around at the children playing, at Dipes and Isaac watching her from the gate, Two men in suits carried a stretcher to a van. Deke lay on the stretcher, his face dead and pale. She glanced at the barbed wire and then across the grounds, at the lake where the dead man had walked, at the crumbling building where crews were frantically hauling equipment up from the basement. Then she looked to the mountains beyond.

What would she say to the police or DSS? That a secret agency had conducted mind control experiments and brought the dead back to life? That insane ghosts had risen from the floor? That she had communicated telepathically with the dead? And that she had helped kill six people, some of them innocent and some of them guilty?

She would end up in the loony bin if she told the truth. It all seemed like a strange nightmare, and even though she could still hear the echoes of Freeman's and Vicky's final thoughts, they were fading, and she couldn't be sure they had ever existed. She couldn't be sure she had visited the land of the dead. And she didn't know for certain which truth was the real one.

Maybe the Trust had already scrambled her memory and she didn't know it.

She shuddered. She hoped, with all her heart, that *God*

knew and understood. And she reminded herself that God didn't send you anything that you couldn't handle.

"Okay, here's the deal," she said to Swenson. "You leave the kids alone. You get rid of Bondurant. They'll shut this place down, but the kids will go to another group home. All of them, together. And I go with them. If your Trust has as much pull as I think, you should be able to swing that easy."

Swenson waved at a panel truck that was coming up the driveway. She motioned it though the gate and watched as it headed down the gravel road, kicking up small clouds of dust that danced like ghosts before being swept away by the breeze.

"Deal. We'll make the pistol disappear, too," Swenson said. "We're good at making things disappear. Remember that."

Starlene's eyes grew watery. Swenson sighed and handed her a wadded-up napkin from her pocket. "Get a grip. Nothing happened, remember? Do your God thing and hold on for *them*. I don't want to have to come after you. I'd enjoy it, but it would be a real pain in the ass."

"I was just thinking of something Freeman told me. He said, 'You carry your dead with you.'"

"Good one. Ought to come in handy during your next skull session. Now, excuse me. I have a lot of work to do. We can't keep this incident secret forever, and we want to make sure the truth ends up just the way we want it."

Swenson started to walk away, but Starlene grabbed her arm. Swenson's face was blank, as impassive as the stones of Wendover.

"Tell them to give it up," Starlene said. "People shouldn't try to play God."

"Who's playing? You set us back a few years, but you know what else Freeman said? On one of the tapes, when he was six, and Kenneth Mills was first teaching him ESP?"

Starlene looked back at the kids. She wasn't sure she wanted to know.

"He said, 'Daddy, is this what it's like when God talks to you?'"

Starlene looked at the sky, a large blue thing stretching beyond imagination, endless and unforgiving, built of impossible pieces.

"Now get the hell out of here," Swenson said. "From now on, this is none of your business."

Starlene went to Dipes and Isaac and put her arms around them. "We need to talk," she said.

FIFTY-TWO

"Charlie."

"Yeah?" Charlie was in a bad mood. Nothing new there. His wife was diddling around with a manufactured home salesman, and the eleven Miller Lites had been great last night, but weren't so hot this morning. He'd busted his thumb with a hammer and, worst of all, this week's paycheck was already spoken for. So the last thing he wanted was a jaw session with Jack Eggers.

Jack wiped gypsum dust from his nose. "Look at this."

Charlie's hip was pressed against a piece of sheet rock, holding the weight until he could get some nails in. "Come on, let's get this room hung and get out of here."

"This is fucked up."

You're the fucked-up one, Jack.

Charlie pounded some six-penny nails into the sheet rock. Once the piece was tacked in place, he slipped his hammer into the sheath on his tool belt. He ran his tape measure to the ceiling. One more sheet and they'd be in the hall. And that was fine with Charlie, because this room was giving him the creeps, even with the quartz work lamps blazing hot enough to spike his eyeballs.

"Give me a hand here," Charlie said. Jack didn't answer. Charlie turned. Dust swirled in the glow of their lamp.

Jack stood in the center of the room, the light throwing his stooped silhouette onto the unfinished gray wall. Jack's hair was white from the gypsum. He was staring at the floor.

"Ain't got time for this." Charlie's hangover pulsed through his sore thumb like a truck barreling through a garden hose. "We got to get it taped and sanded. Painters will be in by Friday, and nobody can fuck up a subcontract like a painter. I want to get my check and be gone, else it'll be 'Fix this' and 'Patch that' till hell freezes over."

Jack continued staring at the floor. "You can cover it up, but it'll still be there."

Charlie shivered, even though sweat trickled down his back, the dust making a paste on his skin. He and Jack had hung a bedroom once for the widow of an ex-cop. The cop had blown his head off with a twelve-gauge, got brains and slime and blood all over the wall. All *in* the wall, because the studs, insulation, and siding had been pocked with dried meat. They'd slapped three-quarter-inch sheet rock over it, taped and troweled the cracks, but that smell of death had been just as strong as before.

You can cover it up, but it'll still be there. That's what the cop's widow had said.

"What the hell, Jack, it's coffee break." Charlie's throat was dry from the dust. He had a couple of fingers of Jim Beam resting in the bottom of his thermos, just waiting for ten-thirty.

"Nobody's been in here, have they?" Jack said.

"Nobody but us chickens." A crew was hanging some windows upstairs in the building's west wing, but they were so far away that Charlie only heard an occasional shouted cussword or dropped tool.

"Then how did *that* get there?" Jack pointed to the floor.

Charlie's tape measure slid into its box, rattling like a metallic snake.

Don't look, Charlie ordered himself. *Damn you, don't look.*

He'd seen plenty enough funny stuff in the two days they'd been hanging this section of the basement. Little movements out of the corner of his eye. Sometimes he'd turn to catch them, but there'd be nothing but the softly spinning dust. That wasn't so bad, he could chalk that up to the swimming eyes that came from hoisting a few too many.

Except he'd heard those rumors about the kids. What had happened here, and why the building's new owners were so desperate to give it a facelift and move it on the market. To make it go away.

Charlie swallowed, the dust like gravel going down.

Jack said, "You're in such a pissy mood today I didn't figure you for jokes."

"I ain't joking today, I'm working. You ought to be, too."

Jack looked up at Charlie. Jack's tongue was set between his teeth as if he were thinking hard. Usually, Jack couldn't get lost in thought if you gave him a Chinese map with nothing but left turns.

"You didn't do it, *did* you?" Jack asked, then turned and stared at the floor again.

"All right, goddamn it." Charlie's voice bounced off the flat, empty walls and the echo slapped his eardrums. He set down the sheet rock and stomped over to Jack. "Now what the hell is it I didn't do?"

Jack pointed.

Charlie looked at the floor. His balls shrank and his heart took an accounting of a lifetime of cigarette smoking.

You can cover it up, but it'll still be there.

Whatever happened here still lived in the walls, just like at that suicide cop's house. Charlie's hands shook, and he knew the two fingers in the thermos wouldn't be nearly enough. He'd be knocking off early today, calling the contractor and playing sick from the safety of his apartment couch. Maybe if he drank enough, he wouldn't be sick anymore. Maybe he'd drink himself sane.

The floor was covered in a fine silt of dust, marked by their footprints.

Among them, scrawled so that the concrete floor showed cleanly, was a single word:

Free.

Feel the Seduction Of
Pinnacle Horror

BOOK YOUR PLACE ON OUR WEBSITE AND MAKE THE READING CONNECTION!

We've created a customized website just for our very special readers, where you can get the inside scoop on everything that's going on with Zebra, Pinnacle and Kensington books.

When you come online, you'll have the exciting opportunity to:

- View covers of upcoming books
- Read sample chapters
- Learn about our future publishing schedule (listed by publication month *and author*)
- Find out when your favorite authors will be visiting a city near you
- Search for and order backlist books from our online catalog
- Check out author bios and background information
- Send e-mail to your favorite authors
- Meet the Kensington staff online
- Join us in weekly chats with authors, readers and other guests
- Get writing guidelines
- AND MUCH MORE!

**Visit our website at
http://www.kensingtonbooks.com**